Praise for *No Way to Die*

'A pulsating action thriller'
   – *Sunday Times*

'Like sitting down in front of the best action movie you've seen this year. A brilliant, gripping thrill ride.'
   – Cass Green, author of *The Killer Inside*

'A thrilling journey across America that channels Baldacci and Crais, all leading up to the classic ticking clock climax. Terrific.'
   – Mason Cross, author of *What She Saw Last Night*

'What an absolute belter of a book. Dempsey reminds me of an amalgam of 007 and Orphan X. A blistering, two-fisted thriller you won't want to put down until you're done.'
   – Neil Lancaster, author of *Dead Man's Grave*

Praise for *Power Play*

'Twist after twist . . . It builds to a brilliant finale.'
   – *Daily Mirror*

'A high-octane conspiracy yarn.'
   – *The Times*

'An intricate, twisty minefield of geopolitics and absolute power gone rogue. Kent has outdone himself with this one.'
   – David Baldacci

'A gripping conspiracy thriller.'
   – Ian Rankin

THE
SHADOW
NETWORK

THE
SHADOW
NETWORK

TONY KENT

Elliott&Thompson

First published 2024 by
Elliott and Thompson Limited
2 John Street
London WC1N 2ES
www.eandtbooks.com

This paperback edition published in 2024

ISBN: 978-1-78396-714-8

9 8 7 6 5 4 3 2 1

A catalogue record for this book is available from
the British Library.

Typesetting: Marie Doherty
Printed by CPI Group (UK) Ltd, Croydon, CR0 4YY

*To Lorne, to Pippa and to everyone at Elliott & Thompson
for making a dream a reality.*

*And to Scott, to Nicola and to everyone at
Ewing Law for making that reality possible.*

'Hell is empty and all the devils are here.'

The Tempest, William Shakespeare

ONE

Kon Frankowski did not register the single bead of hot sweat as it trickled down his cheek. He did not notice as it disappeared into the thickness of his fashionably unkempt beard, nor was he aware of the three further snaking lines of perspiration that followed it.

It was only the fifth droplet – falling from his brow onto the space key of his open laptop – that made him aware of the effect of the midday sun.

He wiped away the wetness as he glanced up from his screen, his concentration replaced by anxiety. Looking beyond his small, otherwise empty table, he tried to gauge if he was being watched by any of the hundreds of people who surrounded him. To his relief, none showed the slightest interest in a heat-swept tech geek and his homework.

Not a care in the goddamn world, Kon thought to himself, resentment stirring in his gut. *Nothing but sun and liquor.*

The Grote Markt had once been a centre for trade, the commercial hub at the heart of The Hague, itself the third largest city in the Netherlands. But like so many historic European centres, that past was long gone and those origins mostly forgotten. Today the old square was the city's prime social destination, encircled by trendy bars and overpriced eateries, all designed to syphon off its patrons' spare cash under the guise of providing fun-filled 'downtime'.

From sunrise until way past sunset, the Grote Markt was guaranteed to be teeming with over-excited, over-stimulated bodies, all high on caffeine or alcohol or, later in the day,

1

something a lot stronger and a lot less legal. Throw in the unusually tall average height across the Dutch population and a man of normal size – a man like Kon – could easily get lost in a crowd like this.

Precisely why he had chosen this location for the meet.

Kon pulled down the brim of his black baseball cap and returned his attention to his laptop, his nervous energy still firing as he refocused on his work. Kon wanted this over. All of it. He wanted his life back the way it used to be, before he got caught up in this nightmare.

He pushed that negativity aside as he studied the open page on his browser again. The information was dense but now familiar, displayed on a secure site of his own creation; a page he had thrown together for this very purpose. The on-screen data was the fruit of seven hours of research, done overnight on the flight from New York to Amsterdam to ensure that every detail Kon could need would be at his fingertips.

Two faces stared back at him, dominating the screen in all their high-definition glory. They belonged to two men, their names, features and personal details now firmly committed to Kon's memory after his in-flight study.

The first picture was of Mendel Prochnik. An Israeli citizen, Prochnik had started life in Hungary sixty-four years ago and every one of those years was etched across the man's deeply lined features. Evidence of hard living or hard drinking, Kon had figured. Maybe of both.

The second image was of Will Duffy. A Scotsman by birth, Duffy hailed from the poorest part of Glasgow and, like Prochnik, he too had moved on from his beginnings; in his case it was London he now called home. He was the younger of the two men by eleven years but the difference between them looked closer to twenty. Duffy's face carried signs of an eventful life – subtle scars and a broken nose – but he seemed to have kept the energy of his youth.

As physically different as the two men were, they had at least a career choice in common. Both were lawyers, even if Duffy didn't look it; he could have been something else entirely, something a lot more physical. Prochnik, though? He looked a litigator to his very bones; his profession would be no more evident if he'd had 'advocate' tattooed across his forehead. Somewhere in the space between his biblically thick eyebrows and the most obvious wig Kon had ever seen on a man.

On any normal day he would have laughed at his own observation. But today was *not* a normal day. How could it be, in a situation like this? There were too many unknowns for the distraction of humour. Too many unseen dangers . . .

Kon's gaze had drifted back upwards and away from the screen, his paranoia once again taking hold as he questioned why he had agreed to *any* of this. But before his thoughts could spiral into anxiety again, his focus was dragged back to the moment. What he had been waiting for had finally arrived.

Prochnik was smaller in the flesh than Kon had anticipated. Five feet five at best. But that was not what stood out the most. Even in the searing heat, he was wearing a blue three-piece suit so well tailored that it screamed both wealth and undernourishment; there was no way the frame beneath the bespoke cotton and wool blend was more than eight stone dripping wet. The build of a man who was busy working when he should have been eating.

Duffy, in contrast, was a little over six feet tall and built like a fighter. Dressed in khaki cargo shorts and an aged white T-shirt that carried a faded picture of a famous boxer, he was in better shape than a man in his fifties had any right to be. And he looked even less like a lawyer than he did in his photo.

More like the other guy's minder than his partner, Kon thought.

Their sudden arrival provided a moment of welcome respite. A break from the constant dread Kon had been experiencing for days. In that instant of recognition he had thought about something other than the danger he was in. Something more than the risk he was taking. For that moment alone, Kon was unburdened.

An instant later and the fear was back.

Kon hesitated as he considered what to do next, unsure of the right approach to take. Now he was here, the situation was even more alien than he had expected it to be. One question, though, now stood out above all else:

How do I bullshit my way through this?

The uncertainty dominated Kon's panicked mind as the two men drew closer, neither their faces nor their body language giving any guide to his best course. All he could read was their air of confidence. For all the incongruousness of their dress – one of them too formal for the hot weather, the other too casual for the seriousness of the occasion – Prochnik and Duffy were all business.

'Konrad Frankowski.'

Prochnik's words were a statement rather than a question, the heavily accented voice much deeper than Kon would have expected from so small a man. They left him in no doubt that Prochnik knew exactly who he was. And that made no sense at all.

It left Kon confused enough to keep him rooted to his seat.

'How did you—'

Prochnik held up his hand as he came to a halt feet away. A clear indication for Kon to stop speaking.

'We're here to meet an American,' he explained, moving around the chair ahead of him as he spoke. He pointed towards Kon's head. 'The Yankees cap. Might as well be a neon sign.'

Kon's eyes swept across the Grote Markt in response. A quick scan that confirmed what Prochnik had noted: as busy as the square was, there was a complete absence of US sportswear. On any other day Kon would have found that fact noteworthy. Grist for those debates about the meaninglessness of a 'world series' when no one else in the world takes part.

Today it served only as an explanation for how he had been spotted so easily. An explanation that did not come close to answering all of Kon's other concerns. His eyes were back on Prochnik and his next question was ready to fire as the lawyer sat down.

'Well, that's not—'

'Do you have it, Mr Frankowski?'

Prochnik's attention seemed focused on the snow-white handkerchief he was placing into his jacket's left-hand breast pocket, rather than on the question with which he had interrupted Kon for a second time. If his intention was to unsettle then it was a success. Kon found himself scrambling for an answer.

'I . . . I'm not sure—'

'You're not sure of what?' Prochnik's unblinking eyes shifted to meet those of his witness. 'You know why we're here, Mr Frankowski. So you know why we need to keep this interaction as brief as possible; this is dangerous business for us all. And so I'll ask you again: do you have it?'

Kon took a deep, calming breath. He had practised this. He knew what he was supposed to say. He knew what he *had* to say.

But he would never get the chance.

The sound was louder – more violent – than any Kon had ever heard. A crack that seemed to split the very air around him and then reverberate from every side of the Grote Markt. Kon had no time to wonder what in the hell had caused it; the answer came before the echo, in the warm jet of blood that soaked his face as Prochnik was thrown violently backwards.

A single bullet had torn through the side of the old lawyer's skull, its immediately fatal impact slamming his body onto the cobblestone floor of the square. Kon was left with no more questions. With no more anxious anticipation. With no more doubts.

He was left with nothing but horror.

TWO

Kon stared with puzzlement at the sight of Mendel Prochnik's body as it lay lifeless on the floor ahead of him. The sight was more than he could comprehend in the heartbeat of time that was available to him. As small as Prochnik had been, a few moments ago he had seemed the very definition of intimidation; a force of nature who had needed only words to destroy Kon's composure and leave him brutally aware of his limitations.

An instant more and the same man was a disfigured corpse, his life's purpose ended by a single bullet.

Kon remained frozen in his seat as he failed to process what he had just witnessed. In all likelihood, he would have remained there longer had he not been pulled to his feet with a force he wasn't strong enough to resist. A single word was screamed into his ear as he was lifted from the chair, before he even knew who had moved him.

'RUUUUNNNN!'

The combination of physical force and the shouted instruction broke through Kon's stunned paralysis, but the numbing shock remained. It took the crack of a second bullet – barely a moment after the first – for his survival instinct to be triggered.

Will Duffy had needed no such additional motivation. He had launched into a near-sprint even before the second bullet had rung out, his large, scarred fist gripping Kon's collar tight and hauling the younger man along in his wake. Duffy's sheer strength had given Kon no chance to resist, but with the incentive of further gunfire, the American no longer needed that encouragement.

If anything, he was now moving quicker than the Scotsman.

At first Kon was so focused on his own escape, he did not notice the movement of the crowd around him. He did not hear the increasing sound of screams as more and more shots rang out, or the wild, uncontrolled pin-balling of bodies as literally hundreds of people began to run for their lives, most fleeing a threat they could not see.

And he did not stop to wonder why people were running in different directions.

But Duffy seemed to be well aware of the chaos around them. He kept his grip tight on Kon's collar, pulling him close just as a man far larger than them both almost crashed between them. That movement sent the giant careering to Kon's right instead, into a small huddle of terrified locals who went down like bowling pins.

'THERE'S TOO MANY OF THEM,' Duffy screamed, his words the first sounds Kon had truly registered other than gunfire. 'WE NEED TO GET OUT OF HERE.'

Duffy's grip on Kon did not loosen as he shouted, nor did his pace lessen. The two men kept moving forwards into a crowd that was now hurtling in every direction. Kon was finally beginning to see the terror-fuelled madness that surrounded him, but any focus he achieved was broken with the sound of every new gunshot.

Sounds that were now coming thick and fast.

'THEY'RE ALL AROUND US.'

Duffy changed direction abruptly as he shouted and Kon now felt himself pulled to the left, turning a full ninety degrees off his path with only the smallest break in stride.

A glance over his right shoulder at where they had been heading gave the reason for the change: even with the crowd between them six deep, he could not miss the sight of two more falling bodies.

Kon flinched at the bloody sight, but he had neither the time nor the stomach to watch further. Duffy was accelerating, passing even those few now heading the same way. Kon could not fathom how the Scotsman seemed to know where to go. How he knew where the danger was and where it was not. Instead he was just grateful for the certainty; for someone with purpose and with know-how, enough to make up for Kon's own helpless terror.

The sound of another shot. The sight of another falling body, close enough this time that Kon felt the heat of the poor bastard's blood as it splattered his own cheek. And then another sudden change in direction.

Had Kon been thinking clearly, he would have realised by now that Duffy was as lost as the rest of them. That he, too, was blinded by panic. By fear and by uncertainty. And that he no longer had any idea of the route to safety. Duffy – Kon would have realised – was running for his life with nothing but the sound of gunfire to direct him.

Gunfire that had so far sent him wrong at every turn.

But Kon saw none of this. His instinct – his need – to survive demanded that he believed in something. In some*one*. And so he had invested his faith in Will Duffy, utterly and completely. It was Duffy, Kon knew, who would keep him alive. It was Duffy who would get him through this.

Until the moment it was not.

With the blood and adrenaline pumping like a torrent through his veins, it seemed there was no way Kon's heart could have beaten any faster. And yet that was exactly what he felt as he heard Duffy call out in pain and stumble to the floor.

The cause of Duffy's fall was immediately apparent; the fast-flowing blood already pumping out of the puncture wound to his calf impossible to miss. A single round, in and out, it would make movement under his own steam impossible.

Kon leaned down towards him, intending to pull Duffy back to his feet. As he moved he was violently buffeted from either side and nearly knocked down himself, the panicking crowd taking zero care as they ran for their lives. It took Kon a second or two to regain his balance before he once again held out a hand to Duffy.

A hand that the Scotsman swiped away.

'DON'T BE A FOOL, MAN,' Duffy screamed. 'THEY'RE HERE FOR YOU, KONRAD. YOU'VE GOT TO RUN.'

Kon felt his head spin as he processed the words. He did not understand what Duffy could mean, nor did he have time to think it through; it was all he could do to stay on his feet as the crowd surged past. An effort not helped as Duffy punctuated his next screamed instruction with a powerful shove to Kon's chest.

'GET THE FUCK OUT OF HERE.'

There was no mistaking the desperation – the fear – in Duffy's voice. He had fought his way back to his feet and had put everything into his physical effort to get Kon moving. It had left him struggling to stay upright on his one good leg, causing him to stumble forwards into the American's arms.

'Trust no one.' Duffy was no longer shouting. His words were now more like a plea, delivered from a distance of just inches. 'You don't know who's behind all this. If you want to survive, you trust—'

Kon felt the crack of the next bullet before he even heard it.

It caused him to flinch in fear, sure that the shooter must be just feet away, and so he missed the instant the round impacted with Duffy. But he did not miss the Scotsman's fall. The weight Kon had borne for just a moment was suddenly gone, as Duffy had hit the floor for a second time.

And this time he was not getting back up.

Kon was on his own.

A fraction of a second later and Kon was moving again. With no one to follow, his base survival instinct shifted gears and fired him into action of his own. He had no idea which direction was safe – no clue even of how many gunmen there were out there – but still his lower brain took hold. It picked a direction and it gave him a single, simple instruction:

Run.

What followed would always remain a blur to Kon. A hazy, bloody and unwelcome memory that would haunt his sleep until his dying day, but one his conscious brain could not even time. He would never recall for how long he ran, how many terrified men and women he pushed aside, how many bullets flew past. All he would remember was fighting his way through hell as he sprinted through the crowd, clambering over the dead and the dying, with bodies and blood and . . . other things, all hitting him as he moved.

It seemed to be hopeless.

It seemed to be endless.

And then it was not.

Kon felt no relief as he pushed through what proved to be the perimeter of the crowd, nor did the sight of open space fill him with anything but fear. To break free of the screaming huddle was, he realised, to make himself stand out. And to stand out was to make himself a target.

And yet Kon knew that he had to take this chance. He had no perception of how long the bullets had been flying and so no way to guess how much longer this could go on. What he did know was that more and more bodies were dropping by the second, a river of blood beginning to flow beneath his feet.

To run into the open was to risk death.

To stay might just guarantee it.

He made the decision without missing a beat, breaking through the slowing confine of the crowd and hitting a speed he had not managed even in his youth. There were others breaking free, too, he now saw; other targets, he would later realise. But in the moment he gave them no thought at all. His focus was on one thing: the road that lay directly ahead, across the square and seemingly unmanned.

The primitive part of his brain – the base instinct that had kept him alive to now – was telling him that *this* was his route to survival. That *this* was his way out of here. It had got him this far; he was not about to ignore it now.

Without so much as a glance at the bloody carnage behind him, Kon ran.

THREE

Sarah Truman's irritation was impossible to hide. She could hear it in her own exhale of breath, made through gritted teeth, as she brushed wet rusk crumbs from the baptism robes of her youngest son.

The damp marks left on the long white silk were most likely invisible to anyone else, she realised. But right now, with all the other stresses of the day, it was a problem she did not need. *And* one that should have been easily avoided.

The sound of footsteps made her look up, just as Michael Devlin walked through the door that led into the main reception room of their West London townhouse. Michael was dressed in his best navy-blue suit and he carried their other son, Liam – older by nineteen minutes than his twin, Daniel – cradled in his arm.

On most days there was no sight that Sarah could have enjoyed more. Tall and slim, Michael was as handsome at forty-one as he had been on the night they had first met. Combined with the primal appeal of a big, strong man holding their baby to his chest, her attraction to him should have only increased.

It usually did.

Today, though, was different. Today was a big day. And right now, whether he knew it or not, Michael was not helping.

'Did you give Daniel a milk biscuit?'

Sarah could not keep the annoyance from her voice as she asked the question. It caused the barrister to sheepishly move his right hand behind his back and out of sight. A reaction Sarah could not fail to notice.

'Now, it's not that I'm saying I did it,' Michael began, deploying that note of disarming charm he was able to inject into his voice at will, 'but why would it matter if I did?'

'Maybe because he's gummed it all over his baptism robes?'

'You're not in Boston now, beautiful. It's called a christening gown here.'

'And you're not in Belfast any more, Michael Devlin, so cut out the blarney.' Sarah tried hard to stay stern, even as she felt a smile threaten the corners of her mouth. 'Now tell me: how is it that I'm down here cleaning up the boys, less than twenty minutes after I finished dressing them? All I asked you to do was keep an eye on them while I got ready.'

'I did keep an eye on them. They're both still here, aren't they?'

'And what's that behind your back, huh?'

'Ah, now you're just changing the subject.'

Michael grinned as he spoke. He knew he had been caught red-handed, Sarah could tell. But still he thought he could talk his way through it. That should have irritated her but somehow it just amused her. As always, she found it near impossible to stay angry with him.

Not that she would ever let *Michael* know that.

'Is it another biscuit?'

'How do you know it's not something for you?'

'Do I look like I eat baby rusks?'

'Are you telling me you've never wondered about the taste?'

'Michael, show me your hand.'

'That'd ruin the surprise. Is that what you really want?'

'Show. Me. Your. Hand.'

Michael's smile broadened and he stepped forwards, towards the same white blanket where Daniel was lying on his back with his tiny head supported by a small, somehow ever whiter pillow. Michael leaned downwards and gently placed Liam next to his brother. For a moment he paused, his eyes fixed on his two sons.

All the while he kept his right hand hidden. Sarah watched him like a hawk throughout, well aware that sleight of hand was not beyond her fiancé.

Finally he straightened up, his full six-foot-one height towering over Sarah's own five eight. Even with her eyes still on his hand, she could almost feel his mischievous expression. And for the first time she began to doubt herself; perhaps it was not a biscuit, after all.

'Well, I was planning to give you this when you were in a better mood. But if it cheers you up then it'll have done its job.'

'Michael, I'm not—'

Before Sarah could finish, Michael held out a flat jeweller's box and opened the top. Inside it was a pendant attached to a delicate necklace. The thin chain was made of gold, Sarah could tell, while the pendant itself was a heart of diamonds interwoven with a Celtic knot of gold and white gold.

The sight made her catch her breath, but her reaction was not because of the gift itself.

It was because she had seen *this* gift before.

'Michael. That's . . . this . . . it's your mother's pendant.'

'And now it's *your* pendant, darling. From me and from the boys. And from my ma, too.'

Sarah felt a tear begin to trickle down from her eye.

'I can't . . . it's your mother's, Michael. I can't—'

'And now it's *their* mother's.' Michael indicated to their sons as he spoke. 'She'd want you to have it, Sarah. We're all that's left of my family. The boys are all there is to carry it on. So it's right that you have this. Besides, *I* want you to have it.'

'What about Anne?'

'Anne knows,' Michael replied. Anne Flaherty was the partner of Michael's late brother Liam. She was also the only living connection Michael had to his past. 'And she's happy.'

Michael reached out and gently wiped the tear from Sarah's cheek. He then removed the pendant from the box, traced the necklace around her neck and connected the clasp. Done, he kissed her on her brow and stepped back. His grin was gone, replaced with a look of total affection.

'It suits you. You look beautiful, sweetheart.'

Sarah struggled for a reply, aware that the tear Michael had wiped away had been replaced by another. When she finally did, it was with a question:

'Tell me what it means.'

'It means there's no beginning and no end,' Michael explained. 'The flow of the knot through the heart represents unity and eternal life. It represents what you made when you made the boys.'

'When *we* made them,' Sarah said.

'Let's not pretend you didn't do the heavy lifting on that one, gorgeous.'

Sarah laughed as she wiped away the tears from her cheek and from her eyes.

'You realise I've got to go re-do my make-up now, right?'

'I hadn't noticed.'

'Meaning you've got to keep an eye on the boys again.'

'Not a problem.'

'And just so we're clear, "keeping an eye" doesn't just mean keeping them breathing. You've got to keep them clean, too.'

Michael's grin widened even further as he raised his left hand. Sarah's eyes shifted to the rusk he was holding between his fingers.

'Then I guess I'll be putting this away until after church.' He looked down towards the blanket. 'Sorry, lads. No more snacking. Yer ma's spoken.'

FOUR

Joe Dempsey crossed the narrow street to the pavement opposite the Church of St Thomas More, placed his hand on his forehead to shield his eyes from the intensity of the sun and looked up.

The church was in London's Chelsea district, just a short walk from the King's Road and only a little further from Michael and Sarah's home in Carlyle Square. It was not what Dempsey would have imagined from the surroundings. The building was surprisingly plain from the outside. Built in unflattering red brick. It looked almost as if a poorly designed factory had been dropped just a stone's throw from the most scenic part of the River Thames, an effect worsened by the pretty, chocolate-box townhouses that surrounded it.

Not that Dempsey was here to appraise the architecture. No. He was here for a far more important task – to take on a duty to which, until just a few days ago, he had feared he was entirely unsuited, but to which he could also not bring himself to say no.

Dempsey's opinion on that subject had been changed by the events of the past week and the lengths to which he had pushed himself to protect the son of his former friend. But that reassurance was the sole positive of what he had just lived through. His experiences in the past seven days – chasing down a dirty bomb across the State of Florida, failing to prevent a prison break in Texas and then leading a pitched battle against a domestic terrorist organisation in the foothills of the Appalachian mountains – had taken a physical and emotional toll that had left him close to exhaustion. And so this rare holiday – his first trip home in four years – was needed more now than ever.

Taking just a few moments more to enjoy the warmth of the sun, Dempsey inhaled a deep, reassuring breath, stepped off the curb and headed towards the church.

The large wooden doors at the front of the building had been left open for the arrival of the christening party, but the church itself seemed deserted. Dempsey was unsure if this was unusual. It had been a while since he had stepped inside a place like this and he could not remember the last time he had done so without it being full. Normal or not, for now he was completely alone.

The question vanished anyway as he paid proper attention to the building's interior, which he now saw was nothing like the outside. It seemed older. As if it predated the exterior, which was of course impossible. But it was something more than that which had grabbed him.

It's what? he asked himself. *A feeling? Or a memory?*

Dempsey looked around as he sought to answer his own question, a strangely familiar discomfort moving within his stomach as he did so. In contrast to the plain walls visible from the street, the nave of the building was filled with a combination of marble, gold leaf and fine art. Like all Catholic churches in England, it paled against the grandeur of Rome. Or even some of those in New York, or at least Manhattan.

But for that, *this* was a church. The kind Dempsey remembered from his childhood. *This*, his father had raised him to believe, was 'God's house'. That thought alone – that rare mental reference to the man who had raised him – explained the gnawing, unhappy feeling deep within his gut. Even one glimpse of that face within his mind's eye brought back a thousand memories. Very few of them were good. And none of them were welcome.

For a moment, in the silence of the nave, Dempsey's thoughts began to drift to a place he had avoided for years. A place he did not want to revisit. He was grateful, then, when they were drowned out by the sound of small wheels on paving stones, and by two very different accents.

Northern Irish and American. Both well-spoken versions, both with the tinge of British colour that years in London will inevitably add. Two voices that made Dempsey happier than he had been in a very long time.

They're here.

Dempsey had not seen Michael Devlin or Sarah Truman in more than two years. Not in person, anyway. One of the few positives of the Covid-19 lockdown was how au fait the world had become with interacting on-screen. And while Dempsey had been less reliant on that tech than most, none of the international journeys his job had required while the planet was closed had brought him home to the UK.

It was via exactly that kind of video link-up that Dempsey had 'seen' Sarah Truman just thirty-six hours ago. From his hotel room back in Philadelphia, to explain why his trip to London had been delayed and to reassure her that its cause had been settled; that he *would* make it to the baptism. But all *that* call had done was to cement how screen contact was no substitute.

No amount of Zoom or Skype would ever replace the physical presence of a friend.

And it sure as hell doesn't replace family.

The afternoon sun beamed powerfully as Sarah reached the

church. It caused the wooden doorway to frame her, creating a full body halo that left her features in shadow, too dark to make out. Not that those details were needed. Dempsey would recognise Sarah Truman in pitch darkness. Right now, he even knew how wide she was smiling.

That happiness filled her voice when she spoke.

'The elusive Joseph Dempsey.'

Sarah's face became visible as she took the few steps that separated them. The grin *was* there, as big as Dempsey had ever seen it, while her striking green eyes were alive with excitement and her arms thrown wide in welcome. An instant later and Dempsey was engulfed in her tight embrace.

'My God it's good to see you.' Sarah spoke into Dempsey's ear as she gripped him harder, every word filled with genuine feeling. 'It's been way too long.'

'I know,' Dempsey whispered. He would have been uncomfortable with this level of physical contact from almost anyone else. But not from her. Dempsey hugged back hard. 'I'm sorry I've not been back.'

'You'll be even more sorry if you don't take your hands off my girl.'

The second voice – male and Irish – came from the sun-drenched doorway. Another silhouette that Dempsey could have identified at a hundred yards, even without the distinctive accent. Dempsey and Sarah each took a step backwards, and Sarah moved to her right to give him a clear view.

Michael Devlin stepped into the space she had vacated. The effect of the sunbeam was less angelic upon him than it had been on his fiancée. Which was, at least to Dempsey's mind, entirely appropriate.

As Michael moved forwards, Dempsey could see a double

buggy behind him, safely stationed in the shade just inside the open doorway. He thrust out his right hand and, with a nod of his head, he indicated the buggy.

'You on parking duty, are you?'

Michael slapped Dempsey's hand aside, took one step closer and threw his arms around his friend's shoulders. It was the same reaction as Sarah's, fuelled by the joy of being together again. And no doubt by sadness that it could not last.

Dempsey returned both the embrace and the sentiment. For the second or two that it lasted, neither man said a word.

'OK. Enough of the emotional bollocks.'

Michael stepped back as he spoke. He looked Dempsey up and down, as if suddenly all business. Dempsey realised he was being assessed for fresh damage. For new injuries, sustained since they had last seen one another. Dempsey knew they were there. He knew where they were. And he knew that most were too old now to affect his movement much, so he was confident that Michael could not spot them.

'I'm not gonna lie, I can't quite believe you're here,' Michael finally said, his grin returning as he spoke. 'I can't believe you really made it.'

'Like I was ever going to miss this,' Dempsey replied.

'It was touch and go for a while there,' Sarah said. 'Any chance we'll ever hear why?'

'No chance at all,' Dempsey replied. 'You know we don't talk to the press.'

'Screw you. When was I ever "the press" where you're concerned?'

Dempsey had no doubt that the outrage was fake and was happy that his answer had diverted Sarah from her question. As much as he loved them both, there were things about his 'other' life that he could not discuss. Not even with his closest friends.

'And there was me thinking my job's just not newsworthy enough for you,' Dempsey joked. 'But what does it matter? I got here, didn't I? I was always getting here.'

'Never doubted it for a second, buddy.' Michael slapped Dempsey's arm as he spoke, then waited a beat. 'Well, maybe for *a bit* of a second . . .'

'Well, *I* was confident about it, at least.' Dempsey laughed. 'I couldn't leave you two hanging on this one.'

'No. No, you bloody well could not.' Michael's smile widened as he spoke. 'Speaking of which, isn't it above time for the boys to meet their Uncle Joe?'

Dempsey walked the few paces to the buggy and for the first time looked down on the small, sleeping faces of the eight-month-old twin boys, just about discernible under their shawls and their hats. They remained motionless, sleeping tight through the big introduction.

Dempsey felt an unfamiliar sensation. Nerves, it seemed to be. Or anxiety. It was alien enough that he was unsure even what to call it, but he felt it now as he looked down on Liam and Daniel Devlin.

On his godsons.

Children had rarely featured in Dempsey's life. He was unmarried, unattached and dedicated to a job that could end his life at any moment. It was hardly an ideal scenario into which to bring a dependent of any kind, let alone a child. But now, as he looked down at Liam and Daniel Devlin, he knew that his doubts about standing for them had been misplaced.

Dempsey *could* do this. He *could* love them. Most of all, if it were ever needed, he could protect them.

'You alright there, Joe?'

Dempsey looked over his shoulder, only now realising that he had lowered himself onto his haunches. He shook his head at Michael.

'Guys, they're incredible. They're just ... they're beautiful.'

Sarah laughed. 'We think so too.'

'Plus it's important you like them,' Michael added, 'because, you know, if anything bad ever happens to us ...'

'Stop that.' Sarah punched Michael in the arm. 'Don't even say that in here.'

'Man's entitled to know what he's getting himself into.' Michael chuckled to himself as he rubbed the spot where he'd been hit. 'So what do you say, Uncle Joe?'

Dempsey looked from Michael to Sarah, and then down to the still-sleeping boys. Two people he loved, suddenly multiplied to four.

He took a moment, then stood back up.

'Godsons or not, they're family. Same as you. And you know I won't let anything happen to my family.'

Dempsey finished with a deep breath, followed by a long exhale. An unconscious effort to expel the seriousness of the moment. When he spoke again, his tone was lighter.

'Now let's get this thing started before I change my mind.'

FIVE

Kon Frankowski's lungs burned with the strain as he burst through the heavy wooden door that barred his way into the Polska Parafia Den Haag. The relief that the church was unlocked caused his legs to buckle a little, but somehow he managed to stay standing.

He steadied himself on the closed left-hand door, pulled shut its right-hand twin and searched for some means to lock the pair. He quickly found it. A large metal hinge bolt, centuries older than the doors themselves if its battered condition was any indication. It would have been more than enough to keep him out, had it been in place.

He pulled down the bolt and checked it was secure. He had no idea if he had been followed. And if he had, a locked door was a weak obstacle to someone determined to find him. But it was better than nothing. At the very least it would slow them down.

Reassured that he was safe for the moment, Kon staggered backwards. He felt his spine hit a tall marble column that stood between the doorway and the aisle and, with his fight or flight instinct now exhausted, he slid down its smooth, cold stone.

He had no idea if he was alone in the white-walled nave of the church. Nor did he care. His focus was on his hands. They were red with blood and they were shaking, even as he rested them on his torn, crimson-stained linen trousers.

But for all of the physical manifestations of his shock, Kon's mind was clear. For the first time since the first gunshot in the

Grote Markt, he could hear his own thoughts. Thoughts which now stretched beyond the next moment. And they left him with one inevitable question.

What now?

He had no answer yet but his mind was working fast. He was sure it would come. In the meantime, he needed to clean himself.

Kon climbed back to his feet and staggered to the ornate stone stoup just feet away, then plunged his shaking hands into the deep pool of holy water inside it. The clear liquid was almost instantly streaked with the red that had caked his skin. The sheer amount of blood first surprised him, and then it worried him: if there was so much on his hands, what about the rest of him?

He thrust his hands back into the water, only this time he scooped out a handful and threw it across his face and his scalp. He did the same thing twice more, rubbing hard at the skin all across his head and neck. Then, after a glance towards the parts of the church he could see to ensure he was still alone, he stripped to his waist and used his black T-shirt as a towel, dabbing away the excess water and with it the streaks of diluted blood that had stained him. Done, he pulled the wet cloth back over his head.

The sensation of the damp T-shirt was almost a relief as it clung tight to his torso. Kon realised now that he had been dripping with sweat as well, brought on by the mix of exertion and heat. And, he guessed, from the flood of adrenaline that had been like nothing he had ever experienced before.

Kon was not sure how far he had run. Or for how long. It was further than it should have been, he knew that much; while the Church of St John Paul II was just three roads from the

Grote Markt, in his manic state Kon had lost his way. But still, it could not have taken him that far out of his way.

And yet right now, despite having covered only a relatively short distance, his legs felt like lead.

That's the terror, he told himself. *Throw that into the mix and even an Olympian would be exhausted.*

His tiredness, though, was hardly pressing. Instead he forced his mind back to the square. Back to the horror he had witnessed. To the bloody executions of scores of innocent people.

The memory was far from complete, but it was too much even so. Kon could feel the shaking of his hands worsen as the foggy images began to coalesce in his mind. Dead bodies littering the ground as he fought his way through the crowd. The horror ... the carnage ... it was more than he could take. And it was made worse by the shame that rose in his gut at his brutally honest assessment of himself.

You thought of no one else, Kon, he told himself. *You thought of no one but yourself.*

And you left Will Duffy to die.

'You're nothing but a goddamned fucking coward.'

He said the last words aloud and so, for the first time, he heard the tears in his own voice as he began to sob. Kon would later realise that this was natural. That this was human; it was just what happens to a traumatised human being when every distraction is gone and they are left with only shock, relief and disbelief.

He would learn all of this in time. For now he could do nothing but cry, his sobs growing more pronounced as grief overtook him. It left him as little more than a shaking heap on the cold church floor, his mind racing with questions:

How am I even here?

Why me, of all people? Why was it me who got away?

Why not Prochnik? Or Duffy?

Why not all those poor people I just stepped over?

The image that came with that final thought made his blood run cold.

Those people he had stepped over, as if they were nothing but an obstacle in his path. Why had they paid with their lives, when he had not?

For a time Kon could think of nothing else; he was lost in despair and debilitating survivor's guilt. And then, just as suddenly as those thoughts had engulfed him, they were gone. Replaced by the words Will Duffy had shouted into his ear:

'THEY'RE HERE FOR YOU, KONRAD.'

Kon's sobs stopped in that moment, that precise, now-vivid memory clarifying in his mind and banishing all others.

It had not occurred to Kon that the shooting was anything but random. Even with Prochnik as the first victim – and even though Kon was acutely aware of the dangers of his situation – his mind had just not gone there. The people he was involved with were military professionals. They were elite. Surgical. *That* was the world Kon had stepped into; one where consequences come without fanfare. Where death is cold and calm, waged without waste of energy or resource.

The Grote Markt was the opposite of that. It was mass murder. Indiscriminate death on a grand scale. A terrorist attack, Kon had presumed. Or just another crazy sonofabitch with an automatic weapon, the kind of thing that happens way too often back in the States.

But then Will Duffy had said what he'd said, and was so sure of it. He had seemed to know immediately what was happening and why. And, since he clearly knew a hell of a lot more about all this than Kon, it was more than likely that Scotsman's conclusions were correct.

'Trust no one. You don't know who's behind all this. If you want to survive, you trust—'

They were the last words Duffy had ever said and they came to Kon now, just as the image of the lawyer's fallen body appeared in his mind. Kon had barely heard them at the time, and he sure as hell had not registered their meaning. How could he, when he knew so little about what 'all this' even was?

But now? As little as Kon understood what was happening, he was convinced that his life was still in danger. Whoever was behind the hell in the Grote Markt, they would still be coming for him. He had to protect himself by following Duffy's instructions, if only because Duffy had sacrificed his life to give them. And Kon knew his best chance of survival was to face that fate alone. It was a terrifying realisation. And it was more than he could take.

His breathing had become more and more shallow in the past few minutes and, with his stress hormones spiking, he began to feel light-headed. The sensation was accompanied by a rush of cold, wet saliva against the walls of his mouth, along with a feeling of weakness in his chin. Kon recognised both as the physical markers that came before vomiting.

He climbed to his feet, his legs unsteady beneath him, and forced himself to take in the biggest lungfuls of air that he could manage. The effect was as intended; the symptoms began to abate and the nausea lessened, and Kon's head began to clear. His legs now steadier, he kept up the deep-breathing technique as he moved back towards the aisle, his vision steadier by the second.

It took just four steps more for Kon to reach the nave of the church, and for the first time he could see the full deserted grandeur of the place. It was a sight that gave him comfort. A left-over, he realised, from a childhood in which his parents' Catholicism loomed large. For a religious boy back in New Jersey, the church was the ultimate safe space. The place to which he could run when he needed to escape the bullies who found sport in tormenting him.

Kon today was far from the shy, bookish child he had been back then. He was successful. He was confident. Hell, he was even an atheist. And yet this was still the place he had chosen when he needed sanctuary. As he moved further along the aisle and saw more of the building – new to him, but as familiar as all Catholic churches tend to be – he began to understand why.

I guess we don't change so much after all.

Whatever subconscious drive had brought him here, it was the respite Kon required. A temporary enclave from the madness he had left behind. It could not last, he knew. The church would have to open soon enough.

But not for an hour. Not for two, even. As long as that door stays locked . . .

He bowed his right knee and lowered his head to the crucifix that hung above the altar ahead, all without thinking. Unconscious genuflection. Another tic from his childhood, maintained even into his ungodly adult years. Then he slipped into the pew to his left.

Kon's eyes remained fixed above the altar as he slid along the hard wooden bench. The effect that the image of the crucified Christ had on him had changed over the years. As a boy it had signified hope. Life after death; the reward promised for faith. And then, as a man, it had meant something else entirely: it had become the visual representation of what Kon now thought of as a two-thousand-year-old cult.

But right now it was neither of those things. It was simply a totem upon which to focus. A fixed point in space at which he could stare while he rid himself of the thoughts – of the memories – that were tormenting him.

For a moment it seemed to work. Combined with his continued deep breathing, he could feel his heartbeat slow and his mental images begin to fade. For a moment, it seemed like he was going to pull through this. Like the horrors of the Grote Markt might not have stained his soul, after all.

For a moment, his mind was empty.

And it was then that the worst fear of all hijacked his every conscious thought.

'Maria.'

SIX

Kulvinder Vic Sethi threw his heavy cricket bag into the back seat of the 2012 Opel Vectra, slammed shut the door and climbed into the front passenger seat, all without even a glance towards the driver. Neither man said a word as the car pulled into the empty lane and began to drive away from the chaos that was visible in Sethi's wing mirror.

Sethi had removed his black balaclava, his assault vest and trousers, his boots and his gloves in an alleyway less than two hundred yards from the square. Along with his AK-47 and two back-up pistols, those items were now stashed in the long sports holdall on the seat behind him.

It had been a risk to change so close to the site of the operation, but neither Sethi nor his three accomplices had any choice. Their assault on the Grote Markt had lasted just minutes, but that level of carnage was always going to attract police attention fast. The sirens were already close when Sethi had called a halt to the attack and so any retreat from the scene had to be short and well-planned.

Careful preparation had ensured it was exactly that.

Sethi's earlier reconnaissance of the location had been thorough. Working against the clock, he had noted the location of every camera that surrounded the square – both local authority CCTV and independent security coverage from the nearby shops and bars – and he had used that information to plot the four clearest routes of escape. Each of these, he had ensured, would lead either him or a member of his group to a safe spot where they could quickly change their appearance unseen, before disappearing back into the horrified crowds.

It was the only safe way for them to exit once the job was done. And in Sethi's case it had worked perfectly. For now he could only hope that the same was true of the others.

By now well practised, it had taken Sethi less than a minute to transform himself from gunman to something a lot less menacing. He had worn his white Hard Rock Cafe T-shirt and bright-yellow, knee-length shorts beneath his assault gear. They combined with his bohemian-style front-and-back sandals to form an already solid disguise, but their effect was improved by his long, oiled black hair and a pitch-perfect Northern English accent in the place of his native New Delhi. He looked like a British interrailer on tour. And his diminutive height of five-foot-two only reinforced his civilian camouflage. No one would take *this* Vic Sethi for the merciless mercenary he truly was. He knew that for one sure and certain reason: in all the years Sethi had been doing this, no one ever had.

With no further thought now needed on his escape, Sethi paid no attention to the long stream of city police vehicles that were driving at speed on the other side of the road. Instead he turned his attention to the laptop he had seized in the square.

It was, he was already sure, the key to all of this.

Sethi pushed the screen up from its near closed position and watched as it came to life. The machine had been open when he'd reached it, on the table closest to the corpse of Mendel Prochnik, and he had been careful not to change that. To close it completely could have triggered the need to re-enter a password that Sethi did not possess. And while he was sure his employer had technicians capable of circumventing that little detail, he also knew that time was not on their side.

He was relieved, then, to see the screen light up as he opened it fully. He even smiled when he saw what was on it. Two faces. Both of them familiar. Both of them now dead at the hands of Sethi and his team.

The smile faded quickly as he navigated away to the laptop's desktop page. Sethi had hoped to see an array of folders there. The haystack in which he would search for the needle he had been instructed to find. To his disappointment there were almost no icons that indicated the presence of files. Instead the dominant image was its default backdrop.

Sethi had expected to spend hours searching the laptop for what he needed. Days, even, depending on how good its owner was. It took less than five minutes to teach him otherwise. The machine was brand new. Purchased and registered within the last forty-eight hours, no doubt intended for today's task and nothing more.

If this guy had the file, it's somewhere else entirely.

It was an unwelcome reality, one that Sethi knew his employer would not take well. And it was with that thought in mind that he turned his head towards a new sound within the car: the buzz of a vibrating mobile, a specialised model that was sitting in the central console between him and the driver.

Sethi had no doubt who was calling. And not for the first time, he found himself wondering if his employer might actually be psychic. He watched as the driver reached out, picked up the phone and offered it to him.

'Is the encryption on?'

'End to end,' the driver replied, his eyes never leaving the road.

Sethi did not even nod in response. He just hit the connect icon and put the phone to his ear.

'What happened?'

The voice was abrupt and to the point. By now Sethi would expect nothing else. In the four years since he had first been engaged by the Monk – the only name Sethi knew for the man – their relationship had never strayed so much as an inch beyond business.

'As planned,' Sethi replied.

'Prochnik and Duffy?'

'Dead.'

'You're sure?'

'Prochnik I hit first. Definite kill shot.'

'And Duffy?'

'One of the musketeers got him.'

The Monk did not ask who he was referring to. Sethi always assigned code names, as the Monk insisted that no team member should know details that could identify the others, a long-standing rule that Sethi obeyed without question. He usually based them on pop culture references, and had decided on the Dumas classic for this team. No doubt used to his code names by now, the Monk made no comment at all. When he spoke again it was as if his attention had been diverted not a jot.

'You're sure?'

'I saw him go down,' Sethi replied. 'And I saw the body.'

'And what about the contact? Did you recognise him?'

'It wasn't someone I knew, no.'

'Did you deal with him? Did you get what we needed?'

'I can't say for sure. I lost sight of him once the crowd went crazy. There's a chance one of the others got him but I'll need to ask them. We hit a lot of people. The contact might have been one of them.'

'Might have been?'

'It's not the perfect outcome, I know. But given the constraints of the plan—'

'The plan was you kill the lawyers and whoever they were meeting, and that you secure whatever the third party was carrying.'

Sethi took a deep breath. He wanted to snap out his response – to give the Monk a reality check – but he knew he had to control his tone. He was speaking to a man who dealt with insubordination as harshly as he did failure. When he spoke again, he kept his tone respectful.

'I understand that. But you also wanted it to seem like indiscriminate, amateur terrorism. That affected how obviously we could target these people.'

The Monk said nothing. As ever, Sethi did not know what was worse: the sound of his employer's strange, roaming accent as it disparaged his efforts, or the silence as the Monk's cruel mind ticked over, no doubt considering the severity of his response.

An instant more and he had his answer.

'Let us be clear on what you are telling me, then. The lawyers are gone. But whoever they were meeting, we have no way to know if he is alive or dead. And more importantly, we have no way to know *who* he is, or track down the file that was the entire point of this operation.'

'Well—'

'DO YOU NOT SEE THE PROBLEM HERE?'

The sudden explosion of anger was unexpected. Not because Sethi had never experienced it before – bursts of fury were common from the Monk – but because it had come so soon. It usually took the man much longer to lose his temper.

'I see it. I do. But you didn't let me finish. There's more.'

Once again the Monk allowed Sethi's words to hang. The long pause seemed unnecessary, but Sethi had learned not to question the Monk's reactions. Instead he waited.

'Go on.'

'I know the contact's name. He's called Konrad Frankowski.'

'How can you know that?'

'Because while I didn't take him down, I did retrieve his laptop. It was registered to that name.'

'You have his computer?'

'Yes.'

'Then you have the file?'

'No,' Sethi admitted. 'There's almost nothing on there. Almost no files or information at all.'

'And yet you tell me this as if it's a positive thing.'

'It has its upsides,' Sethi replied. 'We know who he is. Which means if he survived, we can find him. If he didn't, well, we still have somewhere to start.'

Sethi paused as he allowed that information to sink in. But only for a moment. He knew how quickly the Monk processed information and so he moved on at speed.

'Does the name mean anything to you?' he asked.

'No. But it will. Was the device registered to an address?'

'An American address, yes.'

'OK. Send me it as soon as I hang up. No mistakes. Then wait for my next call.'

'On this handset?'

'On your own. Head back to your room now and wait.'

'And the three musketeers?'

'They'll be told to do the same. I don't know if I'm finished with them yet. I don't know if I'm finished with any of you. Not until I know a little more about Konrad Frankowski.'

'OK.'

'And Kulvinder?'

'Yes?'

'Well done with the laptop. You might have redeemed yourself yet.'

The line went dead once the final word was spoken. Exactly as Sethi expected. The Monk was not usually a man who gave compliments. And he was certainly not one who hung around to discuss them on the rare occasions he did. But still, Sethi could not suppress a smile.

The mission had not gone perfectly, but then what mission ever did?

He had done well.

Next time, he would do even better.

SEVEN

Kon wiped the sheen of cold sweat from his forehead as his fingertips brought his iPhone screen to life. His eyes struggled to focus on the names listed under 'Favourites', the seven entries swaying back and forth under his gaze. His nausea was back. Brought on by fear and panic, sure, but this time also by dread.

How was he going to tell her?

More to the point, *what* was he going to tell her?

The thought of the conversation to come made Kon sick to the stomach and yet he knew he had no choice. If there was even the slightest risk he had put Maria and the boys in danger, he had to warn her. He had to give them a chance to run.

A chance to run.

For a moment the idea seemed ridiculous. The image of his family packing up and running to . . . to where? And from whom? In that instant it struck Kon as absurd. But he knew he could not allow his brain to play those tricks. Even with his world falling apart around him, Kon had retained enough clarity to see what his subconscious was doing.

It's looking for ways out of this, he realised. *For an excuse to avoid the conversation with Maria. It's telling me there's no danger to them so I don't have to make the call.*

But it's wrong.

Those bastards back at the square, they were *there for me. They had to be.*

And after what they did there, they won't stop until they have what they came for.

39

They won't stop until they have the file.

No, Kon would not deceive himself. He was a problem to these people. He had to accept that. Just as he knew now that these were men who solved problems in the ugliest of ways.

And that, Kon figured, made his loved ones a sure and certain target.

He glanced at the clock on his phone screen. It was 1.27 p.m. Almost thirty minutes since the shooting had started. And 7.27 a.m. back home in New Jersey.

The half-hour delay since the Grote Markt attack made the decision for him; Kon couldn't put it off any longer. Not when every additional minute could be putting his family at risk.

Maria has to know.

He tapped the top entry on the 'Favourites' page and put the phone to his ear. It was answered almost immediately.

'Jesus, Kon. Are you OK?'

Maria's tone was urgent, as if she were panicking. Kon immediately thought the worst, his heart rate spiking again as he jumped to the deadliest possible conclusion.

Could they be there already? Could they even know who he was this fast?

His questions were answered – to Kon's relief – when Maria spoke again.

'I just saw what happened on the TV. Literally just this second. My phone was already in my hand to call you.'

Kon took a deep, calming breath. For a moment he had thought . . . he did not even want to admit what he had thought. But that single moment of terror, it put everything into perspective.

His family was safe. That was all that mattered. Nothing else.

And now I have to keep them that way.

'Kon, did you hear me?'

Maria's tone had become impatient. Kon immediately realised why. In his relief that she was safe he had stopped listening and so he had missed what she had said next. It was not the ideal way to start *any* conversation. It sure as hell was not what he wanted for this one.

'Sorry, baby. I didn't . . . I didn't hear what you said.'

'I asked if you were close to where it happened.'

'You mean the shooting?'

'What the hell else, Kon? It's all over the news. I just sat down to watch the TV and dropped my damn coffee.'

'You OK?'

'Am *I* OK? Yeah, I'm OK. Now I know *you're* OK, anyway.'

Kon took another deep breath. It did him no good. His hands continued to shake, a physical manifestation of his fear of what he was about to do. Of how Maria would react to what he had to tell her. When he finally spoke his voice was much quieter than he intended.

'I'm not.'

'You're not what?'

'I'm not OK. I *was* there, baby. I was in the square.'

Maria audibly swallowed at the news. The shock silenced her, if only for an instant. When she spoke again her voice was strained. As if she were afraid of the answer to her inevitable question.

'Were you . . . were you hurt?'

'No.'

'You . . . how . . .'

'I don't know how, Maria. But no. No, I wasn't.'

Kon could hear the inevitable exhale of relief. He knew his wife well enough to guess what was coming next.

'What the hell happened there? All those people.'

'I know. I've never seen anything like it. It was . . . it was just . . . just hell on Earth.'

'Who were the shooters? The news is saying they got away. Were the cops able to tell you anything about them?'

'I don't know. I . . . I haven't spoken to the cops.'

'You haven't . . . Kon, what the hell?'

'I ran, Maria. I just ran.'

'But . . .'

'It was hell, baby. It was . . . it was . . . I can't even describe it. But it was terrifying. So I ran and I hid. I don't know, maybe *that's* how I'm still alive.'

At first Maria said nothing. When she broke that silence, her tone was soft. As if she were speaking to a child.

'OK. I get that, Kon. I really get that. But you have to speak to them. You know that, right? You have to go back. You have to give your statement.'

'Why? Who would that help?'

'The police, Kon. You're an eyewitness to maybe the worst terrorist attack that country has ever seen. They're gonna need every bit of information they can lay their hands on to find those sonsofbitches. They need you, Kon. They need to know what you saw.'

'I can't do it, baby. I can't . . .'

'Of course you can. Look, I can't imagine what you just went through, but it's over. It's safe. You're safe. So now you have to do your duty. You've got to—'

'Goddammit, Maria, I can't do it!'

Kon hardly recognised his own tone as he barked out the

words. He sounded angry. And he was; he was angry at himself. But to Maria, he knew, the irritation would seem directed at her.

An instant later and he was proved correct.

'Just what the hell is wrong with you?' The kind tone was gone. 'What the hell do you mean, you can't?'

'I just can't, OK? I—'

'What the fuck is going on with you, Kon? What *is* all this? You've been a nightmare to live with for months, and now *this*? Jesus Christ, for once in your life be a damned man and do the right thing.'

'I can't.'

'Why the hell not?'

'Because they were there for *me*, OK? *I'm* why those people died. It wasn't a terrorist attack, Maria. It was targeted. And *I* was the target.'

The fact that Kon expected the silence that followed did not make it any easier to take. But how else could his wife respond to what he had just told her? And so he did not press when she said nothing. A full minute passed before either of them spoke again.

'Kon, I . . . I don't . . .'

It was all she seemed able to say. And it was enough.

'I got myself into some shit,' Kon explained, each word feeling like a weight being lifted from his shoulders. 'I got myself mixed up with the wrong kind of people. The wrong person, truth be told. He asked me to do something for him, Maria. I knew it couldn't be straight because, well, because of who was asking. But he was paying me a lot of money. So I said yes.'

This time the silence did not last.

'Are you telling me you've been breaking the law?'

'Not on this, no.' By keeping his answer specific, Kon was telling the truth. He just hoped that his wife's questioning would not widen in scope. 'It was just a meeting. A delivery to two lawyers.'

'A delivery of what?'

'That's not important, Maria. What's important is what happened.'

'You mean the shooting? What, that was around the delivery?'

'It was.'

'And the lawyers?'

'They're dead.'

'But you got away without a scratch?'

Kon detected a hint of disgust in Maria's voice. As if her relief at his survival had turned into distaste. He tried to ignore it.

'I got lucky, baby,' Kon explained. 'That's all.'

'Do they know who you are? The people who tried to kill you? Do they know your name?'

This time he could not ignore the change in his wife's voice. The questions came quickly, in a tone that was now more efficient than anything else. It was almost as if he was being interrogated. It left Kon ill at ease.

'I . . . I don't know.'

'What do you mean you don't know?'

'I mean I don't know anything about these people. Other than that they're way more dangerous than the lawyers could have guessed. Which means I've no damn clue if they know who I am. But we have to plan for the worst-case scenario. We have to assume that they do.'

'And have you thought through what that means?'

'What what means?'

'The fact that dangerous people are hunting you while you're in the wind?'

Kon did not reply. As stressed and as shaken as he was, still Maria's words struck him as . . . unusual.

In the wind?

It was not an expression he would have ever expected his wife to use.

'So have you?' she demanded. The interruption brought Kon's focus back to what mattered. 'Have you considered the consequences of that? The consequences to *us*?'

'Of course I have.'

'So you know that if they can't find you, that they'll come for your family.' Maria was getting angrier by the word. 'Is that why you called me? Is that why you're finally telling me about the . . . the . . . the fucking disaster you've made of your life?'

'Baby, no, of course that's not the only—'

'You need to stop calling me that.' Maria's voice was now close to a shout. Her fury impossible to miss. 'You've put our whole family in danger. You don't get to do that and then call me "baby", like nothing's happened. You got that?'

Kon had no immediate response. And Maria left him no time to think of one.

'Forget that for now. We've got more important shit to get right. First up, you need to know this: if there's even a chance these people are coming our way then the boys and I will be out of this house within fifteen minutes of this call. Twenty minutes at the outside. We'll be gone and we'll be safe and you won't have to worry about us. You understand that?'

The sudden change in direction left Kon reeling.

'But where—'

'You don't need to know where, Kon. And I'm not sure I

trust you enough to tell you. You just need to know we'll be safe, because from this moment on you need to concentrate on yourself, OK?'

Kon felt bewildered by what he was hearing.

'Maria, how . . . I just—'

'Are you listening to me? You need to focus on staying alive. And you can't do that if you're thinking about us. Now what are your plans?'

'My plans?'

'Yes, your plans. You've got to have some idea of what you're going to do?'

'I was . . . I was just going to stay where I am for a few hours. To let things die down a little. Then, I guess, back to my hotel room to—'

'You don't go anywhere near that hotel, Kon. You got that?'

'But—'

'You go back there and you're dead. If they know who you are, they'll be waiting for you there. Do you understand that?'

'I—'

'Do you understand that, Kon?'

'Yes.' Kon followed the reasoning. He just could not fathom how it was coming from his wife. In the last minute she had taken on another persona entirely. It was like he was speaking to a different woman.

How does she know any of this?

'What money do you have?'

The question ended Kon's mental diversion.

'With me?' he asked. 'In The Hague?'

'On you. Right now.'

'I've got eighty euros in my pocket. And my cards.'

'What cards?'

46

'My bank cards. Checking accounts and Amex.'

'How many?'

'Three.'

'What about your passport?'

'It's . . . it's back at the hotel. I need to—'

'It's the last thing you need. Leave it.'

'Maria, seriously, baby, I need you to tell me what the hell—'

'What you need is to listen to me. Where are you now? Where exactly?'

'I'm in a church. A few blocks from where it happened.'

'Then stay there. Not just for a couple of hours. You stay there until it's dark. You need the cover.'

'The cover?'

'Just do as I say. Once it's dark, you get yourself to the nearest ATM and you max out every one of those cards. Get as much cash as you can, then throw the cards in the trash and get the hell out of town.'

'But if I use the cards and they can access bank records, they'll know where I am.'

'They'll know where you *were*. But not where you went next. All it tells them is that you were in The Hague today. They already know that. Once you've got the cash and you've ditched the cards, then you become invisible.'

'What about when the cash runs out?'

'I'm going to wire you more. Tomorrow, once the boys and I are clear of here and safe. Western Union, OK? As soon as they open over here. That way you can pick it up wherever you are, provided you have your ID. You do have some form of ID, right? I know you keep your licence in your wallet? Tell me you've got your wallet.'

'I do, yeah.'

'Good. You can use that ID to draw the cash. Just make sure that when you do, it's not in whichever city you choose to stay in. Google Western Union outlets far enough from where you're hiding that no one would connect the two. Then go there for that reason only, withdraw the money and get out of there. OK?'

'How the hell do you know all of this?'

Maria ignored the question. It was plain she would not be sharing answers.

'It'll be waiting for you tomorrow, OK? Nine a.m. my time. Assuming we're all still safe, anyway.'

'Maria, don't say—'

'And the phone you're speaking on right now, it's your worst enemy, Kon. As soon as this call's over, you break it. You take it apart, you snap the SIM and you don't take any piece of it with you when you leave. Understood?'

'If I haven't got a phone, how can I contact you?'

'You can't. And you won't. You've put us at risk enough already. I won't let you do it again.'

'What are you . . . you mean . . .'

'Kon, I can't be thinking about you after this call. And I sure as hell can't think about *us*. I'll do what I can to keep you alive but my priority is the boys. Whatever the hell you've done, they didn't ask for this. *I* didn't ask for it. You caused it, you deal with it. Then we'll talk. But not until then.'

Kon did not answer. The last few minutes had been a shock. One which lacked the horror of the Grote Markt, sure, but still he was thrown. The change in Maria – the things she seemed to know – was impossible for Kon to rationalise. The way she spoke. Her cold, practical reaction to his predicament. Her sudden transformation from concerned wife to dispassionate problem-solver. It was unsettling in the extreme. And it left Kon with a gnawing fear that Maria would never think of him in the same way again.

Before he could think how to respond – of what words he could say to restore some normality between them – a final curt instruction brought their conversation to an end.

'Make sure you dismantle that phone.'

No wish of good luck or goodwill. No expression of love or affection. Just those six words. And then the line went dead.

EIGHT

Corbin Kincaid stood on the corner of Vlamingstraat and Grote Markt and looked across the police cordon, his mouth open in disbelief at what he saw in the square beyond.

He had known why he was coming here. He'd been told in advance the horror that had taken place and so he knew what to expect. And yet somehow, even with the many atrocities he had witnessed over his thirty years with the Central Intelligence Agency, Kincaid had been unprepared for the sight that now greeted him.

There was no way to disguise the carnage that had taken place in this usually peaceful city, or to conceal the horror of its aftermath. The attack had covered the entirety of the square, the shooting wild and indiscriminate. Its results were everywhere, in every direction. Literal piles of corpses – men and women, most of them young, mown down as they had tried to run – were dotted across the cobbles, connected here and there by rivers of blood.

Such human cost was not new to Kincaid. Hell, he had seen worse. And yet somehow this was hitting him much more deeply than he had experienced in years.

Over three decades Kincaid had worked in every corner of the globe. And in that time he had seen the very worst of humanity.

But he had never seen a sight like this up close in a place that was so similar to home. It was especially jarring in a historic European city like The Hague. The kind of place that had inspired the best of America.

To Kincaid, this kind of death and destruction was more acceptable when it happened in a place he regarded as foreign; when it happened to people he saw as inferior.

Kincaid knew better than to advertise views like that within the Agency. He had no doubt how quickly he would find himself 'cancelled' by the woke generation that surrounded him there. But at this moment he could not bring himself to care. Not while he was looking at people who resembled his own – scores of them – all shot to death in a place such filth should never touch.

It was proof that nowhere was safe any more. The direct result, Kincaid believed, of how weak the West had let itself become.

'How do you wanna play this?'

The question came from Kincaid's right, breaking through the increasing outrage of his thoughts. He turned and glanced slightly downwards, towards the shorter Sean Sutton.

Sutton was younger than Kincaid by thirteen years – thirty-six to Kincaid's forty-nine. Physically, the difference looked less: Kincaid had kept himself in exceptional shape for a man of almost fifty, while Sutton had seemed middle-aged even in his twenties. To Kincaid's mind they resembled nothing more than Fredo Corleone palling around with Steve Rogers, though even he had the good manners not to say it out loud. Sutton was a good man and a hell of an officer. He had earned Kincaid's respect.

'First things first,' Kincaid replied, 'we find out if this really was the Monk.'

'You think there's even the slightest chance it wasn't?'

'There's always a chance.'

'A chance this isn't connected? Seriously?'

Kincaid took a breath, his eyes locked onto Sutton's without the need for a spoken reply. The younger man got the message. This was Kincaid's show and they would do things his way, however cut and dried it might seem.

Because he's not wrong, Kincaid told himself. *This must be connected to why we're in this city. But nothing kills like being complacent.*

'Whatever,' he finally said aloud. 'We still have to check. Even if we are just going through the motions.'

Kincaid reached out ahead of him as he spoke, grasped the police cordon and raised it above both their heads. Sutton ducked under unnecessarily – Kincaid had six inches in height on the younger man and was holding the cordon high enough to pass under it himself – and they began to walk into the square. As they did, they were approached by the closest police officer.

'I'm sorry, no, no, you cannot be here.'

Undeterred, Kincaid reached into his back pocket, pulled out his wallet and offered his identification. Or, more accurately, the identification which best suited his purposes today.

'We're with the US Embassy, officer. Security attachés. We're here to find out if any of our citizens have gotten caught up in all of this.'

The police officer hesitated. Exactly as Kincaid had expected he would. The credentials gave him and Sutton no official authority here at all, but the mere notion of the US government holds a power that often transcends jurisdiction. It would at least prevent them from being ejected from the square. And nine times out of ten, it would achieve much more.

Kincaid intended to discover if this was one of those times.

'Have you been able to identify any of the victims yet?'

The police officer did not answer. He seemed unsure of the correct thing to do.

Seeing the uncertainty, Kincaid decided to push his luck.

'OK, I'll be a little more specific. We're looking for two men in particular. Mendel Prochnik and Will Duffy. We need to know if those two men are among the dead.'

NINE

Michael Devlin leaned across the wrought-iron garden table and refilled Joe Dempsey's white wine glass. He then did the same for the dark-haired woman to Dempsey's right. Two large measures each, judged by eye. An eye which was no longer strictly sober; Dempsey could tell that by the size of the pour.

Dempsey glanced at his watch, aware that his internal clock was not as reliable as usual. The result of three glasses over lunch, too little sleep and the lingering effects of a transatlantic flight.

The weather, too, was a factor. It was still unusually hot, even in the shade, and that disguised how late in the afternoon it now was. Almost evening, really. Which was probably why most of the guests from the christening had already left. Those who remained – three, including Dempsey himself – were few enough that they could all enjoy the coolest spot in Michael and Sarah's garden: a small, sheltered stone courtyard that separated the back doors of the Chelsea townhouse from the exposed lawn beyond.

Dempsey could not miss the intimacy that existed within the smaller group, different to earlier in the day. The church had been busy for the ceremony, with the party afterwards just as well-attended. And while some of those guests who had since left would no doubt still be welcome now, he guessed that most of them would not.

The evening was about family. And, with Michael's all gone and Sarah's back home in Boston, that meant the family the couple had chosen. Dempsey did not need to be told that he was counted in that number.

The other two who remained were both women. The first was Bebe Duffy. A Polish-born chef with an acid tongue and an 'up-front' manner that Dempsey had noted with amusement throughout the day, Bebe was the much younger wife of Michael's closest lawyer friend, Will. She had attended the baptism without her husband, who was working abroad, and had spent much of the afternoon distracted while supervising her hyper-energetic five-year-old daughter. But now she was making the most of the child's early exhaustion and was sat at the far end of the table, deep in conversation with Sarah.

Which left the attractive dark-haired lady to Dempsey's right, now nursing a larger than typical glass of white wine. Dempsey had encountered Joelle Levy briefly before: a single phone call shared several years ago, back when Michael had found himself in need of help that only Levy and Dempsey could provide. It had been the first and only time he had spoken to the Detective Chief Inspector of Scotland Yard's Major Investigations Team before today. Dempsey had been unaware that Levy was still in his friends' lives but, as of around five hours ago, she was now one of two godmothers to Michael and Sarah's twin sons. It made her Dempsey's direct counterpart.

Dempsey was in no doubt why he had been placed next to her for the party. It was no accident, nor was it a 'get to know each other' opportunity for their new shared role as godparents. It was a set-up. The occasional grinning glance from the never-subtle Michael had confirmed that hours ago.

The situation had made Dempsey a little awkward at first; the idea of matchmaking usually left him cold. But, as the day had worn on, he had enjoyed Levy's company more and more, until he'd found himself bowing to his friends' instincts.

This one's going well.

He reached out and picked up his refilled glass. Crystal, he had guessed earlier, based on the weight and by how the light bounced off the ornate cuts to the stem. The wine inside was harder to determine. It was not the same as his previous drink, he knew that much. Or the one before that. But that bare recognition was the extent of Dempsey's insight. He could not tell which wine was better, nor did he have the slightest grasp of which grape had produced which round.

Michael, on the other hand, was a connoisseur of the stuff. Of wine *and* of whisky, though at this hour his focus was still on the former. And for some reason, the Irishman had today decided to convert his less cultured friend.

It had been a waste of effort. Even with the newly imparted knowledge, Dempsey could take or leave the stuff. He had started the day with one opinion about wine and, for all Michael's attempts to educate him, that opinion had not changed: none of it, white or red or in-between, would ever beat a good pint of Guinness.

Joelle Levy had proved a better student. Dempsey had watched as she'd worked her way through every example of grape and vintage that Michael had enthusiastically supplied. And he had noticed how, despite her relatively small size, the intake had affected her no more than it had their mutual friend. Levy's tolerance did not surprise him; Dempsey knew more about British cops than most – he had been raised by one – and so he had expected Levy to be able to hold her drink.

'You're not persuaded by this one.'

The subtle Israeli inflection, an exotic tint to an otherwise soft London accent, broke into Dempsey's thoughts. His mind had wandered – his fatigue was kicking in again, he realised – and so he had not noticed that Michael's mini-lecture on the latest pour had ended and that Levy had returned her attention to him.

It took Dempsey a moment longer to understand the unexpected question, until it was explained by Levy's gesture towards the glass in her hand.

'This? No. It wouldn't be my first choice,' Dempsey replied. 'But sadly there's no sign of a keg.'

'Didn't take you for a beer drinker.' Levy pointed towards Dempsey's flat stomach. 'Usually shows on a guy your age.'

'I doubt I drink enough of anything for that to happen. If you're drunk you're not in control, you know?'

'Is that always such a bad thing?'

'Depends on how you live your life. In mine, yeah. It's a bad thing.'

Levy was silent, which made him regret his words. She knew who he was and what he did. Dempsey was aware of that already. And so any reference to his 'other' life – not least to the danger that surrounded him – was not something she would miss.

Hardly light-hearted first-date chat, he told himself, disappointed in his slip.

He hid his irritation with himself and pushed on, avoiding any further mention of the unwelcome side-topic.

'So how many times have you been subjected to the "Michael Devlin on White Wine" A-level syllabus?'

'Not as often as my BA in "Devlin on Islay Scotch",' Levy replied. 'But more often than the "Devlin on Japanese Whisky" postgrad course he keeps threatening.'

'And which one wins?'

'Ask me once I've passed "Devlin on Vodka and Tonic". That's more my home turf.'

'Home turf it may be, but there'll be no vodka tasting in *this* garden.'

Michael, it seemed, had overheard at least the last line of the conversation. His Irish accent was always stronger when he had been drinking and his strong advocate's voice reverberated off the stone walls that surrounded them.

He seemed oblivious to his own volume as he continued.

'Devil's piss, that stuff.'

'Are you being rude about vodka, Michael?'

The question came from Bebe Duffy, at the far end of the table. Like Michael, her accent had only strengthened as the day and the alcohol had passed. It made Dempsey all the more interested in what might follow.

'And what exactly is wrong with vodka, huh?' she continued.

'Nothing. Nothing at all.'

'But it's devil's piss, you said?'

'Well, then . . . what should I . . . what about devil's urine?'

'And you think that makes it better, do you?'

'Well yeah . . . I mean . . . no . . .'

Dempsey grinned at the sight of his usually uber-composed friend awkwardly backtracking.

'But I . . . I didn't mean *Polish* vodka. I meant Russian. And the French shite. I mean, that Russian stuff, you can't really—'

'You don't change the subject now, Michael Devlin. I know you lawyers. I've lived with one for long enough.'

Bebé began to smile in response to Michael's visible

discomfort; she was clearly unable to keep up the faux anger. And she was not alone in that reaction. The entire table had stopped to watch as Michael tried to remove his metaphorical foot from his mouth.

'I really don't care, Michael,' Bebe said, the act over and her tone friendly once again. 'I can't stand the stuff either; it *is* devil's piss. I just like watching barristers when they stutter.'

'Hey, now. I don't think I was stuttering. Lying through my teeth, maybe. But lying eloquently.'

'You need to learn when you've been beaten, Michael Devlin.' Sarah had decided to join the light-hearted ribbing. 'Take your defeat like a man.'

'And you should know when you've been caught in the act, Sarah Truman.' Michael hardly needed a glance in her direction before he answered. 'What's that you're hiding under the table there?'

'It's a rusk.'

'It's a cigarette.'

'So it is.' She feigned surprise. 'What do you know, huh?'

Michael chuckled at his fiancée's faux-dramatic response but he said nothing. Dempsey took the opportunity to step in.

'I see quitting's going about as well as usual, then?'

Sarah turned to Dempsey, her amusement etched across her attractive face.

'You try living with him without the occasional cigarette.'

'No thanks. You picked him, you keep him.'

'How did I know you'd say that?' Sarah looked back to Michael and then around the table. 'Anyway, enough wine tasting for one day. Who wants to join me in some of that devil's urine?'

'I thought you'd never ask.' Levy downed her glass, pushed her chair back and got to her feet as Sarah rose from the table. 'Let me help you.'

'And me,' Bebe said, a step behind.

Dempsey watched as the three women climbed the rustic-style steps to a kitchen that loomed over the small courtyard garden, his eyelids flickering slightly as they left. He could not fight off a yawn once they had disappeared inside.

'You feeling the pace, buddy?'

Dempsey turned to face Michael, just the two of them now left at the table.

'Are you not?'

'They breed us with more stamina in Belfast. Not like you soft Englishmen.'

'Alright, Ned Stark. I didn't realise winter was coming.'

'Real men. That's all I'm saying.'

'I should have reminded *you* of that before you opened that last bottle,' Dempsey said, laughing. 'Might have stopped you getting drunk under the table by a girl half your size.'

'And yet only one of us is yawning like a toddler on a sugar comedown, eh.'

'I can't argue with that. In my defence, it was a hell of a week.'

'Anything you want to talk about?'

'Not this time. No Catholic guilt to share.'

'No one died, then?'

'No one who didn't deserve it.' Dempsey thought for a moment. 'One way or another.'

'Sounds exhausting.'

'Isn't it always?'

'And for all that you're still here, instead of in your bed. That wouldn't have anything to do with that pretty lady cop you've been chatting to all day, would it?'

Dempsey said nothing, but he could not deny the suggestion.

Levy *was* the reason he was still here. Michael and Sarah too, but Dempsey would see them again tomorrow. And most likely every day after that, until he flew back to New York. But Joelle Levy? She was a curveball. Dempsey had not expected to enjoy their time together as much as he had. It was rare that he made that kind of connection with anyone and he did not know when he would see her again.

Which was why, as much as he needed sleep, he had opted to stay.

And Michael clearly knew it.

'Ah, come on, man. I knew you'd like her.'

Once again Dempsey said nothing. And once again he didn't have to. He could feel the hint of a smile at the corner of his mouth. Something he was sure Michael would spot.

'Are you seriously not going to compliment me on a job well done?' the Irishman asked. 'What are you worried about, that I'll tell your priest and he'll make you hold out 'til your wedding night?'

'You don't know my priest, mate,' Dempsey answered with another laugh. 'Not if you think that's what he'd say.'

'Well then. You're only here a few days. You want my view?'

'Would it matter if I said no?'

'When did you last get any action, Joe? My advice? Get in there lively and make sure you make a good impression.'

Dempsey spat out the mouthful of water he had just sipped

at Michael's final sentence, barely managing to send it sideways instead of across the table.

'Jesus Christ, Mikey. That's your friend you're talking about.'

'Yeah. The only friend with a love life more boring than yours,' Michael answered. 'The pair of you, I swear, it's like your bloody virginities grew back, it's been that long. I can see she likes you, too. So go have some fun, would you?'

'And what does Sarah think about all this?'

'Sarah? Who the hell do you think did the table plan?'

Dempsey rolled his eyes, unsurprised that Michael had not been alone in his plotting. He had more he wanted to say, but the sound of approaching footsteps distracted him before he could speak again.

Sarah and Levy were heading back with fresh drinks in each of their hands, including two bottles of Italian lager. Bebe, it seemed, had stayed in the house. Sarah passed one of the bottles to Dempsey, then the other to Michael.

'Sorry it's not Guinness,' she said.

'As long as it's not bloody white wine,' Dempsey replied.

The seat next to him was filled again by the returning Joelle Levy; Michael's amused expression and sudden focus on speaking to Sarah confirmed that without even the need to turn.

But Dempsey turned anyway. And Levy was waiting.

'So, then,' she said. 'The ISB. When are we going to talk about that?'

Dempsey was taken aback, if only for a moment. After hours of small talk they had come to the elephant in the room: the career that most women would consider a dealbreaker. He was surprised, then, that Levy was raising the subject with no hint of concern.

'Could be a short conversation,' Dempsey replied.

'Because if you tell me anything you'll have to kill me, right?' Levy's smile dismissed any doubts that she was being serious, despite the subject. 'You'd be surprised by the level of security clearance we get in Scotland Yard.'

'I wouldn't. I know all about that.'

'So go on, then. What have you been working on lately?'

'You first.'

'Murder's murder, Joe. And anyway, I beat you to the question. Tell me about your stuff.'

'You really don't wan—'

Dempsey was interrupted by a scream from within the house. The sound banished every effect of the alcohol he had consumed and sent him sprinting for the steps.

TEN

The information that was now displayed on the computer screen earned a rare smile from its reader. Here was a problem, it now appeared, that would have a simple solution. A welcome change from the logistical nightmares that had plagued him and his organisation in recent months.

The name Konrad Frankowski had meant nothing when Vic Sethi had provided it hours earlier. A fact that was as unexpected as it was unwelcome. There was very little in his corner of the world that the Monk did not know, and that included the identities of those players who operated within it. Even the most peripheral of figures were at least vaguely familiar by the time they became the focus of his attention; it was exceptionally rare for anyone to enter the game at this high a level.

Frankowski, then, was an oddity. A complete unknown. And that had presented the Monk with a rare task: the need to construct a profile from nothing that would tell him everything about a hitherto anonymous enemy, especially their key weaknesses and vulnerabilities.

A few hours later and the Monk was almost disappointed in how easy the exercise had proved.

Initially Frankowski had seemed out of place. A forty-four-year-old American computer specialist, former digital security system expert and now the owner of a successful website design company, he was nonetheless an obvious underachiever; his dual 4.0 degree from the Massachusetts Institution of Technology suggested much more potential. But there was nothing in that first search to mark him out as someone who would throw in his lot with Hannibal Strauss. It left the Monk suspecting that Sethi had made a mistake.

That conclusion was quickly dismissed when a little more research exposed the real focus of Frankowski's hard-earned tech skills. With a brief migration across to the dark web, the Monk had discovered just why it was that so sophisticated a mind could be satisfied by something as mundane as web design.

The answer was that it could not. That the design company, for all its apparent success, was a façade. Frankowski, it emerged, was a money launderer. Highly specialised and even more highly valued, he possessed a skill-set so sought after in a world of digital banking, water-tight regulation and instantly transparent movement of funds that he was worth more than the illegal commodities in which his clients chose to trade.

It was a role with which the Monk was intimately familiar. The changes in finance across the past three decades – the efforts made by governments internationally to identify the source and the locations of their citizens' wealth, even if they seemed less enthusiastic to claim their share of it through tax – had made life difficult for people like him. It had forced him to engage men like Frankowski; men who could ensure that the funding of his operation remained unseen and uninterrupted.

And so the Monk recognised *exactly* what he was seeing as Frankowski's true nature began to emerge.

What he discovered was extremely impressive. So much that he found himself questioning how he had not heard the name before; how it was that Frankowski had been engaged by Hannibal Strauss rather than by the Monk himself. But that question was a distraction for another time. The only important thing now was proof of the connection between Frankowski and Strauss.

Vic Sethi had been right.

Frankowski *was* their man.

With that settled – and with confirmation within the last hour that Frankowski was not among the dead or the injured – the Monk had one remaining problem on which to focus: how to lay hands on a man who did not want to be found.

It was a not unfamiliar question. In a career that often involved solving the unsolvable and delivering the most complex and intricate plans, finding ways to compel people to act against their own best interests was unsurprisingly common.

Violence and murder – whether threatened or real – were never the Monk's preferred methods. He found them blunt. A little . . . primitive. But he was also not afraid of resorting to them as an option, and he recognised that sometimes, like today in the Grote Markt, their more civilised alternatives were insufficient.

Sometimes the simplest solution *was* the best solution. And right now, with the clock ticking fast and with so much of his usually abundant resources tied up by the debacle in Ukraine, it was the Monk's *only* solution.

The threat of violence would get him what he wanted from Konrad Frankowski.

But first he would have to find him.

It was, he had reasoned, highly unlikely that the man would be foolish enough to go back to his hotel. And he had to assume that any kind of a criminal, even one whose misdeeds were carried out from behind a keyboard, would know how to cover his tracks. It left a stark reality: with the Monk's resources stretched as they were, there was every chance Frankowski could simply disappear into the night.

The thought angered him. Frankowski was a loose end that

needed to be tied. One of three, along with the lawyers and Hannibal Strauss. And so far only one of those problems was properly in hand.

The Monk would not be happy until all three were out of the picture. They *all* had to go, because this had gone on long enough. It was time this thing came to an end.

If he was going to achieve that, he could not begin some aimless search for the missing man. And to avoid that he needed leverage. Something that would bring Frankowski out of hiding and running towards the bullet he had so far dodged; a willing target embracing his own surrender.

It could be done. The Monk knew that for sure because the Monk had done it before. Many, many times. It was, he believed, his greatest skill: the ability to find the one thing a man values above all else.

Above even his own life.

Everyone has something. And Konrad Frankowski is no different.

The Monk nodded to himself as he looked at the address on the screen. At the address *and* at the picture.

A beautiful woman and her two young sons.

He took no satisfaction in what he already knew would be their fate. They were nothing but a means to an end. Nothing but a necessary tool.

He tapped the screen with his index finger, gently touching the image of Kon Frankowski's wife.

'You'll do.'

ELEVEN

Michael rushed up the steps and into the kitchen. He was barely a step behind Dempsey and so had little obstruction to the sight of Bebe Duffy slumped against the large island unit, her forearm alone resting on the worktop. That point of contact seemed all that was keeping her upright; her legs were bent at the knees, as if they had given way.

Unlike her body, her eyes seemed steady. They were transfixed by her phone screen.

Dempsey stepped aside as the two men entered the room. Michael understood the silent message. With no threat to life to concern them, it made sense for Michael to reach Bebe first, as the one who actually knew her.

Michael did not hesitate, even as he felt his heart rate lessen; his initial panic – the instinct that Bebe's scream had been something to do with the boys – was fast subsiding now that he could see that wasn't the case.

Whatever shocked her, it's on that screen.

'What is it?' he asked. 'What's happened?'

Bebe said nothing. Instead she held out the handset, her fingers trembling violently as she turned the screen towards Michael. He took the phone from her hand and held it up so that Dempsey and Levy could also see.

The images on the screen were from a television news broadcast. One of the twenty-four-hour rolling channels. The footage was shaky as hell, even in Michael's steady hand, but what it showed was clear enough. Something they had all seen way too many times, in way too many reports like this one.

It was the aftermath of a mass shooting.

'Is this today?' Levy asked. 'Where?'

'Somewhere in continental Europe, judging by the architecture.' The answer came from Dempsey, whose view of the screen had to be limited from where he was standing. 'And it has to be today, yeah. No later than midday local time, based on the position of the shadows.'

Levy nodded her head but she said nothing. Michael did not speak either. He was horrified into silence, not quite able to comprehend what he was seeing. The footage had no doubt come with a viewer warning at its outset, but it was still more graphic than was necessary for a news broadcast. It was, he realised, the inevitable result of every smartphone having a professional-standard camera: a population of amateurs transformed into millions of potential paparazzi.

All of the equipment, Michael thought. *And none of the restraint.*

He watched the footage for a second or two more. At first there was little it could tell him. Just jumpy images of blood and bodies; a poor source of intelligence. But then came the breaking news bar at the foot of the page. Two sentences that told him everything:

TERROR IN THE NETHERLANDS.
THIRTY-TWO DEAD, FORTY-THREE INJURED
IN GUNMAN ATTACK ON THE HAGUE.

Michael understood immediately. He passed the handset to Dempsey with one hand and used the other to reach out for his grief-stricken friend, pulling her close into his chest.

'It's Will,' Michael explained over his shoulder. 'He's working in The Hague. Getting ready for a trial at the International Criminal Court. That's why he couldn't be here today.'

Michael turned his attention back towards Bebe, lifting her face up from his chest so he could look into her eyes. Her already pale skin was now deathly white, contrasted against her dark-brown, almost black hair. That alone hinted how close she was to collapse, confirmed by the extra weight that now pressed down on Michael's cradling arm.

Dempsey seemed to sense both Bebe's burden and Michael's own upset at the thought of his friend. He stepped forwards, gently placed an arm on either of Bebe's shoulders and guided her away from Michael, towards the nearest chair. Then he visibly supported her weight as she lowered herself down.

'Are you OK?'

'No. Will. Will's there. What do I do?'

'The Hague's a big place,' Dempsey said. 'What's happened there, it's terrible. But it's just one square in a whole city. The odds on your husband being one of those poor people caught up in all that, they're . . . you've got more chance of winning the lottery.'

'You don't understand. You didn't see what I saw.'

'You mean you saw Will?' Michael asked. Bebe's statement had broken into his own negative thoughts and pulled him back into the moment. 'On the screen? You saw Will in the footage?'

'No. No, not Will.'

'Who then?'

'I saw the man he is working with, Michael. The other lawyer. I saw Mr Prochnik.'

Michael stood up. He felt his own skin go cold, a sign that the blood had drained from his face. Bebe's answer felt like confirmation of his own worst fears.

'Mendel Prochnik? Where did you see him?'

'On the news report. He was one of . . . he is one of the victims they've identified.'

For all her efforts to remain composed, Bebe's emotions and her shock were beginning to win through. Michael could see that, but he still had questions.

'You're sure it was Prochnik?'

'Michael, they named him. They showed a picture.'

'But they didn't name Will?'

'No. But I've been messaging him, Michael. Pictures from today, on WhatsApp. He hasn't looked at them. Not one. And now if this had happened in . . . in the city and he was OK, he . . . he *would* have called me. He would have called to say . . . to say . . . he was fine.'

Michael looked to Dempsey. His sharp lawyer's mind was working again, the combination of alcohol and panic now passed. It meant that he was once again reaching logical conclusions.

He almost wished he was not.

'She's got a point,' he said to Dempsey, his voice low. 'Will's a clear thinker. He *would* have called her.'

'What about you?' Dempsey asked. 'If for some reason he couldn't connect to Bebe, would he have called you?'

Michael nodded his head.

'Maybe. My phone's been off all day. Sarah insisted.'

'Check it now. There might be a missed call or a voicemail.'

Michael needed no convincing. With a gesture to Levy, he moved away. Understanding the unspoken communication,

Levy stepped into the space left by his departure and without a word she wrapped her arms around Bebe, allowing the younger woman to cry silently into her shoulder.

'There is a missed call,' Michael said. He put the phone to his ear as Dempsey approached. 'Just before eleven a.m. And a message.'

'Mike, it's Will. Listen, big man, we've found something out. Something big. We're heading out now to meet this guy and . . . I'm not gonna lie, I'm scared. Because if it's true, well, that means people have been killed to keep this quiet. I can't say more now, we don't know who's listening. But if anything happens to me, I need you to know the name of the guy we're meeting. Konrad Frankowski. He's the key to this, Mike. He's the key to exposing everything. If . . . I know I'll be fine . . . but if I'm not, you have to find him. Get him to tell you what he knows. You've got people who can help you do that. I don't want all this to have been for nothing, Mike. I don't . . . I . . . I know I can count on you. Look, I'm probably being ridiculous. I'll call you back when this is over, OK? Let you know there's nothing to worry about after all. Speak soon, buddy.'

Michael's eyes filled with tears as the voicemail ended, his mind unable to shake the fear that the missed message was now a dead man's testimony.

Not again, he told himself, the thought of losing yet another friend almost too much to take. *Jesus, not again.*

Michael could not keep the emotion from his face, nor could he stop his gaze from drifting to Bebe. The combination was all it took to confirm what she already suspected. For a second time, her pure, primal scream filled the room.

Dempsey stepped forwards, forcing himself into Michael's field of vision.

'Michael, are you OK, buddy?'

The question only half-registered. Like Bebe, Michael had been utterly shaken by what he had seen and heard.

'What was the message, Michael?' Dempsey asked. 'Was it from Will? Is he alive?'

Michael tried to look towards Bebe before he answered, but Dempsey remained in his line of sight and, using his right hand on Michael's jaw, he turned his friend's head to directly face his own. It was a practical act, typical of Dempsey, and it forced Michael to shake off the blow that had just been struck.

'I . . . I don't know,' he finally answered. His head was beginning to clear. 'But it . . . it doesn't look good. He . . . they . . . it looks like he got himself caught up in something, Joe.'

'In what?'

Michael glanced towards Bebe. A silent message that this was not the place.

Dempsey understood.

'Is there something *you* need to do?' he asked, moving the subject on.

'I'm . . . I guess I'm going to do what Will would do. If this was the other way round. I'm going to find him, Joe. Wherever he is – whatever state he might be in – I have to go there and I have to find him.'

Dempsey nodded his head, as if he expected nothing less. Without another word he stepped back, reached into his pocket and took out his phone.

'What are you doing?' Michael asked.

'I'm getting us a flight to The Hague.'

'Us?'

'You and me. People are dead, Mike, and we don't know

why or who's behind it. There's no way you're walking into that without me.'

Michael placed his hand on Dempsey's shoulder and forced the smallest of grateful smiles. But he did not say a word. There was, he knew, no way he was talking Dempsey out of this.

And no bloody way I'd want to.

TWELVE

Vic Sethi sat at the wheel of a Mercedes GLC, his eyes fixed on the Hotel Indigo Palace Noordeinde across the way. He could see the single entrance to the grand, orange-stone building, but only just. The position was less than ideal but it was as close as he could get, thanks to The Hague's strict zoning laws; like so much else of the city, this section of the Noordeinde had followed the growing trend for pedestrianisation.

It had been several hours since Sethi had arrived in the location. He had spent most of that time in the driver's seat with the engine and air conditioning off. Their absence made for uncomfortable conditions, even as the approach of night took the worst of the heat from the air. Discomfort that made the surveillance shift seem much longer than it really was.

It had taken the Monk almost no time to locate Konrad Frankowski's hotel; Sethi had received his call within ten minutes of first providing the name, with both the address and instructions on his next move. Sethi's first instinct had been to rush directly there, in case Frankowski had done the same, assuming the American was not already among the Grote Markt dead. But Sethi had resisted that urge. With the city now on near lockdown, any travelling had to be done with extra care. And that was particularly true when the hotel to which he was heading was spitting distance from the residence of the country's reigning monarch.

Sethi had instead taken his usual professional caution before acting on the Monk's information. He made two changes of transport – both in carefully selected locations not overlooked by any form of camera – and another change of clothes before coming anywhere near the place, and even then he did so alone. The three musketeers were nearby, he knew. Each had been assigned to different elements of the same task; other aspects of the post-Grote Markt clean-up. But even with that common cause, Sethi was sure he would never see any of them again.

Not after today. That would be far too much of a risk.

Regardless of not seeing them with his own eyes, Sethi was grateful now that the team was in place. The downside to his meticulous care was that he had taken longer to arrive than was ideal; the change in cars and clothing had delayed him by over half an hour, providing plenty of time for Frankowski to return to his hotel room, grab his belongings and run.

Thanks to the musketeers, Sethi knew this had not occurred.

Porthos – Sethi's name for the tallest of his three anonymous colleagues – had made his way to Noordeinde alone and on foot, and yet he had still managed to arrive twenty minutes before Sethi. That alone cut down the time Frankowski had to return to the hotel and then leave for good, but still it left a window. And so Porthos had taken care to clear up any doubt. Making the most of the handsome features and bucketloads of Irish charm with which he had been blessed, he had talked his way into Frankowski's room by way of a naive hotel receptionist.

Once inside, he had quickly confirmed that the suite was untouched. Frankowski's clothes were still neatly put away in the wardrobe and drawers, while his passport and valuables were still 'secure' in the too-easily-accessible locked safe.

It was the best news Sethi could hope for right now, because if everything Kon possessed was still at the Indigo, there was still a chance he would come back here. A trained professional would know to cut his losses and run, but the information the Monk had turned up suggested that Frankowski could be something else: a guy dabbling but not immersed in this life. There was no guarantee of that, of course. Could be the guy was as good as they came. But for now they could only play the numbers, and those numbers suggested a novice.

Or, Sethi thought to himself, *they suggest a man who never left that square alive.*

Sethi looked at the encrypted telephone handset he had positioned in the GLC's central console and, not for the first time, he willed the Monk to call. It had been almost three hours since he had last spoken to his employer and that was a lifetime for an operator as uniquely effective as the Monk. There was next to nothing the man could not discover in that timeframe.

So surely he knows Frankowski's fate by now?

And if he does, why the hell am I still sweating like a pig in this damned hot-box?

The question irritated him almost as much as the heat. But nothing bothered him more than the futility of second-guessing his employer. It was a frustration he found hard to take. That even now, even after everything he had done for the man, he was not trusted with the information that mattered.

That he never *really* knew his employer's mind.

It was over four years since Sethi had first worked for the Monk. Four years in which he had been exceptionally well paid to be available at a moment's notice, ready to deal out whatever death or destruction the Monk might require. He was not alone in that role, he knew. Very far from it. But unlike most, Sethi believed he had become essential to the Monk's overarching operation, even if he didn't know its aim. Sethi was, he believed, as close to indispensable as anyone could be.

And he had achieved that by being the best at what he did.

Few men shared Sethi's talent for death. Fewer still his appetite for it. And almost none plied their trade with so acute an awareness of their own strengths and weaknesses. The combination made Sethi a rare asset. And he knew it.

He had learned his value early, back when he had first recognised his insatiable desire to kill. He had trained himself obsessively, to the point that he had mastery over every weapon he could lay his hands on. Kulvinder 'Vic' Sethi would not win any back-alley, bare-knuckle boxing contests. Not at five feet two inches tall. And not against the men in *his* world. But nor would he ever be stupid enough to try, and that was what truly mattered.

Size means nothing when you can stand at the far end of that alley and take out every bastard in it from fifty feet.

His talents had left his bank account rich and his base urges satisfied. But for all that, Sethi remained very aware of his position as a man who took orders. Orders which, he had learned, were not to be questioned. Which was why, after over four hours in the stifling heat of the Mercedes, he had still not picked up the encrypted phone and made the call for himself.

That very thought was crossing Sethi's mind when the handset began to vibrate. He did not question the coincidence. Instead he just reached out, picked up the phone and hit connect.

'Is there any sign of him?' No greeting. Just straight to business.

'No. And I don't think there will be.'

'Why not?'

'Because if he was in one piece, and he had any intention of coming back, he'd be here by now. The police wouldn't keep any uninjured survivor the best part of five hours. He's either dead, hurt or in hiding.'

'There was no Konrad Frankowski among the victims.'

Sethi hesitated. It was not the news he had hoped for. If Frankowski was not dead or incapacitated, then where the hell *was* he?

'So he's not coming back, then,' he finally concluded, cursing the hours he'd wasted in this oven of a car.

'You're sure he hasn't already?'

'One hundred per cent. Porthos checked the room; all of his things are still there.'

'I want him found, Kulvinder.'

'How? We don't have access to his credit cards or his phone. I wouldn't know where—'

'I'm already tracking the credit cards. Any use and we'll know about it. The phone is taking a little longer but I expect to have it within the hour.'

Sethi did not respond. Nothing the Monk did should surprise him by now, he knew. And yet the fact he was already so close to tracking every aspect of Frankowski's life? A name he had never even heard until a few hours earlier? It was ... impressive. Impressive *and* scary.

'In the meantime,' the Monk continued, 'I want you moving.'

'Where?'

'Around the city. Leave ... what did you name him? Porthos? Leave Porthos waiting in the room, in case Frankowski comes back. But we have to assume he won't. That he knows this afternoon was about him.'

'But how could he?'

'I don't know. I don't know what Strauss might have told him. Until I know more, until we have any leads on his location, I want you on the streets finding out whatever you can.'

'Just me?'

'No. One of the team from this afternoon will be doing the same. The Serbian. You have the number for his handset.'

Sethi pulled the phone away from his ear and quickly scanned the short series of entries under 'contacts'. He found what he was looking for immediately. 'Athos'. The second musketeer.

'I've got it.'

'Stay in touch with him. Make sure you're not both searching the same areas.'

'What about Aramis? Three sets of eyes are better than two.'

'The Dutchman has another task.'

'What?'

'Nothing that concerns you. Keep your mind on your job. Frankowski's out there. I want him found.'

The line went dead before Sethi could ask any more. Just as it always did. He cursed himself that he had not asked the questions that were now beginning to bother him. First among them, why the hell were he and the others even still here? Why had they not been ghosted from the city and replaced by a new team for the clean-up, as they ordinarily would be?

As ever, Sethi would ask none of them. He would just do as instructed, as he always did.

He would find Konrad Frankowski.

THIRTEEN

Kon shuffled to the end of the pew, making room for a family of five. They were the first of the congregation to settle onto the bench he had occupied since he had arrived and their appearance made up his mind.

It's time to go.

The building had provided Kon with shelter for longer than he had expected. He had reckoned on just a few hours respite when he had forced his way in. Enough time to get his head together and to consider his options.

Almost six hours had now passed since Maria had disconnected their call. Six hours of monastic silence. That time had kept him alive and it had given him the chance to clean himself up, at least as much as he could, given the limited water and the fact he had only his T-shirt for a washcloth. But in every other way he had wasted those gifted hours. Because even now, as the clock approached 6 p.m., Kon had no idea of what he should do next.

Maria had settled the practicalities, sure. And her remarkable clear thinking had protected Kon from his own naivety, by stopping his intended return to his hotel. But in terms of an actual plan – where he would go and how he would get there – he was no further forwards than he had been at the end of their call.

With his time here now up, that lack of direction could prove fatal.

Kon looked around as he prepared to move. The last of the local parishioners were still filing in, taking up what little space there was in the pews around him, but overall the place was now full.

Saturday evening mass was about to begin, bringing Kon's unofficial holy sanctuary to an end. The thought made him nervous. Paranoid, even.

The thought that there were people all around him, out of his sight-line and free to act with impunity, was hard for him to bear. Kon wanted to look around again. To check for threats among the congregation. But he knew that he could not; he could not risk bringing any more attention to himself.

Not when the city's already on high alert.

That final thought only heightened his fears. Kon already cut a strange figure here. He knew that. A new face with an aura that had kept his pew empty, at least until the others had been filled. It was understandable; even with the efforts he had made to tidy himself – to wash away the blood stains and to hide the tears in his clothing – Kon was still an outsider on a day when anything and anyone unusual would be naturally distrusted.

Some attention, then, was inevitable. Eyes were on him. Perhaps it was the gaze of regular churchgoers, feeling sympathy for a stranger who might be here to search for meaning after the events of the day.

Or maybe it was the sinister scrutiny of someone here looking for him.

Kon had no way to tell.

And nor could he wait around to find out. The thought that among the crowd might lie a hidden enemy had made him begin to panic.

The low buzz of surrounding conversation began to wash over him as he looked at his own trembling hands. It was white noise, no more and no less than there had been since the church had begun to fill; a hundred whispered exchanges, the typical background music of a place like this. And yet somehow, in that moment, the volume seemed to rise to a roar.

He needed to get out, and he needed to do it now.

Feeling as if every eye in the church was on him, Kon rose to his feet and semi-stumbled out of the pew, into the siding that ran parallel to the main aisle. He felt his heart racing as he moved, sending an unwanted cocktail of hormones racing into his blood stream. A sheen of cold, unwelcome sweat clung to the back of his neck as he moved.

Kon registered none of this, his frantic mind now laser-focused on only two things: the exit and the imaginary dangers that could keep him from it.

The distance he had to cover was short, but seemed so much longer than it had on the way in, thanks to Kon's growing fear that he was being watched.

That among the crowd, *someone* must be here for him.

The thought made him accelerate abruptly, causing him to stumble, just as the congregation began to rise as one.

On a normal day, Kon would have seen this for what it was – a sign that the priest had arrived. But in that moment he was no longer in control. His primitive brain that had got him out of the Grote Markt alive was back in command.

And so, in a panic that the entire church was about to turn on him, Kon did the one thing that a man avoiding attention should never do.

He ran.

FOURTEEN

The Monk sat back in his chair, his breathing as consciously deep and slow as any meditation. His eyes were closed, just as they had been for the past ten minutes, and yet he could see clear, interconnected worlds that stretched out to the far horizon.

It was a skill he had learned to hone with the help of his father, a family trait which stretched back generations: the ability to create three-dimensional structures within his own mind – images so real that he could almost touch them – all designed to physically map out and solve the problems he faced.

He could only assume the origin of the technique. His great-grandfather had been his guess: Lieutenant Sergei Sukhotin. The original Monk. Everything else had started with him and so it was logical that this had, too. Before Sergei, their family had been nobodies. Just another dispensable, nigh-invisible offshoot of the Russian middle class. But Sergei had changed all of that. By sheer force of will and strength of character he had aligned himself with his betters. And with them he had changed his family's fortunes.

No one else, the Monk believed, could have done the things his great-grandfather had. No one else could have built what he had built. Controlled what he had controlled. Destroyed what he had destroyed. No one else could have served his country with such unrivalled brilliance. And no one else could have prepared those who followed him to do the same, to carry on his legacy.

And so, like all good things in his life, the Monk believed this unique envisioning skill must have started with Sergei.

Whether he was right or wrong about that, the construct the Monk now faced within his mind was a moving amalgamation of disparate alphabets and images, retreating in and out of focus as his attention moved from one to the other. As a whole it detailed the entirety of his wider operation; a labyrinth of information that stretched across the globe. But for now his attention was on just a small part. The weak, rickety section that threatened the stability of the whole.

The failing corner was — as it had been for over a year — based around the crystal-clear image of Hannibal Strauss. Once one of the Monk's greatest weapons, Strauss had become his biggest threat. And in the process of that transformation, he had managed to disrupt every single thing he touched.

The Monk had attempted to deal with the problem directly. Unusually for him, it had not gone to plan, which is why he'd been forced to the extreme measures of today.

If Strauss had simply done the decent thing and died, none of this would have been necessary. None of the deaths at the Grote Markt would have occurred. Konrad Frankowski would not have become a target. By surviving, Strauss had selfishly sentenced so many to death.

He would pay for that. Of that the Monk had no doubt. He would pay for that, but not today.

Today the Monk's mind was focused on his more immediate arrangements. Following the thread from Strauss's image, he could see Vic Sethi searching The Hague for some trace of Frankowski, while the other operative Sethi had christened Athos did the same.

The code name had amused the Monk. Sethi's choices

always did. The reference to the three musketeers was considerably more highbrow than the last two occasions, when he had used Tom and Jerry and before that the Marx Brothers. The Monk would never encourage Sethi by revealing this, but he had even found himself thinking in those code names himself.

The anonymity rule was designed to maintain control. To ensure that every operative had a connection to one man only: to the Monk himself. It was another tactic inherited from Sergei. Another method that had seen their family's operation thrive for a century. Another reason that it was now so close to its ultimate success. That objective was almost all that occupied the Monk's conscious mind; the obsession that drove him onwards as he fought to complete the family mission.

But right now, inside his head, he considered nothing but the strings that held it all together.

He stayed still as he watched the construct move once again, away from Sethi, and away from Porthos and Athos. Instead he saw Frankowski – the image from his Facebook page – and from Frankowski he followed the connective line to the man's family. To his wife and his sons. And to a solution to this part of the problem: to three faces, all of them familiar, all of them already acting on the instructions he had given.

It was the least concerning element of the plot. The one place in which the stupidity of a power-mad fool had not stretched the Monk's operation to breaking point. He could trust those men to do what was needed. It required no more of his time.

Instead he could focus on the nearest part of the problem. A development only confirmed in the last hour. A problem he had thought already solved.

The thought dragged another image into focus. Aramis. This task would fall to him.

And there could be no failure. Not this time.

Not again.

FIFTEEN

Corbin Kincaid looked at his watch as the last of the four identically dressed figures disappeared from view on the screen.

Two minutes fifty-eight seconds, he thought. *Less than a round of boxing. Long enough for thirty-two people to die.*

He reached out to the time marker on the touch-sensitive screen and pulled it back to the start. The fifth time he had done so. Or was it the sixth? He could not be sure; repeated viewing of the Grote Markt massacre had numbed him to meaningless detail. The only real feeling Kincaid had as the footage reverted to its start was gratitude for the advances of modern tech from the days of VHS; the sight of the shooting on high-speed rewind would have felt like a mockery.

Kincaid had expected to pull every available diplomatic string to gain access to the CCTV footage of the square, and to a private facility in which to view it. But no such effort had proved necessary.

He could only guess as to why, but he was fairly sure that guess was correct. While not permitted to disclose his true position as a senior program and plan officer with the CIA's National Clandestine Service, it was likely still that role that had secured him access to the video suite in the Jan Hendrikstraat Police Station. As he routinely did, Kincaid had portrayed himself to the Dutch authorities as a security attaché to the US Embassy, knowing that anyone above a certain level of clearance would understand what that meant. It was a fictitious embassy position, the go-to for agency operatives like Kincaid and Sean Sutton, and so he assumed someone senior in the local set-up had made the connection.

Never hurts to have the Agency onside when they want a resolution to be fast and decisive, he reminded himself.

Kincaid returned his attention to the screen. He was by now familiar with how events would play out: where the first shot would be; where others would join the fray; how swiftly the scene would move from merriment to mayhem. So what he was looking for now was detail. Small, fast movements he might have missed on earlier viewings.

Something – anything – that might suggest his next step.

Kincaid's eyes moved immediately to the top of the screen as the footage began. To a spot close to the edge of the most densely populated section of the Grote Markt. He had already identified two of the three men on whom he now focused: Mendel Prochnik and Will Duffy.

Naming them had been the easy part. After all, Kincaid and Sutton had met them both in person less than twenty-four hours ago.

The third man, however, was a mystery. An American by Kincaid's guess; a conclusion based on what resembled a well-worn New York Yankees baseball cap and the kind of fashion sense more common to New York than the Netherlands. The grown-out beard was more in keeping with others in the crowd around him, but that was a style not particular to any country or continent these days and so Kincaid did not allow it to influence his assessment.

Wherever he was from, *this* was the guy Kincaid wanted to identify. The reason he was watching the footage again. But as had been the case five or six times already, there was neither the detail nor the time to mark out any distinguishing characteristics which could help put a name to a barely visible face.

Kincaid's eyes flitted upwards at the precise moment the first gunman came into frame. Again, he had seen this play out enough times to know exactly what happened next. From the angle of the camera the gunman seemed short and stocky, and from his movement he seemed absolutely certain of his purpose. His focus never left an oblivious Prochnik as he came closer and closer by the moment, his all-black outfit attracting no attention. Even as he raised his rifle to his shoulder, no one seemed to look.

That changed in an instant as he took aim and fired a single fatal round into Prochnik's skull.

Kincaid had watched this enough times now to be sure of what he was seeing. The shooting had seemed random at first: four gunmen firing indiscriminately into the crowd. But the more he had watched, the more Kincaid had changed his mind. Having watched each of the four shooters individually, he had then watched them in unison. And only through that process, with his brain overlaying the full picture with specific, individual detail, had he seen the pattern.

It was subtle and Kincaid could fully understand why others would have missed it. But once seen, it was forever unmistakable.

They're herding the crowd, Kincaid had realised. *They're corralling them in like cattle.*

The realisation had provided grim fascination, especially when combined with a second, parallel revelation: for all the death and destruction they had caused, the gunmen had fired far fewer shots than Kincaid would expect.

Too few, if their only goal was terror. And far too few for mass murder.

The two factors led him to one inescapable conclusion: that the whole thing had all been for show.

It was that belief that had brought him to where he was now. That had made him return to that first bullet. Because if this had not been a random attack then there had to be a primary target. And if that were the case, he reasoned, they would have taken no chances with their first victim.

With that thought at the forefront of his mind, Kincaid narrowed his eyes as he watched the footage again closely. The answer did not take long.

The gunman had not picked Prochnik arbitrarily. Of that Kincaid was now sure. That shot, that first bullet fired, it was as precise as it was professional. It was exactly what it needed to be.

This was no terrorist attack, he told himself. This was an execution, all dressed up to look like something else. But why?

The question focused his attention on the only evidence that could possibly provide an answer.

Gunman Number One.

With a flick of his finger Kincaid brought the footage back to the start. Keeping his eyes fixed firmly on the small masked figure, he watched first as Mendel Prochnik once again slammed into the ground, dead from the moment the single bullet had hit him. Then he watched as both Will Duffy and the third man ran together into the crowd, fleeing for their lives as the rifle that had killed Prochnik was turned on them.

Duffy had taken the lead in their escape, the unknown male simply pulled along in his wake, with Kincaid briefly losing sight of them both in the suddenly uproarious crowd. A loss which, he was sure, the first gunman had shared; if Kincaid could not see them from his elevated viewpoint, there was no way their would-be killer could do so at ground level.

And it was this that finally convinced Kincaid of his own theory.

He's got his rifle raised, he observed. *It's even aimed into the crowd. But he hasn't fired. Even as the other three are letting off round after round*, he *hasn't fired*.

On previous viewings, Kincaid had been puzzled as to why this shooter had waited so long between shots. Now it was clear.

As the footage continued, the movement of the crowd gave him the further confirmation he did not need. A sudden shift in the tide of frantic, terrified bodies gave him a glimpse – a bare heartbeat's sight – of Duffy and the stranger. After their disappearance into the crowd, they had abruptly changed direction, which is why he'd lost track of them. In that instant, they were visible again.

To Kincaid now and, back in time by a few hours, to the first gunman.

The waiting killer took the shot without hesitation and a tall man next to Duffy dropped to the floor, the victim of a bullet meant for the lawyer. It was impossible to tell at this distance and through the imperfections of the screen, but Kincaid would have placed good money that Duffy had avoided death by mere inches.

And then they were lost from sight within the crowd again.

Kincaid pushed himself back into his chair, his eyes for the first time drifting from the screen.

Prochnik.

Duffy.

They had surely been the targets. And that led Kincaid to his next conclusion.

This was the Monk.

Kincaid was more shocked by the realisation than he had expected. Not by the extremity of the massacre. After all these years hunting the Monk, he had no doubt of the man's absolute ruthlessness. When the Monk was forced to resort to violence, he did so without boundaries of any kind.

It was something else. Something about this that was different.

The Monk was a fanatic. A man of absolute dedication to a cause, who was willing to pay whatever cost was needed to achieve his goal. Everything he did, at least to Kincaid's knowledge, was in the furtherance of his mission. Every bribe he paid. Every word of disinformation he dripped. Every secret he learned. And yes, every death he ordered. All of it was for one thing: the revival of the Russian Empire.

All of it for Mother Russia.

But if the two lawyers had been his targets, then today was not about that. Today was about the Monk himself.

About his own protection.

The thought made Kincaid smile, even in the face of the hell playing out on-screen.

Twenty-two years, he thought. *Twenty-two years and that sonofabitch is finally afraid.*

We finally have a chance.

He leaned forwards, the same excited grin still spread wide on his face. Making no effort to suppress it, he reached for the screen, returned the footage to the start and tapped 'play'.

SIXTEEN

The first things to hit Kon Frankowski as he burst through the church doorway and into the street were sunlight and surprise. He had spent so long inside the poorly lit building that he had expected to step out into darkness.

But it was still only six o'clock. On a typical July day, he would have at least another four hours until dusk. Which meant he had inadvertently ignored Maria's instruction: stay put until dark. Yet another failure to add to those that already weighed him down.

Despite his spiralling thoughts, Kon somehow kept moving. The shock of the sunlight had slowed his pace; a good thing, he realized, as his frenzied flight would have no doubt attracted attention. He could see at a glance that he had not been followed from the church. But still he wanted to put as much distance as he could between him and its occupants.

He looked around as he covered the yards, determined to absorb as much as possible about his surroundings. He did not know what he was looking for. Some hint that he was heading the wrong way, perhaps? That he was about to walk into the arms of the police? Or worse still, some indication that he was being followed. He did not know the answer. But as futile as his efforts might be, they made him feel better.

At least he was doing *something*.

The thought finally began to calm Kon down from the alarm that had gripped him in the church. The realisation that his safety and next steps were in his hands. No longer was he cowering in temporary sanctuary. No longer was he a sitting target, obedient to the instructions of a wife who, for all her bizarre confidence, could well know as little as him.

He was his own man, moving under his own steam. And with every step he felt more like himself again. More confident. More in control.

Still, Kon would not lie to himself. His situation remained very far from perfect. Even now, as he turned left onto a street cast into shadow by the surrounding buildings, he was still *very* visible. If anyone was looking for him it would be easy to spot him. It was surely why Maria had wanted him to stay inside until dark, he realised. At least in that respect her advice had been solid.

Who am I trying to kid? Every damn thing she said was solid.

The thought brought him back to the question that had dominated his mind through half the time he had sat alone in the church. He had tried time and again to dismiss it. To convince himself that it was not important. Not when he had immediate life-threatening issues to worry about. And yet his brain could never ignore it for long.

Every time it came back and every time he asked himself the same thing:

How did Maria know what she knew?

How did she know I was caught up in something?

And how the hell did she know how to keep me alive?

He tried again to force the thought from his mind. There would be time for it on another day. For now he just had to accept that his wife was right: he had to stay focused on his own safety.

On his own survival.

By Kon's reckoning his hotel was to the north of where he now stood, while the Grote Markt was barely a few blocks south-east. And so he chose to head west.

Away from both.

Maria had been correct about his plan to return to his room. As ideas went, it had been an especially poor one. He understood the instinct behind it: the clothes he was wearing were haggard from the square and needed to be changed, and without his passport he could not get out of the Netherlands. But he also knew that to go back there was a death sentence.

The question, though, was how had Maria known that? And so quickly, as if by honed instinct? She was a smart woman – far smarter than Kon was, he knew – but still, for her mind to work so fast when the situation was so alien?

Lost in those thoughts, Kon had not heard the sound of an approaching engine nor seen the flashing lights, so the sudden piercing siren spun him round in shock. A heartbeat later he wondered at its target.

Whether it was him.

He caught his breath at the possibility and at the question that followed: what he should do? Should he run? Or should he take his chances with the police? Perhaps the safest place was with them. The conflicted thoughts left his mind at odds with itself until, seconds later, they were rendered irrelevant. The car began to speed up, a clear signal that its driver had no intention of stopping.

Wherever its task, it wasn't here for Kon.

The car was a marked Audi saloon, a common model for a police cruiser in The Hague. Kon watched it pass, impressed by its speed on the narrow street. Sixty, he would have guessed. Maybe a little less. But whatever the answer, on a road this tight it was damned dangerous. A fact which reminded Kon of the one thing he had not considered until now.

They're still on high alert, the police. This thing isn't even close to over.

Kon had been so preoccupied with his own safety that he had not considered the impact of the shooting on the city around him. What had happened in the Grote Markt must have shaken the locals to their core. Mass shootings just did not happen in this part of the world.

Or at least they were not supposed to.

That fact, Kon now realised, was a threat to him.

Fear breeds vigilance but it also exaggerates danger, and neither of those things were helpful to a man on the run. It was the final factor to confirm the step that Kon already knew he must make.

I need to get the hell out of this city.

SEVENTEEN

The distance between Michael Devlin's Chelsea home and RAF Northolt was just a touch over thirteen miles. A twenty-minute drive at any reasonable speed, the journey had taken Michael and Dempsey almost an hour in the typical Saturday London traffic.

To Michael, sat in the taxi with nothing to occupy him, it had seemed longer. While Dempsey had concerned himself with getting them a flight to The Hague and then arranging both a driver and accommodation at the other end – all perks of his position with the UN's International Security Bureau – Michael's mind had been able to wonder and, inevitably, to think the worst.

Will's message and the fact of Mendel Prochnik's death had left him in no doubt of the danger his friend was in. Michael knew Will well enough to know how fearless he could be in the face of a fight, legal or physical. Will Duffy, he knew, would never have backed down from the threat he was so clearly facing. Nor would he have just left Prochnik to die. Not if he could help it.

Neither factor instilled Michael with much hope for his friend's survival. Taken alone or together, those particular personality traits were not much use against an M16 rifle, or whatever the hell it was those murdering bastards had used on the crowd they had massacred. But if somehow Duffy was alive, Michael would find him. He owed his friend that much.

And he couldn't lose another one.

Michael cast a glance towards Dempsey as the unwelcome

memories crossed his mind. The people who had been taken from him. He had lost so much in a life so far only half lived. His mother and father. His brother. And two of his dearest friends.

With so few people left, he counted Will and Bebe Duffy as part of the family. And Michael was not about to let one of his family die unclaimed on foreign soil.

Dead or alive, he would find Will Duffy and he would bring him home.

The sensation of their black cab slowing interrupted Michael's thoughts, saving him, however temporarily, from the descent into darkness that threatened to overcome him in situations such as this. With the next stage of their trip about to begin, it gave him something concrete to focus on.

'Is this the place?'

The long hedge that bordered the left-hand side of the road had come to an end, exposing the tall chain-link fence behind and beyond it. A few yards more and the fence also ended, replaced by a military-style entrance. It was reminiscent of the army checkpoints Michael remembered from his youth in Northern Ireland.

'It is,' Dempsey replied. He took his identification from his wallet, showed it to the military personnel at the gate and the barrier was lifted without another word. 'And that's our ride.'

Dempsey pointed towards a small jet that was parked at the near end of the single runway. Michael knew next to nothing about aircraft – the fact that four jets make it a jumbo was about the extent of it – and so he had no idea of the make nor the model of the plane Dempsey had procured for the journey ahead.

What he *did* know was that it did not look cheap.

'Seriously. That's just for us?'

'There weren't any direct flights left,' Dempsey explained. 'It was this way or wait until tomorrow.'

'How much is this costing you?'

'Nothing. It's on the ISB.'

'Why?'

'A shooting in The Hague, Mike? A skip and a jump from the International Criminal Court? That's ISB business.'

Michael gave Dempsey a grateful smile. The shooting alone would not have taken his friend from London to the Netherlands, he knew that. Dempsey was going there for one reason only: so that Michael did not have to face this alone.

And if claiming it as ISB business got them to Duffy sooner, Michael would take it.

They climbed out of the cab and Michael paid the driver while Dempsey headed towards the plane. Within moments he was heading back.

'Is it ready to go?' Michael asked.

'Needs to top-up on fuel,' Dempsey replied, 'then we're good. Ten minutes.'

'Agent Dempsey.'

Dempsey turned at the sound of his name. A female member of RAF ground-crew was walking across the tarmac towards them.

'It's still a short wait, sir. Can I escort you and your companion inside? It's a lot more comfortable there.'

Dempsey looked towards Michael and shrugged. A clear question.

'No,' Michael replied. 'No thanks. We've been sitting long enough in the cab. I need some air.'

Dempsey turned back to the officer.

'We're good, thanks. We'll stick it out here.'

'OK, sir. Your call. But if you need anything—'

'I know where to find you.'

'Sir.'

Dempsey turned to Michael as the officer moved away, and it dawned on Michael that this was the first time the two men had been alone since Michael had listened to Will Duffy's voice message. First there had been Bebe Duffy, then the black cab driver who had driven them here from Chelsea. Neither Michael nor Dempsey had wanted to discuss anything delicate in earshot of either.

Now that they were alone, Dempsey wasted no time in getting to the point.

'What did you make of the voicemail?'

'I honestly don't know. But it's not good, is it?'

'No. He sounded scared. Like whatever was going on was no empty threat. You think he'd walk into trouble if he knew it was there?'

'He'd run in. If he thought he was doing the right thing. Especially if someone on his team was there already.'

'Like Prochnik?'

'Like Prochnik.'

'Shit.'

'Exactly.'

Dempsey took a deep breath.

'OK. So we have to assume he was caught up in the shooting too.'

'We do.'

'And that the shooting was targeted.'

'Seems that way.'

'So how do you think this is going to play out? If he's dead, Mike, or hurt. What do you plan to do?'

'Whatever condition he's in, I want to find whatever sonofabitch put him in it. Then I want to repay the favour.'

Dempsey nodded his head. He did not seem surprised by the sentiment.

'And how do you think we go about that? What leads do we have?'

'The name Will gave us. We find that guy, we're halfway there.'

'I couldn't make out the name, could you? The message broke up at the end.'

'Maybe the reception dropped out. Here, listen again.'

He handed the phone to Dempsey. His friend's expression was blank as he listened to the part he had already heard.

But as the message came to the end he saw the colour visibly drained from Dempsey's face. The sight was a shock. Michael had never seen Dempsey physically react to . . . well, to *anything*.

'What is it?'

'Konrad Frankowski.'

Dempsey seemed distant as he said the name. As if his mind was somewhere else.

'You know him?'

'I know someone with that name. Or at least someone I know does.'

'You think it's the same guy?'

'Probably not. He lives in America. But I need to find out for sure.'

'Why?'

'Because if this Frankowski is the key to everything, chances are he's in danger. And maybe anyone connected to him.'

Michael felt his eyes narrow as he scrutinised his friend.

What Dempsey was saying made sense. But it was what he was *not* saying that bothered Michael.

'And if it's the guy you know?'

'I don't know him. I know his wife.'

Michael could not miss the look in Dempsey's eyes. It was one he had never before seen in his friend.

It was more than concern. It was fear.

And in that moment he understood.

'His wife?'

Dempsey met his gaze, his face a mask but his eyes still a giveaway as he replied.

'His wife.'

EIGHTEEN

The sound of gunfire, while muffled by the noise-dampening headphones Eden Grace was wearing, was still physical in its impact. The range was deserted save for Grace herself and so no shot came as a surprise. Each and every one corresponded with her own pull of the trigger, and yet each one still sent an imperceptible jolt through her tensed body.

The difference between range shooting and a live-fire situation was not lost on Grace. One was controlled and even a little contrived, designed with every safety precaution in place and every distraction excised. The other was life and death, when – ideally – the combination of adrenaline and training kicked in to give agents like Grace the advantage.

The adrenaline came naturally. The training? That took time. Which was why she was here now, in the secure bowels of the United Nations Secretariat Building in Manhattan.

Two more trigger pulls and all fifteen 9mm rounds from Grace's Glock 19 were spent. She dropped out the magazine and placed the pistol flat on the counter ahead of her, facing into the range, before activating the target recall. Grace had set the target halfway between the fifteen- and twenty-five-yard markings. Twenty was as far as she could fire while guaranteeing a degree of accuracy; years of practice told her that she would not improve on that, but with enough work she could minimise the odds on a stray shot at this distance.

The target retracted slowly and so Grace had time to consider her grouping from a distance. Even she had to admit that it was impressive. Fifteen shots. Three to the head, ten to the chest in a cluster. And the two that had slipped away were still clean shots; one to the abdomen, one to the right shoulder.

Better than yesterday.

Grace had seen all she needed to by the time the target was fully retracted and so she did not waste time with an inspection. Instead she replaced it with a fresh paper silhouette and sent it back to the same twenty-yard spot, before picking up the Glock and inserting a second fifteen-round magazine.

She was ready to go again – pistol raised and her stance settled – when she felt the buzzing of the phone in her front trouser pocket. A moment later and the Glock was back on the counter, the phone by her ear.

'You're supposed to be on holiday, Boss.'

'Change of plans, Eden.' There was a tone of concern in Dempsey's voice. Something Grace was not used to. 'Did you see what happened today in The Hague?'

'That's a long way from London.'

'You'd think, wouldn't you?'

'Are you there?'

'I will be within an hour. I'm just about to fly out.'

'Why?'

'A few reasons. I need your help with one of them.'

Grace did not like what she could hear. Dempsey was unflappable. It was the man's defining characteristic. Yet right now he did not sound calm.

'Anything, Boss. What is it?'

'It's Maria.'

'Who?'

'Maria Parker, Eden. My old . . . the friend I once told you about.'

Dempsey was not a man to share personal information

lightly and so Grace could not claim to know everything about him. No one could. But they *had* become close – as close as was possible with a character like him – and Dempsey had shared some details about his life which, Grace guessed, few others knew.

'You mean the doctor?'

'Yeah.'

'What does she have to do with The Hague?'

'Hopefully not a thing. But you remember I told you she was married now?'

'Yeah.'

'Well, her husband's name is Konrad Frankowski. Someone with that name is caught up in all this.'

'In a terrorist attack?'

'It might not have been terrorists. I've received some intel that puts Konrad Frankowski at the heart of everything. And that puts his family at risk too.'

'You don't think that's a bit of a stretch, Boss? That it's Maria's husband. It would be one hell of a coincidence.'

'You're right. It's probably not him. But I need to know. To be sure.'

Grace felt herself nodding. She could understand Dempsey's concern, no matter how long the odds. And besides, she was hardly rushed off her feet today.

'So what do you want me to do?'

'I want someone to find out everything there is to know about Maria's husband. I want to know if there's anything that can connect him to what happened this afternoon. If there's anything that can connect him to The Hague.'

'And when you say someone, you mean someone *other* than me?'

'I do, yeah.'

'OK. Which means I have another job.'

'It does. I don't want to regret taking chances here, Eden. I want you to go check on Maria. Take Dylan and Sal with you, please, and give their family home in New Jersey the once-over.'

'Boss, are you—'

'I'm sure, Eden. Please, just play along with this one. Put my mind at ease.'

Grace nodded again, as aware as before that Dempsey could not see her agreement down the phone line. She knew that Dr Maria Parker – or Frankowski, as she now was – had once meant everything to him. Maybe she still did. And after all Dempsey had done for Grace, she could do him this favour.

'OK, Boss. What's the address?'

'They live in Park Ridge, New Jersey. You'll find exactly where on the voter roll.'

'You don't know it?'

'I'm an old friend, Eden. Not a stalker.'

'Right. I'll head out there with Wrixon.'

'Take Sal, too.'

'Sal's on leave. Back home. He's a whole lot closer to you right now than he is to Jersey.'

'I forgot about that. What about the others?'

'Shui is chasing down a lead on one of her cases. But Kate and Adama are at their desks upstairs. Or they were an hour ago, anyway.'

'In that case, take Adama. Leave Kate to deal with the Frankowski research. And tell her to keep an eye out for any news on the names Will Duffy and Mendel Prochnik, too. I need answers as soon as possible, so tell her to call me direct.'

'What about you? What's your plan?'

'I'm going to get myself to The Hague and find out what the hell's going on there.'

'And how do you think you'll do that?'

'Same as always. I'll stick my nose where it's not wanted and see what turns up. If there's trouble, it'll find me.'

'It usually does.'

'Pretty much. Now get yourself to Jersey, Eden. Let me know she's safe.'

Grace slipped her phone back into her pocket. She hesitated for just a moment, her gaze settling on her pistol, as she thought through what lay ahead.

Or, more likely, what did not.

There's no way Maria's husband is the same Konrad Frankowski. No way.

And yet in the back of her mind, Grace could not avoid the question:

But when does Dempsey's gut ever steer him wrong?

NINETEEN

The Gulfstream G150 was a bigger plane than was necessary to transport just Dempsey and Michael the two hundred and fifty miles from London to The Hague. Built for far longer journeys and for up to eight passengers to fly in comfort, the private jet became the definition of luxury air travel when occupied by just two.

On any other day the experience would have been one to savour. But right now, as the engines pushed the G150 past five hundred miles per hour and towards the east coast of Sussex, the plane's two passengers barely noticed their surroundings.

Michael had hardly spoken since boarding. A stark change from his demeanour at the airport. Dempsey wondered if perhaps he was a nervous flyer; it only now occurred to him that, as close as they were, they had never travelled together. Whatever its cause, Michael's silence had provided an opportunity for the Irishman to get lost in his own darkest thoughts.

And that, Dempsey knew, was never a good thing.

For all his outward respectability and his elevation to the highest ranks of the English legal establishment, Michael was far from a typical lawyer. Dempsey knew more of his friend's past than most – he had played a role himself in some of its most traumatic moments, after all – and so he knew the places that Michael could go when lost in his own mind.

What he also knew was the effect those descents into darkness could have upon the man. The demons they could bring out. Fiercely intelligent and a natural gentleman, when the black thoughts took hold, Michael could become something else altogether. Something far less . . . civilised.

Dempsey could see hints of that now and felt the need to intervene.

'What's the case Duffy's been working on?'

Michael did not react to the question, his eyes fixed ahead in the blankest of stares.

'Michael?'

Dempsey shifted himself just slightly as he spoke, enough to break into his friend's line of sight. The movement had the intended effect.

'Sorry, what?'

Michael seemed confused for a moment, as his thoughts came back from wherever they had taken him. Dempsey had no wish to find out where that place was. They were heading into the unknown and that required a clear head. For that, Dempsey needed Michael Devlin the lawyer, not Michael Devlin the fighter.

In Dempsey's reckoning, work was the subject most likely to bring Michael's professional mind back to the fore. Even if it was not technically *Michael's* work.

'Will Duffy's case in The Hague,' Dempsey continued. 'What is it?'

Michael took a few more moments before answering. Long enough, Dempsey could see, to properly focus his mind. It seemed a near physical effort, but soon enough he was back.

'It's a war crimes trial,' Michael said. 'A totally new kind of thing for Will. He's an old-fashioned blagger's brief, villains and gangsters. But earlier this year he got himself wrapped up in this instead. I told him it was a bad idea from the beginning.

Just not his field. But he wouldn't listen. And once he became convinced of the guy's innocence, then there was no talking him out of it.'

'But how did it come to him?' Dempsey asked. 'It's not exactly interchangeable work, is it? The Old Bailey to the International Criminal Court?'

'Not even slightly. But Will *is* a hell of a lawyer. And the advocate – Mendel Prochnik – he needed someone great on this one to back him up. Someone fearless. And fearless is pretty much the first line on Will's CV.'

'And Prochnik found Will how?'

'A retired Jewish gangster, by all accounts. Old client of Will's who had a few close escapes back in the day, before sailing off into the sunset and retiring in Israel. Never forgot the guy he owed for his freedom. He got to know Prochnik in Tel Aviv and, when he heard the kind of help Prochnik needed with Strauss, he introduced him to Will.'

'Strauss?' Dempsey's attention zeroed in on the name Michael had just dropped. 'You mean Hannibal Strauss?'

'Yeah. You know him?'

'I know *of* him,' Dempsey replied. 'Our paths crossed a few times over the years. Strauss is Will's client?'

'He is.'

'But you said Will was convinced his guy's innocent?'

'He is.' A look of sadness crossed Michael's face. 'Or he was, anyway.'

'Then he's wrong.' Dempsey shook his head as he spoke. 'Strauss is a mercenary, Mike. A large-scale military operations specialist and a murdering bastard who works for the highest bidder. There's no way Strauss isn't guilty of what they say. That and God knows how much more.'

'How can you say that? You don't know anything about the case.'

'I know enough. A few years back his highest bidder was the Tripoli government, fighting for control of Libya after the fall of Gaddafi in 2011.

'They recruited Strauss to do the things their military couldn't in the war with the Tobruk faction, which hadn't been going so well. By 2017 Strauss had turned the table and Tripoli was winning. The Tobruk forces had all but retreated to the border to Tunisia, but instead of letting them go and claiming the win, Strauss followed.

'Eventually he pinned what was left of them down just outside the town of Wazzin. They tried to surrender there but Strauss refused to accept it. Instead he massacred them. Nearly fourteen hundred men, wiped out with sarin gas. You know the kind of death that stuff causes, Mike?'

Michael had not broken eye contact with Dempsey through his friend's recap of the case. Nor had he interrupted him. But even so, he did not seem inclined to answer Dempsey's question.

'OK. So you *do* know a bit about it, then.'

'I work for the UN Security Council. You think we don't get briefed on these things?'

'Of course you do. But that doesn't mean everything you're told is correct. Some things aren't as simple as they first appear. You know that better than I do.'

'But where's the room for confusion on this one? Strauss led an army to Wazzin, trapped his enemy soldiers inside and a day later they were all dead. Who the hell else gassed them?'

'Will was certain of his innocence, on these charges at least.

That's all I know. And Will's not naive, Joe. Not by any stretch of the imagination. So that's enough for me to allow room for some reasonable doubt.'

'Then who did it?' Dempsey asked. 'It's the middle of the bloody desert. There was no one else there.'

Michael shook his head.

'How can you be so sure of that? How are you so sure the intelligence is accurate?'

'Because sometimes a duck is just a duck.'

'Oh, don't come at me with cliches.'

'Why not? When you live in Strauss's version of the world as long as I have, you learn there's a whole lot of truth in cliches. Sometimes things are exactly as they appear. Sometimes the maths just adds up.'

Michael nodded his head.

'Alright. I'm not an idiot. I know it doesn't look good. But Will knew all this stuff too and he *still* didn't think it was a true bill. He absolutely believed that Strauss was innocent.'

'Then he didn't know Hannibal Strauss.'

Dempsey took a deep breath, giving his mind time to access the reams of information it held on Will Duffy's client. A second later and he was ready.

'Take it from me, Strauss is one of the most ruthless men to walk this Earth. Gassing over a thousand surrendering soldiers? That's the same evil shit he's been pulling his whole life, just on a bigger scale. The man is a walking nightmare. Where he is now – in a prison cell – is exactly where he should be. And it's exactly where he needs to stay.'

Michael's eyes narrowed.

'You seem to know a lot about the man for someone who only crossed his path.'

'Well, I haven't met him face to face. But I suppose maybe those crossings were a bit more eventful than most.'

'What does that mean?'

'You ever seen a picture of the man?'

'I have. Looks like a mean sonofabitch.'

'Those looks aren't deceiving. But they did used to be a little more attractive.'

'What does that mean?'

'You didn't notice the missing left eye and ear?'

'How could I not?'

'That happened in Cambodia. 2009. The lucky bastard got called away moments before the bomb was set to explode. It still did some damage. Just not as much as it was supposed to.'

'That was you?'

Dempsey nodded.

'I put him out of action for a while, but not for long enough. He was back at it within six months. Hardly a missed beat in the grander scheme of things.'

'What had he been doing in Cambodia?'

'Bad things.'

'Classified?'

'Completely.'

'And after the bomb? Was he still doing those things there?'

'No. I put a stop to all that.'

'Then the grander scheme of things doesn't matter. You helped the people you could help.'

'I guess so. But now your friend is helping *him*.'

'Everyone deserves a defence. Especially if they're wrongly accused.'

'The guy's a piece of shit. He's guilty as charged.'

'One of those things doesn't aways follow the other.'

Dempsey exhaled hard. He could see that he and Michael were about to hit a philosophical impasse: Michael's idealistic views on justice against Dempsey's vivid, close-up experiences of what evil could do. Such a dispute was neither necessary nor helpful – especially not now – and so it was best avoided.

Dempsey turned away without another word, reached into the seat pocket beside him and took out the large tablet he had carried with him from London.

'How long left?' Michael asked. He seemed just as keen to put the debate behind them.

'About twenty minutes,' Dempsey replied, keying in his password as he spoke. 'It's not been long but Kate Silver's good. She might have some news for us. That's why I'm checking my emails.'

For a few moments only the sound of the engines filled the fuselage as Dempsey navigated his tablet. It took little time to see his inbox was empty. Disappointed, he slipped the device back into the seat pocket.

'Nothing yet?' Michael asked.

'Nothing.'

Dempsey watched as the Irishman's eyes began to wander around the jet. They seemed to focus on features that did not warrant his attention. Dempsey knew his friend well enough to recognise when there was something he wanted to ask.

'What is it?'

'What's what?'

'The thing that's on your mind. Whatever's making you uncomfortable. What is it?'

Michael hesitated, for a moment unsure, until he seemed to make up his mind.

'Frankowski's wife,' he said. 'What do I need to know about her?'

Dempsey had not expected the question. He did not know why – in the context it was near inevitable – but still it made him hesitate. And as he did, an image of Maria forced its way to the front of his mind. The mental picture of her face made him smile. Not wide and only for a heartbeat, but long enough that someone as sharp as Michael could not have missed it.

'Chances are you'll need to know nothing,' Dempsey finally replied. 'The odds on it being the same Konrad Frankowski are tiny.'

'Yeah. I suspect you're right. Dime a dozen, those Frankowskis. You can barely swing a cat without hitting one.'

'The name's not so rare in Poland.'

'It's not John Smith anywhere, though, is it?'

'Maybe not.'

'And so? Frankowski's wife? The one you *do* know?'

'Her name's Maria. And I didn't say know her. I said I *used* to know her. A long time ago.'

'When the mere thought of a woman puts *that* expression on your face, even in these circumstances? That's more than someone you simply "used to know", Joe. How long ago was it?'

'Nine years.'

'And she's still got that grip? Shit. That's no casual ex.'

'We were engaged.'

'And?'

'And then we weren't.'

'Come on, man. It's me. How do I not know about this girl?'

'I don't like to dwell on the past.'

Michael could not prevent a laugh at the answer.

'Are you serious? If you had a theme tune it'd be called "Living with the Things I've Done".'

Dempsey shook his head wryly at the response.

'Fair enough. But now's not the time, is it?'

Michael paused for a beat.

'Fine. But when this is all over, you're bringing me up to speed. Got it?'

'Do I have a choice?'

'Does it sound like you do?'

Dempsey smiled again.

'No. Not at all.'

TWENTY

Corbin Kincaid shook his head as he looked around the small workspace located less than half a mile from the International Criminal Court. The location of the office was convenient; with the Hannibal Strauss trial imminent, it made sense for his legal team to be so close to its venue.

The condition of the place, on the other hand? If Kincaid did not know better, he would have assumed that it had been raided and ransacked by whoever had hunted down Mendel Prochnik and Will Duffy earlier that day. The only factor that convinced him otherwise was the fact that burglars would have no need to leave this level of disarray.

He stepped forwards into the room, towards what he assumed was a desk; both its position and the strewn pile of papers that concealed the surface beneath them suggested that use. Plus Kincaid thought he could spot the grey metal sheen of a laptop exposed by a gap in the accidental quilt that otherwise covered every inch of the worktop.

'How can anyone work like this?'

The question came from Kincaid's right. From Sean Sutton. Kincaid had been expecting the question. Sutton was just about the most fastidious man Kincaid had ever known – more so even than Sutton's father, with whom Kincaid had worked as a newly qualified officer – and so he knew that the condition of the office would offend him. Not that Kincaid disagreed. He was nowhere near the neat freak his younger colleague was, but this was a little much even for him.

'You'd think with a team of hotshot lawyers, most of

this would be digital these days. The evidence and all that stuff.'

'I think it is,' Kincaid said. 'Or at least it's served that way. Which means these guys must have printed all of this shit, instead of just working off a screen.'

Kincaid gestured with a wave of his hand as he spoke, the movement taking in all of the room and the piles of paperwork and files that filled the space. By his estimate, they were looking at one hundred thousand pages at least. Perhaps a lot more. All of it stored via a unique filing system that could only be labelled 'mayhem'.

'Old dogs, new tricks,' Sutton replied, his tone making his disdain perfectly clear. 'I guess that's what you get for choosing old lawyers.'

'Less with the old. Duffy's only four years older than me.'

'Precisely. And he's the younger one. At least you have me to drag your creaking feet into the twenty-first century.'

'Don't flatter yourself, kid. Age is just a number.'

'Well, *their* number adds up to a hundred and seventeen. You ask me, that's pretty damned old for a legal team.'

'One hundred and fifty-seven, if you include me.'

Kincaid and Sutton turned at the sound of the new voice, which had come from the office door. Kincaid immediately recognised the speaker: Alastair Compton, the third member of Hannibal Strauss's legal team. Compton was British like Duffy – English rather than Scottish – and his appearance here was not a surprise to either of the Americans; Kincaid had arranged it.

What *was* a surprise was that Compton was not alone.

'You're Yuri Shevchuk,' Kincaid observed, his recognition instant as the man who had been standing just behind Compton stepped into view.

'I am.'

Shevchuk stepped forwards as he spoke, his hand outstretched in greeting to Kincaid. He was another small man, not much bigger than Mendel Prochnik and around the same age. The physical similarity between the two men was marked.

Kincaid took Shevchuk's hand and gripped it tight. The man's presence bothered him – it bothered him a lot – and Kincaid was in no mood to disguise that fact.

'And just what the hell is the International Criminal Court's prosecutor doing at the offices of Hannibal Strauss's lawyers? And *with* defence counsel, as far as I can tell?'

Shevchuk's eyes narrowed at the question. As if he had not expected to be challenged.

'What sort of a question is that?' Shevchuk's English was flawless. Even when outraged. The Ukrainian lawyer yanked his hand out of Kincaid's grip as he continued. 'Men are dead, sir. Good men. You think that fact does not cross party lines?'

'I think it's damned unusual whatever the circumstances,' he replied. 'It's your job to prosecute Hannibal Strauss, for crimes just as bad as what happened today. You think you and what's left of his legal team should be palling around? You think that's a good picture?'

'Hang on Mr . . . Mr Kincaid, is it?' Compton interrupted. 'This reaction is way over the top. Yuri and I, we're professionals. It's perfectly possible for us to be in one another's company and not discuss the case.'

'Even when the rest of your team was just murdered?'

'Well, of course we're going to mention Mendel and Will. But that's hardly discussing the case, is it?'

'And what if they were murdered *because* of your case?'

'That might be more problematic.' Shevchuk's tone was

almost dismissive. 'But it's not, is it? So let's not waste time with hypothetical scenarios.'

'There's nothing hypothetical about it,' Kincaid replied. 'Prochnik and Duffy are dead because of Hannibal Strauss.'

He turned to face Compton.

'And the only reason you're alive is because you weren't in the Grote Markt with them. I'll be straight with you, that's the sort of coincidence that usually concerns me. Knowing that, are you still comfortable having this conversation in front of your prosecutor?'

'This is ridiculous,' Shevchuk snapped, as Compton looked on, stunned. 'What happened today was a terrorist attack. Mendel and Will were tragically unlucky to be there, just like all the other poor souls who were lost. It had nothing—'

'You're Ukrainian, correct?'

Kincaid turned towards Sutton. He had not expected the interruption. Nor did he know where the younger man was going with the question, but he was intrigued to find out. Sutton's mind worked in a way very different to his own. The results were often effective.

'What does that have to do with anything?'

'I would have thought a man from your country, with all that's happening there right now, you'd recognise that not everything is always as it seems.'

'I don't see how the invasion of my homeland should have any bearing on how I perceive what happened today.'

'You have relatives there?'

'Some. Very few. My close family were lucky enough to escape as the tanks rolled in.'

'Among the fortunate few. So there's no one there you speak to?'

'There are some.'

'And what do they tell you? Does it match what we're seeing in the media?'

'What's your name, sir?'

'Sean Sutton.'

'Mr Sutton, I have been the senior prosecutor for the International Criminal Court for five years. Before that I was a specialist United Nations war crimes prosecutor. I know better than you, young man, how a false flag works. I know better than you the way the media can contort what we see. I need no such education from a novice.'

Sutton smiled at the insult.

'Then let's just call it a reminder, shall we? Because that thing you know all about, that's what happened today. The police don't know it yet – maybe they never will – but believe me, the shooting in the Grote Markt was targeted. The gunmen were there for Prochnik and for Duffy and, we presume, for someone else. Everything else was a distraction.'

'And so I'll ask you again,' Kincaid said, taking the verbal baton and redirecting the focus back towards Compton, 'do you want this conversation to carry on with Mr Shevchuk present, or do you think the time has come for prosecution counsel to step outside?'

For a moment Compton said nothing. Then, slowly – hesitantly – he turned to Shevchuk. When he spoke his words were quiet. As if he had been stripped of all confidence.

'Yuri, they're right. I need to do this alone.'

'You need to do nothing of the sort.'

Kincaid concluded from Shevchuk's tone, combined with his attitude so far, that the man was used to being the final authority in his professional life. He did not welcome being challenged.

But Compton, it seemed, was no pushover.

'It's my choice, Yuri. Please. Wait outside.'

For a moment Shevchuk looked as if he would protest again, his eyes darting from Compton to Kincaid and then to Sutton. His mouth was even open at one point, only to be met by an exaggerated grin and wave from Sutton, which seemed to break his resolve. Or cause him to almost lose his temper. Either way, he changed his mind. Turning without a word, he left the office.

Kincaid did not take the time to watch him go.

'Why were you not at the Grote Markt for the meet this afternoon?'

Compton looked confused. Perhaps by the speed of the question. Perhaps by its subject matter.

'I . . . I . . . didn't know there was a . . . what meet?'

'With Hannibal Strauss's source,' Kincaid replied. 'Why were you not there?'

'His source of what?'

'Don't play coy, Mr Compton.' Sutton this time. 'Today was a key part of the deal. *The* key part, really. So why were you not there? Did you know what was coming?'

The confusion on Compton's face seemed to increase with every word. It bothered Kincaid. It was either genuine or Compton was one hell of an actor.

Based on Sutton's question, the next words Compton said would tell him which.

'I . . . I'm . . . look, I'm sorry but . . . what deal?'

Kincaid felt the answer like a punch to the gut. It was not what he wanted to hear.

'Are you saying you were unaware of the deal Strauss was negotiating?'

'I've no bloody idea what you're talking about.'

'So when I called you an hour ago and told you about Duffy and Prochnik, you seriously had no idea who I was?'

'I'd never heard your name before in my life.'

'Neither of them ever mentioned me or Sutton?'

'No.'

'The CIA?'

'What the hell does the CIA have to do with any of this?'

Compton's accent was beginning to change. Less polished, more working class, it betrayed his origins. To Kincaid, it was a sign the man was becoming irritated rather than acting. Which in turn suggested that his confusion was not faked.

Kincaid ignored the question.

'What about Strauss's list? You heard of that?'

'His list of what?'

'The list he was planning to trade for his freedom.'

'What?! Look, this is getting ridiculous. Just what the fuck are you going on about?'

'This was happening, buddy. And your colleagues were in on it right up to their necks. Which is why someone put a bullet in the both of them. Are you really trying to say you knew nothing?'

'Do I look like I know anything? One minute you're telling me the people I work with are dead, now you're talking about the sodding CIA. You want to know what I know, Mr Kincaid? I know so little that I lost you at question one.'

Kincaid looked towards Sutton. The glance was intended as both an indication that he was done and permission for the younger man to say whatever his unusual mind was cooking up. Sutton understood.

'Are you saying that your own team kept you in the dark?'

'I guess they did, yeah.'

'Did they not trust you?'

'Evidently not.'

'Why?'

'How the hell would I know? It's only right now I'm finding out they didn't.'

'So they gave no indication that they had an issue with you?'

'None.'

'Up until this moment, it was smooth sailing?'

'I didn't say that.'

'So they *did* have a problem with you?'

'No. Not them.'

'Who?'

'Strauss. He didn't trust me. He's refused to interact with me for the last month or so. Ever since he was attacked in prison.'

Kincaid was aware of the incident. The official line was that Strauss had killed three guards in an unprovoked incident. Kincaid knew that Strauss told that story differently; he claimed to have been defending himself. Compton's use of the word 'attacked' suggested that he believed the alternative version. A fact which left Kincaid even more inclined to accept that Compton was a straight shooter in all this.

He said nothing. Instead, he just watched as Sutton continued.

'Do you know why he shut you out?'

'Because he doesn't trust anyone he didn't hand-pick himself. The guy's a control freak.'

'And he didn't pick you?'

'No. I was court-appointed, when he was first brought to the ICC. And once he'd selected Mendel and Will and secured them to act for him, Mendel insisted on keeping me on board. So they weren't constantly playing catch-up.'

'That was what, eight months ago?'

'Around that, yeah.'

'But it's only been a month since he stopped engaging with you?'

'Yes. He tolerated me until then. He wasn't happy I was a part of things but he trusted Mendel's judgement. Then, after the attempt on his life, he pulled back. After that it was Mendel and Will and no one else. I wasn't welcome at the prison.'

'And did this change how they treated you?'

'Mendel and Will? No. No, I didn't think so. Although I guess it's hard for me to say that now, isn't it? If there was some sort of immunity deal going down with you guys that I knew nothing about.'

Kincaid had heard enough. Compton, it was clear, was even more in the dark than they were. If they were going to find out who Prochnik and Duffy were meeting, they would need to look elsewhere.

The sound of the door opening interrupted Kincaid's frustrated thoughts. This time he was expecting no visitor and so his nerves were heightened. As, it seemed, were Sutton's: both men had reached for their concealed firearms in an instant. And both immediately saw that the reaction was unnecessary.

It was Shevchuk.

'You were told to stay outside,' Kincaid began. 'So why—'

'I have news you'll want to hear.'

'What?' asked Compton.

'It's Will Duffy. He's alive. He's badly hurt but he's alive.'

TWENTY-ONE

The Monk glanced to the top corner of his computer screen and noted the time.

8.13 p.m.

It had been two hours since he had spoken first to Vic Sethi and then to Luuk Jansen. Or Aramis, as Sethi had christened him at the outset of all this. As the only Dutchman in the four-man team tasked with the Grote Markt assignment, that fact alone had made Jansen the most suitable candidate for what the Monk needed next.

Constrained to a choice of only four. How has it come to that?

It was an unnecessary question; the Monk knew exactly why his resources were stretched so thin. The situation in Ukraine – the madness, as it was better described – had left Russia vulnerable. Her limitations exposed for all the world to see. That in itself was no bad thing; the worse the invasion went for the military, the weaker the government would become. But for the Monk, the timing was poor.

To those few Russian officials who even knew of the existence of the Monk and his organisation, he was a patriotic asset. A man with the goal – and the means – to bring his country back to its rightful position in the world. And while that much was true, it was also less than half the story.

The legend told how the Monk's organisation – the Mladorossi – had existed for a century, created by the Monk's ancestor, Sergei Sukhotin. He had been a patriot so loyal to the Romanovs that he had orchestrated the murder of Grigori Rasputin, the icon whose malign influence he had seen as a threat to the rule of Tsar Nicolas II. And it told of how Sergei and his co-conspirators had seen themselves banished for those necessary actions, an injustice which had inadvertently saved them from the horrors of the October Revolution.

That was the legend. And it was mostly true. But there was so much more. Details that were known only to a very few.

With the Tsar and his family murdered by the Communists, Sergei had vowed to see the wrong made right, and – having seen first-hand the failures of the civil war that had followed – he knew he needed to find another way. That he and his heirs would have to play the long game.

It had become the obsession of Sergei's life. A single, absolute focus that led him to fake his own death in 1926 and to dedicate the rest of his years to creating the weapons – the resources – that would be needed to achieve his goals, even after his real demise years later.

The first few decades were spent on this key task. Sergei had been the first to use the identity of the Monk; an ironic weaponisation of the myths that had grown around the 'mystical' and 'un-killable' Grigori Rasputin and the whispered legends of his return. Seizing on the mystique and the fear that surrounded it, Sergei had utilised the persona well; positioning his own mysterious and charismatic 'holy patriot' to redirect the incalculable sums of money that had been pumped into the Union of Young Russia by European aristocracy and anti-communists in the 1920s and 30s, he had used those funds to begin the recruitment and training of spies and covert assets he would place around the world. Chess pieces to be used by the future Monks, first in Russia and then across the globe.

By the end of the Second World War, the organisation had become a shadow network powerful enough to offer its invaluable services directly to the Soviet state. And in doing so it pulled off its greatest coup: it had secured the funding that guaranteed its future from the very regime it existed to destroy.

It was the perfect cover. Their key Russian government connections had no way to know that by supporting the efforts of the Mladorossi to undermine their country's enemies, they were also financing their own demise. Sergei Sukhotin and his descendants *had* created a global force for the advancement of Russia. An ideology that *did* necessitate the weakening of rival states, by whatever means necessary.

But it went much further than that: to the Monk – as to those of his ancestors entrusted to hold that identity before him – ultimate success did not stop with the pre-eminence of their mother country. It required something more. It required nothing less than the restoration of Russia to its true former glory.

A Russia that stood astride the world unrivalled, under the leadership of those who had been born to rule.

And *that* required the return of the Romanovs.

To that end, the very first Monk had identified who he believed to be the rightful Tsar. And while that royal never found his way back to the throne, in the century that followed the Mladorossi had protected his line, ready to restore it when the time was right. When the final government that stood in the way could be removed.

In the sixty-plus years since the death of Stalin, the Mladorossi and the leaders who had preceded him had pursued the same unwavering agenda that now drove the Monk. And they had done so with incredible success. With their network ever growing and their effectiveness ever greater, the network had undermined the West at every turn, earning them the gratitude and the loyalty of their 'superiors' back home in Moscow. And yet, unknown to their bankers, every step of the way they had used the same techniques and the same tactics to weaken each successive Russian government. By weaponising superior intelligence, utilising skilled misinformation, employing long-term embedded operatives and – when necessary – by resorting to violence and even murder, the Monk and his forebears had undermined regime after regime, from the 1950s to the present day, preparing for the return of their country's rightful ruler.

And by doing so they had kept the Soviet and later the Russian leadership insecure, all while convincing them to pay generously for the seeds of their own destruction.

None of that had changed since the Monk had taken over the reins of the organisation. He had followed the path mapped out by other men and he had added his own spin to what had already proved so effective. He had worked tirelessly and yet despite everything – despite literal generations of effort – he could now see how his own eight years of sowing disunity in the Western world had succeeded a little too well.

He could see that things were destabilising too quickly for his plans.

A previously unimaginable insurgency in the heart of Washington DC, bringing the United States closer to civil war than at any time since 1865.

The foundations of NATO shaken to the point of collapse, with America placed at odds with its European allies.

The dramatic decline of relations within the European Union, with continental neighbours now at each other's throats through the epic mishandling of Brexit.

The Monk's network had played a major part in all of this and more, using their practically unlimited funding to feed the exponential growth of usually small, ineffectual extremist groups. The dissolution of the Soviet Union in 1991 had done little to stop the flow of money from the state; the change in regime had simply diverted the funds, so that now they came from the oligarchs, a stream of billionaires granted obscene wealth on the understanding that most of that money belonged to their political paymaster.

With such deep pockets, the Monk had deployed his Mladorossi network to infiltrate and abuse both traditional and social media to spread misinformation on a scale never before seen. And he had ramped up his own favourite tactic – using foreign politicians to give that misinformation credibility – to a level that had never previously been achieved. It was a triumph of which he was particularly proud, a success based on his own innate understanding of human nature. The Monk's predecessors had purchased these tame statesmen and women in the old-fashioned way: via their compromised morality or their empty pockets. The Monk, though, had found a different way. He had seen the vulnerability in overriding ego and in the lack of the self-awareness necessary to spot manipulation.

In other words, he had utilised populist, vote-hungry media darlings for his own purposes. And they did not even know it.

It could only have happened in the modern world. A time that was more ripe than any other point in history for an actor with bad intentions to get his message to as wide an audience as possible. As the Monk liked to think of it, social media had industrialised his greatest weapon and had allowed him to deploy it as his predecessors could only have dreamed.

And it had worked. The institutions that upheld the illusion of global stability – the myth of world peace – had begun to crumble. Given time, the Monk did not doubt that they would have collapsed altogether.

Except that megalomaniacal fool in Moscow didn't give them enough time.

The truth of it was that the invasion of Ukraine had been the Monk's plan from the beginning, but it was never his intention that it should have happened so soon. He had always intended for the invasion to fail – it was designed to be the nail in the coffin of an increasingly uncontrollable Russian leader, signalling the end for yet another regime – and so in *that* respect it had been a success so far. But had it happened in a few more years, as the Monk had planned? When his many other efforts around the globe had enjoyed more time to bed in? More time to foster unrest and friction and division? *Then* it would have rocked the world more thoroughly. It would have exposed weaknesses in many more countries.

It would have done exactly what the Monk had intended.

Instead, by moving prematurely, Russia's president had achieved the undoing of what should have been the Monk's greatest triumph. His actions had served to unite the Western world in opposition to his aggression, shoring up and strengthening a hitherto faltering NATO alliance and even defrosting relations between Britain and the EU. Without time for the animosity and distrust the Monk had created to truly take root, the West had reverted to form.

And now the Monk – like Russia herself – was paying the price.

With the Russian state and many of its wealthiest oligarchs under international sanctions, the Monk's ability to call on his usually unlimited funding had taken a big hit. And what finite monies he did have were now directed elsewhere, to support the various Russian paramilitary groups he had since unleashed on their own government.

It was a massive drain on his diminished resources and so, for the first time in his experience, the Monk had been forced to pick which short-term goal would receive his fullest attention. And that, in reality, was no choice at all.

The need for a new Russian leader had to take precedence over everything else.

Even over the Monk's own personal safety.

Even over the security of his network in the West.

It was for this reason that he now found himself cursing the enforced limitations that stifled his operations. Limitations that had never been more evident than they were right now.

His men must have noticed, he was sure. Sethi certainly had; the surprise in his voice when ordered to search the streets for Konrad Frankowski confirmed that. Sethi would have expected to be bunkered down in some secure bolt-hole after today's atrocity, waiting for the heat to die down before he could quietly leave the country. Instead he was out on another assignment, working – in a break with all previous tradition – with members of the same team.

It had long been a tactic of the organisation, predating the Monk by decades, that operatives would meet only once. They would be assembled as a team, they would be briefed, they would do the job and then they would disband, never to see one another again.

But right now, it was a luxury the Monk could not afford.

He looked again at the clock.

8.15 p.m.

It could not be long now, he was confident. But even that level of uncertainty was not acceptable to the Monk. As ever, he could only be comfortable if he knew every last detail. Especially when something was *this* important.

He reached out for his encrypted phone, found Jansen's handle – the name under which he was registered in the system – and placed the handset to his ear.

It was time to add the exact moment of Will Duffy's death to his plan.

TWENTY-TWO

Eden Grace took the phone from her ear and placed it into its holster. Like the two she'd already made in the last forty minutes, the call to Kate Silver back at United Nations Secretariat Building had revealed nothing of interest.

'Still no news?'

The question came from Dylan Wrixon, Grace's ISB colleague. Wrixon, along with Grace and Kate Silver, was one of the three Americans who made up half of the elite Alpha Team, the unit hand-picked and led by Britain's Joe Dempsey.

'None,' Grace confirmed.

'Well, that's great. Not like we need to know what we're walking into anyway, huh?'

'Like I keep saying, it's probably nothing. Dempsey's just covering his bases.'

'And it takes three of us to do that?'

'It takes as many of us as Agent Dempsey orders.'

The intervention came from Adama Jabari, one of Alpha Team's four non-American operatives. Jabari was seated behind Grace and Wrixon, in the back seat of the black Chevy Suburban they had loaned from the FBI field office in nearby Woodland Park. The vehicle had been needed to transport them from Colony Field – the temporarily closed baseball field that had proved the closest landing space for the Bell 525 Relentless they had flown from Manhattan to Park Ridge – to the Frankowski family home.

Wrixon fixed eyes on Jabari through the rear-view mirror.

'What, I'm not allowed to question orders now?'

'Question whatever you like,' Grace replied. 'But keep your eyes on the road while you do it.'

'This place is dead,' Wrixon replied, his attention nonetheless returned to the street ahead. 'I couldn't hit another car if I tried.'

'Let's not test that theory out.'

Wrixon said nothing in return, but the resulting silence did not last. Instead it was filled by Jabari's smooth, melodic voice.

'This country, it never ceases to surprise me.'

They were not the words Grace was expecting from her colleague but they provided a welcome distraction from the tension. Not for the first time, she noticed how soothing Jabari's slow, carefully enunciated Ethiopian tenor could be. Which was, she suspected, exactly the effect he intended.

'Just thirty minutes from the most frantic city on this planet,' Jabari continued, 'and we're here, surrounded by peace and by quiet and by the most beautiful green. So close and yet so far, all at once. All in one incredible place. It truly is special.'

'Let's hope it stays that way.' Wrixon's tone of irritation had not changed. 'Quiet, I mean.'

Grace could appreciate Wrixon's frustration at not knowing what they could be heading into. That was natural. But what she could *not* stand was his apparent belief that she knew more than she was letting on.

'Look, if you think I'm holding something back here—'

'Are you?'

'No, of course not.'

'Then why don't we know anything about this family we're going to check on?'

'It's fresh intelligence – literally within the hour

– and Dempsey isn't even sure it's on point. In fact, he thinks it probably isn't.'

'Yeah, so you said. What I want to know, though, is why Dempsey's briefing you directly and then leaving it to you to pass on. Instead of speaking to us all.'

'He was getting on a goddamned flight. This whole thing is a rush job; he literally had minutes.'

'And what, your number's the only one he has these days, is it?'

'Enough.' Jabari again. His voice was just as calm as before and yet it now carried an authority that both quietened Wrixon and stopped Grace from replying. 'You are not children and Agent Dempsey is not your father. Who he chooses to call and how much he chooses to tell? They are his decisions. They are not for us to second-guess.'

Grace noticed Wrixon's eyes shift to the rear-view mirror once again, the irritation in his expression impossible to disguise. But he said nothing. The two men were equal in rank – bar Dempsey, the whole of Alpha Team operated on the same level – but somehow Jabari always seemed senior. Not just to Wrixon but to them all. Grace had never been able to say why that was. Perhaps it was his extra years; for all that he never seemed to physically age, Jabari was the oldest member of Alpha Team by a distance. Or perhaps it was just natural gravitas.

Whatever it was, Wrixon's silence confirmed that he felt it, too.

'It's the second right ahead,' Grace said. The instructions were unnecessary – the satnav system was on – but saying something was better than continued silence. 'Then about halfway down Johnsvale Road.'

Wrixon nodded his head, as if grateful for the change in subject, but he still said nothing. His eyes were now fixed ahead on Pascack Road. The amount of vehicles on the road and the number of municipal buildings bordering it had changed in the last half mile, suggesting they were now reaching the centre of town.

To describe what they were now passing as 'built up' would be wild hyperbole; the commercial buildings amounted to only a small mini-mall and pizzeria to their left, followed by the local high school. But compared to everything else they had seen so far, those few features were a hive of activity.

They were also an anomaly. A few more seconds and the school was behind them, with nothing but scenic suburban greenery and large, set-back residential houses ahead, for as far as Grace could see on the long, wide road that stretched out into the far distance.

'Beautiful.'

The comment came from the rear of the car. Jabari again, this time seemingly to himself. His voice made Grace smile. He really did seem to like the place. It only now occurred to Grace how different the foliage-heavy surroundings must be to Jabari's home city of Addis Ababa, and she wondered if that explained his reaction. Life in one of Africa's most densely populated, least green cities could make even a middle-of-nowhere New Jersey suburb seem like an oasis.

The thought was still occupying Grace as Wrixon took the right-hand turn into Johnsvale Road, the short residential street on which the Frankowskis' registered address was located.

Grace surveyed their surroundings at a glance.

The first half of the road was entirely visible from the junction with Pascack Road, with her view even beyond that point only slightly obscured by a small kink in the road. And so Grace immediately spotted the Park Ridge Police Department cruiser that was parked just past the bend, outside of what she guessed to be Number Six.

Maria's place.

'Pull in behind the squad car.'

'Thanks. I never would have thought of that.'

A moment more and Wrixon had done as asked, with all three ISB agents out of the Suburban just seconds later.

Grace had called ahead to the local police department before leaving Manhattan, to arrange for them to send officers to the address ahead of the team's arrival; with Dempsey as concerned as he was, she was taking no chances. The call had not been as straightforward as she had hoped – the local police chief had been less than happy to receive orders from some random intelligence agency in the city – and so she was relieved to see that officers had been dispatched.

'They must already be inside,' Grace said, realising as she approached it that the cruiser was empty.

'If they are then they just got here,' Wrixon replied. 'I can hear the engine still cooling.'

'I made that call almost an hour ago. Police chief making a point, I guess.'

'Looks that way.' Wrixon turned to Jabari and smiled. 'See, buddy? Even the best places are full of assholes.'

Jabari did not reply. Instead he held up a hand, his eyes narrowing as he listened for . . . something. Grace did not know what, but she *did* know that only a fool dismissed Adama Jabari's instincts.

She reached silently for her holstered pistol and saw Wrixon doing the same. Jabari did not follow suit. His focus was elsewhere; honing in on whatever had spooked him, Grace assumed. She watched as he subtly lowered his body, into a semi-sprint position, just enough to allow for a burst of speed if he had to move. Grace matched his movement; she was still oblivious to what the threat might be, but she was increasingly sure one existed. Like Dempsey, Jabari was rarely wrong about these things.

Her eyes moved from Jabari to Wrixon and then back again. The Kentuckian was as uncertain and so as tense as Grace herself, while the Ethiopian seemed in no hurry to bring either one of them up to speed.

As the seconds ticked passed, Wrixon's patience finally failed. Grace saw him open his mouth – to ask just what the hell was going on, she assumed – but neither she nor Jabari would ever hear his question.

Whatever Wrixon said was drowned out by the sudden sound of gunfire, shattering the idyllic silence of Johnsvale Road.

TWENTY-THREE

Grace sprinted towards the property's driveway to her right, Jabari a few yards ahead of her. Wrixon took the more direct route, hurdling the hedge that separated the lawn from the manicured verge that bordered the road.

The large house was an unusual shape, Grace had noticed. What would usually be described as its 'front' did not face the street. Instead it faced outwards across its own drive and then to the east, which left its side wall presenting onto Johnsvale Road. Wrixon's direction of travel, then, inadvertently covered the side and rear of the house, while Grace and Jabari were heading towards the entrance and, just beyond it, the rear garden.

The two gunshots had sounded out from inside the Frankowski house less than three seconds earlier. No more had followed in that time and Grace had no way to know whether they had been fired by the officers who were presumably inside, or by someone else entirely.

Neither she nor either of her colleagues allowed that uncertainty to slow them. Until they knew otherwise they would assume the worst, and that meant being ready for lethal resistance from within the house.

Grace and Jabari moved with smooth and practised precision. There were many things that set Alpha Team apart from the rest of the ISB. Its members very selection was one of them; Dempsey chose only the best of the best. Their experience was another; as the bureau's elite team working under its lead agent, they saw far more action than any of their peers.

But most of all it was practice. Hour after hour after hour spent honing their skills, both separately and together, until each and every one of them could react to any scenario with a level of choreographed and complementary movement that could be admired as an art form, if only its results were not so inevitably bloody.

Two vehicles were parked on the drive as they approached the house. Both were potential obstacles; hiding places from which clean shots could be taken as they moved. Grace recognised both from her research – the 2020 Toyota RAV4 was registered to Maria Frankowski and the 2019 Jeep Renegade Altitude to her husband – and this, along with the fact that the shots had come from inside the house, made it less likely that either was being used for an ambush. But less likely was not the same as certain, and so she and Jabari still had to clear them as safe before moving on to the property.

Twenty seconds later and that task was done. Five more and Jabari had blasted through the secure deadlock on the property's front door with a single, precise pistol round, kicked the obstacle to one side and covered his half of the entrance hall in one precise scan with his Glock 19. Grace was through the doorway just an instant behind him, moving in a near-squat that reduced her height by a third, keeping her below Jabari's line of fire. She covered her half section of the visible space with an identical wide sweep of her own pistol.

With the immediate vicinity identified as safe, Grace had just a moment to take in the smaller details. It confirmed the absence of any imminent threat, but what she saw was still unwelcome.

In the long entrance hall there were three ransacked side-tables, their contents strewn across the hardwood floor. Her limited view of both the kitchen and the lounge – straight ahead and to her right respectively – suggested that both of those adjoining rooms had been subject to the same messy search.

'It seems Agent Dempsey was correct,' Jabari said.

'Not about everything, I hope,' Grace replied, almost to herself. She raised her voice when she spoke again. 'Let's move in.'

The two agents pressed forwards with the same careful sweeping patterns they had employed to enter the house, protecting one another with every step and each taking care to cover the angles that the other could not.

Grace felt her heart beat harder with every step. The combination of gunshots and the evidence of a violent search left her in no doubt that she and Jabari were heading into danger. Whoever had fired those rounds was almost certainly still here, given the timeframe. And the state of the house strongly suggested that, when found, they would not be friendly. But with Maria Frankowski and her children under the same threat, Grace and Jabari had no choice.

They had to keep moving inwards.

Their progress was slow and careful, as it had to be, and it took them first to the lounge, where Grace's initial impression was confirmed. The room, now empty, had been thoroughly turned over. Grace saw that in an instant. A few moments more and she reached a further, more welcome conclusion. There were no signs of a struggle. For all the damage, it was evident that the detritus had come from drawers and cupboards being overturned and upended, rather than from bodies being slammed against furniture.

It was a small mercy at best, one Grace only briefly registered in her tense apprehension. She saw the same thing when they reached the kitchen. As with the lounge, the damage done there was explicable from a search alone.

'You thinking what I'm thinking?' she asked.

'No signs of violence yet,' Jabari answered.

'Exactly.'

'Don't get carried away. It's only two rooms. And we know a gun has been fired.'

'Still better than the alternative. At least we're not seeing bodies yet.'

'Just so.'

The exchange ended as they moved again, their eyes taking in every detail as they searched for even the slightest hint of danger. Their movement by now was almost a dance, rhythmic and instinctive and absolutely without hesitation. It swept them back through the hallway and towards the room that had been to their left upon entry: a seemingly underused dining room that was dominated by a round table wide enough for ten.

A room which, they could now see, did not seem to have been searched.

Grace noticed the detail in an instant but, before she could mention it, Jabari pointed to his own nostrils.

'Gunpowder. Can you smell it? The shots came from in here.'

'I can smell something. But it could be *your* shot,' Grace said. 'From the front door.'

'Trust me,' Jabari replied. Then he tilted his head before nodding towards the far side of the table; he had noticed something. 'More to the point, trust them.'

Grace followed Jabari's eyeline and spotted what he was referring to. Two pairs of feet, both clad in shiny patent leather shoes. She did not need to crouch down to confirm they belonged to the bodies of two uniformed Park Ridge cops, but she did so anyway. From this angle she could not see where either had been shot — a single bullet each, presumably — but their open, lifeless eyes said enough.

She slowly rose to her feet, her attention now fixed on a closed door that sat in the far corner of the room, ahead of where the bodies lay. Thanks to the unusual shape of the house, she could not even guess where it might lead.

'You think?'

Grace understood the vague question. It meant that Jabari had reached the same conclusion; that whoever had shot the two officers moments before the two ISB agents had entered the house had likely gone through that doorway.

'Seems likely,' Grace replied. 'Shame we don't know where it goes.'

'If it goes anywhere. If it doesn't, how would they know?'

Grace redoubled her grip on her Glock, her gaze fixed unblinking on the doorway. Jabari made a good point. If it led to another room or to a cupboard — rather than to an exit route — then the shooter was unlikely to have known that when going through. Leaving an even chance they were still in there.

She stepped backwards, towards the exit that led back to the hall. When she reached it, she lowered herself down to one knee and steadied her aimed pistol.

Once Grace was in place, Jabari moved around the far end of the table and to the other corner of the room, opposite Grace to his right and the closed door straight ahead. Once in place he positioned himself like Grace, halving his own height by dropping to a knee. Both agents knew if anyone came through that doorway, they would likely look to head level first. It was natural human instinct, to seek out the eyes, and it could gift the agents a micro-second's advantage if they were lower down than expected.

Often enough, that tiny advantage would be the difference between life and death.

Grace looked towards Jabari. An exchanged nod of heads confirmed that both were ready. Then she turned back to the closed door.

'Federal agents,' she called out, her voice firm. The words themselves were not strictly true, but that identification required less explanation than 'ISB'. 'We've got your exits covered. Drop your weapon and step out.'

Nothing.

Grace gave it a moment, listening for any hint of movement. When there was none, she called out again.

'We know you're in there. We know what you did. There's no way out, so let's stop wasting all of our time. Throw down your weapon and step out.'

Nothing again.

Grace looked at Jabari, unsure of what to do next. They had no way to know what – if anything – was behind the door. Which meant that, for all the confidence Grace was injecting into her voice, she was unsure if anyone was even there to hear her.

Her uncertainty must have been evident on her face; Jabari raised his hand and shook his head. Grace took it as an indication to stay calm. Jabari confirmed that with a wave of his raised hand; silent instruction to go again.

She took a deep breath.

'There's no good way out of this. The house is surrounded and we can wait as long as we have to. Sooner or later you're coming out. Either voluntarily or because an assault team comes in. One of those stories ends with you still breathing. Make the right choice.'

There was still no answer, but this time Grace thought she heard something. The faintest sound of movement from within. She glanced across at Jabari, who nodded his head in confirmation. He had heard it too. Someone *was* behind there.

Grace steadied her aim as her heart rate increased.

This is going to happen.

In that moment her focus was total. All that mattered was the person in that back room. The person who had killed two Park Ridge police officers. The person who, she was sure, had come here to kill Maria Frankowski. Whoever he was, he had Grace's full attention.

And that would prove to be a mistake.

The intruder in the hallway had been silent enough that even Jabari – a man with the senses of a wolfhound – had heard nothing. Or perhaps he had attributed the sound to the room on which he, too, was so completely focused. Whatever the reason, neither of them expected the series of gunshots that suddenly filled the dining room, all coming from the open door to their right.

Grace saw movement a moment before she heard the first bang. Timing that probably saved her life. She jumped forwards instinctively, placing herself beside the room's wall instead of in its open doorway. If she had moved even an instant later then the wildly splaying collection of shots could hardly have missed her.

Grace did not count the rounds but the gunfire was over almost as soon as it had started. The shots had come, she quickly realised, as the gunman sprinted past the dining room and through the open entrance that led out of the house. A desperate attempt to escape rather than an attempt at a distraction.

But *as* a distraction, intended or otherwise, it had worked perfectly.

Jabari had turned at the first shot, his pistol sweeping away from the closed door and towards the source of the gunfire. It was too late to draw a bead on the running man – a heartbeat at best before the shooter was gone from sight – but those same moments were long enough to leave him vulnerable.

Just seconds earlier the inner doorway had been impassable, fully covered by two laser-focused, highly trained marksmen. But in a situation where danger is measured in milliseconds, those seconds were a lifetime. With Jabari and his pistol now facing the wrong direction, the closed door burst open and a second figure emerged, his own gun blazing before he even had a target in his sights.

It meant that the rounds that now hit Jabari were a matter of luck, the first striking him in the left shoulder, the second hitting his chest. Desperate shots fired without any thought to aim. Not that it mattered. A hit was a hit and Jabari went down hard.

Grace would never know if the gunman had seen he had two opponents to deal with. Because the moment *she* could see *him*, Grace did what Grace was trained to do.

A single shot to the forehead from barely fifteen feet away. There was no way she could miss and so she did not even watch him fall. Instead she was already moving, towards Jabari, ready to assess his injuries. But before she was even halfway there, Jabari was shaking his head.

'The other shooter,' he said, his voice far stronger than Grace had expected. 'Go.'

She hesitated for a moment, but only that. Jabari was right. She had to catch the first guy if she could. Plus Wrixon was out there somewhere, with no idea what was coming his way, and

Grace would not risk the shooting of another teammate. With a final glance towards Jabari, she broke into a run and headed for the front door.

She managed just four steps beyond its frame.

The sound of gunfire was more distant this time, but instinct and training still sent Grace diving for cover behind the wheel of Maria Frankowski's Toyota. She came to a rest with a roll that brought her back to one knee, her pistol already aimed in the direction of the shots. It gave her the clearest possible view of Dylan Wrixon, his own pistol expertly trained on an unmoving body spread prone on the driveway tarmac.

Wrixon kicked the body to ensure death. Satisfied, he looked back towards Grace with an almost nonchalant expression.

'Peaceful town my ass.'

TWENTY-FOUR

Grace looked at the deep red stains on her hands as she flicked the excess water into the sink of the Frankowskis' guest restroom. She had scrubbed at her skin for almost five minutes, doing her best to wash Adama Jabari's dried blood from her skin. All but a few streaks remained, but those last traces were proving stubborn.

Like the man himself, Jabari's blood did not give up easy.

With the second gunman dead and no one else yet on the scene, Grace and Wrixon had quickly split responsibilities. While confident that the number of gunmen was limited to two – any third man would have surely made a break for it as all hell broke loose, they had reasoned – they still needed to be sure, and so Wrixon had taken on a search of the house.

Grace, in turn, would tend to the injured Jabari.

It was only when back at his side that Grace had realised the full extent of Jabari's wounds. Her earlier view had been fleeting and Jabari's show of strength had misled her to think the hits had been relatively superficial.

The shoulder wound she *had* seen, but the chest wound she had missed.

And that one was the problem.

Grace was sure that the bullet had missed everything essential – the fact he was still alive suggested that – but the holes it had left on either side of his torso were causing a significant level of blood loss. By the time Grace had reached him, Jabari was already passing in and out of consciousness as his blood seeped away.

Grace had done everything she could to stem the flow, but even the emergency medical training she had received in the Presidential Protective Division of the US Secret Service had left her unequipped to deal with the injury. She had been relieved, then, when police units had begun to arrive within just minutes of the final shooting – no doubt responding to reports of gunfire – followed by three sets of paramedics.

The upsides of a small town, she had thought at the time.

The police had removed Grace from the premises as soon as Jabari was stabilised and able to be moved. They did so with a lot more force than necessary, which did not surprise Grace at all; they had lost men – good friends, no doubt, in a place like this – and so they were in no mood to play friendly. For the same reason it took Grace longer than usual to prove her credentials, but ultimately a call from ISB headquarters – from Henry Yale, the assistant to the director – had resolved that problem.

With her cuffs off and her status confirmed, Grace had first chased an update on Jabari. Only once she was sure he was in the best possible hands did she attempt to clean herself. And now – with the remnants of his blood still on her skin – she finally stepped outside to speak to Wrixon.

It did not take her long to find him. He was at the far end of the driveway, his backside leaned against the hood of their loaned Suburban. Even at that distance he seemed a little jumpy, as if filled with nervous energy. The four cigarette butts on the floor by his feet and the fresh one between his fingers confirmed that impression.

'You OK? I've never seen you smoke like that.'

Wrixon looked up as Grace approached. He had clearly not noticed her before she spoke.

'Helps kill the jitters,' he replied. 'Old sniper's trick. Dempsey never teach you that?'

Grace was instantly concerned. As contrary as he could be, there was one thing Grace could guarantee from Dylan Wrixon and that was calm under fire.

'Since when do *you* get the jitters?'

Wrixon shook his head as their eyes met. He looked almost afraid.

'Since I shot an FBI agent twice in the head.'

'What?' Grace almost laughed as Wrixon's words hit her ear. 'What the hell are you talking about?'

'The guy who came out shooting, turns out he was FBI. Local, too. Out of Woodland.' Wrixon slapped his open hand on the Suburban's hood. 'Same damn office as loaned us this car. Hell, the sonofabitch has probably driven it.'

For a moment Grace said nothing, struck dumb by a mixture of shock and confusion. What Wrixon was saying, it made no sense. And yet there was no way he would make that up. Not here and not now. For a moment she felt light-headed, as if the world had slipped a little off-kilter.

'You look pale.' Wrixon held out his cigarettes. Lucky Strikes. 'Trust me, they work.'

Grace ignored the advice.

'That can't be right,' she said, still unable to accept the development. Or what it could mean. 'It can't be, can it? It makes no sense. What the hell would the FBI be doing in there? And why would they shoot at us?'

'That's what *they* want to know.'

Wrixon pointed back towards the house, to a man and a woman who Grace had not seen before that moment. The couple were standing together, near the main door to the house.

Federal agents, Grace was sure. *Right down to the identikit sunglasses.*

They must have arrived while she was washing up.

'A Fed,' Grace was now speaking as much to herself as to Wrixon. The knot in her stomach seemed to have tightened at the sight of them, causing a rush of what she could only describe as dread. 'What the hell have we walked into?'

'A whole lot of trouble, feels like.' Wrixon lit another Lucky Strike. 'Need one now?'

Grace reached out without answering, her own hand now noticeably unsteady, and took both a cigarette and Wrixon's battered Zippo. It had been nearly seven years since she'd quit. After so long, the welcome calming effect hit her almost immediately.

'Tell no one,' she said, holding up her hand so that Wrixon would follow her meaning. 'Natasha would kill me.'

'You think a sly smoke is the story we'll be telling about today?'

'No. No, I guess not.'

The two ISB agents fell silent as Grace took the spot next to Wrixon on the Suburban, and for the next minute or so they watched the comings and goings outside of the house. None of it told them a thing, but that was not the point. Between them they had seen enough already.

They just needed to put that jigsaw together but, as always, that was easier said than done.

'How do you think he's doing?' Wrixon finally asked. 'Really?'

'You mean Adama?'

Wrixon nodded.

'They reached him in time.' Grace exhaled a flume of

smoke, conscious that the initial nicotine calm was now being followed by the light-headed feeling she had long forgotten. 'They stopped the bleeding. He's lucky they got here so quickly.'

'He's lucky he had you until they did.'

'Barely.' Grace took a final drag on the half-smoked cigarette and threw what was left into the gutter. 'Now that's a habit I don't miss.'

They were silent again for half a minute, until a thought occurred to Wrixon.

'What if they were *both* Feds?'

'You mean the guy I shot, too?' Grace had not asked herself that question and so she gave it due consideration. It did not take long. 'No. No, I don't think so. He didn't look it to me. Have they not identified him yet?'

'No. Which I guess means at the very least he's not local. But he could have been undercover, maybe?'

'Who the hell knows. But does it even matter? One dead FBI agent is bad enough, surely?'

'Two would be worse.'

Grace nodded her head but said nothing. Already she was rationalising their position. The rights and wrongs of what had gone down both inside and outside of the house. When she finally began to speak it was as much to herself as it was to Wrixon.

'You didn't have a choice,' she said, still mentally assessing the situation. 'Federal agent or not, that guy was up to no good here. Either he killed those two cops in there or the guy he was with did. Whichever way round it is, that makes him dirty.'

'You sure about that?' Wrixon asked. 'There's no sign of Maria here, or the kids. What if someone came by earlier, killed the cops and took them? What if these two guys were just Feds? Normal investigators working a case?'

Grace looked at Wrixon. She could see the concern in his eyes.

'That's not what happened here,' she said, sounding more firm than she felt in the hope the projected confidence might be contagious. 'I identified myself loud and clear and yet both of them came out shooting. There's no way Feds on an official job react that way. And besides, the first shots that brought us inside? They were fired just after we arrived.'

'I guess.'

Wrixon still looked unconvinced and Grace had little else to offer. On this subject, at least. She needed to switch his focus; to get his mind back on the case.

'There's one other thing still bothering me,' she offered. 'One thing I don't get at all.'

'What's that?'

'That Maria isn't here. It doesn't look like she was taken, so where the hell is she?'

Grace watched Wrixon's brow visibly furrow. It was the reaction she had hoped for.

'What makes you think she didn't leave under her own steam?'

'The Frankowski family have two cars. They're both still on the driveway.'

'And you're ruling out they weren't taken earlier?'

'Not completely. But it's unlikely as all hell. That search of the property we stumbled on had only just started.'

'OK. Well, in that case, what's to say she hasn't just walked somewhere? Her and the kids. Into town, maybe? Main Street's only a stone's throw.'

'Yeah, it is. Which is why every single person *from* Main Street is now bunched behind the police cordon at either end of the road.' Grace pointed at the mass of onlookers in the distance, as if to prove the point. 'If Maria was in that crowd she'd have seen by now that it's her house where everything is happening. She'd at least try to approach, surely?'

'Maybe not.'

'I think she would. It's the natural thing to do. So if she isn't out there on foot and she hasn't taken one of the two cars, where is she?'

Wrixon took a moment to consider the question. As he did, a new one – an entirely new line of enquiry – appeared as if out of nowhere to derail Grace's train of thought.

'The Fed,' she said, not even sure herself of where this was going. 'The dead guy. He was running away from the road when you intercepted him, right? Towards the back yard?'

Wrixon nodded.

'Where do you think he was going?'

'Cover of the greenery back there?' Wrixon suggested. 'Harder to see him there, with the bushes and such.'

'But where does that ultimately take him? It's no use to him just hiding in the yard. It'd gain him what, a minute or two at best? And for that matter, where's his car? It's not out front, so how did he even get here?'

Wrixon thought for a moment.

'I went to the back as you guys headed into the house, to cover anyone trying to exit from the rear. When I was there I saw the back yards on this street join onto another identical bunch of yards from the next road over. The houses seem pretty much the same as these ones, from what I could see. They're just facing another road. So maybe he was heading there?'

'You think maybe their car was parked on the other street? It'd be less obvious there than parking outside on this road, the way we did. Especially if they didn't want to attract attention to themselves from anyone inside the house.'

'Could be,' Wrixon replied. 'In which case it's less likely they were here on official business. Feds don't do covert, not on jobs like this. But we can't be sure. I didn't go far enough to check for a vehicle. Once I heard the shots I headed back to you guys and ran straight into Special Agent Fuck Head.'

'But if they did park there, the car might still be there.'

'Worth a look, I guess.'

'Let's go then,' Grace said, standing up from her perch on the car.

'Might have to leave that to the Feds,' Wrixon said, gesturing towards the agents headed their way. 'Looks like these guys want a word with us.'

TWENTY-FIVE

The night air was hot as Michael stepped down from the Gulfstream G150 and onto the tarmac of Rotterdam-Hague Airport. With solid ground beneath his feet, he turned back towards the pilot, who was holding out the leather hold-all Sarah had packed before they had left London. Michael reached out and took it.

'Beats the hell out of the luggage carousel,' he commented, unsure of what else to say.

'All part of the service, sir.'

'Thanks.'

Michael turned and stepped away from the plane towards Dempsey, who had exited first.

'So this is The Hague?'

'Rotterdam,' Dempsey replied. 'It's the closest airfield to The Hague. Fifteen miles or so. There's a car waiting to take us the rest of the way.'

'Thanks, mate.' Michael was genuinely grateful for all that his friend was doing. 'I don't know what I'd have done without you right now.'

'Exactly the same thing, probably. It would have just cost you a lot more, taken you a lot longer and your intel and access would be a lot worse.'

'You're not wrong.' Michael glanced at Dempsey's bag as he spoke. It reminded him of what Dempsey had inside it: the tablet that connected them to the ISB office in Manhattan and their lifeline to locating Will Duffy. 'You think there's any news yet?'

'I'll check once we're on the move.'

As if summoned by Dempsey's words, a sleek, two-tone Mercedes-Maybach S-Class swept towards them across the tarmac. It was just feet away before Michael even noticed it; the roar of its own massive road engine was lost within the overwhelming cacophony of the jets that surrounded them.

The driver opened the doors for his two passengers before placing their luggage in the boot. Michael instinctively deferred to his friend's authority here and took the rear right-hand door for himself, leaving Dempsey to sit up front. Within thirty seconds of its arrival the luxury limousine was moving again, passing through otherwise prohibited security checkpoints with just a flash of the vehicle's United Nations credentials.

It was not until they had left the airport grounds that Michael broke the silence that had fallen between them.

'We need to decide what we do once we get to The Hague. We'll need to drop off our stuff, whatever happens. But what then?'

Dempsey did not answer and, on closer inspection, Michael realised why. Dempsey was once again navigating the tablet he had used on the plane.

Michael waited as Dempsey accessed his inbox and opened the three unread emails highlighted at the top of the page. The ISB agent read each one of them in seconds. He then returned to the first and opened it as a full page, so that it was the only message visible on screen. Then he handed the tablet to Michael.

Michael read the email as quickly as Dempsey. The content made his heart rate spike, which in turn sent a torrent of cold relief rushing downwards; an endorphin rush unlike anything he had ever experienced. He read the message again, to be sure. Then once more.

'He's alive. Jesus Christ, Joe. He's alive.'

TWENTY-SIX

The drive from the airport to the emergency department of HMC Westeinde took precisely twenty-five minutes and sixteen seconds. Dempsey had practically counted every second. His impatience for the journey to end bordered on desperation.

The email he had shown Michael was one of three he had received from Kate Silver back in New York. It was the only one he intended to share. It was also the only one that contained good news.

Silver had located Will Duffy and had confirmed that he was alive. His condition was still deemed life-threatening and he remained in an induced coma, with the prognosis hardly positive. Duffy had survived the shooting, but it would be a fight to survive the recovery.

None of which mattered in the moment. For now, the fact he was alive was enough.

The second and the third emails had been less welcome. Both were short and scant of detail, and both required an urgent debrief that Dempsey could not undertake from the front seat of an occupied car. But each had said enough to concern him deeply.

The second confirmed that the name Konrad Frankowski was not the coincidence Dempsey had hoped for. Not unless multiple fatal shootings at the man's family home back in the US were also miraculously unconnected.

It *was* the same Frankowski, Dempsey was sure of that now. And so he was equally sure Maria's husband had somehow managed to get wrapped up in the Hannibal Strauss trial, and in doing so had put himself at risk. In normal circumstances Dempsey would regard that as foolish, but it became something else entirely when that risk stretched to Maria and to their children.

It becomes unforgivable.

But for all of that, it was the third email that had concerned Dempsey most. It was a short, matter-of-fact update informing him of two things: that Adama Jabari had been hospitalised in the shooting at the Frankowski home; and that Maria Frankowski and her two sons were nowhere to be found.

Dempsey had struggled to focus on the screen the first time he read that. The sensations of panic and helplessness were alien to him, and yet in that moment they had combined in a physical, nauseous reaction. Silver had included no further reasoning or possible explanation for Maria's whereabouts. The team's updates never did; Dempsey trusted his agents and their ability to think for themselves, and always preferred as little information crossing cyberspace as possible.

But this time? This time he cursed that protocol. He wanted to know more and he wanted to know it now.

Because if Maria's hurt . . .

The very idea was unthinkable, made less bearable by the delay as Dempsey waited to reach the hospital and the opportunity to make a private phone call to New Jersey. He was grateful, then, that Michael had his own good news to focus on during that time, as well as a confirmed destination. It saved him any need to plan what their next steps should be.

With that discussion now unnecessary, Dempsey could retreat into his own thoughts.

He could focus on staying calm.

The Mercedes came to a halt in the drop-off lane that sat immediately outside of the Emergency Department entrance. The location alone made the driver's intention clear: he planned to leave his passengers at the hospital while he took their belongings to their accommodation, after which he would return and wait until they were ready to leave.

Dempsey had other ideas.

'I need you to park up here and accompany Mr Devlin inside the hospital,' he said. 'I want someone with them in there.'

The driver seemed surprised.

'But I . . . that's not . . . I can't leave the vehicle here. It is prohibited.'

'The ISB will pay the fine,' Dempsey replied. 'I can't go in with him yet. And without UN credentials to back him up, the hospital will refuse to let him in at all. So I need you in there with him. To wave your ID around when the time comes. OK?'

'Why can't you—'

'I have an urgent call. An emergency. I don't know how long it will take and I don't want Mr Devlin to have to wait for me when *he* has urgent business inside. So I need you to do this.'

The driver still looked unsure, as if he wanted to argue further. A shake of Dempsey's head put a stop to that. He had given more of an explanation than he had intended already. The driver seemed to understand the message and, in return, he nodded his head weakly in agreement.

'Thank you.'

Dempsey smiled politely as he spoke, but he was already turning to Michael before he had finished. He had no time left to waste.

'Did you catch that?'

'I did,' Michael replied. He sounded concerned. 'You OK, buddy?'

'Too early to say. But when I know, you'll know. Now get in there and find your friend.'

Dempsey turned back without another word and opened his door, ready to step out of the car. As he did, he felt Michael's hand grasp and squeeze his shoulder. It was intended to be reassuring, Dempsey realised. But in that moment it meant so much more than that.

He was about to face his greatest fear. A threat he could not fight, not from where he was right now. And he had no idea what he would do if the news was bad. But from the reassuring strength of his friend's grip, he at least knew he would not face it alone.

TWENTY-SEVEN

The Park Ridge Police Department Headquarters was closer to Johnsvale Road than Eden Grace had expected. A ten-minute walk at most, so maybe ninety seconds in a car. The realisation irritated her. Why had it taken the local police an hour to send a patrol car that minuscule distance, from here to the Frankowskis'?

Sixty minutes earlier and maybe none of this would have happened.

Grace and Wrixon had been allocated a bare, mostly unfurnished office within the building, ostensibly for their use while the initial investigation into the shooting took place. The room was devoid of technology and of any comfort beyond a single bunk, a chipped wooden desk and three cheap, plastic foldaway chairs.

It was also where they had been asked to remain for as long as they were in the building.

Both knew the reality of their position. The isolation was the closest thing to custody that law enforcement could risk when dealing with ISB agents. As the intelligence arm of the United Nations Security Council, the ISB outranked all other agencies within each UN member state. Technically, even the Feds had no authority over Grace or Wrixon.

This meant that the FBI agents from the Frankowski home could not compel them to remain, nor could they confiscate their weapons or their phones. All they could do was ask for the ISB team to cooperate, which was exactly what they had done.

Grace and Wrixon's options, in turn, had been to comply or to refuse. In the circumstances – with a federal agent dead and with Wrixon responsible for the shooting – Grace had taken an executive decision. Instead of pulling rank, she had agreed they would stay and confine themselves to the office.

At least for now.

In the meantime, Grace had tried to use the empty hours productively.

First she had checked on Jabari's treatment at the nearby Valley Hospital Emergency Room, using a reluctant officer of the local police department to make the call for her. The news from there had been good: Jabari had reacted well to blood transfusions and, with his wounds treated, he was considered to be out of the woods.

Satisfied that Jabari was safe, she had next used her own phone to contact the ISB office in Manhattan and update Kate Silver on all that had occurred.

Silver had taken the details, added them to her own research on Konrad Frankowski and Will Duffy, and she had assured Grace they would now be sent directly to Dempsey. And so for the next twenty minutes, in the knowledge that her boss was about to find out that Maria Frankowski was still missing, Grace had been waiting for the inevitable call.

With all tasks complete, there was nothing to distract her from the thought of Dempsey. Of what he would want to know. And of what little she could really tell him. Determined to be as helpful as she could, she tried to focus on want she *did* know, and on the possible scenarios that now faced them.

Possibilities that seemed to increase at every step.

Every answer to every question seemed to lead to two more as Grace thought through their situation, with potential scenarios spreading outwards in all directions. With so little real information to work with, her ability to reach any firm conclusion was effectively stalled.

The frustration was difficult for her to take. Grace wanted to be in a position to help. She knew that Dempsey would be worried and unlikely to be as effective as usual, given his personal connection to Maria Frankowski. And she realised now that her situation, confined to this room, was preventing her from doing all she could to help him.

To Grace, that final fact was simply unacceptable.

'Screw it.'

She rose to her feet, fast and without warning. Wrixon started at the sudden movement. He placed down the Zippo lighter he had been fidgeting with and lifted himself up to his elbow.

'Screw what?'

'This,' Grace replied. 'All of this. I'm done with this bullshit. I'm done with being stuck in this goddamned room, unable to do anything. We've got a case to be working.'

'What the hell are you talking about? Right now we *are* the case. And besides, it was you who agreed to this.'

'Bad decision on my part, then. But neither one of us was thinking real straight, were we?'

Wrixon smiled as he dragged his feet off the bed and sat upright. He seemed amused by the fresh hint of insubordination. It seemed to overcome the nervous energy that had affected him for the last hour.

'No. No, I guess we weren't. So what do you suggest?'

'I reckon if the FBI wants to speak to us then they can do that now. We get it over with and then we get back to work.'

'You think that's a good idea?' Wrixon was now on his feet, his tone mischievous. 'Not that I'm planning to talk you out of it.'

'Good or bad, it's the *only* idea. I'm done sitting around.'

Grace's mind was made up and she was walking even as she spoke. The door to the office was barely feet away and it was, she was sure, unlocked; otherwise the illusion of captivity would have crossed the line into fact, and that would have been a step too far.

She was close enough to reach out for the handle when she heard the ringtone.

Grace turned back towards the familiar sound, realising that she had left her phone back on the desk. Wrixon was already there. He picked up the handset, took a look at the screen and threw it to Grace.

'Too late with the change of heart,' he said. 'It's Dempsey.'

Grace had already caught the phone and glanced at the screen before Wrixon's announcement. She hit connect.

'Boss?'

'How's Adama?'

'He's OK,' she replied. 'He's still in the ICU, but he's OK.'

'And you and Wrixon?'

'We're both unhurt.'

'Good. Now what the hell happened down there, Eden?'

Grace answered the question, as quickly as possible without missing out detail. She knew from experience that Dempsey's mind worked fast. She also knew it was fuelled by as much information as she could provide.

When she was finished she turned to Wrixon.

'Did I miss anything?'

'Not that I noticed.'

Grace nodded her thanks and turned her attention back to the telephone.

'So what do you think, Boss?'

'I think we don't know nearly enough. I need you back on this, not hanging around in some backwater while the FBI plays silly buggers.'

'But what about the dead agent? That's going to be an issue without being able to prove he was dirty.'

'Firing shots blind into a room? That's not protocol of any kind and it sure as hell isn't standard practice. That was a man getting the hell out of there before anyone stopped him. And before anyone had a chance to ID him. Assuming they're acting in good faith, the FBI will have reached the same conclusion already.'

Grace nodded her head in agreement. The logic made perfect sense and yet, as happened so often, she found herself surprised that Dempsey could be so confident so quickly. It was, she always thought, the biggest benefit of experience.

'So what do you want me to do?'

'Get in a room with them and answer their questions now. You need to put this distraction to bed and get yourself out of New Jersey. There's somewhere else I need you to be. Both of you.'

'Where?'

'Same place I'm about to send Kate and Shui. They'll get there ahead of you; I want the place covered as soon as possible so I'm telling them to leave right away. But ultimately I want you *all* there, Eden. This isn't over.'

Grace could detect the usual confidence returning to Dempsey's voice. She had expected him to be devastated at Maria's disappearance. Or at least distracted by it. And yet he had not even raised that as an issue.

The omission had been a surprise but now, based on his last few words, Grace was beginning to understand.

'Boss, do you have some idea of where Maria might be?'

'Maybe. But even if I'm right, she and her kids are still in danger. If these guys will come for her at home, then they'll come for her wherever she goes.'

'But the cars were both still there.'

'She's no fool, Eden. She would have known her own cars could be too easily traced. She was with me for a long time, remember? Back when there were a lot of people who would have happily used her against me.'

Because no bad guys want you dead these days, Grace thought to herself.

She resisted the urge to say the same thing aloud. Instead she focused on the here and now.

'So what? You taught her how to disappear?'

'I taught her how to survive. Stuff she'd never forget. And she wasn't exactly a novice to begin with. Fact is, if she was going to run, she wouldn't leave any trace. So the fact we haven't found her yet, that doesn't mean something bad's happened to her. Not yet, anyway.'

'But how are we going to find her before it does?'

'I know the one place she would go if her and her kids were at risk. If they needed protecting. I'm looking into it now. If she has gone there, she's safe. For now, anyway. And you'll be taking that trip I just mentioned.'

'And if she's not there?'

'Well, then I *will* be worried. So let's hope it doesn't come to that.'

TWENTY-EIGHT

Dempsey took a deep breath as he disconnected the call, his nerves calmed by what Grace had told him and by his own knowledge of Maria Parker.

It had taken every ounce of his self-discipline to keep the exchange with Grace professional. He had even forced himself to ask the appropriate questions first: as Alpha Team leader, he had to begin by enquiring after the health of his agents. Especially with Adama Jabari injured in the line of duty.

Truth was he would have been happier to leave that for later. From the moment Grace answered, all he really wanted to know was whether Maria was safe.

Thankfully Grace had not dragged out the information drop and Dempsey was relieved by the details she had given him. He could understand her concern about the cars being in the driveway. After all, what ordinary civilian fleeing their home would leave their most convenient transport behind?

But Dempsey knew Maria. If she had been aware of an imminent threat, she would have done exactly as he had taught her. She would have run, and she would have left no trace or trail behind.

If there was a chance she had been caught off guard then he still would have been worried, but that was no longer a possibility. In the time it had taken him to speak to Grace, Kate Silver had acted on his earlier instructions and the results were waiting in his inbox.

Dempsey read them now, his heart lightening by the second.

Among the many tasks he had given Silver was a check of

Maria's phone records. Contrary to too many bad movie plots, information like that was not instantly accessible to just anyone with a warrant. Often it could take days – even weeks – to secure.

But not for the ISB. The technology available to the organisation allowed it to exert its all-pervading jurisdiction to the fullest possible extent, including the ability to secure telephone records in something close to real time. It had therefore taken Silver just hours to check for the interaction between Konrad Frankowski's and Maria's mobile phones.

The result was exactly what Dempsey had hoped for: a seven-minute call between Maria's phone and her husband's, taking place within thirty minutes of the Grote Markt massacre.

Approximately 7.30 a.m. New Jersey time.

More than six hours before the shooting in Park Ridge.

Dempsey did the reasoning fast.

If the call was made by Frankowski thirty minutes after the killings in The Hague – and assuming he realised the attack had been targeted – then it was most likely he was making it to warn Maria of danger. More importantly, he was doing it early enough to give Maria time to escape, hours before the arrival of the crooked Fed and the other gunman.

And there's no way Maria would have taken hours, he told himself. *Not when she had those boys to think about.*

It was enough to assure Dempsey of Maria's immediate safety. Whatever else had occurred at their home, she and the boys were already long gone.

And Dempsey was sure he knew where they were headed.

With relief flooding through him, he lifted his smartphone, found Kate Silver's name and prepared to give her the only address to which *his* Maria would ever have run.

TWENTY-NINE

Michael felt a tear roll down his cheek as he looked at the unconscious Will Duffy. He wiped it clear with his left hand and then brushed away the wetness onto the leg of his jeans, his right hand gripping his friend's deathly cold fingers throughout.

Will's condition had hit Michael hard. Much more than he had anticipated. Having prepared himself for the worst – having convinced himself that Will had been killed in the shooting that afternoon – Michael had allowed the news of his friend's survival to warp his expectations. Sure, he had been told that Will was in an induced coma. But that was just like being asleep, he had told himself.

The sight that had greeted Michael as he stepped into a large room dedicated solely to keeping Will Duffy alive was enough to dispel that notion.

Instead of the strength and vitality that usually marked Will out for his age, Michael was now seeing his friend at his weakest. The injuries he had sustained had visibly diminished him. Will seemed older. He seemed smaller. And above all else, he seemed utterly vulnerable.

But it was none of this, Michael realised, that had affected him so much. Instead, it was a detail as simple and as innocuous as Will's jawline. Usually square and strong, in his comatose state Will's chin had somehow dropped inwards and down. Of everything Michael had seen so far, it was this feature – this medical irrelevance – that struck him the most.

And Michael knew why: it reminded him of death.

Michael had seen too many dead bodies in his lifetime and there was one thing he had always noted in the aftermath: the way the jaw of a corpse seems to collapse, as if it cannot be held properly in place in the absence of life.

Michael had seen that detail every time he could remember. And he saw it now.

The effect was both unexpected and profound; Michael found himself losing hope that Will would pull through. He had entered the room with nothing but optimism – however unrealistic that was – only for it to be dashed by what his mind could only see as a death mask.

The feeling persisted as another tear threatened Michael's eye. What had begun as shock was now an almost physical sensation, as if his darkest thoughts had been made manifest and were weighing him down. It was that same old feeling and it led to the same old fear. One that Michael was all too used to. And one that, every time, he wished to never experience again.

The threat that despair would drag him to a place he did not want to go.

At forty-one years of age, Michael was sufficiently self-aware to spot the signs. He had been controlling what he saw as 'his other self' for as long as he could remember, and even more so since he had left Belfast behind. Years that had been spent tempering the more savage side of his nature. It had become much easier as time had passed – Michael had become better at the tricks that helped – and so he was determined to shake it off now, just as he always did.

He released Will's hand and got to his feet, breathing deep and slow and reminding himself that a fit of rage right now would help no one. Stepping back from the single chair that occupied a space to the right of the bed, he began to pace around the room as he tried to focus his mind on something – anything – that could distract him from the fate of his friend.

Breaths. Steps. Even just small meaningless details that he could find within his line of sight. Whatever it took to send his mind in a different direction. A lighter direction.

It was a tried and tested technique. But right now it wasn't working. For his efforts to succeed, Michael needed to distract himself from Will's condition, from the very reason he was here. But every last detail of his surroundings was related to his friend's fight for survival.

The room was surprisingly spacious – twice the size of what he would expect from a similar facility in London – and yet every inch of it seemed to be occupied by machines that were, together, fighting to keep Will alive. There were far more of them than Michael had noticed when he had first been shown inside by the nurse; he had hardly registered anything beyond the bedside IV and the kind of beeping monitors that seem to feature in every hospital TV show.

But now? Now he could not miss the sheer quantity of medical wizardry around him.

It left no room for distraction. No way he could think of anything but how close his friend must be to death.

For a moment he considered stepping outside – into the corridor of the intensive care unit – but he dismissed that as an option. Things out there were frantic. The emergency department downstairs had seen twenty-one critically injured patients rushed in after the shooting that afternoon. Not all of them had made it and some remained close to death, but those who were now relatively stable, if still critical – like Will Duffy – had been moved to the third floor. Their number well outweighed the dead and dying and for that, Michael was sure, the medical staff were grateful.

But it also meant that the ICU was being pushed far beyond its limits.

All of this combined to make the corridor outside a nightmare for Michael; far too much activity to calm himself. Plus he realised what an unwelcome obstruction he would be for the doctors and nurses who were trying to do their job.

That left him with only two choices: to leave Will altogether and step outside the building; or to get a grip of himself here and now.

To a man like Michael, that was no choice at all.

Moving to the far corner of the room – as far from Will's bedside as the space allowed – he placed a hand on each of the two walls that met there and rested his head against their cold rendered surface. It was the one spot where he could see nothing to remind him of where he was. The one place where he could close his eyes and focus.

The sound of the opening door interrupted his efforts. In his agitated state, the sudden noise that spilled into the room from the corridor outside made him spin around.

The white coat and the name tag marked out the man who had entered as a doctor. Not one Michael had seen outside on his way to the room, but that meant nothing; there must have been scores of them on duty after the horrors of the afternoon. He was around six feet tall, maybe a little more, with blond hair and an athletic frame. In many ways he resembled Michael himself, just ten or so years younger.

He also appeared entirely unaware that Michael was in the room.

Michael waited a moment to be noticed. But as he did, he

was struck by a sense – by a certainty – that something was off.

'I'm sorry, Doctor.' Michael stepped forwards as he spoke. 'Am I in the way here?'

The doctor turned sharply at the sound of Michael's voice, clearly surprised that the room was occupied by anyone but Will Duffy. A perfectly natural reaction, Michael accepted. Why would he have expected to find a civilian hiding in the corner? But still, there was something about the man that bothered him.

'I'm . . . what . . . who are you?'

The doctor seemed unsure of himself, as if he had been caught somewhere he should not be. It was a reaction that heightened Michael's mistrust. His instincts were telling him something – they were screaming to him that something was wrong – but could he rely on them? Was there something not right here, or was Michael's animal brain now just looking for a reason to lash out?

He pushed his inner conflict aside as he answered the doctor's question.

'I'm a friend of Mr Duffy. Is there something you need to do?'

'I . . . what I . . . no, no, I'm just here to check . . .'

The doctor's words trailed off. He still seemed nervous. As if he'd been caught in the act. It was that impression that caused Michael's instincts to take over.

'To check what?' he asked.

'To check . . . I'm just . . . I've got to review the IV mix. Got to make sure your friend's meds are correct.'

Michael moved closer. As he did, he surveyed the doctor and the details he noted only strengthened his suspicions. The broken nose on the otherwise handsome face was one indicator.

Not the best one, he had to concede; the man was fit and any number of sports could account for that. The visible long-term damage to the medic's knuckles, though? That was harder to dismiss.

'Isn't that a job for a nurse?'

The supposed doctor hesitated for just a moment, then he shook his head.

'Usually it would be, yes. But today, it's a crazy time.'

The answer was a good one. An obvious one. But his mind was made up.

'What's the mix?'

Michael took another step forwards as he spoke, rounding the end of the bed.

'I'm sorry, what?'

The man did not look back as he answered. His attention stayed focused on the drip.

'The drugs in the IV. I was here when the nurse came in and set that up a little while ago. I asked *her* that question. I'm just wondering if you'll give me the same answer.'

The man said nothing. Instead he turned slowly to face Michael. And this time he no longer looked flustered.

He looked angry.

'Why are you asking me that?'

'Why are you not answering?'

'Are you questioning my authority? I'm a doctor in this hospital,' he said, though his voice lacked conviction. As if there was no longer any expectation that it would be believed.

'It takes more than a coat and a name tag. So what's in the mix?'

The doctor said nothing, but Michael could see the telltale signals of what was about to happen. A slight shift in foot placement, to maximise forwards movement from the stronger side. A slow, steady closing of the right hand, ready to form a fist. And the slightest sign of tension in the neck, an indication that this was a man who saw his head as a valuable extra weapon.

The man looked Michael up and down. No doubt carrying out the same assessment. No doubt noticing Michael's own unconscious signals. Whatever he saw, it did not seem to concern him.

An ugly smirk spread across his lips.

'Do you really know what's in the IV mix?'

'Not a clue.'

'Then what? I could have said anything and walked out of here?'

'Maybe.'

The man nodded his head.

'*Goed Gespeeld*,' he said, his voice quiet. 'Well played.'

And then he exploded into motion, like a sprinter off the blocks. It would have caught Michael off guard if he had been unable to read the early warning signs.

As it was, Michael was ready.

He wanted this.

He *needed* this.

The fake doctor reached him in a fraction of a second, his body aimed like a crude but effective battering ram, his head lowered to maximise the damage of their impending collision.

His aim was perfect, his execution immaculate. If Michael had been standing where a less experienced fighter would have been – or if he had reacted as most brawlers would, by attempting to meet the rush with a blow of his own – then that one movement could have ended their confrontation.

But Michael knew better than that..

To stand in one spot was an invitation to unconsciousness.

To throw a punch, ineffective and a guarantee of injury.

Instead Michael picked the only sensible option. He used the man's devastating momentum against him. Stepping barely an inch out of his path in the instant before impact, Michael spun his body clear. And then, using the rotation of his own movement to maximise his power, he hit the back of his passing head with a wide-open left-hand slap.

The blow did exactly as Michael had intended. Connecting hard with the man's crown, Michael maintained contact and turned the strike into a powerful shove. It was enough to send his assailant stumbling sideways, his footing wild as he careered into the life-saving equipment lined up on the room's left-hand wall.

The impact damaged at least one of the machines, but Michael had no time to wonder at the effect that would have on Will. He was too busy closing the gap between them.

Moving fast, he pounced on his opponent before he could turn to defend himself. There was no time for fair play. No time for gentleman's rules. This impostor had come here to kill Will Duffy. That made him a professional, and Michael had fought professionals before.

To win this, he would need to take every advantage.

The younger man was still off balance as Michael hit him from behind, his right fist driving hard into the nape of his neck – a clean, powerful shot. Next Michael threw a twisting left hook into his kidney, followed by a hard straight right to his spine. He delivered his punches fast, one after the other, as he pummelled the exposed back of his friend's would-be killer.

Michael's blind rage drove him on more than any cold or

calculated fight plan, but even so, as he rained down blow after blow he could feel himself begin to tire. He needed to finish this.

He halted the barrage of punches, ignored the bloody mess they had made of his fists and stepped back, intending to lift his leg and drive it into the back of the man's knees; the only sure way to bring him down. That movement paused his attack for barely a moment – too quick, even, for him to catch the breath he now badly needed – but even that was too long. Somehow in that fleeting intermission, his adversary was able to throw himself backwards with every ounce of strength he could find.

The man's body collided hard with Michael and this time – whether intended or not – his head succeeded where it had earlier failed: it struck Michael fully in the face and sent him reeling backwards.

With his right leg off the floor from his attempt to kick out his opponent's knees, and with his eyes watering from the impact of the bastard's rock-hard scalp, Michael could not stop himself as he first stumbled backwards and then fell to the ground, dragging the still unsteady hitman down with him.

Michael hit the floor hard. He felt the back of his head collide with the hard concrete that was barely cushioned by the room's thin carpet. An instant more and the full weight of a heavy body landed on him from above, causing the same impact to repeat.

For a moment neither man moved as both recovered their senses. But a heartbeat later they were struggling again, this time grappling on the floor as the fake doctor did his best to turn and face him, while Michael did everything he could to stop that happening.

What little breath he'd had left had been knocked out of him by the fall and so Michael's strength was disappearing by the second, but still he fought, trying hard to get his arms under the man's jaw, only his anger and his desperate will to win keeping him in the fight.

Even with his opponent's weight now pinning him to the floor, Michael retained the advantage for as long as the guy's back was against him; it meant that of the two, only the Irishman could potentially inflict the damage that was needed to win this.

The other man seemed to realise the same thing and so, though surely just as weakened by their struggle as Michael, he did not let up for a moment. He was relentless as he fought off Michael's attempt to grip his neck, all while trying to twist his body around to where he could do some damage of his own.

It was a desperate effort and, to Michael's horror, it was working.

Michael knew that he had to do something to regain his position – his only edge – and so in desperation he reached down, seized the man's ears and pulled at them with every last jot of strength he had left.

If Michael had been fresh then those ears would have been ripped clean off; all it would have taken was a firm grip, a violent twist and a powerful jolt of his arms. But he had almost nothing left at all. And so it was with just a fraction of his natural strength that he had thrown his Hail Mary pass.

A moment later and he knew his prayer had been ignored. His attempt to fight dirty had only made things worse.

Too tired to think straight, Michael had not considered the natural consequence of failure: the pulling motion had brought his opponent's body level with his own. And now he would pay the price.

Michael did not see the reverse headbutt coming, but he sure as hell felt it land.

The first *and* the second.

By the third, his head was too groggy and his face too bloody to register very much at all.

It was with that final crashing blow that Michael's weakened grip on the fake doctor was finally released, his equilibrium a victim to the assault and his vision now blurred by the blood that seeped from the wound it had caused above his right eye. For a moment that combination seemed to extinguish the fight Michael had left and he felt himself fall back limply onto the cold floor, his hold on his own consciousness unsteady.

It was a temporary surrender, no more than a heartbeat; that same survival instinct that had brought Michael this far would not allow it. A voice somewhere deep within his psyche, somewhere out of reach and beyond his own control, was telling him to get up. It was telling him to fight on.

To not become another victim.

Michael would later rationalise what his subconscious must have been telling him. He would recall how he had felt the man scrambling to his feet. And how he had seen him reaching into his white doctor's coat. It was a movement Michael recognised even through the haze. One he had seen too many times in the past. He was going for a gun. A weapon he'd had no chance to pull out during the short, intense battle he had fought against Michael.

The realisation gave Michael a final burst of desperate energy. If the guy had time to draw then Will was a dead man. Michael too, most likely. It was not an equation that needed much working out so he was moving in an instant.

After everything he had just been through, it was faster than Michael had any right to be.

It also saved his life.

Michael's movement pulled the man's focus back to him, causing him to hesitate for just a moment. An instant later and he was reaching for the gun again, this time with his full murderous intent on Michael. But as his hand moved so did his feet, backwards and towards the door.

The movement exposed his uncertainty.

He was unsure if he had time to draw the weapon.

And he was right to worry.

Michael's speed surprised them both. As he lunged forwards he knew that he would reach the would-be assassin before he could aim.

And the younger man knew it too.

Abandoning the fight, he turned, threw open the door and burst through it, into the corridor outside.

'STOP HIM!' Michael did not pause for even a moment, somehow finding enough air in his hitherto empty lungs to call out for help as he stumbled through the door. 'STOP HIM. HE'S GOT A GUN. SOMEONE STOP THAT SONOF—'

The first gunshot cut him off.

The first of three, all fired in quick succession.

By the sound of the third, Michael was down.

THIRTY

*B*ang. *Bang. Bang.*

Dempsey felt his pulse-rate spike at the unmistakable sound of gunfire. From the cocoon of a moving hospital elevator it was impossible to gauge distance or even direction, and yet he had no doubt about his first instinct:

Michael.

Who else could it be?

Dempsey's pistol was already drawn and ready as he punched at the floor controls. It was a desperate effort to make the mechanism move faster, and even as he did it Dempsey knew it was pointless. The buttons, once pressed, could do nothing more. And yet he continued to hit the already illuminated number 'three' as the lift moved upwards.

The elevator's progress felt agonisingly slow as Dempsey listened for more shots. None came, the silence in no way reassuring. But Dempsey knew he could not let himself dwell on hypothetical scenarios. It would remain Schrodinger's shoot-out until the lift doors opened and he could see the reality for himself.

A reality now just seconds away.

He moved fast as the lift came to a halt at the third floor. With his gun held out ahead of him in his right hand and his left cupping its butt, he stepped into the corridor and scanned the scene with one long, uninterrupted sweep of the barrel.

Of all the possibilities that had run through his mind, what he saw now would not have been Dempsey's bet. In an instant he reached three conclusions simultaneously:

Michael's alive.

The CIA are here.

And we could be half a second away from a bloodbath.

Recognising the last thought as his immediate priority, Dempsey made a show of releasing his grip on his weapon and allowed it to fall to the floor. In the same movement he raised his hands above his head and then joined his fingers just above his scalp, all while lowering himself to his knees.

The speed of his decision did exactly what Dempsey had intended.

It saved his life.

THIRTY-ONE

$\mathbf{F}$ ive minutes later Dempsey was back on his feet, leaning against the corridor wall as he surveyed the fallout from the shooting. On the floor ahead of him, further along the hallway that made up the bulk of the intensive care unit, was a six-foot-long object covered by a sheet.

The corpse, Dempsey now knew, of a professional killer sent to finish Will Duffy.

Just past the body were the two men who Dempsey had identified as CIA. The younger of the pair was responsible for the three gunshots Dempsey had heard from the lift, and through them the lifeless obstacle that was now cluttering up the busy hospital ward. But as Dempsey watched them now, as they conferred with one another and barked orders at doctors and security alike, it was clear that the older man was in charge.

As close as they were, Dempsey could not hear what was being said over the background noise of the ICU. And there was only so much body language could tell him. Satisfied that he had learned all he could for now, he turned his attention back to Michael.

The Irishman had already brought Dempsey up to speed on what had happened. How he had been in Will's room alone, while the UN driver had gone downstairs to fetch coffee for them both. How this had led to Michael taking on the fake doctor without the help the driver could have otherwise provided. And how he had managed to chase Will's would-be killer from the room before the man could draw his gun, a pursuit which had sent the assassin headlong into the two armed Americans and the tight volley of bullets that had brought him down.

That debrief had been Dempsey's focus moments earlier but now, with time to spare, his concern was for his friend. Michael was seated a few feet away on an otherwise empty gurney with his long legs dangling and his back unsupported. It was an intentionally casual posture, Dempsey suspected. An attempt to suggest he was in better shape than he looked.

'How's the eye?'

'I'll live,' Michael replied. A painful grin spread across his face as he nodded his head towards the covered figure on the floor. 'You should see the other guy.'

Dempsey smiled back, amused by Michael's enjoyment of his own joke. Amused and relieved. It suggested that any injuries weren't too severe.

'They say you need stitches?'

'Glue, apparently.'

'That close to your eye?'

'I doubt I'm the first.'

'Still, rather you than me.'

'This from the man who cauterised a bullet wound by igniting gunpowder?'

'Different thing entirely. I wasn't in a hospital.'

'Well, I am, so how about we don't second-guess the doctors?'

'Your choice.'

'It is, yeah.'

Dempsey looked away, satisfied from the exchange that the beating had done nothing to dampen Michael's fire. He found his eyes drifting back to the 'other guy' while his thoughts returned to what had almost occurred in his absence.

The Americans had managed the situation efficiently. That much was undeniable. He would have preferred they had taken Michael's attacker alive if only to answer some of Dempsey's questions, but he doubted he would have done better if he had been in their position. They had been confronted by a fast-moving situation that included three unknown men, two of them armed, and they had managed to leave two of the three alive – and the right two at that – *and* protected a packed ICU in the process.

As he considered the hectic scene before him, he noticed that the taller of the agents was heading their way. A man in a sharp suit who had already identified himself as Corbin Kincaid, a security attaché with the US Embassy to the Netherlands. It was a position that had confirmed Dempsey's suspicions, because only CIA operatives ever claimed to be something so nondescript.

Kincaid was walking towards them with a sureness that spoke of absolute confidence. It was a familiar trait. One Dempsey had seen in every CIA case officer he had ever encountered. The only difference was Kincaid's look. He was tall – an inch or two more than Dempsey's own six feet two inches – blond and handsome; a comic book's idea of an American secret agent. Thirty years younger and he would have been an absurdity of a cliche, but even in his fifties he looked like he had just stepped off a film set.

Kincaid's much younger companion – shorter, slighter and darker-featured with a heavily receding hairline – looked far more like the real-life spies Dempsey had encountered across his two own decades in the job.

Dempsey pushed himself off the wall as the agent approached, bringing himself to his full height. Kincaid was a typical alpha male, he could already tell that. If Dempsey wanted to retain any control here – which he certainly intended to do – he had to counter the man's instinctive aggression with his own assertiveness.

He stepped forwards, meeting Kincaid halfway across the floor.

'I have a question,' Dempsey said, interrupting the American a heartbeat before he could speak. 'What authority is it you think you have here?'

'You really need to be told that twice, buddy?'

'Humour me,' Dempsey replied. He knew what Kincaid was referring to: the barked identification he had given while Dempsey had been on his knees.

'All you need to know is that this ICU is under US protection following today's events. Which means you and anyone else in here answers to me.'

Dempsey could not suppress a smile at the response.

'I'm well aware of *my* chain of command,' Dempsey replied, throwing in a casual shrug that was calculated to infuriate the agent. 'And you're not in it.'

Kincaid looked furious. He took a step closer, into Dempsey's personal space. It was, Dempsey recognised, an attempt to intimidate. It did not work, but Kincaid did not seem to notice.

'The point is, we've got this. The US doesn't need any help from the United Nations or from any jumped-up little agency they might send here. Not now. Not ever.'

'Your president would disagree with that,' Dempsey replied. He did not move back so much as an inch as he spoke. 'And I'm fairly sure he outranks you, Officer . . . sorry, what did you say your name was again?'

Dempsey's use of the term 'officer' was deliberate. And it had exactly the effect he intended: it made Kincaid hesitate, if only for a heartbeat.

'It's not Officer anything, Mr Dempsey,' Kincaid said, his jaw clenching in anger. 'You want the full title, it's Colonel Corbin Kincaid.'

'Of course it is. So how long have you been with the Embassy?'

'That sure as hell isn't any of your business, mister.'

'I'm sorry, I thought that was our theme today. Stepping in where we don't belong. Because this hospital, *Colonel* Kincaid, it sure as hell isn't any jurisdiction of yours. This is Dutch soil. Which means the CIA has no authority over what goes on in this ward, anywhere else in this building or even anywhere else in this country. And *that* means, contrary to what you seem to think, right now you're in charge of nothing.'

Kincaid made no effort to correct Dempsey's mention of the CIA. Nor did he continue to insist on a rank of colonel. Neither man was in any mood to keep up the charade. And neither was about to back down.

'Is that right?' Kincaid asked, his nose now inches from Dempsey's. 'Well, you sound a lot more English than you do Dutch, Mr Dempsey. So I've got to wonder, what makes you any more relevant here than me?'

'The ISB has a multinational remit. Our jurisdiction spreads to every United Nations member state, based on consent. Like the CIA, we go everywhere, only we've actually got the authority to do that.'

'You really think the Dutch would say no if we pushed it?'

'Probably not. We both know it's easy to be a bully when you're the biggest kid in class. But do you really think you'd still be in a job once this gets back to the White House? Because believe me, your biggest boss is no fan of this kind of thing.'

'And how would you know that?'

'Look me up. If your security clearance goes high enough, you'll find out.'

Kincaid hesitated again. He seemed to be connecting some mental dots. He took a step back as he did so, putting some physical distance between himself and Dempsey.

The younger CIA officer did the opposite. He stepped forwards, level with Kincaid.

'You're *that* ISB agent?' he said, his voice lowered and uncertain. 'The one involved with the White House shooting?'

Dempsey turned to face the smaller man, surprised that he had spoken his thoughts – *those* thoughts – aloud.

'We don't need to go over any of that.' His words stopped any more unwelcome statements before they could be made. 'I didn't catch your name?'

'Sean Sutton, Mr Dempsey.'

Sutton took another small step forwards, holding out his hand in greeting. Dempsey took it and shook back.

'Thanks for what you did here,' he said, indicating towards the covered body that still lay just feet away. 'Your handiwork, right?'

'Could have been either of us,' Sutton replied. 'I was just closer.'

'Still, that was a skilled situation assessment. You made that decision quick.'

Dempsey turned back to face Kincaid.

'Look, all the posturing aside, I'm glad you were here. You guys did a good job. You stopped more people dying today. But I have to know: what brought you here?'

Kincaid and Sutton looked at each other for a moment. An unspoken communication that Dempsey could not read. When they turned back to face him, it was the senior man who spoke.

'There are US citizens in this ward,' he said. 'American victims hurt in today's shooting. When our people get wrapped up in these things then so do we. We might not have control here, but we're a part of this. Whether you like it or not.'

Dempsey resisted the urge to shake his head. There was much more to the presence of the CIA than Kincaid was willing to admit, Dempsey was sure of it. And so he was disappointed that the lead officer had not chosen to play things straight.

'Whatever you say,' Dempsey replied. 'I'm not planning to go over your head or even get in your way. Just make sure you stay out of ours.'

Kincaid held Dempsey's gaze, his face a mask that gave no hint of his true feelings. The American had played this game enough times to know all the tricks, Dempsey realised. He was not about to give himself away now. That fact alone threatened to trigger a stoic stand-off between the two men, but it was broken before it had even begun by the shocked sound of Michael's voice.

'Clubber? What the hell are *you* doing here?'

THIRTY-TWO

Michael stared at the newcomer in confusion. The sight of Alastair Compton was so surprising – so completely out of context – that Michael almost missed the signs of equally baffled recognition that dawned on 'Clubber's' face.

'Devlin?'

It took that single word for Compton to confirm his years of dislike for Michael; the tone of his voice said it all. It was a reaction that neither bothered nor shocked the Irishman. The two lawyers had known one another for almost twenty-one years and the poor regard was mutual.

'You're bleeding.' Compton's eyes scanned Michael as he spoke, no doubt picking up on the other visible injury. 'What happened here?'

Michael ignored the question. He was still a little disoriented by Compton's unexpected arrival, which was now made all the more bizarre by the presence of yet another familiar face: Yuri Shevchuk.

Michael had never met the International Criminal Court's prosecutor but Shevchuk was the closest thing to a celebrity that a lawyer can be, at least outside of the US. It left him in no doubt as to the man's identity.

Still less than clear on the connection between the new arrivals, Michael turned back to Compton.

'Seriously, Clubber, what are you doing here?'

'I live here, Michael. You're the one who's hundreds of miles from home. And the one who looks like he's gone ten rounds with Mike Tyson. I should be asking you that question.'

Michael had to admit that, on this occasion, Compton was correct.

The Englishman was eighteen months older than Michael, which had made them direct contemporaries at the criminal bar. The two men had cut their teeth alongside each other in the courts two decades earlier, before crossing paths – and swords – many times in the years that followed. Compton's bruising advocacy style, as well as an unusually aggressive style of robing-room chat, had long ago earned him the nickname 'Clubber'.

All of which was half a career ago. It had been more than ten years since Compton had left behind the practice of domestic criminal law and his multiple professional rivalries, and since then he had been practising in The Hague as a defence advocate on appointment by the International Criminal Court.

As his surprise at Compton's unexpected appearance lessened and his composure returned, Michael quickly reasoned how to play this from here. Maintaining the old animosity was out; it would be as counterproductive as developing new ones. And so Michael chose to do the sensible thing. Compton was a potential resource, he now saw. One that could be utilised if Michael could leave the past in the past and see what help Clubber could provide.

'You're right,' he said, his tone intentionally softer. 'It is me who should be explaining. I'm here for Will Duffy. He's a friend.'

Compton nodded his head.

'I didn't realise that, Michael. He didn't mention you.'

'You know him?'

'Know him? I was working on the case with him, and with Mendel Prochnik. I was Mendel's junior. That's why we're here: to make sure Will's OK.'

Michael could not hide his surprise at the new information. Will had not spoken about the Hannibal Strauss case in much detail – to do so would have been inappropriate because Michael was not involved – but Michael would have expected his friend to mention that an English barrister was Prochnik's back-up.

He would have guessed we at least knew of each other, he thought. *So why the hell did he not mention it?*

The question was perplexing, making Michael hesitate before replying. Yuri Shevchuk quickly filled the silence, his enquiry directed behind Michael at the agents.

'How is Will? Is he awake?'

'He's not, Yuri, no,' Sutton replied. 'He's in an induced coma, critical but stable.'

'And not helped by the attempt that was just made on his life,' Kincaid added.

Michael watched the exchange with interest. A quick glance towards a plainly bemused Dempsey told him that his friend shared his thoughts.

'You called him Yuri,' Michael said. 'You guys know each other?'

'What business is that of yours?' Kincaid replied.

'What does it matter?' Shevchuk cut in impatiently. 'Yes, we know each other. We're all here to check on Will. Is that so shocking after what's happened?'

'It wouldn't be, no. Except your friend here said they were in the hospital to check on US citizens,' Dempsey said, looking pointedly at Kincaid. 'And Will ain't that.'

Kincaid said nothing. To Michael his silence sounded like an admission.

If Shevchuk had noticed the same thing, he decided to

ignore it. 'And just who the hell are you?' he snapped, his full attention now on Dempsey.

'He's with the International Security Bureau,' Michael volunteered. Tempers, he saw, were getting them nowhere fast, and so he saw no use in risking Dempsey's. 'Another branch of the UN. Only his one outranks yours.'

The prosecutor looked from man to man, as if looking for some disagreement about Dempsey's status. When none came, he took a deep breath before he spoke again.

'All this . . . this bickering. It is doing no one any good. We are all here for Will Duffy. To see that he gets through this, yes?'

'At least some of us,' Michael replied.

'Then let us focus on that. So, is there any update on his condition?'

'None. He's still critical. The doctors are in there now, seeing if any additional damage has been done. They'll be able to tell us more once they're out.'

'And the odds that he might wake up?'

The question caused Michael to pause before he gave his answer. It seemed a strange thing to ask – a strange way to say it – and while he suspected that it was nothing more than a language glitch from a non-native speaker, he was still unsure of how to respond. He was grateful, then, that Dempsey stepped in.

'They don't know the answer to that. They said there's no way to tell.'

Dempsey placed his hand on Michael's shoulder as he spoke. It was an unusual gesture; Dempsey was one of the least tactile people he knew. Combined with the lie he had just told – the doctors had said no such thing – and Michael understood the message.

Follow my lead, Dempsey was saying, *because we don't know who we can trust.*

'In that case, there doesn't seem anything we can do here at the moment,' Shevchuk said. 'If Will already has his friends here to look out for him.'

'Someone in his position can never have enough friends,' Dempsey replied. 'Especially not friends with influence like you.'

Shevchuk hesitated.

'What does—'

Dempsey did not wait for him to finish the question. He had already turned to Compton.

'I'm sorry, I didn't catch your name. I assume it's not Clubber?'

'No, it's not. No one else has called me that in years. My name's Al. Alastair Compton.'

'Pleasure to meet you, Mr Compton. I'm Joe Dempsey of the ISB, here to investigate what went on this afternoon. I'm just wondering, do you know what Will and Mendel Prochnik were doing in the Grote Markt this afternoon?'

It was clear to Michael that Compton had not anticipated the question. The sudden change in subject made him stumble over his words as he attempted to answer.

'I . . . well . . . no. No, I've no idea.'

'So it wasn't case related?'

'No, definitely not. I didn't even know Duffy was still in the country. Not until I heard the news. I thought he was back in London for the weekend.'

'You didn't know he'd changed plans?'

'Not until I got the call from Yuri.'

'And you're sure they weren't there for work? For the case?'

'If they were then I'd have been there, too.'

Dempsey glanced at Michael. The look on his friend's face was impossible to read, but Michael could at least make his own assessment of Compton's response. And he believed him. Whatever else he might be hiding, Compton really *was* unaware of why Duffy and Prochnik were in the Grote Markt.

And that means Will didn't trust him.

'What does it matter why they were there?' Kincaid asked irritably.

'I'd have thought a man of your trade would appreciate knowing everything that's worth knowing,' Dempsey replied.

'I do. But I also don't waste my time with things that *ain't* worth it. And why two lawyers were unlucky enough to be in a public place when four terrorists started shooting it up, I don't see how that's something *I* need to know.'

'Are you seriously going to pretend you buy that? That this was a random terrorist attack?' Dempsey indicated to the corpse on the corridor floor. 'After he came here to finish the job? Drop the pretence, Kincaid. You're fooling no one.'

The American once again said nothing. To Michael, he looked like a man weighing his options. Considering if it was time to tell the truth. But before he could come to a decision, it was taken out of his hands.

'I do not even understand this conversation,' Yuri Shevchuk said. 'These conclusions. These . . . these conspiracy theories. The nature of the shooting this afternoon could not be clearer. Mendel Prochnik and Will Duffy, they were unfortunate to find themselves there when these . . . these madmen attacked. Mendel is dead, Will is lucky to be alive. That is all there is to say. And since Will is in no condition to see any of us, I would suggest we all agree that this evening is over.'

On those words Shevchuk turned and walked back towards the elevator, his body language mimicking his words. The message was clear: he was done here.

Compton hesitated for just a moment before turning to follow. Michael stopped him with a step and gently pulled him aside.

'Hannibal Strauss, Clubber. Do you think he's guilty?'

'I'm defending the man, Devlin. I can't answer that question.'

'We're not in court now, mate. It's just us two and these four walls. Did Strauss do it?'

Compton looked uncomfortable as he looked back towards the agents, then in the direction of Shevchuk. For the moment they were all out of earshot, as long as he kept his voice low. For a second or two more Michael still doubted he would get an answer, but when Compton finally spoke he did so with certainty.

'Man to man, for old times' sake? Yeah. I think he's as guilty as sin.'

'What about Will and Prochnik? What did they think?'

'They thought the same. We were going through the motions on this one. There's only one verdict coming at the end of all this and it's not one that sees Strauss walking free.'

Michael nodded his head.

'Yeah. Yeah, that was kind of my take too. See you around, Clubber.'

Michael returned to where Dempsey was still standing, the exchange with Kincaid and Sutton still focused on the nature of the Grote Markt shooting. Beginning to feel his tiredness setting in, Michael chose to play no further part.

'I'm going to head back into Will,' he said. 'To see what else the doctors have to say.'

He nodded an absent-minded goodbye at the CIA agents and headed back down the corridor, uninterested in what was being discussed behind him. Michael had learned all that he could for now and it left him with a lot still to consider. But there were three things he already knew for sure:

Kincaid's lying to us.

Shevchuk wants us gone.

And Will didn't trust Clubber as far as he could throw him.

THIRTY-THREE

Kon Frankowski peeled two fifty euro notes from a small wad of paper money and handed them to the desk clerk, tucking what was left into the tight front pocket of his newly purchased jeans. The skinny, pale kid behind the counter took the money without a glance at the new guest and, seconds later, pushed back a single plastic key card and thirty euros in change.

'Room 109,' he said, his English as perfect as Kon had come to expect. 'No lift, so take the stairs behind you.'

Kon turned without a word. The curt, almost rude attitude didn't bother him. A lack of interest in their guests was exactly why he had chosen this place. That and the price; with cash limited and no credit cards, seventy euros per night was as much as he could afford right now. But while the no-frills nature of the Hotel Olympic offered the barest of hospitality norms, it did come with some advantages: no ID, cash payment only and, it seemed, very few fellow guests. In other words, it provided exactly the anonymity Kon was looking for.

If there's anywhere I can be invisible, it's in a shit-hole like this.

He was pleased with his decisions so far. Impressed, even. His moves had been careful, considered and – he hoped – effective. They had also mostly been his own.

Once on the street, Kon had begun by following Maria's most urgent instruction by disposing of his phone. It had been a seminal moment, representing a line which, once crossed, gave him no way back. No phone meant no contact. No lifeline.

From that point on, Kon had only himself.

It was that very thought that had focused his mind. That

had made him remember *he* had talents, too. And as he'd started to follow Maria's instructions, useful though they were as a starting point, he realised that they were insufficient. If he was going off-grid, as she had suggested, then it was not enough to just throw away his phone, dispose of his bank cards and get the hell out of town. Not in a world that was now so covered by electronic surveillance.

Not in a world of cameras.

Kon had spent his twenties and much of his thirties working in every aspect of every automated system that made twenty-first-century life worth living. He knew better than almost anyone the technical infrastructures that kept modern cities running smoothly. And how much it was all monitored. He needed to make himself harder to spot.

And so he had kept on walking as he'd left the dismantled phone behind, keeping to the shade when he could and always aware of the danger he was in, not stopping until he'd found what he was looking for: an open charity shop.

When he emerged from the store twenty minutes later, Kon was carrying a ragged rucksack that he had filled with clothes he would never ordinarily wear. He had picked his new look carefully. A dark faded T-shirt. The kind of long-sleeved checked shirts that would embarrass a lumberjack. Denim trousers that were marginally too short for his height and way too tight for his already slim build. And a pair of boots more suited to a building site than a city street.

With a single pair of bright-red suspenders and a battered fedora to complete the ensemble, he knew that the outfit would do its job perfectly; he would look every inch the hipster he had never been. All he needed to do now was to lose the one hipster feature he already possessed: his beard. It might have suited the look, but it was a key identifying feature; even he could barely remember what he looked like clean shaven.

That, though, would have to wait. First Kon had to deal with the contents of his wallet.

Even at second-hand charity rates, the clothes purchases had almost exhausted the limited cash he had been carrying and that left him no choice but to move to the next stage of Maria's plan: it was time to max out his daily limit on every bank card he carried, then dispose of the plastic and get the hell out of town.

An easy enough decision that came with one not-so-simple question: where the hell would he go?

Kon had already accepted that an American citizen travelling without a passport – and, in his case, one who sure as hell could not go to the US Embassy for a replacement – could not leave the Netherlands. Wherever he was going, it had to be inside the country's borders. That left him few transport options: train, coach or car.

The last he ruled out in seconds. Hitch-hiking was much too dangerous in the circumstances and he could not hire a vehicle without using his ID and leaving a paper trail.

So rail or road. Neither was ideal. Both would involve overcrowded, easily accessed terminals. Places where the bastards no doubt out looking for him would surely have men in place already, waiting to put an end to the threat they believed Kon to be. But one of the two options, much more than the other, suited Kon's quickly evolving plan.

A bus was the logical choice. Kon concluded that almost immediately. On a bus he could keep other travellers in sight much more effectively than he could on a train, while the lack of 'private' areas made unseen violence against him much less likely. Even more importantly, a bus could be stopped at any point, should the need arise.

As comforting as it was to have made the decision, it came with a worry of its own: if Kon could see the sense in his choice, then surely those who were looking for him could do the same? They were professionals. It was their job to anticipate how a target thinks. Which made it necessary to somehow counter that conclusion: to create a misdirection compelling enough that it would convince even them.

At first it had him stumped. Every idea – every deceit – seemed too obvious. Too transparent.

And then it came to him.

With no way to access the internet, Kon had been reduced to a paper bus schedule. He had used it to identify a local bus route that would take him to within a block of a small rail terminal near the outskirts of the city. Named Den Haag Mariahoeve Station, he had first noticed it when reading a guide book the previous night and had planned to travel there for a selfie to send Maria; a light distraction in an otherwise hellish trip. Those plans were long gone but his interest in the place had changed, albeit it for a very different reason: the fact that Den Haag Mariahoeve was nowhere near a bus terminal.

Taking care to stay away from the small rail hub itself, Kon had visited an ATM a little over a block away and it was there that he maxed out the daily limit on all three of his cards. Two hundred and fifty euros in cash for each one. Seven hundred and fifty total. Dispensed in less than two minutes, all in full view of an ATM camera that would show a Kon Frankowski identical to the man who had fled the Grote Markt.

A man who, minutes later, would look very different.

Kon had bought a tourist map of the city and studied the

area before boarding the bus, and so he knew how close Den Haag Mariahoeve Station was to a small, unlit park area called Ooievaarsveld.

Ooievaarsveld was both central to Kon's plan and the part on which he had to take the biggest risk. He had known it would be dark enough for his purposes by the time he got there, that much was inevitable. But he had been uncertain if it would be sufficiently empty. He had guessed it would – the park was famous locally for a population of storks, so he figured that suggested a lack of human footfall after dark – but still it had been a risk. Kon had been relieved, then, when he found himself proved correct.

Entering the park from the east, he found a secluded spot and quickly set about changing his outfit. The next task, however, had taken a little more time than he would have liked. In an effort to conserve his cash, Kon had bought the cheapest beard trimmer he could find and so he'd had to take particular care as he used it to remove his facial hair.

It was a far from perfect job. The combination of Kon's open-air surroundings, the lack of either light or a mirror and the inadequacy of the equipment combined to make the process painful and no doubt messy. But it did what needed to be done. It removed Kon's most distinctive feature and left the relatively clean-shaven man who exited Ooievaarsveld via its west exit bearing little resemblance to the guy he had been just ten minutes earlier.

Confident enough in his disguise, Kon had then embarked on the final stage of his plan: with his pursuers presumably alerted by his card use and racing to Den Haag Mariahoeve to intercept the train they would think him to be taking, Kon boarded another local bus and headed back to town.

To his *real* route out of The Hague.

He would never know if the next few hours played out exactly as he had intended them; if his carefully laid bait was taken as completely as in his imagination. But for now he decided to think positively, if only to give him a much-needed boost of confidence in his *own* instincts and skills.

Plus it didn't really matter anyway, he reasoned. Whether the misdirection was complete or just a temporary distraction, it had worked well enough. Kon had found his way back to the centre of The Hague with no sign of a tail. He had then boarded a coach out of the city, not from the terminal but from a full quarter of a mile along its route, where he had stood in the centre of the road to force the driver to stop.

No way to make friends, he had thought at the time, as the angry driver berated him for the risk he had taken. *But definitely the best way to stay off camera.*

Less than two hours later and Kon was in Eindhoven and heading for the dangerous, run-down part of town he and Maria had stumbled on by mistake four years earlier, on the one time they had been in this country together.

Kon had never forgotten the neighbourhood of Het Ven. And he had never forgotten that night; the twenty minutes he had spent with his heart racing, rushing to get himself and Maria out of the only spot in the Netherlands where he had felt unsafe.

Until today, anyway.

Looking back, he thought how privileged he had been until this trip. That those twenty minutes of danger should be so unusual that they should stick in his mind so clearly after a full four years. Before the Grote Markt, it had been one of the most dangerous moments of his life.

And now it looks like a sunny afternoon stroll.

Het Ven, he reasoned, was the very last place they would look for him. With no knowledge of his most fleeting connection to the neighbourhood – and no way to trace his journey to Eindhoven in the first place – they could have no reason to look for him here.

The thought made him smile for the very first time since he had watched Mendel Prochnik fall.

His plan had worked.

THIRTY-FOUR

'Come with me.'

The short, stocky federal agent did not wait for a response. Neither did he acknowledge that he was here at Grace's insistence. Instead he turned and left the room, leaving the door open behind him, as if his appearance in the temporary ISB 'office' had been his own choice.

The discourtesy irritated Grace more than she wanted to admit, but she did her best to suppress it. She had wanted out of the room, out of the police precinct and out of Park Ridge itself even *before* speaking to Dempsey. A desire that had only increased since listening to what he had to tell her. It was because of this that, following the call, she had finally had enough.

If *they* would not put this charade to bed then she would, and so she'd informed the FBI that they spoke in ten or they did not speak at all.

It was one hundred per cent bluff, but it did the trick.

Grace was certain that neither she nor Wrixon had crossed any lines back at the Frankowskis' home. A fact that no amount of dead federal agents was going to change. But politics required her to explain those conclusions to the agents investigating and so she and Wrixon could not just leave without a word, no matter how much they wanted to.

With that need in mind, Grace did as the obnoxious agent had instructed. She exited the room in the same direction as he had done, with Wrixon just behind her.

Their procession was a short one. The FBI team were also

playing away from home in the Park Ridge Police Department and so had commandeered the office next door. It was twice the size of the room Grace and Wrixon had just left and not nearly so bereft of technology, but its furnishings were barely an improvement. The chairs to which Grace and Wrixon were directed were identical to the cheap, uncomfortable plastic seats they had left behind.

'Seems the cops here like you about as much as they like us.' Grace indicated to the chairs as she spoke, an attempt to warm the cold reception. 'What's the seating budget in this town anyway?'

'I don't think this is a time for jokes.'

The rebuke came from the back wall, from a man Grace had not seen before. He was seated away from the table that dominated the centre of the room. Intentionally separated from what was to follow, Grace presumed.

'Sorry,' Grace said. 'Never was very good at small talk. Maybe we should try some introductions instead, get this thing back on an even keel?'

'We already know who you are, Agent Grace.'

The reply came from the agent who had brought them here. He had stayed standing while everyone else sat. It was an intimidation tactic that Grace recognised; it required him to loom over the prisoners while he was questioning them. It would not work: Grace knew the technique herself, neither she nor Wrixon was a prisoner here and they sure as hell were not about to be interrogated.

And it's damn near impossible to loom when you're five seven.

Grace kept the thought to herself; what they were here to discuss required at least a show of respect. She kept her response polite.

'In that case you'll do me the courtesy? Since you have the advantage?'

'You really think you deserve a courtesy?'

'We paid you one. We stayed when we didn't have to. And we're letting this whole exercise happen right now, aren't we? So yeah, I think we deserve to know who we're talking to.'

The agent hesitated. He seemed uncertain of the right response. His partner had no such problem. A tall, slim woman who was seated across the table, she was older than both her male colleagues and she already gave every indication that she enjoyed both seniority and superior intelligence.

She reached out her open hand across the table and towards Grace, who reciprocated.

'I'm Special Agent Harris. Jane Harris. My less forthcoming colleague is Special Agent Brooks. And the gentleman behind us—' she poked a thumb over her own shoulder without looking back, towards the rear wall '—is Special Agent Tyson.'

'Pleased to meet you.' Grace took back her own hand. 'Sorry it's in these circumstances.'

Wrixon stayed silent, and nor did Harris offer him her hand. His eyes were fixed on the senior agent but his face was free of any expression. Grace read the disengagement as consent for her to take the lead. Harris seemed to read it the same way and directed her full attention to Grace.

'They *are* unfortunate. And I'm sorry that it's led to you being . . . detained here for so long.' Harris paused before using the 'D' word. Grace understood why. It revealed the fiction of the last hour. 'But it was necessary. As you know, one of the men who lost his life today was a member of the local Bureau office. Special Agent Ben McDonald.'

'We didn't know his name,' Grace replied.

'You know it now.'

The comment came from Tyson, who was still seated against the back wall. From the bitter tone and the anger that underlined his words, Grace could guess why he was here. She made eye contact over Harris's shoulder.

'Special Agent McDonald was your partner?'

'He was that. And he was my friend.'

'Then I'm sorry for your loss.'

'You mean you're sorry for his murder, don't you?'

'Careful, Al.' Harris turned in her seat as she spoke. The first time Grace had seen her look directly at Tyson. 'Either keep your emotions in check or go elsewhere. Understood?'

Tyson said nothing but his expression spoke volumes. He was unhappy with the rebuke, but he was also outranked. The interaction interested Grace. It suggested that Harris and Tyson were seeing the whole thing in very different ways.

Harris turned back and continued.

'You'll understand that Special Agent Tyson is a little upset right now. Please excuse him.'

'Of course. But if I can ask, is the fact that Agent Tyson is here at all appropriate? If this were an official interview, it wouldn't be.'

Harris nodded her head, her expression giving nothing away.

'No. No, it wouldn't,' she said. 'But we both know this *isn't* an interview, don't we?'

'We do now.'

The answer confirmed what Dempsey had predicted. In the short time they'd had to investigate, the FBI had reached the right conclusion on their dead agent. A conclusion that Special

Agent Tyson seemed to resent. Grace could understand that. No one wanted to believe that a friend was dirty.

As long as that's all it is, Grace found herself thinking. *Because there* is *another obvious possibility when one half of a partnership is dirty . . .*

She looked beyond Harris and towards the back wall.

'Agent Tyson, do you know what Agent McDonald was doing at the Frankowskis' address this afternoon?'

'You're not here to ask questions, lady.' Tyson was angry. Too much to hide it. 'You're—'

'I don't think you got the memo on this one, Agent,' Grace cut him off. 'I'm sorry you lost a friend, but this is *not* an interrogation. This is a debrief. And we're here to help with an ongoing investigation in which we're all engaged to some extent. So I *will* answer your questions and I'll tell you anything you need to know, within the parameters of security clearance. But it also means you'll answer mine. That way we all help each other, you see?'

'That's not how this works.'

It was Brooks this time. Grace had almost forgotten he was there. She glanced upwards.

'It might not be how *you* work, Special Agent Brooks,' Grace replied without missing a beat, her attention switched in an instant, 'but it is how things are going to proceed here today. So maybe stop wasting everyone's time, put your ass in that chair and join the grown-ups.'

Brooks looked to Harris, the expression on his face one of livid anger; if anything, he was now closer to the edge than Tyson. His urge to respond was so all-consuming to be almost visible, but Harris did not allow it. With an irritated frown, she indicated for him to take a seat.

'Thank you.' Grace turned back to Tyson. 'So, again, do you know why Agent McDonald was at the Frankowski property today?'

Tyson hesitated for a moment. Grace thought that she knew why: the man had no explanation for his partner's actions. He just did not want to admit it.

'Maybe he was responding to the gunfire that was coming from that house,' he finally suggested, his tone bitter. The answer was desperate. A stretch for any justification Tyson could find. 'Like any good agent would do?'

'Unlikely.' Grace kept all emotion from her voice. 'Given that my colleagues and I were already there when the rounds were fired and that he certainly didn't arrive after us, I think we can safely conclude he was already *in* the house by the time the shots went off. Which brings us back to why he was there in the first place. If you can't help with that then what about this: was he even on shift this afternoon?'

'What the hell does that have to do with anything? He's a goddamned federal agent. I don't know about *you* people, but *we're* never off-duty.'

'Of course you're not.' Grace was already satisfied that she had the truth. Tyson knew nothing. 'But that doesn't answer the question. Was he on shift?'

Tyson hesitated again. He looked towards Harris, as if looking for help.

'Answer the question, Alan.'

He looked back at Grace. His anger was still there but now it was tempered a little. He reminded her of a child, forced to admit the one truth that he wanted to avoid.

'No,' he said, his voice now low. 'No, he wasn't on duty.'

'Does he live near to Johnsvale Road?'

'You mean *did* he? Before your friend there killed him?'

'Yes. That's what I mean.'

'No, he didn't.'

'Any friends or family nearby?'

'Look, just what the hell is this?'

The violence that was bubbling beneath the surface was threatening to blow. Grace could see it coming. But she wanted this over.

When Tyson did not respond she glanced towards Harris.

'Would you, please?'

'Answer the question, Al.'

'No. No, there were no friends and family nearby. Not that I know of.'

'So what was he doing there?'

'How the hell should I know that?'

'You were his partner. You told me that just a minute ago. You were his partner *and* his friend.'

'That doesn't mean I know what he does twenty-four-seven.' Tyson pointed towards Wrixon. 'Do you know what *he* gets up to on his off-days?'

Grace ignored the question.

'And was he a driver, Mr McDonald?'

'Of course he drives, he's a federal agent. He *was* a federal agent, I mean. Why?'

'Because there was no car connected to Special Agent McDonald found anywhere near the address, that's why. The only vehicles parked up were the police cruiser and the Suburban that my team had been driving. So how did Special Agent McDonald even get to the address, whatever he was there for?'

Tyson said nothing.

Grace turned away from him, satisfied that she had given the FBI agent food for thought. It was clear that there had been a third man. A driver. But it would be for the FBI to find out who. Grace's curiosity had already moved on.

'I have another question,' she asked, her focus now fixed on Harris, 'if you'll allow me?'

'Please.'

'Last I heard, the other gunman – the one shot inside the house – was unidentified. Is that still the case?'

'It's not.'

'Can you tell me who he is?'

'I can't,' Harris replied. 'That's our little corner of the investigation, I'm afraid. We can't disclose any specific information at this stage. I'm sure you understand?'

Grace did. She took a moment to think.

'What about who he *isn't*?' she finally asked. 'Can you tell me that?'

'What do you mean?'

'I mean that, without telling me his name, can you tell me if he was another federal agent?'

'He was not.'

'Was he law enforcement of any kind?'

'He was not.' Harris hesitated. 'Or to answer that question in as helpful a way as I can without breaking any rules . . . he was quite the opposite.'

'The *opposite* of law enforcement?'

'That's all I can say.'

Grace took a few moments to consider the answer. It was a new puzzle piece, part of the growing jigsaw she had been building in her mind. No one else spoke to break the silence, giving her time to think. For her to pull the strands together as best she could, while at the same time considering what Harris's answer confirmed.

Harris, it told her, had been straight with them from the outset of the debrief. Even with the undeniable hostility of the atmosphere, the meeting really *was* the collaboration Harris had described. One which Grace had now hijacked completely.

When she finally spoke, Grace was as sure of her conclusions as she could be. But there was one of which she was even more certain than the others. Exactly as Dempsey had been when they had spoken on the phone.

And it was a certainty she knew she had to share.

'I'm sorry to say this,' she began, 'but I think the only conclusion available here is that McDonald was in Johnsvale Road *with* the other dead guy. And I believe he was there looking for Maria Frankowski. Except Maria Frankowski and her children weren't there when they arrived, so they'd started to ransack the place, to find some clue of where she might be. That's what they were doing when the patrolmen turned up and that's why the dining room hadn't been searched yet. The cops interrupted them and were killed for it.

'Unluckily for them, we arrived moments later. McDonald and his pal tried to do the exact same thing to us, only they came off worse second time out. It's that simple, I'm afraid. McDonald's dead because he was dirty.'

Harris had watched Grace intently throughout her analysis. When Grace was done, the FBI agent sat back into her chair and placed her fingertips on the table ahead of her. Then she began to slowly nod her head.

'I think I agree with you.' She glanced apologetically towards Tyson as she spoke. 'Everything you just said, that's where I was heading. I was just moving a little more slowly, so thanks for the turbo boost.'

'I doubt it would have taken you much longer.'

'Maybe not, but every second counts. We don't have time for slow on this one. Not when there are so many questions still to answer. I suspect you might know the answers to some of them.'

Grace frowned. For the first time she seemed to be behind the pace.

'What questions?'

'Just what you'd expect. Who are the Frankowskis, for one thing? Who's after them and why? What's the ISB's interest in them? I assume by the fact you're here that you must know something? And sure as hell more than us.'

'I do know a little,' Grace admitted. 'Though I don't have all the answers yet. Or anything even close. But I'm sorry, I can't tell you any of it. You have your investigation, Agent Harris. And we have ours.'

Harris nodded. She could hardly complain that Grace was withholding information when she was doing the same thing, but Grace was still relieved when she didn't push it. There was no time for a stand-off on this.

The FBI would press ahead with their inquiries, and they would leave Grace and Wrixon free to do the same. And right now Grace had one question she wanted answered above all others.

Just where the hell are *the Frankowskis?*

THIRTY-FIVE

G race stepped out of the makeshift office with that final question still on her mind.

Just where the hell are the Frankowskis?

She knew the answer was coming. Dempsey seemed to have a line on them almost half an hour ago and at the speed he worked she was sure he would have nailed that down by now. Which meant she would be brought up to speed as soon as she was out of here.

Still, she could not pretend that she wasn't a little frustrated. Had the meeting been as collaborative as both Grace and Harris had pretended it to be, then Grace would have shared what she knew. It was not much – not yet, anyway – but it would have at least given Harris a little direction.

But that was not what had happened and so, with little left to discuss, the debrief had come to a natural end; Special Agent Brooks – silent and still seething from Grace's earlier rebuke – indicated as much by showing Grace and Wrixon towards the door.

Harris had stayed seated as they'd left, her attention switched within an instant of her polite goodbye to the papers that were laid out on the table ahead of her.

The sound of a chair being scraped backwards at the far side of the room had told Grace that Agent Tyson was leaving too. Heading inevitably in the same direction. The only exit.

Aware of Tyson's close proximity and his less-than-ideal mood, Grace had turned as she'd stepped through the open door. She suspected that any words from her would be unwelcome, but it felt like common courtesy to try.

'I just want to say one more time, Special Agent Tyson. We really are very—'

'You can keep your apologies.'

Tyson seemed to make no effort to avoid his shoulder colliding with Grace as he stalked past. The impact was slight and maybe unintentional, but his grim expression suggested otherwise. He paused after a few more steps, then turned back to face her.

'I know what you people were pushing at in there,' he said. 'All that shit about the missing car. I know what you were suggesting.'

'That wasn't what I was saying at all,' Grace lied. The fact was, Tyson had taken her meaning exactly as she had intended it. He just hadn't realised that it had been designed to shut him up. 'It was just an observation intended to help with the investigation.'

'Yeah? Well, that observation sure as hell felt like it was pointed at me.'

'I can see you're upset. I understand—'

'You understand nothing. My friend died today. That's bad enough. And now I have to hear that maybe he wasn't who I thought he was. Do you know how that makes me look? How people are gonna read that? What they'll say?'

'Agent Tyson, I . . .'

'I'll have this hanging over me the rest of my career, you know that? *Did he really not know?*, they'll ask. *Was he really that dumb?* You think that's not enough for me to deal with, without you trying to finger me too?'

'We didn't—'

'Don't waste your breath. You know what you did and so do I. Screw the pair of you.'

Grace resisted the urge to reply as Tyson turned his back and continued on his way along the corridor. The man was in no place to be placated; he was emotional and he was hurt. He was also right. Grace had done exactly what he accused her of and she had done it for her own reasons.

And now, having seen the impact, she was beginning to regret it.

'Forget him.'

The words came from just behind her. Grace turned in response and faced Wrixon. His jittery body language betrayed his impatience to leave.

'We don't have time for this,' he said, confirming her impression. 'We've got to catch up with Dai and Kate.'

Grace nodded in agreement. He was right. And there was nothing she could say to comfort Tyson. Or to calm him. And she was sure a message would already be waiting for them by now anyway, with instructions on where to go to meet the two colleagues Dempsey had sent ahead.

It left no room for further attempts at inter-agency diplomacy.

'OK. Let's go.'

Alan Tyson walked fast in the opposite direction to the departing ISB agents. Determined to speak to no one as he went, he found that he did not have to avoid eye contact. He was wearing his anger like a cloak and the path ahead of him cleared as a result.

The building's rear exit was at the far end of the corridor. He reached it quickly. With a final display of fury he threw the door open, smashing it against the exterior wall. Once through he slammed it closed behind him.

His obvious rage would have warned off even the most curious spectator, and so he was sure that no one within the building would risk following him. Nor was there anyone outside who would come near enough to eavesdrop as he visibly seethed, seemingly on the brink of explosion.

Tyson knew that for sure because Tyson was careful. He knew the kind of behaviour that would make even hardened cops steer clear. And he knew how to fake it.

Satisfied that he was being neither overheard nor overlooked, he took out his phone. His breathing, erratic to the point of frenzy just moments before, calmed as he hit the switch that swapped his handset's settings from his contract SIM card to its encrypted alternative and pressed the only contact saved to the phone's secondary system.

The voice that answered spoke English, but with a trace of a Russian accent.

As ever, the Monk was all business.

'Is it done?'

THIRTY-SIX

'No, it's not damn well done.'

The Monk bristled at the insolence in both Alan Tyson's words and in his tone. It was something that he would mark down for a future date, when his own position was less precarious. Right now, though, he needed every resource, and that made a reprimand risky.

But still he could not entirely let such insubordination slide.

'Why the hell not?' he demanded.

'Because this whole thing is a lot more complicated than you had us believe.'

'Complicated by what?'

'Complicated by the fucking International Security Bureau, that's what. You never mentioned anything about the fucking UN being involved in any of this.'

The Monk inhaled sharply. It was an involuntary reaction to the news. One he hoped Tyson had not heard. He did not want the American to realise how unwelcome the mention of the ISB was.

How had they worked out Frankowski's involvement so quickly? he asked himself. *Let alone already tracked down the man's family.*

'You need to watch your language, Mr Tyson.' The Monk kept his tone flat as he changed the course of the conversation. 'Remember who it is that you're talking to.'

'And just who *am* I talking to?' Tyson replied. 'I've never even met you.'

It was not the response the Monk was expecting. Nor

one he had ever received before. Most of his 'resources' were happier that their paths would never cross. Some worked for him for money. Some for belief in his cause. And some because to do otherwise meant death, for them or for the people they loved. But whatever their motive, his underlings had one thing in common when it came to him: fear.

They all knew and feared the reach and the ruthlessness of the man for whom they worked.

Tyson, for some reason, was different. He was a nihilist motivated solely by money and, in the short time he had been engaged, he had not shown the Monk the respect that was due. Tyson's was an attitude badly in need of adjustment that the Monk intended to provide when the time was right. But he was also a man of resource and extraordinary usefulness. And now, more than, ever, the Monk needed both.

For all of those reasons the Monk chose to ignore the question.

'Tell me what happened.'

'We did what you said,' Tyson explained. 'We went with Mancuso to the Frankowski home. The plan was to show our badges, tell the woman we were taking her and her kids with us, for their own protection. But she wasn't there. No one was. So Mancuso and McDonald searched the place for the item while I waited with the car.'

'And what happened?'

'The local cops showed up. Two of them. Turns out they'd been sent there ahead of time at the request of the ISB, but we didn't know that then. I caught sight of them at a distance so I warned the others and drove away; too many questions if they'd found me sitting there and chances are they'd have called in my plate. I parked around the next street over waiting for

McDonald and Mancuso to get out of the house and jump the back fence, but it never happened.'

'What did?'

'The cops got into the house before either of them could get out, I guess. Whatever the reason, one of them opened fire and killed the cops. But those UN fuckers were already there by then and they got involved. They took out Mancuso *and* McDonald.'

'They killed them both?'

'Yeah. One of them took a couple of bullets, but he's alive. Our guys, though? Very dead.'

The Monk said nothing for a moment. This was not what he wanted to hear. Not by a wide margin. His mind was racing fast as he considered how the ISB action in Park Ridge fitted into the bigger picture.

'You still there?' Tyson asked.

'Of course I'm still here.'

'So what do we do?'

The Monk thought for a moment more.

'Do the ISB suspect you?'

'No.'

'Does anyone else?'

'No. I played up the whole loss of McDonald thing. Made out like I was angry and grieving over my friend.'

Tyson sounded as if he was expecting a compliment for his deception. The Monk knew that Tyson and McDonald could hardly bear one another; only mutual corruption had made them a pair. It was through McDonald that Tyson had come to the Monk's attention.

The Monk chose not to acknowledge Tyson's comment; he was in no mood to massage egos. Especially not that of Alan Tyson.

'Where are the ISB now?' he asked.

'They've just left the police headquarters.'

'To go where?'

'How should I know?'

'Because I pay you to know. Find out.'

'How?'

'Use your initiative. Just do it fast.'

'How much is it worth?'

'Call it repayment for a job not yet done. Now get to work.'

The Monk disconnected the call before Tyson could speak again and placed the handset on the table beside him. His mind was racing fast. The involvement of the ISB in The Hague was unfortunate enough; their presence in Park Ridge complicated things further.

The arrival of Agent Joe Dempsey had been more than unwelcome. Their paths had never crossed and yet Dempsey's was a name the Monk knew well. He was a dangerous man, one who would prove a serious complication even at the best of times. And right now – with so much at stake and with the Monk's resources stretched like never before – Dempsey's involvement could prove fatal.

The Monk had made that assessment before the wheels of Dempsey's plane had even touched down in Rotterdam. Warned by one of his sources that the agent was on his way, the Monk had been considering how best to take this new player off the board. He had run through the possibilities in his mind, building a succession of imagined three-dimensional constructs to play out each complex, decisive scenario.

None of them had gone the way he had hoped, and the likelihood of success seemed to be decreasing with every new development in The Hague. It had left the Monk less confident than he had ever been, but still he had believed that he would find the solution. That he would envisage a neat way to deal with Dempsey without resorting to violence.

But now? With the involvement of Dempsey's ISB team in Park Ridge?

As long as Dempsey was breathing, the man was an unacceptable threat.

It would have to be violence after all.

THIRTY-SEVEN

Michael placed two steaming cups of strong tea onto the small table that stood against the bare wall of the serviced apartment kitchen. He had heard Dempsey move from the shower-room to his bedroom a few minutes earlier and had timed the hot drink for how long he thought it would take his friend to dress.

The estimate was near perfect, with Dempsey walking through the open kitchen doorway within moments of the cups touching down.

Michael gave him time to take a seat and then a sip before he asked the question that had been on his mind since they had first arrived at their accommodation.

'Did you make the arrangements?'

Dempsey put his cup down, sat back in his chair and pushed his fingers through his short, dark hair before he spoke. As if he was taking a final moment of respite before he had to start thinking about work again. Done, he fixed his eyes on Michael.

'Yes,' he said. 'For now we've got local armed police outside Will's room. Best we can do for a few hours. But by morning my man will be here.'

'That soon?'

'He was on holiday in Italy. Visiting his family. I asked him to cut it short.'

'And you trust him for this?'

'Sal Gallo's part of my team, Mike. Hand-picked. He's also as close to being a damn brick wall as any human can be, so once he's there we can stop worrying about Will.'

Michael smiled his thanks. The second attempt on Will's life had taken more than just a physical toll; there had been few moments since leaving the ICU when he hadn't worried for his friend's safety. Even the thought of a police guard did little to allay his fears. If whoever wanted Will dead could get a man into the ICU posing as a doctor, could they trust the police guard was on the level?

Dempsey's faith in who was coming to replace them, then, was a relief.

'And what about Maria?' Michael asked. 'Do you know yet if she's safe?'

Dempsey had told Michael only a little about the events in Park Ridge. Just enough for Michael to know that Dempsey's first fear had been confirmed: against all the odds, it *was* the same Frankowski at the Grote Markt. And Maria was nowhere to be found.

They had not discussed it further since that short summary, but now Michael wanted to know more.

'Not yet,' Dempsey replied. 'But I will soon.'

'What does your gut tell you?'

'Maria had hours of warning, if I'm right about that call from her husband. That's hours more than she'd need to be sure she and her family were safe.'

'You sound pretty certain of that. It's been a long time. How do you know she's even the same person any more? People change.'

'Perhaps. But the way Maria was raised, she had better instincts than ninety-nine per cent of professionals I ever worked with. If she'd not been a medic she'd have made a hell of an agent.'

Michael nodded his head. He knew that Dempsey would

not take her safety lightly and so his confidence was telling. It was also intriguing. One day Michael would want to know more about the ex who still had such a grip on his friend, but now was not the time.

There were much more pressing matters to consider. One in particular.

'Is there a reason we didn't mention Frankowski back at the hospital?'

'I didn't see you rushing forwards with his name,' Dempsey replied. 'You tell me.'

'You testing me, Joe?' Michael asked. 'You want to know if my instincts are good enough to keep up?'

'You've already proved that tonight. There aren't many who would have clocked that doctor for a fake. So no test, but I am intrigued. Why did *you* not mention the name?'

'I felt like I didn't have a clear enough idea of what was going on then. Still don't, truth be told. And since no one's being straight with us so far, well, it felt best to keep our cards close to our chest. At least until we have a better clue who we can and can't trust.'

'And what's your gut telling you about those four?'

'Well, Clubber's easy. He's not my cup of tea at all. Never has been.'

'Why?'

'Just who he is. He's ambitious and unethical. And I know that's a bit rich coming from me with some of the things I've done, but he was an unethical prosecutor and that's much worse. We came up against each other a lot and I didn't trust him. A prosecuting barrister, they're not supposed to be there to win. They're there to make sure they achieve the correct result, which is guilty for a guilty man, not guilty for a man who's not.

I don't think Clubber ever learned that. With him, unhelpful evidence – the stuff that didn't suit his case – too often it'd mysteriously disappear.'

'You mean he was bent?'

'And then some. But he was also a dyed-in-the-wool prosecutor, so when he suddenly became the big defender in these war crimes trials, I never understood it. None of us did. And after tonight I still don't.'

'Why do you call him Clubber?'

'Goes back to how he prosecuted cases. He'd bludgeon defendants until they were battered and bruised. Subtleties like truth and rules of evidence, they didn't mean so much. Not when he could just smash up a defendant in front of a jury. And he could, because he was bloody good at his job. Even with all his faults.'

'OK. And there was me thinking he was yet another brawler lawyer like you.'

'Oh, he was that, too. I don't know what he's like these days but he was a handful when we were young. He grew up working the family farm so he was way more physical than you'd expect from one of us. The nickname would have suited him regardless, I guess.'

'And now? What's your feeling about him on this?'

'Will didn't trust him. Prochnik neither. If they did, he'd have known they were meeting Frankowski.'

'Maybe he *does* know. Maybe he just didn't want to tell us?'

'If he's lying about it then he's doing a hell of a job. I'm a good judge of bullshitting and he didn't seem like he was. But either way, there's a trust issue. Either *they* didn't trust him, which I think is most likely since they went without him. Or *he* doesn't trust *us*. One way or the other, that puts us at odds. It means we don't need to be sharing intelligence with him.'

Dempsey smiled.

'Intelligence, Mike?'

'That's what you call it, right?'

'I guess so. I just didn't expect you to dive in head first.'

'Alright, piss-taker. Information, then.'

Dempsey ignored his own amusement as he moved the analysis on.

'What about Yuri Shevchuk?' he asked.

'His reputation is that he's a fair man,' Michael replied. 'A fair prosecutor. But on this one, according to Will, he's been dogmatic as hell. Refusing to give an inch, determined to convict Strauss at all costs. That's maybe not unusual for some prosecutors, but it's out of character for Shevchuk.'

Michael paused.

'And then there was that question he asked tonight.'

'The one about the chances of Will waking up?'

'Yeah. In the context and the way he did it, the way he asked it, it just . . . it seemed weird, right?'

'I thought so.'

'I mean, it's not like Will could tell them anything if he was awake, is it? If it *was* just a random shooting. And even if he could, Shevchuk's not a part of that investigation. He's an international prosecutor, not a Dutch one. So why would he need to know what Will knows?'

'There would be a few possibilities,' Dempsey replied, 'if we took the time to think about it. But not many of them are good ones. So yeah, I agree, that guy puts the hairs up on the back of my neck. What about the other two? What's your take on the CIA boys?'

'Less sure,' Michael replied. 'They're your world.'

'Still. Humour me.'

'Well, they're sure not playing this straight. That whole "there for American citizens" bullshit isn't fooling anyone.'

'Agreed. They were there for Will. And they were there *with* Compton and Shevchuk. But why? What's that about?'

'You think they know about Frankowski?'

'There's no way for us to know that.'

'But what do you think?'

'I think they must at least know there's someone *like* Frankowski. I think they know that Will and Prochnik were meeting someone about the Hannibal Strauss case.'

Michael paused again as he considered the answer. An answer that just led to another question.

'Why do you think Will and Prochnik were meeting Frankowski? What does he have to do with Strauss?'

'We're as in the dark as anyone on that, Mike. All we have is a name.'

'Do you think the CIA agents might know?'

'Maybe. Like I said, at this stage there's no way to tell.'

Michael took a moment to sip at his cooling tea, wishing now that it was something stronger.

'What did you make of Kincaid?'

'He's proper,' Dempsey replied. 'At least he once was. I don't know about now, not with how the world's changed. But game recognises game. Kincaid used to be what I used to be. He was a lone man with a gun, sent to silence problems. I can spot us a mile off.'

'But not any more?'

'Unlikely. But men like us don't disappear. We move on, to where our talents are still valuable. I do what I do. And I imagine Kincaid does his own version of that. Most likely for the CIA's National Clandestine Service.'

'Clandestine? Like secret ops?'

'Exactly that. My guess is he's a Senior Program and Plan Officer. Which means he's not pulling the trigger any more. But he *will* be arranging it where others still do. That and worse, I imagine.'

'OK. Let's assume that's right. Why are the CIA interested in Hannibal Strauss? You think they think he's innocent?'

'They couldn't care less either way. The CIA isn't interested in the justice of a courtroom. And those two are not here to ensure the right result.'

'Then why *are* they here?'

'I already told you, there's no way to tell. Not yet anyway. We'll get to the bottom of it, Mike, but until we do we've got no more reason to trust them than we do Compton or Shevchuk.'

Michael nodded in agreement. He hated not having an answer to a question – it went against his very nature – but he also knew that Dempsey was right. There were no more answers right now. And so they would have to go out and find them.

He took another long sip of his tea. Dempsey did the same, the two men sitting in a comfortable silence for several minutes. It was only with each cup drained that either spoke again.

'It's been a long day,' Dempsey said, 'and it's getting late. It's time we turned in. We need to be in Scheveningen by eight a.m.'

Michael frowned in confusion. Dempsey had not mentioned any such plans.

'Where's Scheveningen?' he asked.

'Not far. Just on the outskirts of town, by the coast.'

'And we're going there why?'

'Because it's where they're holding Hannibal Strauss.'

This time Michael was genuinely shocked.

'You want us to speak to *Strauss*? After everything you told me about him?'

'If we're going to get ahead of this thing then we don't have a choice. We need to find Frankowski, that much we know. I already put some feelers out but, from what little I've had back on him, he won't be so easy to find. Which means we need some help. The way I see it, Strauss *is* that help.'

'What have you found on Frankowski?'

'There's no sign of him at his hotel, his phone has gone dead, he's maxed out his bank cards. All little things that add up to one big thing.'

'What's that?'

'The man knows how to hide. And with him missing, with Will unconscious and with no one else we can trust, it seems to me that Strauss is the best bet we have for some insight into what this is all about, or where our missing man might be. At the very least, maybe he knows why they were meeting this afternoon.'

Michael took a moment. Dempsey's logic was sound, but the work that had taken place without Michael's knowledge was a surprise.

'When did you find the time to do all this?' he asked.

'All what?'

'The checks on Frankowski?'

'I put that in train before we even landed,' Dempsey replied. 'Then once we arrived and established he wasn't among the dead or injured, I had the urgency stepped up.'

Michael was unsure why but the fact Dempsey had been

working without involving him made the Irishman feel a little put out. He knew it shouldn't. Dempsey was the professional here, not him, so why would he involve a civilian in every single step of an operation? But still, it somehow made Michael feel less essential than he would like.

He forced the unhelpful thought out of his mind and instead focused on the practical.

'You really think Strauss will speak to us?' he asked. 'That he'll speak to you?'

'He has no choice. If Will was right and Strauss really didn't do this – if there really *is* something else behind it all – then he needs someone on his side. With his legal team taken out, and with the enemies he's made through his life, I'm betting he doesn't have a whole lot of options right now.'

'But what about . . . you know?'

Michael touched his own eye and then his ear as he spoke. A reminder of Dempsey's last encounter with the man they were going to see.

'I doubt Strauss knows it was me who did that. Not for sure, anyway.'

'And if he does?'

'If he does then he'll just have to put a pin in it. We can circle back to any problem he has with me once we've found out who tried to kill Will. And who went after Maria. Until then, Strauss's whole future depends on staying friendly and playing ball. Even if that's with me.'

'You're speaking like he's a rational man.'

'A man doesn't live the life Strauss has without knowing how to put his own interests first. He'll help us. Because doing so will help him.'

Michael climbed to his feet, picked up his cup and

Dempsey's and placed them both in the empty sink. He then headed to the kitchen door before turning around to face his still seated friend.

'Let's hope you're right.'

'I will be,' Dempsey said with a grin, his voice utterly devoid of uncertainty.

The absence of doubt – of even a hint of it – gave Michael comfort. It was the most reassuring part of his friend's character: his unwavering confidence. Right now it was on full display and, with all that was happening around them, it was exactly what Michael needed to hear.

THIRTY-EIGHT

The journey from Park Ridge, New Jersey, to the area of Cooperstown in New York State was almost precisely one hundred and seventy miles. Over three hours by car on a good run, the same distance took a little over fifty minutes by chopper.

It was lucky for Grace and Wrixon, then, that the Bell 525 Relentless that had brought them from Manhattan was still waiting at Colony Field. Barely an hour door-to-door had not been what Grace was expecting but it was very welcome. With her blood now up, she had dreaded the prospect of a long journey on Maria Frankowski's trail.

Grace had called Kate Silver within moments of leaving the police station and had been provided with an address that was seven miles outside of Cooperstown. One of the only working ranches left in the area, that property was a full six hundred acres of grazing for both cattle and sheep. Unimpressive by the standards of the super-holdings common in the likes of Texas, in mid-state New York – where prices per acre averaged four times as high as in the Lone Star State – the Golden Calf Ranch was as big as they came.

Dempsey was certain that the ranch was where they would find Maria, though he had not told Silver why. As far as Grace could establish, the place was wholly owned by a single individual: David Burton, a sixty-five-year-old former US Marine Corps major who was now a cattleman. Burton had purchased the place thirty-four years earlier and had only one dependent on record, a thirteen-year-old daughter named Leisha.

For all that Grace had studied what information they had, she could see absolutely no connection between Burton and Maria Frankowski, Maria Parker or any other identity Dempsey's former partner might have used throughout her life. The same was true of the eighteen permanent staff registered at the address, none of them any more connected to the Frankowskis than Burton himself.

But Grace trusted Dempsey. He had earned that much and she had no doubt he knew his ex better than she did. And so she and Wrixon had boarded the chopper and flown the near two hundred miles without question.

As instructed by Dempsey, the Relentless had ultimately landed in an open field three miles from the ranch, leaving Grace and Wrixon to finish the journey by car. It seemed an unnecessary extra effort since there was nothing but clear landing ground on the ranch itself, but Dempsey had insisted that things be done to his exact specifications.

Perhaps he's worried that landing a chopper right by the ranch might spook an already on-edge Maria, Grace reasoned. *Seems fair. If a little over-cautious.*

Just as particular were his orders about where Grace and Wrixon should rendezvous with Silver and Dai, and what should happen when they did. The where was on a roadway adjacent to the ranch perimeter, still well out of sight of the property's buildings. While the what was for Grace to then go to the ranch alone and make first contact. Only once she had established Maria was there and it was safe were the others to join her.

Grace and Wrixon were out of the GMC Yukon as soon as it came to a complete stop at the meeting point, with Grace instantly noticing the sheer heat of the night. It was still uncomfortably warm; more so even than in Park Ridge, despite being so much further north.

Dai and Silver were out of their waiting vehicle just as swiftly, exiting a typically dark Suburban that had not moved an inch in almost two hours. The four agents met at the hood of the Yukon and Kate Silver took the lead.

'How's Adama?'

It did not surprise Grace that Jabari was Silver's first thought. She and the older Ethiopian agent had been regular partners since the formation of Alpha Team, just as Wrixon and the absent Salvatore Gallo had, and more recently Grace herself with Shui Dai. It was natural that she would be concerned for her friend.

'He's through the worst of it,' Grace replied. 'He'll be out of action for a few months but he'll be back. It won't slow him down.'

'Nothing ever does.' There was a real sense of relief in Silver's voice. An affection she made no attempt to disguise. 'I can't believe someone got the drop on him.'

'It was just bad luck. Our focus was elsewhere.'

'And the shooter?'

'Dead.' The answer came from Wrixon. 'You're welcome.'

Silver glanced towards the Kentuckian as he spoke, then back to Grace without a reply. It was a look of disdain Grace had seen her use before, almost always with Wrixon. Grace did not know the cause but, uniquely among the agents of Alpha Team, there was no love lost between the two.

Grace ignored the silent exchange and instead focused on what Silver could tell her.

'Dempsey tells me you're fully briefed on this one.'

'On the subject of Maria Frankowski generally,' Grace replied. 'But on this particular location, not so much.'

'So you don't know the connection between the mark and this place either, then?'

'No. But Dempsey seems certain she's here. That this is where she'd run. So is he right?'

'We can't say,' Silver replied. 'We've been here for nearly two hours, including an hour before sundown. No one has come in or out and there's been no sign of Frankowski or the kids outside of the main building, from what we can see of it. If they're here, they've got to be inside. And we have no eyes in there.'

'Then I guess I knock on the front door and ask.'

'And what? Assuming she *is* there, you think she'll just trust that you are who you say you are?'

'She will when I tell her who sent me.'

THIRTY-NINE

The drive from the gates of the Golden Calf Ranch to its main residence was like a country road all of its own. Long and meandering, it took a full three minutes at twenty miles per hour for the Yukon to snake its way through pitch-black fields and small hills.

At almost 9 p.m. and forty minutes past sunset, Grace could only imagine what the surrounding land must have looked like in the light of day. In her mind she could picture only reruns of *Dallas*. One of her mother's favourite shows, it had ended not long after Grace was born but old episodes were rarely absent from their TV screen at home.

Grace's idea of ranch life came entirely from there. Images of multi-millionaires playing at being cowboys on miles of perfect green fields, all of it hemmed in by exquisitely maintained white fences. Totally divorced from reality, most likely. And yet so strong in her mind that, in the darkness, Grace could picture little else.

At least until her SUV peaked the first hill and she spotted the house.

The main residence looked nothing like the fictional Southfork homestead. The building was enormous. Too big for a family of twenty, let alone a father and daughter alone.

Built from dark materials without a hint of white wood anywhere, it was only as Grace came nearer that she could see the details. The property was most likely made of brick, but with exterior wooden panelling that made it more resemble timber. The centre of the residence lay directly ahead, three floors high and with an equally huge wing jutting off at either side. Together, they framed a large, circular driveway that led in from and then back out to the road that Grace was still on, with an offshoot heading out to a series of massive buildings that were barely illuminated in the distance.

Stables and barns, Grace guessed. *A real working ranch.*

The sheer scale of the properly distracted Grace as she neared and so at first she did not notice the large male figure exiting the central door to the main house and walking in the direction of her vehicle. And even when she *did* see him seconds later, it was dark enough that it took another moment to register the long metal and walnut object he was holding at waist level.

Grace brought the Yukon to a stop at the far end of the main driveway, still thirty yards from the approaching figure. Any closer could seem like a threat, she feared, and that would have been unhelpful in the circumstances.

Grace got out of the car slowly, her eyes focused on the long, ornate shotgun in the man's thick, weather-damaged hands. She raised her arms to shoulder height, palms facing forwards in the air. It was the clearest possible signal that she offered no threat.

'YOU DON'T NEED THAT, SIR.'

Grace shouted the words with care, determined that nothing she said would be misunderstood or would go unheard.

'You reckon not?'

The answer was loud in turn, but not quite a shout. The man raised the weapon to his shoulder, the lethal end of the barrel now trained directly on the trespasser.

'You wanna tell me why I should believe that from a

stranger I find driving on my property in the middle of the night?'

Grace kept her hands held high as she replied.

'All due respect, Major Burton, but it's only nine p.m.'

A quizzical look passed across David Burton's gnarled but still handsome face. It lasted no time at all. When he spoke again, it was with no hint of uncertainty.

'Who told you to call me that?'

'Call you what?'

'What you just said. Who told you to call me Major Burton?'

'Your military jacket, sir. I'm with the International Security Bureau. I was briefed on you on the way down here from Manhattan, exactly as you'd expect. Which means I know that you're Major David Burton, US Marine Corps, sir.'

'That was a long time ago you're talking about, missy. A lifetime and more.'

'Marine Corps is for life, Major. My father taught me that.'

'Your daddy serve?'

'SEAL Team Six, sir.'

'That's impressive credentials, if that's true. Gotta say, though, I've met a whole lot more people claiming to be SEALS than there ever was space for 'em.'

'So have I, sir.'

'How do I know you're not one of them?'

'How many of the fake ones died under fire, Major?'

Burton ignored the question, instead throwing in another one of his own.

'Where'd you say you were from again?'

'The ISB, Major. United Nations intelligence service.'

'Strange job for an American.'

'Plenty of us there, sir. Seemed the logical step for me after the Secret Service.'

Burton lowered the shotgun just slightly. Not enough that a discharge would be any less fatal, but enough to suggest he was listening.

'You were with the service?'

'Presidential Protection.'

'And now you're international? A UN spy?'

'Covert intelligence operative.'

'Tomato, tomato.'

'I guess.'

Burton nodded his head as he considered what he had just been told. For a moment Grace felt his hostility lessen. A heartbeat later and it was back as he pulled the shotgun butt into his shoulder.

'All sounds pretty damn convenient, missy. If you'd done your homework and you were looking to impress a man like me, you're saying all the right things.'

'I can't help that, Major. It is what it is and I am who I am.'

'So just what the hell do you want?'

'I need to speak to Maria, Major.'

'Maria who?'

'Maria Frankowski, Major. Formerly Maria Parker.'

'Never heard of her. Either of 'em.'

'I doubt that, sir.'

'You know how little I care about what you do and don't doubt? I could tell you, but then I wouldn't be much of a gentleman.'

'This is very important, Major. This is life and death.'

'My privacy's important, too, missy. And the sanctity of my personal property is important. *They* could be life and death, too, if you play this wrong. So time's past now for you to get off this land.'

Grace could see that she was getting nowhere. Whether Dempsey was right or wrong about Maria's presence at the ranch, David Burton had no intention of playing along. And Grace knew far too little about the guy to gauge how she could change that.

Maybe next time Dempsey could help a little more with getting past the gun-toting gatekeeper.

Grace dismissed the complaint and instead focused on the problem. She would not allow the first obstacle to beat her, even if that obstacle did have a lethal weapon pointed right at her. She would try another tactic.

'I was sent here by Joe Dempsey, Major.'

The reference to Dempsey was a Hail Mary. Grace had no idea if the name would mean anything to Burton; Dempsey had not suggested that it would. She had been saving it for Maria herself, the one person she *knew* would respond to it.

But she caught the fleeting glimpse of startled recognition on the man's face. He knew Dempsey's name. And he hadn't expected to hear it.

Encouraged, Grace continued:

'Dempsey believes that Maria and her children are in danger. Imminent danger. He sent me and my team to protect you all, sir. And he told me to mention the Carlisle Hotel in New York to Maria. He said if I did that, she would know I really was sent by him.'

'I don't know what the hell that means, lady. And I've never heard of anyone called Dempsey or anyone called Maria Frankowski. But I *have* had just about enough of this. It's time you got your ass—'

'I'm sorry, sir, but I don't believe you. You recognised Dempsey's name when you just heard it. I saw it in your eyes. You know who I'm talking about. You know Maria too, and you know that she's in danger. Now please, stop this charade and let us help you.'

'I won't tell you again, there is no Maria.'

'Sir, we don't have time for this.' Grace's voice was raised in growing desperation. 'Maria doesn't know this but the people she's running from, they already came for her. Back in Park Ridge this afternoon, after she'd fled the house. It's only a matter of time before they end up here, too.'

'And how do I know they ain't already?' Burton took a step forwards, the shotgun now held rock-steady. 'How do I know that's not who *you* are?'

'Because she wouldn't know to use Joe's name, Daddy. And she wouldn't know about the Carlisle. No one would.'

The new voice was soft but confident. And somehow, as it carried across the hot evening air, it calmed the anger that had threatened to ignite.

Grace turned her head in the direction of the speaker and she knew in an instant that she was looking at Maria Frankowski.

Dressed down in a pair of beaten-up jeans and a checked shirt made for someone twice her size, the woman's long, thick hair cascaded down her back and her hazel-green eyes seemed to pierce right through Grace as she looked at her intently. Grace was taken aback by the reality of her physical appearance, mentally comparing it against the picture from the doctor's file. That photo had been of an attractive woman but it did not do Maria justice.

Slightly shorter than Grace herself, Frankowski was also a little thicker set. Her build suggested the ranch-honed strength that would be useful in her chosen career as a trauma surgeon, and yet that obvious power took nothing away from her femininity.

Dempsey had never described Maria physically – he had said very little about her at all – but Grace did not need his confirmation to know that this was the woman he had loved.

The *only* woman.

'You're Maria.' It was not a question.

'For my sins. Or maybe for someone else's.'

Grace stepped forwards and held out her hand.

'I'm Eden Grace. I work with Dempsey. I'm also . . . well, we're—'

'I'm happy to meet you, Eden.' Maria took Grace's hand and shook it. 'How did . . . how did he know I needed help?'

Grace was unsure of how much she should disclose. Of what Dempsey would want Maria to know.

'It's, erm, it's a case we've been working on. He connected some dots and, you know . . .'

'But he didn't come himself?'

'No, ma'am. He couldn't. He's in Europe.'

'In The Hague?'

'Yes,' Grace confirmed. She could not tell a direct lie. Not if she wanted Maria to trust her. 'But he still wanted you protected, so he sent me. Me and the rest of his unit, in fact.'

'So you're with the ISB, then?'

'How do you know that?'

'I heard you introduce yourself to my father. But I already knew where Joe was working.' Maria's eyes shifted guiltily towards Burton. 'Daddy always stayed interested in him.'

Burton looked back sharply.

'Just me, was it?'

Maria said nothing.

'Well, OK then. Just me.' He turned to Grace. 'I liked the guy. He was a real man. Shoot me for wishing good things for my girl.'

'And yet you never mentioned Agent Grace, did you, Daddy?' Maria shifted her focus back to Grace. 'For what it's worth, I'm happy he has you.'

For a heartbeat Grace found herself confused. Then she realised Maria's meaning.

'No, no, that's not what I meant earlier,' she rushed to explain. 'We're not ... Dempsey and I ... I'm engaged to someone else. We're friends, that's all I meant. Dempsey's my friend. And so he's told me about you, Maria. Not a lot but ... you know ...'

For just a moment Maria was silent, but the look of relief on her face was unmistakable.

'I know,' she finally said. 'He doesn't say much, does he? So if he's told you *anything* then yeah, you must be friends.'

Grace was relieved to have cleared up the misunderstanding. With the awkward moment over, her mind returned to the mission.

She turned to David Burton.

'Sir, I'm sorry if I got under your skin just then. I couldn't—'

'You were obeying orders. No explanation needed.'

Grace gave a grateful smile.

'But,' Burton continued, 'what I do need to know is what danger my girl's in. And my grandsons. What's coming our way?'

Grace took a deep breath and instinctively looked into

the distance. Towards where she knew Dai, Silver and Wrixon were waiting. Then she turned back to face both Maria and Burton.

'Truth is, sir, we don't yet know who it is. But we *do* know what they're willing to do. And we need to be ready.'

FORTY

Vic Sethi glanced at his watch as he silently approached the main entrance to the Gezellig Appartements, nestled in the heart of the Escamp district of the city.

It was 3 a.m.

The hour gave Sethi some increased confidence but he knew there was no safe time for what he and his two companions were here to do. Not in The Hague's most heavily populated neighbourhood, and sure as hell not while the city remained on high alert.

For all that, there was far less that could go wrong here and now than there had been at the Grote Markt. There were two targets this last time and there were no other obstructions. No crowds of civilians. No potential heroes. No swarms of cell phones.

And no need to make it look like anything but murder.

It was a logistical cakewalk in comparison to their last assignment. But still Sethi remained nervous, his heart rate raised more than was usual.

The Monk had warned him of the danger posed by Joe Dempsey. A man perhaps more lethal than Sethi himself, he had said. And while that suggestion would always be a challenge to an operative with Sethi's ego, the rational portion of his mind had overcome those adolescent instincts and forced him to listen. Sethi had never known the Monk to be afraid of anyone or anything; problems were never more than obstacles to the man, there to be overcome.

But this time he had sounded genuinely concerned.

And if he's *worried about the guy*, Sethi had rationalised, *then there must be good reason.*

It had unsettled Sethi enough to spend the next hour on due diligence, researching his target as best he could. What little he found did not assuage his anxiety.

After years spent operating in his dark and dangerous world, Sethi had built up contacts and sources of intelligence that were second to none. Or at least that was what he had believed them to be, until tonight.

His inability to find any meaningful information on Joe Dempsey had changed that belief. And it worried him deeply. Dempsey's bare record of employment had been easy enough to locate, but it had told him next to nothing. All Sethi had learned was that he had been employed by the UN's International Security Bureau since 2018, before which he had been with the British Department of Domestic Security and before that the British Army.

There was nothing more.

No citations.

No awards.

No medals.

Nothing.

The complete absence of detail, even within the security-cleared databases to which Sethi had access, told him two things:

Dempsey's a covert agent.

And he operates at a level so high that even I can't access it.

The realisation was frightening. Sethi could admit that to himself alone. But with fear came something else. Something that had been missing on the more routine assignments that made up his recent working life.

It was accompanied by exhilaration.

Few men were as skilled as Sethi with a bladed weapon. Fewer still with a gun. And tactically he was yet to meet his equal. But what really set him apart, he believed, was the sheer joy he found in his work. Vic Sethi loved what he did – he revelled in it – and he was never more alive than when a job carried an air of genuine danger.

Joe Dempsey was dangerous. He was a challenge. And Sethi was determined to enjoy it.

He turned to Porthos and Athos behind him, reassuring himself that his back-up was still close at hand. It was an unnecessary safety check. They had already proved themselves reliable. That he did it at all just reminded Sethi of his own uncertainty.

He forced a confident smile, then turned his attention back to the glass door ahead of him.

The Gezellig Appartements had been secured at Dempsey's request by admin staff at the International Court of Justice, an organ of the United Nations that was based in The Hague. The Monk had told him that information at the same time as he had provided the number and exact layout of the apartment in which the UN had lodged Dempsey and his friend. As ever, Sethi did not ask the source of his employer's intelligence.

He just accepted it as accurate.

It always was.

He looked back over his shoulder again, this time with purpose. He needed Athos for what had to happen next because, of the three, Athos was the least physically distinct: his average height wasn't remarkable compared to Sethi's memorable five-foot-two and Porthos's looming six-four. That fact alone made him less likely to be recognisable on any camera footage that might cover the building's lobby.

'Knock on the window.'

Sethi indicated to the building's sliding glass door as he gave Athos his instruction. It was the sole entrance to the apartment block and it lay just a few feet ahead of them, beyond the wall that for now provided much-needed cover.

He took off his own oversized baseball cap as Athos stepped past him. He wore it to hide his joora – the topknot of hair that his religion forbade him to cut – when he wanted to avoid 'short Sikh guy' as an immediate description. But right now it was Athos who needed a disguise.

Sethi reached up and pulled the cap onto the younger man's head.

'Get the guard's attention. And keep your face down.'

Athos did as he was told, expertly affecting the common gait of a 3 a.m. arrival: a young man who had enjoyed the surrounding bars a little too much. It was well done, and for all the faux-intoxication he was still careful to expose little of his face to the lobby door. By keeping his eyes down, he increased the cover provided by the cap's brim.

'Hey, man?' Athos's drunk US accent was perfect – Californian, Sethi noticed – as he called through the glass to the lobby's night guard. 'Hey, buddy? Hey? I lost my key, man.'

Sethi and Porthos stayed out of sight, just behind Athos. Each had a blade in their right hand and a balaclava in their left, ready to use the moment the door was opened.

'C'mon, buddy. You gonna let me in or what?'

Sethi kept his eyes fixed on Athos's back, looking for some physical indication that he was getting the desired response from inside. It came almost immediately. He could tell from the tightening of the traps around his neck that Athos was preparing to move.

The guard must be coming.

Sethi pulled his balaclava onto his head. A glance over his shoulder confirmed that Porthos had done the same.

The next few seconds moved as if in slow motion, every detail playing out exactly as it already had in Sethi's mind.

The door slid open and the night guard stepped out. He was a large black man – not as tall as Porthos, but half again the width. No doubt one of the countless immigrant workers who filled the service industry night-shifts that were less attractive to the local population.

The night guard's grin disappeared in an instant as his eyes drifted past Athos and to his two companions, both of them with their faces now hidden by their masks.

His eyes snapped back just as Athos thrust his knife straight upwards at a speed too fast to avoid. It entered the man's broad chest at dead centre, forcing him backwards and into the far side of the door frame as his knees gave way.

Sethi was already moving, ready to act if the lobby was occupied by anyone else. Once inside he saw that it was not – the building's reception area was deserted – but that did not rule out danger. He headed straight for the desk and, beyond it, the complex's back office.

Ten seconds later and Sethi was back, fresh blood wiped off his blade and onto his black trousers.

'How many back there?' Porthos asked.

'Just one,' Sethi replied.

'No alarm triggered?'

'She didn't even have the lobby displayed on a screen. She didn't see me coming.'

Athos – now wearing a balaclava of his own, to hide his features from the lobby cameras – stepped through the open doorway and into the wide reception area. Sethi pointed towards the guard's body as soon as he saw him.

'Drag him into the back room and dump him with her. Then close and lock that front door and turn off all the alarms and all cameras. I want to have this over and the three of us clear in eight minutes. Understood?'

Porthos and Athos nodded and got on with their task.

Everything was going to plan.

FORTY-ONE

Appartement 3B was on the third floor of the building. It was the second of five serviced flats that occupied the corridor to the right of the lift that Sethi and his team had not used.

Determined to keep noise to a minimum and to avoid the death-trap that an elevator could prove to be, Sethi had instead deactivated all staircase alarms from within the building's ground-floor control room. He had then led Porthos and Athos up the short three flights that would take them to Dempsey's floor.

The three had moved quickly. Barely three minutes had passed since the death of the night guard and already they were outside the door of 3G. All well within the time frame that Sethi had set for their assignment.

Sethi's heart raced as he approached the locked door, his adrenaline heightening every sense better than any drug. He kept his excitement in check as he positioned himself on one side of the entrance, his two companions on the other.

He gave a silent instruction for both men to draw their pistols. Up to now they had been dealing with civilians, making bladed weapons both preferable and sufficient.

Preferable because they avoid making any noise that would warn Dempsey of what was coming.

And sufficient because ... well, that speaks for itself.

From this point, though, things were different. Even with time and surprise on their side and as unlikely as it was that they would meet resistance, with Dempsey they could take no risks.

His reputation demanded their respect and there was too much riding on his death.

With his own SIG M17 already drawn and a universal room key in his free hand, Sethi gestured for Porthos to take position in the centre of the doorway. The tall Irishman did as he was instructed, his weapon raised to meet any threat that might lurk on the other side of the apartment's entrance.

Seconds later and they were inside.

The door had opened with only the barest click to indicate the release of the electronic locking mechanism. Otherwise there was silence as first Sethi, then Athos and finally Porthos made their way into the short corridor that separated the various daytime areas on the left-hand side, and the flat's three bedrooms on the right.

The Monk's briefing had been thorough and the layout of the apartment was exactly as he had described. It gave Sethi confidence in the final piece of intelligence he had imparted: which man was sleeping in which room.

Coming to a halt outside the first of the two closed doors, Sethi indicated for Athos to pass him and head to the far end of the hallway. To the room that was occupied by the lawyer. Porthos had already stopped just beyond the apartment entrance, in position in case anything went wrong and either target made it into the hallway.

Sethi took a moment to examine his chosen doorway: Dempsey's room.

It opened inwards, just as the Monk said it would. That was helpful. It would allow him and Athos to synchronise their entry, without the risk of fumbling a handle and causing even a moment's delay before they could fire.

With the hinges on the inside, all it would take was a well-placed kick to the locking mechanism.

Sethi stepped back. A short stride, just enough to create clear space between himself and the door. He glanced to his left, to confirm that Athos had done the same. Then to his right, to ensure that Porthos was ready.

Satisfied, Sethi faced his own doorway once more, lifted his pistol and took a long, deep breath. It was calming. It also gave him a moment to think. Time to consider what the Monk had said about Dempsey. The memory of his employer's warning made him smile.

He held up his left hand, closed into a fist. Then he raised his index finger.

One.

His middle finger.

Two.

And finally his ring finger.

Three.

On the pre-agreed signal, Sethi and Athos stepped forwards and kicked the doors that faced them. Each crashed open, though the sound of that destruction was instantly drowned out by deafening gunfire.

Dempsey was exactly where the Monk had said he would be in relation to the entrance, his bed straight ahead and butted against the rear wall. It provided a target that Sethi could not miss.

The first three of Sethi's shots hit in quick succession, fast enough that he did not register anything unusual about the impact.

It was not until the fourth round that he sensed something was wrong.

And the sixth that he registered what that was.

It's too soft.

That's not ...

Sethi's thought process went no further, the bite of cold metal against his temple demanding his full attention. His grip on his pistol loosened with dread, just as the sound of gunfire from the other room came to an end.

In the sudden silence, whoever was holding the pistol uttered the last words Sethi would ever hear.

'You try to kill a man in his sleep, you better be damn sure *where* he sleeps.'

FORTY-TWO

A single 9mm round tore through the small man's temple, decorating the room's far wall with the contents of his skull. There was no question the shot was fatal and so no need to check his vital signs. Not that Dempsey had time to do so.

A lifetime of violence had immunised Dempsey against the paralysing effects of surrounding gunfire and so his mind was working clearly. He analysed the situation as effectively as he would in exam conditions.

His conclusion was both immediate and certain.

The dead man's unusual physique matched one of the Grote Markt shooters.

The body had barely touched the floor as Dempsey spun round to face the open bedroom door and dropped to one knee, all within a heartbeat of his first shot.

As fast as he was, he was only just in time. He had barely felt his kneecap hit the thin carpet when a second figure appeared in the broken doorway. He was dressed identically to the first man, all in black with his face covered by a balaclava and his pistol raised.

And like the smaller man, he was also too slow.

Two shots took him down the instant he entered Dempsey's line of fire. One round to the chest. One round to the head. Both unquestionably fatal.

Dempsey was moving towards the doorway even as the second shot hit its target. The likelihood of at least a third assailant was high. Someone to cover the main entrance.

He paused in the hallway to peer around the corner and

avoid running headlong into a barrage of bullets. As he did, he caught sight of another man escaping through the apartment's main door.

He had chosen to run, which suggested to Dempsey that he was the last man in the apartment. Were he not, standing his ground as part of a crossfire was by far the safer course. As a professional, he would know that. Just as Dempsey did.

Dempsey made the assessment so quickly that he was already running before the thought had settled, exiting the flat in time to see the fire door at the end of the corridor closing. It made a clear shot impossible and so Dempsey could only sprint towards it, covering the ground in little more than a second before bursting through into the lift foyer, his pistol raised to meet any resistance.

There was none. Just the sight of a second exit marked staircase, its door already drifting shut. The sound of footsteps came from just beyond.

Dempsey was through the door in a flash and heading down the bare, concrete staircase three steps at a time. His target was moving just as fast; he could tell that from the sounds ahead. Spurred on by a desperate will to live, the man was moving like a springbok. But Dempsey was relentless. He did not slow for a moment as the floors passed by at speed.

The gunman would reach the lobby first. Dempsey knew that, and so he knew he had to be close enough for a clear shot before the man could escape through the main glass door and into the night.

The guy was fast and Dempsey had not gained an inch in the chase. But neither had he lost one, and as he burst through the lobby doors he raised his Glock and aimed at the fleeing man's back as he hurtled towards the entrance.

He was ready to fire in that instant.

Until he saw he did not need to.

The fleeing man had come to an abrupt stop in front of the glass sliding doors, skidding to a halt to prevent a collision.

The doors did not open automatically as Dempsey had assumed they would. Perhaps they were routinely locked at night. Or perhaps they had been deactivated by his attackers, to secure the building against any surprises during the botched attempt on his life.

Whatever the reason, it left his prey helpless.

'HANDS UP AND TURN ROUND.'

Dempsey studied the gunman's body language, fully prepared to be ignored. The man was tall and he seemed slim through his nondescript clothing. Athletic, too; he had moved fast and yet he was breathing easy.

'I SAID HANDS UP.'

This time Dempsey's instructions were followed. The gunman lifted his hands to shoulder height. One of them was empty. The other carried a Glock 19 identical to Dempsey's own.

'NOW TURN.'

The gunman did as he was told. His movement was slow and deliberate. Taken with care. In seconds he was facing Dempsey, only his eyes and the bridge of his nose visible beneath his black balaclava.

'DROP THE GUN.'

This was where the obedience stopped. He shook his head, slowly and deliberately. The pistol stayed held in the air. It posed no threat – its barrel was closer to the gunman's own skull than it was to any part of Dempsey – but its very presence caused the stand-off to continue.

'DROP THE GUN,' Dempsey bellowed again, 'OR I DROP YOU.'

'Knock yourself out, fella.' The man spoke in an Irish accent. 'Easier for me that way.'

The response was not what Dempsey had expected. The tone of resignation indicated a man who had reached his end.

'This is your last chance.' This time Dempsey spoke instead of shouting. 'Drop the damn gun.'

'It's not happening, man. You do what you have to do.'

Dempsey shifted his grip on the pistol but he made no attempt to fire. Not yet.

Not while there were things he could learn.

He took a step forwards.

'Who are you working for?'

'No chance.'

'One way or the other, you're gonna tell me.'

'You think?'

'I know.'

'No. No you don't.'

Dempsey took another step. They were now separated by half the width of the lobby. Four metres, maybe a little less.

'Just give me a name.'

'You know what would happen if I did? I've got people that matter to me. He knows that. And he knows who they are.'

Who is he?

Dempsey wanted to ask the question, but at the same time he could not allow his ignorance to make him seem weak. Not with the promise he was about to make. If it was going to work, he needed to seem in complete control.

'I can protect you from him,' Dempsey promised. 'He's nothing to be afraid of. I can protect you. I can protect you all.'

'Like bollocks you can.' The Irishman's voice carried no trace of doubt. 'But *I* can protect *them*.'

Dempsey tightened his grip as he heard the words. The telltale tremor in the man's gun hand had caught his eye. It was a precursor to movement he had seen many times and so he was sure of what was coming next.

The Irishman was going to draw down and force Dempsey to kill him in self-defence. Suicide by cop, they called it. It gave Dempsey hope; he was sure he could take the man down without killing him, and before a shot was fired in his direction.

He was wrong, because the Irishman had surmised the same thing. And so he took the quicker route.

Before Dempsey could react he had shifted the pistol the bare two inches to his own brow and, with not even an instant of hesitation, he fired a single round into his own temple.

There would be no need for a second.

FORTY-THREE

G race followed the sound of hushed conversation through
the warren of the Burton homestead.

She could make out three voices. Two of them she
recognised: Maria Frankowski and David Burton. The third
she did not but as the speaker was twice as fast as the others
and several octaves higher, Grace concluded that it must be
David Burton's thirteen-year-old daughter, Leisha.

The main building of the ranch was both huge and
labyrinthine – it gave even the White House a run for its money
in the latter category as Grace struggled to find her way around,
and tactically that was a negative. The isolated location of the
residence gave them the advantage, sure: long, clear views in
every direction made an unseen approach nearly impossible.
But the sheer size of the place was a double-edged sword.

If any hostiles *did* reach the building, there were not enough
agents in Alpha Team to defend each point of access.

Thankfully this was unlikely to be a problem for tonight.
Whoever was coming after Maria and her family, they would
not find this place *that* soon.

And after that, Grace told herself, *the ISB will fill the place
with reinforcements. By 10 a.m. tomorrow morning, this place will
be damn near impregnable.*

The voices grew in volume with every few steps Grace
took and in seconds she had found them, in a room she entered
via a short flight of three steps. It was a kitchen, Grace realised
as she stepped inside. And a working one at that. The lack
of ornate furnishings and the industrial-sized appliances

set it apart from every other room she had seen in the house so far.

'You guys hiding in here?'

Her question stopped their conversation in its tracks. David Burton looked irritated by the interruption, though he tried his best to hide it. And the girl – his younger daughter, Leila, Grace assumed, though she was tall and pale with fuzzy brown hair and not a single feature in common with her sister – seemed merely curious at the new arrival.

Grace absorbed these details instantly, but her main focus was on Maria. She seemed more downbeat than when they had parted company just thirty minutes earlier.

'Is everything OK?' Grace asked. 'Has something happened?'

Maria forced a smile in reply to the question. It was an act. Grace could see that. But it was a good one.

'It's as good as it can be, Eden,' Maria replied. Her voice was neutral and steady. Which left it at odds with the emotion Grace could see in her eyes. 'It's not ideal, what's happening. But we'll come out the other side.'

'You sure there haven't been developments I should know about?'

'Does there need to be?' David snapped. He seemed less friendly than when Grace had left him. 'Her husband's put her and her boys in danger before turning tail God knows where. Lady's entitled to a moment, ain't she?'

'Daddy, I told you, he ran because I told him to run.'

'No offence, sweetheart, but a man don't go hide on no one else's say-so.' Burton turned to Grace. 'You think Joe Dempsey would have run?'

Grace held Burton's gaze for a moment. She knew the

answer. They all did. But giving it would hardly be helpful. Finally she turned back to Maria.

'All I know is that you're dealing with this better than anyone could expect. Especially when you've got the boys to worry about, too. I won't lie, I expected to find you a wreck.'

'A wreck doesn't keep my kids safe,' Maria replied. 'That's all that matters to me.'

'That's exactly why *we're* here. For them *and* for you. You're not in this alone.'

Maria smiled again. Only this time it seemed genuine.

'Is everyone settled in?' she asked. A very deliberate change of subject. 'Your team, I mean?'

'As much as they can be, in the circumstances.'

'Are the bunks not comfortable?'

'Yes, of course. What I meant was that we can't *get* settled. Not on an assignment like this. We're taking shifts, two agents at a time. One inside, one outside. To make sure the perimeter and the interior are secure. That's what I came to tell you: that you shouldn't be concerned if you see one of us stalking the halls, because we'll be doing it all night.'

'You think your numbers are enough?'

Grace shifted her attention to Burton, who had asked the question. A military man, he had no doubt reached the correct conclusion already. Grace had no intention of lying.

'No, sir. No, I don't. Not long-term, anyway. But we'll rectify that first thing in the morning. For tonight it's all we've got.'

'And if something happens tonight?'

'It won't. The only way *we* traced Maria here was through Dempsey.'

'Who's Dempsey?' Leisha chimed in.

Grace had almost forgotten Burton's other daughter was present.

'Never mind,' Maria said, answering her sister without a glance.

'He your ex, M? Is he stalking you?'

'No, Leisha,' Maria answered firmly, 'he's not stalking me. He's just looking out for me. Making sure I'm safe.'

'Sounds like stalking to me. Does Kon know about this guy?'

'I told you it's not important.'

Grace could tell from the snap in Maria's final answer that her emotions were nearing the surface. But Leisha was little more than a child and could plainly read none of the same signs. She opened her mouth to speak again. This time she was beaten to it by her father.

'Leisha, you've been told. Now get your backside up to bed.'

'But Daddy—'

'Now, young lady.'

There was no room for argument when he barked the final orders. Nor was there any chance that Leisha would disobey. She jumped out of her seat and headed out the door as the final word left his lips.

'I'm sorry.' Burton reached out and gripped Maria's shoulder. 'She's just a kid.'

He turned back to Grace.

'You were saying?'

'I was saying that we only knew to come here because Dempsey knew of the connection between you two,' Grace replied. 'No one else could possibly work that out so fast. So I'm as sure as I can be that we're good for tonight.'

'That's what I thought too,' Maria said. 'That's why we came here. I wouldn't have put Daddy and Leisha at risk. Not if I thought they could find us. I figured we could disappear here for weeks if we had to. But then you showed up. And as welcome as you are, now I'm not so sure we should be here. Maybe it *is* too easy to track me to here.'

'It's not, trust me,' Grace reassured her. 'I don't consider myself a novice when it comes to background checks and I couldn't find anything to explain why Dempsey was sending us here. Anyone else is going to have the same trouble.'

She paused, hesitant to ask her next question.

'Do you mind me asking why that is? Why there is literally nothing to connect the two of you? Leisha's the only child you've got on record.'

'That's because Maria's not my biological daughter.' Burton pulled Maria closer as he spoke. As if to reassure her despite his words. 'Neither is Leisha. Maria's mother Susan and I, we weren't married. We got together when Maria was three years old. There was no other man in the picture so, as far as I'm concerned, I'm her daddy. Even if I'm not her father. Always been that way.'

'But you all lived here together for decades?'

'That's right.'

'So how is there no record at all? This would have been Susan's registered address? Maria's school file would have the Golden Calf as her residence at least, surely?'

Burton and Maria looked at one another. An unspoken exchange that resulted in a silent decision.

'My service,' Burton began, 'was not one hundred per cent typical.'

'Meaning?'

'Meaning that a lot of people would have liked to see me dead for the things I did for my country. We don't need to say more than that, just that I got some protection as a result. When Maria was young, we were kept off the radar. No records. No voter roll. No licences in my name, even. That's why me and Susan didn't get married either. All those years when Maria should have been connected to me, there was no trace of me to connect to. Ain't true no more; any enemies I had are long gone. But back then? Yeah.'

Grace nodded. Now she understood. And she was intrigued by the growing similarities between Maria's father and her former fiancé.

'And Leisha?'

'Daughter of a couple who worked for me for years and years. Good people, her father was from my old unit. They died in a car wreck when she was eight months old. Leisha came out without a scratch, no one else made it. Poor kid had no family left, so what else could we do? We took her in.'

'But you formally adopted her?'

'I did. I've always regretted that I couldn't with Maria.' Burton glanced towards his older daughter as he said the words. 'But it was Susan who insisted. Before we could do it, she got sick. And she went quick, before we could do anything, but she made me promise. She made me swear I'd be Leisha's official father. So that's what I did.'

'Hence why we could connect you to Leisha but not to Maria.'

'Silver lining to every cloud, Agent Grace.'

'Please, sir. It's Eden.'

'It's only Eden if I'm David. Agreed?'

Grace reached out for the hand that Burton had offered.

'No spit to seal the deal?' she asked.

'This ain't a John Wayne movie, Eden.'

Burton's hand was predictably calloused and powerful as Grace shook it. She almost commented on the fact, but before she could say another word she felt the phone in her pocket vibrate.

An instant later and the handset was in her hand, a single name displayed across its screen.

Dempsey.

FORTY-FOUR

Dempsey was alone in the office that sat just off the Gezellig Appartements lobby. He had respectfully covered the two corpses he had found there – both employees of the complex – but had left them otherwise untouched. Their forensic examination would come later. But right now he needed the space for himself.

It had been almost twenty minutes since he had dealt with the three men who had been sent to kill him. The sound of gunfire had woken the entire building. Probably most of the surrounding neighbourhood, too. It was inevitable that so many of the apartment's residents would find their way downstairs to investigate, and that most would immediately call the police.

It was also unnecessary, because Dempsey had made that emergency call within seconds of the Irishman firing the final bullet.

The Hague's law enforcement night shift had arrived shortly after. Dempsey had just had enough time to call Michael, who was alone in an apartment in a separate, unconnected complex across the street. Dempsey had moved them both there within ten minutes of their arrival at the Gezellig Appartements, as soon as he was satisfied that the UN driver had left.

The move had been an extra precaution. One that Dempsey had hoped was overkill. He had wanted the United Nations team to be reliable. For them to be trustworthy. But he was also a realist. The attempt on Will Duffy's life could only have been ordered by someone with inside information: how else would they have even known he had survived the Grote Markt attack?

Combined with the corruption of at least one FBI agent in the US and the inference was clear. Whoever they were up against, their tentacles were everywhere.

To ignore that would have been reckless, and so Dempsey had used the opportunity to test just how compromised they were.

The result was not what he had hoped, but it was better to know and to be disappointed than it was to be ignorant and dead. And besides, now he *did* know, the rules of the game had become clear.

Until this is over, we can only trust our own.

This was why his first call had been to Michael. With no idea who was compromised, Dempsey could risk neither the gathering crowd of residents nor the fast-approaching police presence. With no institution or organisation safe, he could not risk Michael turning up in response to the gunfire and finding himself in some unknown assassin's crosshairs.

Having warned his friend to steer clear, Dempsey had met the police alone. Their interaction had been quick. It took Dempsey ten minutes to explain what had happened, what they would find in the apartment upstairs and who they should call to confirm his status with the ISB. That speed was helped by the fact this was not the police officers' first experience with UN immunity; as a city in many ways dominated by the international organisation, the guys on duty had encountered it enough to know the drill.

It made the process painless.

With the debrief over and only the UN confirmation outstanding, Dempsey had retreated to the privacy of the back room to make the only call that mattered more than his warning to Michael.

Grace did not answer as quickly as he was used to and Dempsey found himself growing apprehensive as he heard the rare fourth ring. His nerves remained even as he heard the line come to life.

'Is everything OK?' he asked.

'Nice to hear from you too, Boss.'

'Is that a yes?'

'It's a yes.'

'So you're with Maria?'

'Literally. She's two feet from me. So is David. You gonna say hi?'

Dempsey hesitated. He had expected Grace to answer the phone alone; that she would know to step away before doing so. He had not considered the possibility of having to actually speak to Maria.

The thought made his stomach turn over. Something even the earlier gunfire had not achieved.

'Boss?'

Dempsey knew he had no choice.

'Put her on, Eden.'

He held his breath after saying Grace's name. And even though he was conscious of that reaction, he did not exhale until he heard the voice he had missed for a decade.

'Joe?'

One word. It was all it took to banish the anxiety.

'Maria. How are you?'

'How am I? I'm talking to you, aren't I? To Joe goddamn Dempsey? After . . . after everything. There's only one thing that could've made that happen.'

'World's gone to hell.'

'Precisely.'

'Look, I'm sorry about all this. I'm—'

'Why the hell are *you* sorry? It's the asshole I married who put his family at risk, not the asshole I *didn't* marry.'

Dempsey let the insult pass. He deserved it. And right now it did not matter.

'I know, but . . . well . . .'

'All I know, Joe, is that my boys and I are in danger. And somehow you've stepped up to protect us. So thank you. Because whatever else you are, you're the best man in the world for this job. Even if you're not here yourself.'

'I'd be there if I could.' Dempsey hesitated again, the clearest picture of Maria forming in his mind. An image he had avoided for so long. 'Or maybe it's best I'm not. But Eden and the team, they're as good as it gets. There's nothing I could add.'

'Well, that last part's bullshit and we both know it. But I'll swallow the rest. I know they must be good. You picked them.'

This time it was Maria who hesitated. When she spoke again her tone had changed. Dempsey realised that she had steeled herself to ask a question she knew she could not avoid.

'So tell me, Galahad. What kind of danger are we in here?'

Dempsey almost laughed at the sound of that name. Galahad. It was the nickname coined by his old friend James Turner – the man who would later call himself Joshua. He had used it with disdain, especially once their friendship had deteriorated into bloodshed.

But Maria? She used it because she had believed in it. She believed in *him*. That he could be more than he was. That he could be a protector instead of a killer. It had been Maria who had instilled that same belief into Dempsey himself. It had changed his life.

It had changed his very being.

Dempsey had forgotten that she had called him Galahad. It was one of a million details he had erased from his mind in order to live without her. Hearing it now brought back a thousand conversations at once. Thoughts that made him happier than he had any right to be.

But he had to put them aside. This was not the time for emotions. Right now, Maria was not Maria. She was an assignment. He could only protect her if he treated her as such.

He forced himself to focus on her question.

What kind of danger are we in?

'It's impossible to say. Maybe none at all. There's nothing anywhere to connect you to the ranch. You've got no social media presence at all, and even . . . even your husband's pages have nothing on them about the place.'

'Thanks to Daddy,' Maria replied. 'He wouldn't allow it. Told Kon he didn't want strangers and crazies looking at his private property.'

'The right call. Generally *and* for now. Which means there's nothing obvious to place you there. I assume there's still no paper trail connecting you? Nothing's changed?'

'Hang on.' The volume of Maria's voice increased. 'Daddy, is there any paperwork that has my name on it along with yours?'

'Just a will. Paper only. Sealed in a lawyer's office.'

'You hear that?' Maria asked.

'I did. It means you're going to be near impossible to find. We can't rule it out – that's why the team are there – but I don't see it. I don't think they can track you down.'

'But if they do? How bad would it be?'

'They won't be coming for a friendly chat. Not from what

I've seen. Until they find Kon, the danger is very real. You're bait, Maria. All three of you. And bait rarely sees the finish.'

'Thanks. That's real uplifting.'

'You wanted a lie?'

'If I did I'd have asked someone else.'

'You need to know the truth. But you also need to remember who's there for you. My team. They'll protect you if they have to. You, your sons. Everyone. Anyone comes for you, they have to go through Eden, through my team and through your dad. And trust me, Maria. No one's that good.'

'I do.' Maria's voice had lowered. 'I do trust you. Thank you.'

'Don't ever thank me. You never need to do that.'

'Whatever. It means a lot that you've got my back.'

'I'll do everything I can,' Dempsey promised. 'But right now I need to track down your husband. Do you have any idea where he is?'

'Not at the moment, no,' she said. 'I told him to get out of The Hague, but God knows if he even listened. If he makes contact, I'll let you know.'

'OK. Let's hope that happens. In the meantime, go get some rest. I need to speak to Eden.'

'OK, Major. Speak to you soon.'

Dempsey could picture a mock salute as Maria said the final words. It was something she used to do to tease him. The sadness in her voice made it very unlikely that she was doing the same thing now, but still, he enjoyed the image. The memory.

It did not last long, banished by Grace's voice.

'Boss.'

'Move away from them, Eden. Get out of earshot.'

Neither spoke for several seconds as Dempsey listened to the sound of movement.

'What's the problem?'

'Have you scoped out the whole residence yet?'

'Of course.'

'Which means you're planning to bring in reinforcements?'

'First thing, yeah.'

'Have you made the call?'

'No. We got here pretty late.'

'Good. I don't want you to do that. I want no one in this loop outside of Alpha Team.'

'Why not?'

'The UN's been compromised, Eden. The accommodation they arranged for us was just attacked.'

'Shit. Is everyone OK?'

'Not if "everyone" includes the guys who thought they had the jump on us.'

'Any survivors?'

'No. But I only took two of the three. The last one killed himself.'

'What? What the hell—'

'I know. Whoever's behind this, their own people would rather die than cross them. That takes a very particular kind of evil, and this one's got people everywhere. Your FBI guy today. My UN driver tonight. Even a guy in the hospital to mop up loose ends. That means they have embedded operatives on two different continents. And gunmen willing to fake a terrorist atrocity to cover up a murder.'

'Jesus Christ.'

'Exactly right. That's why we have to batten down the hatches. We trust ourselves and no one else from here on out. Understood?'

'Fully, Boss. But there's only one problem with that.'

'What?'

'There's no way four of us can defend this property. If they come in numbers, we don't win this.'

'Then there's only one thing for it.'

'Let me guess: you're gonna kill the sonofabitch before he ever gets anywhere near here?'

'Him and any fool dumb enough to follow him. No one's going to hurt her, Eden. No one.'

FORTY-FIVE

Michael took a mouthful of his thick, lukewarm black coffee and immediately winced. The taste was close to rancid, made worse by the slightly metallic tang that came from the open cuts within his mouth; a hangover from last night's action.

He had ordered the strongest brew the vendor sold, knowing how badly he needed a caffeine hit after the broken sleep of the night. But he had not counted on how extreme the Dutch sometimes took their java. The liquid that was now on his tongue was like nothing available back home. He was grateful, then, for the metal bin a few feet away.

Michael rubbed his hand across the stubble of his unshaved chin, mopping away the escaped residue of the unwelcome sludge he had just struggled to swallow. The aftertaste was just as bad as the actual, but at least his need for a stimulant had been banished. The shock of the coffee's flavour had broken through his sluggishness.

'No good?'

'Does it look like it was?' Michael answered. He pointed to the bottle of mineral water in Dempsey's hand. 'Here, let me have a sip of that. Get that bloody taste out of my mouth.'

Dempsey did as asked, handing the plastic container over with a smile. Michael took it gratefully and downed a slug before offering it back.

'Keep it,' Dempsey said. 'I'll pick up another one inside.'

Michael took another long sip by way of reply, his eyes staying fixed on his old friend as he did so. Dempsey, he had noticed, seemed as alert as he had yesterday, even before the christening. That fact fascinated the barrister. Here was a man who had enjoyed even less sleep than Michael last night, barely hours after a gun battle that had left three professional killers dead.

That's surely more than most agents achieve in a year, Michael surmised. *He does it all in one bloody night. And then he gets up in the morning, fresh as a daisy.*

The resentment he was feeling was light-hearted, but it *was* resentment. He pushed past it.

'Where are we meeting your man?' Michael asked.

'He's already upstairs,' Dempsey replied. 'He got here an hour ago.'

'And he's as good as you say?'

'There is no one on this planet I'd rather have protecting me,' Dempsey replied. 'Sal's a freak of nature. He's a near giant, but even for that size he's biblically strong. With him watching over Will, the only thing that could end his life is God himself.'

'He sounds . . . unique.'

'He is.'

Dempsey stepped into the hospital without another word and headed for the elevators.

Less than two minutes later and they were back in the main corridor of the ICU.

It was much quieter than it had been last night; it was no longer crawling with cops as they investigated the fallout of a shooting, and nor were there as many medics rushing from room to room. The aftermath of the Grote Markt attack was, it seemed, under some semblance of control. Michael guessed that those who had been teetering on the edge of death had either stabilised or passed.

It left all the focus on the survivors. On the people like Duffy.

The lack of visible staff gave them an unobstructed view into the unit, down to and beyond the door to Will Duffy's room. It was the direction Michael had instinctively looked the moment he'd exited the hospital lift and so he'd noticed the figure seated halfway along the corridor.

From the sheer scale of even just the upper half of his body, he could only be the man Dempsey had described.

Salvatore Gallo.

Michael and Dempsey walked shoulder to shoulder along the empty hallway, towards Duffy's room. Gallo had noticed them the moment they had stepped out of the elevator and as they came closer he began to rise to his feet. It was a slow process as he unfolded his unnaturally huge body upwards. The closer Michael came and the taller Gallo stood, the more the Irishman was aware of the Italian's immense stature.

'Boss. It is good to see you. Here, of all places, eh?'

Gallo thrust out an enormous hand as he spoke, his voice so deep and his accent so heavy that at first Michael thought it was an act. It was a fleeting instinct, dismissed as he observed the biggest hands he had ever seen engulf Dempsey's own.

'Good to see you too, Sal,' Dempsey said. 'And sorry for calling you in. I know it's supposed to be your vacation.'

'You would not if you did not need me, Boss. It's good.'

'Still. Lucia must want to kill me.'

'She will kill the bambinos first, without me there to distract them. Then perhaps my mother. Until then, you're safe.'

Dempsey smiled; he seemed grateful for Gallo's

understanding. Then he took back his hand and gestured towards Michael.

'Sal, I want you to meet Michael Devlin. Michael is more than a friend to me, OK? He's the closest thing I have to a brother.'

'I understand.'

Dempsey pointed towards Will Duffy's room.

'And that man in there, he's family to Michael. Which pretty much makes him my cousin. You follow?'

'You want me to look out for him as I would look out for your family.'

'Exactly.'

Dempsey placed a hand on Michael's shoulder and gently guided him forwards.

'And with that clear, Mikey, please meet Salvatore Gallo. One of the best men I've ever worked with.'

'And one of the biggest, I bet.' Michael grinned as he held out his own hand and felt it lost in Gallo's massive paw. 'A pleasure, Gallo.'

'Please, call me Sal. And please know, from his moment you have nothing to fear for your friend. Family is family, yes?'

'Exactly. And the man in there, he's—'

Michael was interrupted by the sound of an arriving elevator. He turned towards the noise and saw Sean Sutton step out and into the corridor. Unlike the previous evening, the younger of the two CIA men was alone.

Dempsey turned to Gallo.

'I have to deal with this guy, Sal. Then we'll speak more, OK?'

'Sure, Boss.'

Dempsey turned next to Michael.

'Let's see what he wants.'

Sutton was striding along the corridor but he did not wait until reaching them before he spoke.

'Are you both OK?' Sutton's tone carried genuine concern. 'We just heard about the shooting.'

'News travels slow round here,' Dempsey said. 'That was hours ago. We've had a night's sleep since then.'

'We weren't in The Hague last night,' Sutton explained, 'so we were only told this morning. Kincaid sent me here to find you.'

'Why?' Dempsey asked.

'In case there was anything we needed to know.'

'What could *you* need to know?' Michael asked. 'I thought you were only here to check up on American citizens?'

Sutton threw Michael an impatient glance. A silent acknowledgement that they all knew the line was a lie.

'He was also concerned about you both,' he said.

'Really? Kincaid doesn't seem like much of a bleeding heart to me.'

Sutton ignored Michael's comment and focused on Dempsey.

'And he's worried about Mr Duffy. After last night, the chances of another attempt on his life are high.'

'Why is the CIA so concerned about that?'

'Duffy might know things we don't. It's in our interests that he stays safe.'

'And he will. The ISB has made arrangements.'

'Is that safe? As I understand it, what happened to you guys last night was caused by a leak from within the UN.'

'The UN is not the ISB. From now on this is a bureau operation. And *we* don't have weak links. That's why I've replaced the security detail with my own man. From this moment onwards that's *his* door.'

The comment made Sutton look past both Dempsey and Devlin for the first time, towards Gallo.

'Holy fuck,' he said, his reaction unquestionably genuine. 'Is that a man or a bear?'

'Bit of both,' Dempsey replied. 'That's Agent Salvatore Gallo from the ISB. Anyone goes near Will Duffy – even medical personnel – they do so with Gallo at their shoulder. That clear?'

Sutton took a step back.

'Look, I can see we've started this on the wrong foot. But I don't have the authority to tell you anything that Kincaid doesn't want you to know and so I've no choice but to toe the line on why we're here. Even when we all know it's bullshit. But trust me, we want Duffy alive as much as you do. If you choose to increase his protection, we support that.'

Dempsey said nothing. Michael wondered why. Had Sutton surprised him by being so frank? Or was Dempsey just so unimpressed that he had nothing to add? Either way, it gave Michael the chance to ask a question that had been bothering him.

'What is it that you think Will knows?'

Sutton turned towards him.

'I can't answer that.'

'Why not?'

'Operational parameters. I'm sorry. We could help each other, I'm sure. But that's just not how Kincaid works.'

'Who gives a shit about Kincaid? That guy's a—'

'I know he's unlikeable. I know he's arrogant. But his loyalty's beyond question. Kincaid is one hundred per cent focused on the mission. One hundred per cent dedicated to the protection of the United States. That's all his country can ask of him.'

'Even if the way he works is getting in the way?'

'He's the senior officer. He's running this operation. And together we're as close as we have ever been to achieving the objective of our assignment. As long as that's true, I have to work within the framework he sets. I'm sorry that doesn't suit you.'

'Say what you like,' Michael replied. 'As far as I'm concerned, the man's a prick.'

'I didn't say he wasn't. I just said it didn't matter.'

Sutton turned to Dempsey.

'Can I ask what you plan to do next?'

'When you won't even tell us the objective of your assignment? Cooperation's a two-way street.'

'I get that. But I *do* think we can help one another. You guys are in someone's firing line. Last night shows that. The time could come when you need help. We can provide it. You've got Kincaid's number.'

It was all Sutton had left to say. With a nod he turned and walked away, back towards the elevator, leaving Michael and Dempsey to watch his exit in silence.

FORTY-SIX

It was near 8 a.m. as Michael and Dempsey arrived outside of Penitentiaire Inrichting Haaglanden in the Scheveningen region of the city. The second of PI Haaglanden's two main locations, Scheveningen Prison housed two unique international custodial facilities: the United Nations Detention Unit and the International Criminal Court's Detention Centre.

They were here for the latter.

The ICC Detention Centre was a purpose-built unit constructed within the much older building that surrounded it. Unlike the rest of the prison, it was managed and staffed by ICC officials and operatives, and it existed only to hold a maximum of twelve prisoners at a time, all of them either on or awaiting trial at the ICC. For that reason, every man and woman held within was treated as innocent until proven guilty.

With The Netherlands taking a more liberal approach to criminal justice, that status gave the inmates far more freedom than they would ever experience as remand prisoners in the UK or the USA. Each prisoner was provided with a room of their own, a personal washroom and access to not only a gym but to personal training. They also enjoyed unfettered computer access plus training if needed, and regular private contact with their family and their friends. All within the confines of the centre.

That regime was very different from the grim facilities that Michael was used to back home, and it was a whole world away from the nightmare the US federal prison system offered to those who could not afford to meet bail.

The two men walked the short distance from the car park to the main entrance of the prison in silence. The building that lay ahead of them would have been foreboding to most people, Michael realised. But to him, it was an everyday sight.

The large, arched central wooden gate was the height of three tall men, but it was still dwarfed by the two stone turrets that shouldered it on either side; they stood at twice that height, and they led to an eighteen-foot-tall sheer stone wall that extended fully around the entire complex.

There were three ways into the structure. This main gate and two smaller doors that bookended it on either side: one for staff, one for visitors.

Michael and Dempsey took the one on the right.

The interior decor of the ICC's Detention Centre was not exactly what Michael would have expected from the more traditional exterior, but neither was it unfamiliar.

As a barrister specialising in serious criminal trials, Michael rarely represented a defendant who was not remanded in custody. The various jails in the South of England and beyond had become frequent early-morning destinations.

The budget of the International Criminal Court was massive, which put it in direct contrast to the meagre crumbs the UK government used to fund its own crumbling criminal justice system. And yet the centre looked no more hi-tech and no better maintained than some of the already creaky new builds back home.

It was, he had to admit, a surprise.

But maybe inevitable when you build something new inside such an old structure.

The thought occupied his mind as he and Dempsey moved through the corridors that would lead them to Hannibal Strauss, right up until their escort – a female guard whose dark hair and slightly tanned skin reminded him of Joelle Levy – took the right-hand turn just ahead of them and stopped barely six feet into the new corridor.

She gestured to an open door on her left.

'Take a seat, gentlemen.' Her English was predictably perfect. 'And make yourself comfortable. Mr Strauss will be brought up shortly.'

Michael stepped inside ahead of Dempsey as the guard locked the door behind them. Even in the Netherlands, the concept of custody involved bolts, bars and secure barriers. Like it or not, they were about to be locked in this room with a man even Dempsey considered a threat.

FORTY-SEVEN

There are some who do not photograph well. The camera adds ten pounds to some. To others, it captures imperfections less obvious to the naked eye. To others still, the picture can look like someone else entirely.

For these men and women, the digital lens is not a friend.

Hannibal Strauss was not one of them.

The tall Hungarian was the living image of what Michael had expected. At six foot two he was the same height as Dempsey and just an inch taller than Michael, but his stature was much closer to the barrister's than the ISB agent's. At least twenty-five pounds lighter than the thicker-set Dempsey, Strauss was lean, taut and naturally powerful. He was physically what Michael could have been if extreme physical fitness had been as essential to his survival as it so clearly was for Strauss.

Strauss moved to the centre of the room. Even with his hands cuffed securely ahead of him and with a guard at either arm, he had a charisma that was hard to describe. The Hungarian's presence didn't so much fill the room as engulf it completely. Michael found himself fascinated by every detail of the man as Strauss took his seat on the other side of the screwed-down metal table.

The same interest was not being returned in his direction.

Strauss's single, grey, unblinking eye was fixed on Dempsey. That did not change as his cuffs were removed, nor as the two guards stepped back. Instead he just stared, his silence a weapon. It was a skill Michael had always wished to possess: the ability to capture a room without even a word.

'I know you.'

Strauss's voice was deep and throaty. As if he found it a strain to speak. A sign of too many cigarettes, perhaps. Or a combat injury. A moment of study and Michael had settled on the latter. There was no other sign that Strauss was a smoker; no telltale lines around his lips, no staining of his fingers.

The thought passed in a moment, his attention refocused by Dempsey's response.

'And who do you think I am?' Dempsey asked.

At first Strauss said nothing. Instead he slowly raised his hand to his own face and touched the black patch that covered his missing left eye. He then traced a path with the same finger until it gently stroked what was left of his ear.

All three men were silent as Strauss ran his fingertips across the decade-old bomb damage. It was only once he had dropped his hand that Strauss spoke again.

'I was intrigued what you could want with me, Joe Dempsey.' His raspy voice gave no hint of whatever emotion he was feeling. 'So openly, at least. A man like you, he would usually come unannounced.'

'And what sort of man am I?'

'A killer. And the man I once thought responsible for this.' Strauss gestured again to his damaged face. 'When someone tries to kill me, I do my research.'

'You thought that was me?'

'I did. Once. Not any more. I was . . . educated as to the truth.'

Dempsey's expression remained blank. The perfect poker face.

'Educated by who?'

'A man who had every reason to want you dead. Which is

why I believed him when he directed my attention elsewhere. Had it not been for him, well . . . perhaps I would have made a costly mistake.'

'Costly for which one of us?'

'Who knows. It would have been interesting to find out.'

Michael felt himself pushing back into his seat; a subtle attempt to put some distance between himself and the intensity of the exchange. It was like watching two lions circling a carcass, each assessing his dominance over the other before risking a bite. Both Dempsey and Strauss were used to being the alpha male in any room. Neither knew who held that status here.

'So who was it?' Dempsey finally asked.

'The bomb? A nobody from Chechnya. He paid his price.'

'That's not what I meant.' Dempsey did not miss a beat, as if the man who had died in his place meant nothing. 'Who was it that wanted me dead?'

'A man who should have let the blame remain on you. He paid his own price for your survival.'

'That makes him one name on a very long list. Why don't you do us both a favour and narrow it down for me.'

Strauss smiled for the first time. It was not unwelcome; the expression seemed genuine and far warmer than Michael would have expected. The break in the cold, stern facade revealed a more handsome face than the one he had worn 'til now. But the reason behind the grin spoke to the cruelty of his character. Dempsey's casual reference to the violence and death in his life had either amused or impressed him. Maybe both.

'You make a good point,' he finally said. 'I presume, however, that the name Joshua once meant as much in your world as it did in mine?'

For the first time Michael noticed Dempsey hesitate. He

understood why. The name had shocked him, too. It was, Michael knew, one of the few that could have thrown Dempsey.

Strauss saw the same reaction.

'You *do* remember him.'

'Vaguely.'

'Vaguely doesn't earn that response from a man like you. You knew him well.'

'So what if I did?'

'It says much about you. Were you friends?'

'Why would that matter?'

'Because if you were, it reveals the man you are. For you to have done what you did? To consign him to rot in that American hovel? It takes a ruthless man to do that to a friend. Are you that ruthless, Mr Dempsey?'

Consigned to rot? Michael could not suppress a frown of confusion. *What could that mean?*

Joshua was dead. Michael knew that. Killed by Dempsey a full five years ago in the Republic of Ireland. He could not stop himself from turning towards Dempsey. Now was not the time. Michael knew that. And yet he could not help himself.

Dempsey met his questioning gaze and shook his head. When Michael did not look away – when he did not accept the message – Dempsey said one word. A word that Michael could tell he had wanted to avoid.

'Later.'

The dry, triumphant laugh from across the table brought both sets of eyes back to Strauss. Even dressed in a prison-issue jumpsuit and locked in a room from which he could not escape, he was the one who looked victorious.

'So you're not the only one who knew him. But you *are* the only one who knew he was still alive. Tell me more, gentlemen.'

The direction of the exchange was now troubling Dempsey, Michael could tell. His friend, usually so unflappable, seemed less than composed. And Michael felt responsible. He knew he should not have reacted to what Strauss had said. He had allowed the man to get under their skin.

It was a trap he would not have fallen into if this had been a cross-examination. And now that he had realised that, he knew how to rectify the damage he had done.

By treating this like *a courtroom.*

He fixed his gaze on Strauss, determined to redress the imbalance he had created.

'What makes you think we're here to tell you anything?' Michael asked, his 'barrister's voice' deployed.

Either the question or the change in demeanour intrigued Strauss. His good eye narrowed; he was now viewing Michael as something more than mere furniture.

'And just who is Michael Devlin?'

'So you know my name. Am I supposed to be unnerved by that?'

'Most would be.'

'Only those who don't know you have to approve your visitors. You saw my name on the manifest. Same as you saw Agent Dempsey's.'

'It's Agent Dempsey, now, is it? Last time I looked him up he was a Major.'

'That's not how this works, Mr Strauss. We ask the questions. We choose the subjects.'

Strauss grinned again.

'You're a lawyer. I can spot the . . . technique.'

'Which is precisely why we're here. You know what happened to your legal team yesterday?'

'Of course I know. Why?'

'What do you know about it?'

'I know that my lead advocate is dead. And I guess my solicitor is at least badly hurt or he'd be the one visiting me this morning, would he not?'

'But that leaves one more alive and well.'

'Compton? He is not my lawyer.'

'The court record says otherwise.'

'What it says is irrelevant. I will not speak to that man.'

'Why?'

'Not your concern, counsel. I suggest you move to your next question.'

Michael did exactly that.

'Do you believe that Mendel Prochnik and Will Duffy were victims of a random mass shooting?'

Strauss let out a short, angry guffaw.

'What do you think?'

'So you believe they were targeted?'

'Not your concern, counsel. Next.'

'Do you think they were targeted because of Konrad Frankowski?'

This time it was Strauss who was caught off guard. He had plainly not expected to hear that name. That reaction, visible for barely an instant, confirmed that Michael was on the right path.

A moment later and he was unsure if it was a path he wanted to walk.

'Who the hell *are* you?' Strauss's voice was a violent hiss. The change made him even more intimidating. His one grey eye glared at Michael with the menace of a hungry python, poised to strike.

Michael refused to bow.

'I'm a friend of Will Duffy,' he replied. 'A good friend. I want to know who tried to kill him and I'm as sure as I can be that it's got something to do with your case. He believed you were innocent, he told me that himself. So maybe we can help each other.'

'*Tried* to kill him? You mean he *is* alive?'

'Yes. Like you surmised, he's in intensive care, badly hurt but alive.'

'That won't last for long. You think he can't get to Duffy in a hospital bed?'

'He?' The dropped pronoun was the first hint that Strauss had any useful information to share. Michael could not ignore it. 'Who's he?'

Strauss did not answer. He simply stared at Michael, his irritation at his own verbal slip impossible to hide. He held the gaze for seconds before suddenly rising to his feet.

'This visit is over. I want you out of here and I do not want you to return. Understood?'

Michael stood too, more slowly and with none of the physical menace.

'Mr Strauss, we can help you. Whatever Will and Prochnik knew – whatever you told them – it made them innocent victims here. We want to know what happened to them and we want to know *why* it happened. We can't do that without you. So please, what did you tell them?'

'Do you really expect me to just accept that you are who you say? That I should share with you the information that keeps me alive? What sort of fucking idiot do you think I am?'

'What information?' This time the question came from

Dempsey. Unlike Michael and Strauss, he made no attempt to stand. 'What information is keeping you alive?'

Strauss smiled again, but this time the warmth was missing. It was grim and menacing and he looked down at Dempsey as if ready to pounce. Michael felt his own legs tense, preparing to physically intercept Strauss if he moved on his friend.

Dempsey seemed less concerned.

'I know you've no reason to believe us,' he said. 'You've no way to know if we're here to protect Duffy. You've no way to know if Michael has ever even met that man, never mind whether they're friends. You can't know any of that. But you *do* know me. Or at least you know *about* me. You know my reputation. You know what I used to do and who I used to do it for. And so you know I don't play games, Hannibal.'

'People change, *Agent* Dempsey.' Strauss emphasised Dempsey's title, to prove his point. 'You're not that man any more. But who are you now?'

'I'm a man who's willing to risk his own life for your trust. It's our only way to stop this.'

'To stop what?'

'To stop the killing. And, I guess, to release you. Because this isn't just about Duffy and Prochnik. Other people are at risk. Innocent people. Until I find out who's behind this, I can't protect them. And believe me, I *have* to protect them. That's why I'm willing to do this.'

'To do what?'

'To tell you something that could kill me when this is over.'

Michael finally realised what Dempsey meant. He felt a cold chill run down his spine as his friend continued.

'Joshua lied to you, Hannibal. The man you murdered – the Chechen – he wasn't the one who tried to kill you in Cambodia.'

Strauss's hand once again rose to his damaged face.

'What are you saying?'

'You know what I'm saying. I'm telling you a truth that could cost me my life, because right now I need your trust. It was me, Hannibal. The bomb that nearly killed you. It was me.'

FORTY-EIGHT

Dempsey's admission was a risk Michael would never have taken. He would never have created a situation that put him so firmly in someone's future crosshairs. And sure as hell not when that someone was Hannibal Strauss.

And yet he knew that the disclosure was exactly what it would take to convince Strauss.

At first Strauss was silent. A full two minutes, his gaze fixed on just one of the two seated men. Neither Michael nor Dempsey said a word as Strauss fought his own internal battle, his mind clearly racing as he weighed his sudden desire to kill Dempsey against the fact that this man now represented his best chance at freedom.

They both knew this had to play out in Strauss's own head.

They also knew there could be only one outcome.

His visible fury dissipated slowly, his breathing finally returning to normal. There was no longer a contest of dominance, not as far as Michael could detect. The identity of the alpha now mattered to neither man. Both had bigger issues to navigate.

For Dempsey, it was the safety of Maria Frankowski.

For Strauss, his freedom.

It was Dempsey who spoke first.

'So, what's it going to be?'

'I have some ground rules,' Hannibal replied.

'Which are?'

'The understanding that what lies between you and me,

it's not over. Whether I leave this place a free man or I die a prisoner, I will ensure you pay for what you did. I need you to know that before we move forwards.'

'Why?'

'Because whatever you may think of me, I am a man of honour. My *own* honour and my *own* ideals. I need you to understand that if we work together now, the time will come – once this is over – that I will kill you.'

'You'll try.'

'Unlike you, Mr Dempsey, I never just try.'

'I can live with that. But for now, you trust us?'

'What other choice do I have?'

'Not much. Not if you ever want to get out of here.'

'And I do. Now more than ever. Now that I have things to achieve.'

Michael could see the blood rising again in both men. It was natural in the circumstances but it was also a distraction he could not allow. He needed to keep them focused on something other than each other.

'Why don't you tell us about the man you mentioned?' Michael asked. 'The one who can still get to Duffy. Who is "he"?'

Strauss looked directly at Michael. Then to Dempsey. Then back again. Whatever he had to say, he was struggling to spit out the words. Finally his eye settled on the table, as if he was resigned to what he had to do.

'He . . .' Strauss spoke slowly, his harsh voice as quiet as Michael had heard it '. . . is the Monk.'

He sat back into his chair as soon as the name had left his lips and Michael could see that he expected it to mean something. A quick glance at Dempsey showed that it did. But the deep frown on his face suggested that meaning was not what Strauss had expected.

'The Monk?' Dempsey sounded angry. 'Are you kidding me? The Monk's a goddamn myth.'

Strauss looked up, his expression angry once again. But before he could say anything in response – something likely to fuel another confrontation, given the mood of both men – Michael made sure to speak first.

'Who's the Monk?'

'The Monk is the boogeyman of Cold War espionage,' Dempsey explained. He sounded less angry now, more irritated. 'He's an urban legend in the intelligence community. Has been for decades.'

'And what is he supposed to be?'

'The story is that he headed up a network of embedded Russian sleeper agents all over the West. The Mladorossi, they were called. Russian fascists or communists, depending on who was telling the tale. But in whatever version, their mission was to bring Russia to prominence. To superpower status, to the detriment of the rest of the world. Politicians, scientists, soldiers, journalists. You name the place, the Monk was said to have his people there. Men and women stationed their whole adult lives in democratic nations, ready to be activated at any moment.'

'You mean like that old Kevin Costner movie?'

'I only ever saw his Westerns,' Dempsey replied, 'but possibly. There were some who gave the Monk credit for pretty much everything the Soviet Union pulled off during the Cold War, and for a whole lot they had nothing to do with. Sabotage. Blackmail. Disinformation. Assassination. His organisation was responsible for the lot, if you believe the bullshit.'

Michael's eyes widened as he took on board the details. Things which were, he noticed, a little too close to home.

'And you don't believe any of it?'

'Why the hell would I? It's a legend.'

'But what about everything that's happened so far? The UN. The FBI. Joe, isn't that exactly what you just described?'

Dempsey took a moment to think. It was clear to Michael that in his rush to reject a myth, he had not made that same connection. He visibly considered it now, but only for a moment. Then he turned back towards Strauss as he continued.

'The problem with all that is no one's ever seen this person. Not in all those years. No one's ever spoken to him. There's no official line on him. In all the decades that have passed since his name was first whispered, not one person has ever been connected to him. There has never been one single iota of evidence that he actually exists.'

He turned back to Michael.

'There's plenty of explanations for the past twenty-four hours that don't involve believing in monsters under the bed. And besides, the Cold War ended thirty years ago. Even if the Monk *did* exist once upon a time, at the most generous estimate a man operating in the fifties and beyond would now be, what, ninety-odd? And yet we're being asked to believe that he's still an active player in that world? Dangerous enough to scare a man like *him*?'

Dempsey pointed his finger at Strauss as he said the final word. Strauss, in return, did not waver for a moment.

'I assure you, he is no myth. The Monk is *very* real. The Mladorossi are *very* real.'

Dempsey exhaled hard. He seemed intensely irritated.

'What use is this, Hannibal?' he demanded. 'It helps none of us if you insist on lying.'

'I am not lying. You say that no one has ever seen him. *I* have seen him. With what *were* my own two eyes. He is real.'

'You're telling me you've met a ninety-year-old master-spy?'

'You think so small, Joe Dempsey. In so . . . so few dimensions.'

'What does that even mean?'

'It means that you are focused on the Monk as a person. An individual. But he is more than that. He is a symbol.'

Michael could not stop himself from frowning as he listened to the answer. He was lost and he could not hide it. One glance and he could see that Dempsey was equally confused.

'Do I really have to take you by the hand?' Strauss asked, exasperated. 'The Monk is just a title, adopted by the head of the Mladorossi. The man who currently calls himself that name, he is not ninety years old. He is just the latest to play the role. A role that goes back even further than your cynical storytelling suggests.'

Michael could see a change in Dempsey. His expression remained irritated – as if he was still unlikely to believe what he was being told – but his interest been caught.

'And how the hell do you know any of this?'

'How do you think my career began?'

'You started off working for the Monk?'

'I was an independent contractor, let's say.'

'When?'

'Thirty years ago for the first time. And many times since.'

'But you're not a Russian agent.'

'Very few of those who do his dirty work are Russian agents. Do you know the time and training and expense it takes to develop an embedded Mladorossi operative? Why would he risk exposing or losing them when he can simply hire in help? The Monk uses hand-picked mercenaries. Men like me. He always has.'

'When did you meet him?'

'In person? A long time ago. Long enough that he was a different man back then.'

'You mean literally?'

'I mean literally. The man I met, he was my first Monk. I am on to my second. I have not met this one face to face but I'm not afraid to admit that I preferred his predecessor.'

Dempsey fell silent, assessing the information he had just been given. It gave Michael a chance to ask a question.

'What is it you did for him? For them?'

'Whatever I was asked,' Strauss replied. 'At first. Small jobs back then. As the years went on – as I became more successful – my tasks were on a grander scale.'

'You mean you were too successful a war lord to take the small jobs any more,' Dempsey said.

'I was. In fact, I have killed almost as many people as you have, Agent Dempsey.'

'You've done your homework.'

'Like I said, a man should know his enemies.'

Michael could only watch in silence as two of the most lethal men on the planet glared at one another across the narrow table. The atmosphere felt charged with electricity and it would clearly take little for that charge to become something more. An explosion none of them could afford.

It was time to move this on.

'But the deaths that landed you in here?' Michael asked. 'You're saying you're innocent of those?'

'I am.'

'So what really happened there?'

'You already know the allegation. That I took the Tripoli military into the city of Wazzin in pursuit of the Tobruk faction. That I pinned them down and that when they attempted to surrender, I used sarin gas to murder over fourteen hundred of their soldiers in cold blood.'

'That's what they say,' Michael replied.

'Well, I did pursue them. I did lay siege to Wazzin. But the sarin gas? Do you think I'm a fool? You think I don't know that to do this is a war crime?'

'It wouldn't be your first,' Dempsey commented.

'That's a matter of opinion. I have been convicted of nothing. But believe me, whatever else I have done in my life, I did not do this. *He* did it. The Monk.'

'What?'

'The Monk ordered for the sarin gas to be deployed. Whatever his plans were, he needed the conflict between the Tripoli and Tobruk factions to be at an end. And so he instructed me to finish it with the gas. I refused. It was a crime that could *only* come back to me. It could *only* result in the situation I am now in. And so I refused. Not for moral reasons but for self-preservation.'

'But it *did* happen,' Dempsey said. 'Those deaths were no hoax.'

'It did. But by the hand of others from among the Mladorossi. Not by mine.'

'And why would he do that?' Michael asked. 'What did he have to gain from killing soldiers who were already trying to surrender?'

'I don't pretend to know his plans. His motivation, yes: it's always Mother Russia, everything for the advancement of his country. Whoever assumes the role of the Monk is a fanatic, it seems. But I don't know how Libya served his plan. I *do* know he was involved in the revolution. In deposing Gaddafi. He used disinformation and rabble-rousing and bribery and all of his other dirty little tricks to ensure that occurred. And I know that the Tobruk resistance to the new regime continued for longer than he expected. But the motive behind it all? I cannot help.'

'So he set you up to take the fall? Even though you know the truth?'

'That was not his first choice. At first he wanted to punish me, to force me back into line.'

'How?'

'The Monk, he does not just hire and trust that money buys loyalty. He looks for leverage. Absolute, ultimate leverage. He will find what his contractor values most in life and he will use that thing. The loyalty of those who work for him, it is *bought* with money but it is underwritten with the blood of their loved ones. You accept his coin once, you are on the hook for life.'

'And what leverage did he have on you?'

'Nothing, as he soon found out.' Strauss's expression was grim. 'When I refused his orders, he had my mother taken. When that did not have the effect he wished, he took one of my two sisters. And then my son. After that, he accepted I was different. That I value no one and nothing above myself.'

Michael stared at the man in growing horror as the meaning of his words took root, unable to fathom how he could speak so coldly. With a young family of his own – the three people in his life who meant quite literally everything – he could not comprehend what Strauss was describing.

Or *how* he was describing it.

He glanced across at Dempsey and found his friend nodding. The Englishman seemed less outraged, instead focusing on what he was beginning to understand about the man who sat across from them both.

Strauss had noticed it too.

'This is making some sense to you, yes?'

'Maybe. Someone tried to kill us in our sleep last night.'

Strauss raised an eyebrow.

'And they failed. His standards must be slipping.'

'I cornered one of them,' Dempsey said. 'I gave him a chance to give himself up. Instead he shot himself.'

'Predictable.'

'Why? Because the Monk would have killed his family if he'd been taken?'

'Someone would have, yes. Without hesitation. And the fact his peons know that is what buys the Monk their absolute loyalty. It's how he recruits martyrs without the incompetence that comes with fanaticism. It's a rare prize.'

'Clearly doesn't work on true monsters, though, does it?' Dempsey said.

Strauss ignored the jab.

'So the Monk ordered the massacre,' Dempsey said, 'not you. And having realised he could not control you, he ensured that you got the blame and that you ended up here.'

'Exactly.'

'But why not just come after you directly? It seems a big risk to leave you alive in here where you're free to tell people what really happened.'

'He has tried. Both before I was in here. And since.'

'You're referring to the three guards?'

Michael turned at Dempsey's interruption, realising quickly that his friend was referring to the prison guards Strauss had killed. An incident which was not, he now guessed, the unprovoked attack that had been reported.

'They were his, yes,' Strauss confirmed. 'He should have sent four.'

'Clearly,' Dempsey replied. 'You'd think he'd know better. He's met you, after all.'

'Are you testing me?' Strauss leaned forwards as he spoke, his forearms on the table that sat between them. 'You still do not believe me?'

Whatever Dempsey believed, to Michael what had seemed ridiculous just a few minutes earlier now sounded almost plausible. He also noted that its credibility was bolstered by one simple question: what motive did Strauss have to deceive them?

He was beginning to buy it. But that didn't mean he had no more questions.

'But what does any of this have to do with Will Duffy and Mendel Prochnik? Why would someone like the Monk be interested in them? Enough to stage a terrorist attack in the middle of a city just to get to them?'

Strauss shifted his gaze back to Michael.

'The Monk *wants* me dead. But he *needs* the allegations against me to be the accepted truth. That way the lie becomes history and his role in it is hidden. He must have discovered that

I told them the truth about Wazzin. I told them what had really occurred there. And I told them how to prove it.'

'How?'

'I told them the man they needed to find to prove my story. The Monk killed them to keep them from Kon Frankowski.'

FORTY-NINE

The room went silent at the mention of Frankowski's name. It made Dempsey sit more upright in his chair, a reaction he knew Strauss would notice. It could not be helped; his heart rate had spiked in that instant. Whatever the Hungarian made of it, *this* was what Dempsey had been waiting for.

He would finally know how Maria's husband had tied himself into this nightmare.

'Tell us about Kon Frankowski,' Dempsey said. 'Who is he to you?'

'He was intended as my safety net. My . . . what is it you call it? From the board game? My "get out of jail" card. He has an item of mine. Something I intended to use to secure my freedom.'

'What is it?'

'It's a list, Agent Dempsey. A record of every embedded agent within the Mladorossi. In the right hands it could bring down one hundred years of Russian espionage. Every resource they have – every operative in every hard-won position – would be exposed in an instant. It would cripple them.'

Dempsey shook his head. Strauss had almost convinced him. But this last claim went too far.

'You can't be serious.' Dempsey did not try to hide the derision in his voice. 'Why would anyone take the risk of keeping all of that information in one place? Let alone a supposed genius spymaster.'

'You are thinking like a Westerner,' Strauss replied. 'You need to think like a Russian. For all of the technological skill of their hackers, for all of the international ambition and even sophistication of their oligarchs, it is their leaders who do not live in the twenty-first century. They are paranoid and they are volatile and they are unpredictable. But most of all, they are basic.'

'If they have a weapon, they want to see it. Rockets? They want to see them fire. Fighter jets? They want to see them fly. And so one of their greatest weapons – the Mladorossi, a network of agents across the world – they want *that* at their fingertips also. Safe, encrypted and unconnected to any aspect of the internet. But accessible to *them*. Another weapon, even if one only they can see.'

'And the Monk just allowed that, did he? Despite the obvious dangers?'

'In some things I guess he has no choice. What he does, these people fund it. Is it any surprise that now and again they would wish to see some records?'

Dempsey said nothing to this. It was, he had to concede, a fair point. If the Monk was real, then even he had to be accountable sometimes.

'And yet somehow *you* have it? This all-knowing list. Somehow you got your hands on it.'

'I did.'

'How?'

'Years and years of deceit and planning, Agent Dempsey. Much more than you need to know. Much more than you would ever believe, even. It cost me a lot. Almost everything. But finally I obtained it.'

'For what reason?'

'Protection. What else? With everything I have told you about the Monk, you don't see why I would need that? I always expected him to turn on me one day. That something would go wrong and I would be made to pay the price. The list, it was my insurance policy.'

'Then how is it that you're in here regardless?' Michael interjected.

'Because it is, as you say, my nuclear option. I didn't want to use it until I had no other choice. I was willing to give him time to unpick the mess he had made for me. But in the meantime, I had to pass the list to someone else. For safekeeping.'

'Kon Frankowski.' Michael said the name an instant before Dempsey.

'Yes.'

'Why him?' Dempsey asked. 'How do you even know him?'

'Frankowski took care of my money. Funds are an Achilles heel in my business. The wealth generated by what I do, it is substantial. But it is not . . . shall we just say it is not necessarily legal? I had many different outlets to deal with that and Frankowski was the most effective. Actually, that does the man an injustice. He was a magician. A few taps on *his* keyboard and my money was safely on the other side of the world, untouchable and untraceable.'

'And that qualified him to hold onto the list? It's hardly the same thing.'

'I needed someone who could transfer the list across the dark web without detection. Without the Russians intercepting or tracing it. I also needed someone I could trust with my business dealings, and I didn't have a whole lot of time. If there was one man who I knew could achieve both those things, it was Frankowski. And so I made him an offer. Five million dollars to transfer the file to a physical hard drive in the US, to then remove all trace of its existence online, and to safeguard that hard-drive file until I called for it.'

'And he agreed to that?'

'Of course he agreed. For five million dollars, wouldn't you? It was hardly much different to the work he already carried out for me.'

Dempsey had to hide his distaste at the picture he was forming of Frankowski. His disbelief that Maria had somehow married a man caught up in . . . in all this? Who had put her *and* her children – *their* children – in danger.

Maria's safety was the reason Dempsey had ended their relationship. For her to then marry a man who had dragged her into the shadows of this world anyway?

It was more than infuriating. But Dempsey could not allow himself to show it.

'So that was why Frankowski was here? To deliver the hard drive?'

'Yes.'

'And Duffy and Prochnik were involved?'

'Yes. That's why they were meeting Frankowski. To retrieve the hard drive.'

'But why did you wait so long?' Michael asked. 'You've been in here for over a year.'

'As I said, revealing the list was my last resort,' Strauss replied. 'At first I was willing to negotiate.'

'So you were in direct contact with the Monk? From in here?'

'He has people. I have people. And I am not yet a convicted prisoner, so I get to see mine. Through them, I made it known what I possess. And I informed him that if I was found guilty, the list would find its way to the Americans. I accepted that this would take time. That I would remain here while the slow process of my exoneration was carried out. And so I waited, safe in the assurance that the Monk had agreed to my demands.'

'But that changed.' Dempsey could now see where this was headed. 'And you had to find a different route. One that involved Duffy and Prochnik. What was it? The guards?'

'Correct. When they paid me their visit I realised that the Monk had no intention of playing by my rules. They were sent to my cell to beat the information from me. To force me to give up the list. I can see why the Monk thought that might have worked. I was a man willing to lose family for my own safety. Why would I not fold when it was my own life at risk? Maybe he would have been proved correct, if only he had sent better men.'

'You're not afraid he'll try again?'

'Of course he will try again. And as confident as I am in my own abilities, if I remain here then sooner or later he *will* succeed. That is why I told Duffy and Prochnik everything. I knew it had become my only option.'

'Why only those two?' Michael asked. 'Why not Compton?'

'Because I never trusted him.'

'Why not?' Michael asked.

'He was not my choice; he was appointed by the court to defend me, before my people found Mendel Prochnik. I was persuaded to keep Mr Compton on the team for continuity, but he is part of the establishment and he is far too close to the other side. Something like this, I did not want him near it. I gave clear instructions to the others that he should not be involved.'

Strauss sat back in his chair as his explanation came to an end. He seemed satisfied that he had convinced Dempsey and

Michael of the truth. That he had given them enough. And as far as Dempsey was concerned, he was right.

Dempsey had been incredulous at the start. Dismissing even the chance that the mythical Monk could actually be real. But if what Strauss had suggested was correct – if the Monk was more than one man – then what had seemed impossible became something a whole lot more plausible. Still some of Strauss's story seemed insane but, as a whole, it was now making sense to Dempsey.

Michael, though, appeared to have more questions.

'There's one thing I don't understand about any of this,' he began. 'How would getting the hard drive to Will – to your lawyers – help you with this case? Sure, the whole spy ring gets exposed. The Monk and his men get dragged in or eliminated or whatever the hell else happens in that world. But how does that help you? How does that stop you being responsible for what happened in Wazzin? The two things don't seem connected.'

'And outwardly they are not,' Strauss replied. 'Which is why I struck a deal. With the CIA.'

Dempsey leaned forwards at the mention of the Agency. He was now sure he knew what was coming.

'My legal team had already met with the agents,' Strauss continued. 'Without Alastair Compton. It had already been agreed how the case against me would be arranged to fall apart, provided the Americans received what I had promised. That was stage one. The meeting with Frankowski to collect the hard drive was stage two. They would collect it and they would deliver it to the agents, followed some respectable time later by my release. Everything was in place. It should have gone like clockwork. But somehow the Monk found out.'

'And let me guess,' Dempsey said, 'those CIA agents, they go by the names Kincaid and Sutton?'

'I see you've already run into them,' Strauss said.

Dempsey gave just a curt nod in reply, his mind already occupied with a thousand other thoughts.

Every one of which finally made sense.

FIFTY

Yuri Shevchuk slumped into his seat as he watched Dempsey and Michael exit the final doors of the penitentiary. The facility's car park was large and Shevchuk's vehicle was well away from where he had watched the two Brits park ninety minutes earlier. That made it unlikely that they would pass his location as they returned to their car, but Shevchuk was taking no chances.

It was strange enough that he should have shown up at Will Duffy's hospital last night with Alastair Compton, he realised. But for the ICC's prosecutor to turn up at the Detention Centre? A facility that currently held a single prisoner, and him a man who Shevchuk was personally bringing to trial?

That would be a step too far, Shevchuk knew. That would be the end.

He was relieved, then, as he watched the two men retrace their earlier steps, taking them in the opposite direction while each focused on his mobile phone.

He was safe.

At least from them.

At least for now.

The respite lasted no more than an instant, his fear of discovery replaced almost immediately by the all-pervading dread that had dominated his life for the past six months. Dempsey and Devlin had been a welcome distraction. Having something else to fear – something other than the man who had been plaguing him – was the closest thing he could remember to relief.

Now, with them out of sight, Shevchuk's mind returned to the single thought that had occupied him for so long.

The Monk.

He pushed himself back upright with a long, winded groan. His ageing body was not made for the sort of contortion he had just demanded of it. A man of his years and of his status had no place hiding in cars. He had no place in *any* of this. But he also had no choice.

As much as he despised the idea, Shevchuk had become a tool. A resource for the most ruthless man he had ever known. It was not the end he had envisaged for himself.

And however this thing went, it *was* the end, of that he had no doubt.

He glanced towards the encrypted mobile phone that sat in the central console of his Mercedes GLC. A slim, sleek and harmless object, to Shevchuk it carried all the threat of a sleeping viper. His hand moved towards it hesitantly, his half-outstretched arm visibly shaking. He did not want to make the call. He never did.

But the decision was not his.

A moment more and the phone was at his ear, the only entry in its contact list selected and the connection made. It was answered almost immediately.

'What do you have for me?'

Shevchuk felt his mouth go dry as he heard the cold, menacing voice.

'They have just left Scheveningen Prison,' he said. 'They have been with Strauss.'

'How can you be sure?'

'They were inside for an hour and a half. If he had refused to see them it would have been quicker.'

'In that case we have to assume that they know everything. Which makes Joe Dempsey an even greater threat than he seemed. He needs to be addressed.'

Shevchuk felt his heart begin to race. Fast enough to give him physical discomfort. The thought of what the Monk might be about to ask of him was terrifying.

'You know ... you know ... I ...' He took a breath to compose himself. 'You know *I* can't help with that? There's nothing I could—'

'Of course there's nothing you can do; at best you would provide him with target practice. No. I have others for this side of things.'

Somehow the answer did not offer Shevchuk the relief he had hoped for. Not while the greater threat remained.

'I have to ask: do you know who Joe Dempsey is? Dealing with him, it is no simple thing. He is no easy prey.'

'Have you been doing your homework for me, Yuri?'

'He works for the United Nations. For the International Security Bureau. I have heard enough over the years to know.'

'And so have I,' the Monk replied. 'But I will be dealing with him, regardless of reputation. You can count on that. Dempsey's time is coming.'

Shevchuk felt his heart sink at the last comment. He had considered himself bound to tell the Monk what he knew of the ISB man, if only to avoid the consequences of not doing so. But he had hoped to be ignored. More than anything, he had hoped that Dempsey would find the Monk and put a stop to the bastard once and for all.

But with the Monk already aware of what he was up against, that outcome seemed unlikely. And so Shevchuk's nightmare seemed set to continue.

Still, he needed to know his role.

'If you're dealing with him, what do you want me to do?'

'Go back to the office. We don't want anyone asking where you are.'

'And Strauss?'

'Proceed as before. Until I say otherwise, he is to face trial and you are to do absolutely everything within your power to ensure his conviction.'

'But all of this . . . everything that's happened and that's happening . . . is this trial even going to go ahead?'

'Not if I have my way, no. Because he won't live long enough for that. But we have both seen how plans can go awry and until you hear that Hannibal Strauss is ready for burial then you will remain my contingency. Until I tell you otherwise, you are to prepare this trial as if your life depends upon it. Your life and others.'

Shevchuk took a deep, soul-strengthening breath.

'And my family? When—'

'When this is over.'

The line went dead with that final answer, leaving Shevchuk feeling no better than he had before the call. No further forwards. No more reassured.

As it had been for half a year, he would continue to do exactly as the Monk instructed.

FIFTY-ONE

The Monk disconnected the call and brought his fist down hard on the table ahead of him. For all of his emotionless poise when speaking to Shevchuk, the problem posed by Joe Dempsey was now a very serious concern.

His survival after last night's attack had been unexpected. Vic Sethi had always been reliable, if never *quite* the talent he believed himself to be. But he and his team should have been enough to kill a man as he slept.

And yet Dempsey was not only alive and well, he was closing in.

At any other time, with the Monk's usual resources, it would be Dempsey and Devlin against an invisible army. They would not have stood a chance. But the war in Ukraine had stretched him to breaking point.

The reality of his situation irritated the Monk beyond measure. And nowhere was it better illustrated than through Yuri Shevchuk.

Shevchuk had been 'recruited' for a single purpose: to ensure the vital conviction of Hannibal Strauss. The plan had always been to kill Strauss before it began, but as ever the Monk was prepared for all eventualities, including Strauss's survival.

It was for this reason that he had targeted Shevchuk. The invasion of Ukraine had put the prosecutor's family at risk; a Ukrainian himself, he was left desperate as he saw reports and footage of Russian tanks entering his home country and shattering the safety that his closest relatives had always enjoyed.

The predicament had made Shevchuk an obvious target, easily susceptible to the Monk's brand of manipulation. A promise of his family's protection, in exchange for the aggressive prosecution of a man Shevchuk already believed was guilty.

Or at least that was how it had begun.

The Monk had been as good as his word. He always was. But it was in the unspoken that he wielded the dagger. There had been no discussion of what would become of Shevchuk's family once they were clear of Ukraine and so the Monk had broken no agreement by keeping them in his own custody. They were leverage to ensure that Shevchuk did not change his mind once their extraction was achieved.

And now, they were the motivation for Shevchuk to do more than he had ever agreed.

The Monk did not *want* to use the prosecutor as a surveillance operative. It was a risk of a valuable resource, and well beyond Shevchuk's particular skill-set. Ideally the man would have one role only, his focus entirely on Hannibal Strauss. But the Monk no longer had a choice.

With no one else available to tail Dempsey and Devlin – not in The Hague nor anywhere else in the Netherlands, at least not today – it had been Shevchuk or no one. It was an operational position the Monk had never been in before. And not one he wished to repeat.

But it left him with a problem: If Strauss *had* told Dempsey everything, the Englishman would now be hunting for the player who was missing from the board.

Dempsey cannot find Kon Frankowski before I do, he thought. *And there's only one way to ensure that outcome.*

The Monk needed to expand options. He needed a new

'recruit'. It was not a new realisation but it had been made more urgent by the increasing threat posed by Joe Dempsey. The ISB agent's arrival had forced the Monk into action and so the first stage of acquiring his new asset was already underway.

With the clock ticking fast, it was time to close that deal.

FIFTY-TWO

Will Duffy's new room within the ICU was not built for guests. The same large bed he had occupied in the previous room now dominated the much smaller area. He was still surrounded by what looked like an armoury of medical equipment dedicated to his continued recovery, but it now left space for a single chair.

Between Michael, Dempsey and Sal Gallo, they filled almost every spare inch within the room. It made for a physically uncomfortable meeting, but also a private one.

Dempsey wasted no time in bringing Gallo up to speed. And Gallo was just as quick in his own understanding and analysis. The two agents interacted well together, Michael noticed; their sharp minds seemed to work in unison.

'Does Frankowski know what he has?' Gallo asked.

'There's no way to know that yet,' Dempsey replied. 'But if he does, he's kept it to himself. He certainly hasn't mentioned it to his wife.'

'You're sure?'

'I spoke to her last night. If she knew anything about this, she'd have mentioned it. I'll make sure later today, but she wouldn't have held anything back.'

'And you are certain of all this?' Gallo asked, after taking a moment to consider. 'That Frankowski has the copy of this list for sure?'

'You mean do we believe Strauss?' Dempsey asked.

'Yes. Exactly that.'

'Strauss has no reason to lie and every reason to tell the

truth. As long as he's in custody, his life is at risk. They've already tried once. They'll try again. And next time they'll send more men. Better men. Strauss knows he needs to get out of there as soon as he can, and so I believe Strauss when he says Frankowski has the list. That will have to do for now.'

Gallo said nothing in return, while his furrowed, almost Cro-Magnon brow suggested why: he was considering Dempsey's logic. It did not take long.

'In that case,' he said, breaking the short silence, 'we need to find this Frankowski, yes?'

'And quick,' Dempsey replied. 'Because if we don't, we have to assume the Monk will.'

'And you really believe this man is real?' Gallo's eyes had narrowed to slits as he spoke. 'This Monk. After all this time, you think he is more than just a legend?'

'Like I said, Strauss had no reason to lie,' Dempsey replied. 'And every reason to tell the truth.'

'But the word of *that* man?'

'I don't intend to just take him at his word. There are ways to confirm what he told us.'

'How?'

'The CIA agents we met last night,' Michael said. 'Kincaid and Sutton.'

'Exactly,' Dempsey nodded. 'If Strauss *is* telling the truth, Kincaid will jump at the chance we're offering him. And if he doesn't jump, well, that tells us all we need to know about Strauss's story.'

'But what *are* we offering him?' Michael asked. 'We've no clue where Frankowski is.'

'Not yet we don't,' Dempsey explained, 'but we do have access to the one person who knows him better than anyone else. He ran after speaking to Maria. Maybe she can help us work out where he ran to.'

'Maria?' Gallo asked, looking confused.

'Maria is Frankowski's wife,' Michael explained.

'And you think she would help us to find her husband? To put him at risk?'

'She's also Joe's ex. So it's more than a little bit complicated.'

Gallo's expressive eyes widened in disbelief. They stayed that way as his head slowly turned towards Dempsey but he stayed silent.

He knows Dempsey well enough not to ask further, Michael thought.

'It is what it is,' Dempsey said curtly, 'so let's keep our mind on the job. I want Frankowski. And I want him today.'

FIFTY-THREE

Grace pinched the bridge of her nose with her thumb and forefinger. A meaningless movement that did nothing to banish the tiredness she had been unable to shake since waking at 4 a.m.

She had taken to her bunk just after 11 p.m., once she had settled the rest of the Alpha Team contingent into their accommodation and then debriefed Maria and her family. Grace had known then that she would get five hours at best – the length of the security shift taken by Kate Silver and Shui Dai – and so she had wasted no time in getting to sleep.

It was a lesson Dempsey had taught her:

Sleep when you have the chance, because who the hell knows when you'll get another.

Last night that lesson was unnecessary; it had been a long day. False flag 'terrorist' attacks. International conspiracies involving the infiltration of key US law enforcement. Shoot-outs with federal agents in leafy, well-heeled suburbs.

Even for a member of the ISB's Alpha Team, it was far from a typical stint at the office.

Five hours had proved insufficient to recharge Grace's depleted inner battery and so she had paced the grounds for the last three hours, struggling to keep her eyes open and her mind focused on the task at hand.

She could only hope that was about to change.

Long since bored by the monotony of her task, she was grateful when it was time for Dylan Wrixon to take his turn. Not least because the already scorching morning sun was well on its way to unbearable as she approached one of five rear doors to the ranch's main residence. The heatwave of recent weeks was still clinging on. It made the prospect of indoor rounds in the air conditioning of the main residence a whole lot more attractive.

'Sun's up with a vengeance.' Grace spoke as Wrixon stepped out of the doorway and onto the long, wide patio just beyond. 'You're gonna be hot.'

'What's new there?' Wrixon replied. He indicated back into the property with a jerk of his thumb. 'The family's awake. All of them. Including the kids.'

'You look happy to be getting outside.'

'Crying pre-schoolers ain't for me.' Wrixon smiled. 'You'll handle it better. More your scene.'

'That'll be the ovaries,' Grace replied, her tone unmistakably sarcastic. 'They make us all born childminders.'

'Pretty much.'

'Screw you, Wrixon. It's not the seventies any more.'

'Pity. Better times.'

'How the hell would you know? You were born in the eighties.'

'I got a TV, don't I?'

'At least you said TV. If you said books I'd have known you were lying.'

Grace stepped inside without another word. They were both tired, she realised, and more irritable than usual. The only sensible course was to walk away.

A second later and the exchange was forgotten, with Grace's attention caught by a sense of movement as she closed the door. Turning quickly, she spotted Maria rushing across the hall, towards the kitchen they'd been in the previous night.

Maria was dressed in poorly fitting white cotton pyjamas

that were designed for practicality, not appearance. As unflattering as they were, the crumpled outfit did nothing to diminish her striking good looks. She was make-up free, her long, light-brown hair set loose down her back and her feet bare: the Hollywood version of a harassed mother, as if she had been expertly made up to appear superficially dowdy, the beauty still clear beneath.

But this was no performance and Maria was exactly what she appeared to be: a frazzled, harassed mother, doing her best to keep life normal for her children in exceptional circumstances. If Grace had doubted that for even a moment, the sight of Maria stumbling over an inconveniently located golden retriever would have changed her mind.

'JESUS FUCK!'

Maria had glanced back as she went down the three steps into the kitchen and hadn't spotted the family pet lounging at the bottom.

Grace ran towards the doorway as she saw Maria fall, passing the fleeing dog as she went. By the time she reached the steps Maria had regained her balance and was leaning against the kitchen island, bent over and massaging her injured ankle.

'Are you OK?'

She looked up at the sound of Grace's voice, her eyes tearful.

'I'm . . . it's just . . . it's everything. Nothing's going right, Eden. It's all so goddamned hard.'

Grace stepped forwards, but then she hesitated. Her first instinct had been to place an arm around Maria and give her the opportunity to cry, but she pushed that aside. Grace had no idea if Maria would welcome that; they hardly knew each other, after all.

Deciding on a less tactile approach, Grace instead moved around the island, grabbed a tall kitchen stool and carried it to where Maria was standing.

'Take the weight off.' Grace placed the stool down as she spoke. 'You need to elevate the ankle.'

The advice made Maria smile wryly and Grace instantly realised why. How to manage a sprain was hardly something an emergency room surgeon needed to be told.

'Thank you.' Maria took the seat. 'But don't worry, it's not bad. It'll walk off. It's just . . . you know . . . it's just on top of everything else.'

'I understand.' Grace moved back to the far side of the kitchen island as she spoke. She placed both hands palm-down on the worktop as she faced Maria. 'What you're going through, it's a lot. It's too much.'

'It is that, but what choice do I have? Whatever Kon's got himself into, I can't allow my boys to become collateral damage. I need to keep them safe.'

'I know that. And you will, Maria. *We* will. That's why Dempsey sent us. He won't let anything happen to you.'

Maria brightened a little at the mention of Dempsey's name, just as she had done the previous night. It was a reaction Grace could not miss, but one she knew she had to ignore. Instead she focused on a different subject.

'You sound angry with Kon.'

'Wouldn't you be? With everything he's putting us through?'

'I get that. But you don't know the full story yet.'

'Not all of it, no. But I've got no doubt Kon caused this, Eden. Because this isn't about just the last twenty-four hours. He's not been himself for a very long time. I've tried to ignore it. To deny it for the sake of our marriage. But there's no getting away from it. Not now. He's changed since the business started doing well. A different guy.'

'In what way?'

'He was sweet, you know. He was no Joe Dempsey, that's for damn sure. But in his own way he was . . . he was good. A good man. He was hard-working and loving and there was nothing that was too much for him, if it made the family happy.

'Then, a few years ago, the nice, patient man I married seemed to disappear. The bank balance started to increase, sure, but as it did he . . . he became . . . arrogant, somehow. He was stressed all the time, and he started putting on this kind of alpha male bullshit. I mean, Jesus, he was a computer nerd. But there he was acting like the wolf of goddamn Wall Street.'

Grace nodded sympathetically.

'But I tried to get past it. To make the best of it. For the sake of the boys, you know. I didn't want them to come from a broken home. And he was still out there providing for the family. He was working hard.'

'How long was this all going on?'

'At its worst? The past two years. But really, it started way before that. He's not been himself for I don't know how long. Four, five years?'

Grace was shocked by the answer.

'Five years? Holy shit, Maria. That's a long time to live with something like that. To be unhappy, I mean.'

'It is when you stop and think about it. I guess I was just trying to make the best of it, you know? Just like I always have.'

'Like you *always* have? What does that mean?'

Maria hesitated. Grace could tell she had said more than she had intended. But after a moment Maria continued, and when she did it was with an air of relief.

'What I mean is that I've always made the best of being with Kon. He . . . he wasn't exactly my first choice.'

Grace said nothing. This was not where she had expected their conversation to go. And now that it was, she was unsure it was something she wanted to hear.

'I don't mean what you probably think,' Maria continued. 'Kon wasn't a replacement for Joe. How could he be? Joe Dempsey is kind of a hard act to follow, you know? Poor Kon was never going to live up to *that*. But then he was never supposed to. He was supposed to be a fling. A nice, harmless guy, perfect to ease my way back into dating.'

Grace remained silent. Maria did not seem to notice. The one-way conversation was, Grace realised, almost a long-overdue therapy.

'When Dempsey and I split in 2012 it was like a death, Eden. We were so close. He was . . . he was everything to me. And when it ended I mourned him. For three years. I didn't look at another man for *three years*. It . . . it wasn't healthy. I realised that and so I tried to do something about it. To get some semblance of a life back. My first date? Kon. Like I said, nice, unthreatening, no pressure. He was supposed to be the gentle route back.'

This time Maria stopped speaking, leaving Grace with no choice but to ask the obvious question.

'So what happened? How did he go from a single date to a husband?'

'Do you really need to ask? Eddie happened. Our son. I got pregnant and that's all she wrote.'

'You married Kon because you had a kid on the way?'

'I know what it sounds like. I know what you think: it's not the 1950s any more. I could have brought Eddie up alone. I mean, if I'd done that we sure as hell wouldn't be where we are today, would we?'

'But why didn't you?'

'Because I was a mess. I was still screwed up by Joe. I was madly in love with a man I couldn't have and with my head all over the place like that, I wasn't thinking straight. So I did what I thought was best. I settled for the nice guy. Then I spent the next seven years trying to make it work.'

Grace said nothing. Maria had shared more than either woman had expected, and in doing so she had answered a lot that Grace had not asked. But the 'therapy' had taken its toll, leaving Maria visibly tearful. Seeing that, Grace stood up and walked to the cupboard behind her, to give her a moment to compose herself.

'How about a coffee?' Grace asked, taking out two mugs and a tin of instant granules as she spoke.

'You haven't asked the obvious question.'

Grace closed her eyes at the comment, disappointed that the coffee distraction had not worked. She already knew more than she really wanted. All the same, there was no way she could stop this now.

'Which is what?' she asked.

'You didn't ask if I ever loved him.'

Grace took a breath, realising that Maria now wanted this to be a two-way deal; it left Grace with no choice but to actively fill the role of therapist. Taking her time before re-engaging, she slowly filled the thick iron kettle from the tap and placed it on the lit stove. Then she returned to the kitchen island and looked Maria in the eye.

'So did you?'

'I don't think I did, no. Not as I look back now. I think I convinced myself I did at the time. But it was never real love.'

'What then?'

'I think it was a friendship. I cared for Kon. I still care for him. I don't want to see him hurt. But love, like in songs and poems and movies and all that fairy-tale bullshit? No, I don't think I ever did.'

'But it's not fairy-tale bullshit, is it? It does exist.'

'For some people, maybe.'

'It did for you. You just told me that.'

'Oh yeah, and that worked out brilliantly, huh?'

'Just because it didn't work out doesn't mean it wasn't real. You clearly loved him. And he was sure as hell in love with you.'

'You think?'

'I don't just think. You were his world, Maria. You meant every bit as much to him as he did to you. He loved you. And no one else has ever come close since then. No one.'

Grace noticed a tear forming in Maria's eye and so she turned her back for a moment, making a show of adding milk to the still empty coffee cups. When she turned back, the tear was gone.

'If he loved me so much,' Maria said, 'then where was our happy every after? Fairy tales don't end how we did.'

'That's because Prince Charming doesn't have to put his life on the line every day. You know his reasons, Maria.'

'He told you?'

'He told me he couldn't walk away from his job. Not when he had so much bad shit in his past that he had to make up for. Not when there were so many wrongs he needed to put right. *And* he told me he couldn't put you through the living hell of fearing for his life every single time he was sent away. He ended things so you wouldn't have to suffer through all that. More than anything, he wanted you to be happy. You know that, right?'

At first Maria could not answer. The tears were back, only this time they were no hint. Grace could not even pretend to miss them. When Maria finally spoke, her voice was tight. As if she was trying to speak when all she wanted to do was sob.

'That *is* what he told me. I just . . . I just never believed him. I thought it was an excuse.'

'It was no excuse. He couldn't walk away from that life, Maria, but he knew *you* could. So that's what he made happen. He thought it was the only way you could have a normal future. How you could have a normal husband and a family. Even if it meant putting himself through hell.'

Grace stopped speaking as Maria began to break down, her face now streaked with free-flowing tears. For a moment she was unsure of what to do, until her first instinct finally won through. Stepping forwards, she put her arms around Maria and allowed her to cry the tears she had held back for so long.

FIFTY-FOUR

Checking the integrity of every door and window inside the Golden Calf's central hub and its two wings was essential to ensuring that the property was secure. An interior patrol that took a full twenty minutes when done correctly, and correctly was the only way Grace knew how to do her job.

She had completed the circuit twice since her conversation with Maria, in which time she had thought of little else. The revelation that Maria remained as besotted with Dempsey as Dempsey was with her had come as a surprise. But having listened to Maria describe it in her own words, Grace had no doubt that the decade apart had not dented the feelings of either one.

That knowledge left her in a quandary: what should she do with this new information?

Do I tell Dempsey?

Would Maria want me to do that?

Is that maybe why *she shared it?*

And would Dempsey even want to know?

It was not the type of problem Grace usually faced, so she had no instinct for what the correct answer would be. Nor did she have time to think on it further as the vibration of her phone distracted her from the problem.

It was Dempsey.

'Everything OK, Boss?'

'We're making progress. How are things there?'

'All quiet on the Western front.'

'No sign of any problems?'

'Not a one. Any news from your side?'

'Some. We think we know who we're up against.'

'That's something at least. Progress. Who is it?'

'A whole lot of trouble. I'll explain later. Right now I need to speak to Maria about her husband. It's urgent.'

Grace did not hesitate for a moment. Dempsey had barely finished the sentence before she had turned and headed back in the direction of Maria's room, where she knew Maria had gone to compose herself following their conversation.

'I'll take the phone to her now,' Grace said, moving up the central staircase. 'What is it you need to know?'

'I need to find Frankowski. And I need her help.'

Maria visibly held her breath as Grace placed her phone on the tall dressing table that stood between them and converted the handset's setting to loudspeaker. It was clear that she had not expected to speak to Dempsey again so soon.

Or with me standing right beside her.

Her eyes said everything they needed to, boring into Grace as the two women waited for Dempsey to speak. An unspoken but clear message passed from one to the other, and in doing so it took some of the pressure from Grace's shoulders: *Please don't repeat a thing*.

Grace replied just as silently, a clear nod of her head all it took to convey her answer.

'Are you both there?'

The sound of Dempsey's voice broke through the silence, causing a visible reaction in Maria. Once again she seemed to brighten, and in that moment Grace realised that for her there was no longer anyone else in the room: there was just her and Dempsey.

'I . . . I am, yeah,' Maria answered. 'I'm here.'

'OK. And Grace?'

'I'm still here too, Boss.'

'Good. OK, to start. Maria, I need your help with something. But there's something else you need to know first.'

Dempsey sounded a little unsure of himself. It was not a tone Grace had heard before. She listened carefully as he continued.

'I need to find Kon, Maria. And I need to do that quick. Now I think you can probably help me with that, but first you need to understand the consequences.'

The final word caused Maria to look away from the phone and towards Grace. She looked confused.

'What consequences?' she asked. 'What does that mean?'

'For Kon. And so for you and your family too.'

'I don't understand?'

'There have been some allegations made against him, Maria. Suggestions that he has been laundering funds for some very unsavoury people. And if it's true then he will go to prison. Which means that if I find him – if you help me to find him – he could end up behind bars.'

'WHAT?!'

Grace watched Maria carefully as she reacted to the news. Her shock, she could see, was genuine.

'That can't be right,' Maria continued a few moments later. 'Kon's a web designer. What the hell would he know about money laundering?'

'Maybe you're right,' Dempsey replied, his voice gentle. 'Maybe he is just that. But the allegations against him, they're being made by people who believe them to be true. So you have to at least consider it, Maria. The possibility he's been lying to you.'

'No. No, I can't . . . I know he's . . . he's gotten himself mixed up in something. But he's not a criminal. He can't be a . . .'

Grace noted the expression on Maria's face as she trailed off. As if realisation was dawning. As if things were finally making sense. For a few seconds there was nothing but silence, until it was broken by a voice from the phone that did not have time to waste.

'Maria, are—'

'Why are you telling me this?'

The question was snapped out. As if Maria suspected some bad motive in what Dempsey had just told her. Grace knew she did not mean it; it was only human nature that she should react defensively after what must seem right now like an attack on her family life.

Dempsey could not have missed the tone either, but it did nothing to dispel the calm in his own voice. He was not going to allow this to become bitter.

'I'm telling you because I need your help to find him, Maria. But I won't trick you into thinking I'm there to save him. You deserve to know where finding him could lead. That way, I've given you every chance to refuse.'

Maria hesitated again. Just a second or two this time.

'And if you *don't* find him? What risk does that have for my kids?'

'As long as Kon is out there, the Monk will be looking for him. And as long as that's the case, you and the boys are at risk. It's like I told you yesterday. You're leverage.'

'Who the hell is the Monk?'

'That's a long story. I'll tell you on another day, when all this is done. I promise you that. For now, all you need to know is he's the other guy who's looking for your husband. And he *isn't* looking to bring him in alive.'

Grace's gaze never left Maria's face as Dempsey answered her questions and so she could see that Maria understood. His straightforward honesty made it impossible to do otherwise. A few more seconds and she had made her decision.

'OK. What do you need to know?'

'First one's a long shot. Do you know the name Hannibal Strauss? Did Kon ever mention him?'

'Never,' Maria replied. 'And I'd remember a name like that. Sorry.'

'That's fine,' Dempsey replied. 'Like I said, it was a long shot. And the next one is more important anyway. I need your help to find Kon.'

'I've no idea where he is. I wasn't lying when I said that last night. If I could help you find him, I would. Believe me.'

'I don't think you were lying, Maria. But I do think maybe you can help, even if you don't realise it. Wherever Kon went, he went without his passport and without travel documents; they're all still in his hotel room. That means he can't have left the Netherlands. His mobile phone hasn't been used – not even a background ping – and he's made no attempt to access social media or emails or any other kind of messaging service that could help us locate him. Plus there's been no card use on any of his accounts since yesterday evening in The Hague, when he maxed out his daily withdrawal limit on every one of them. That tells me he's living on cash right now, to avoid any trace. Any of that sound familiar to you?'

'They're all the things *you* taught *me* to do. In case I ever had to disappear.'

'I'm glad you remember the lessons.'

'Me too. If I didn't, I might have driven my own car to Dad's place instead of loaning my neighbour's. I doubt we'd be having this conversation now if I had.'

'Lucky you're a good student.'

'I had a good teacher.'

'And my guess is that you became one yourself. A teacher, I mean. You told Kon what to do, right?'

'I did. Kon called me after the shooting. He didn't tell me much, but said he was in trouble. So I told him what I had to, to keep him alive.'

'You did a good job. And so has Kon. He seems to have followed your instructions to the letter. But right now that's a problem for me.'

'I won't apologise, Joe. Whatever Kon's done, he *is* my husband. For now, at least. More importantly, he's the father of my boys. However things pan out between me and him, that last one's forever. So I had to do whatever I could to protect him.'

'I'm not criticising you, Maria. I'd have done exactly the same. But the seven hundred and fifty euros he withdrew isn't enough money to hide for long. Did you arrange to send him more?'

'Yeah. Yeah, I did that, too. I told him that once I got to where I was going, I'd deposit a chunk of money with Western Union for him to collect.'

'Which outlet?'

'We didn't specify one. And I didn't want to know anyway. I was angry, Joe. I was angry that he'd put me and the boys *and* himself at risk. So I didn't ask. And I don't think he even knew then where he was headed.'

'OK. Well, at least we know something. And Western Unions, they're not as common as they used to be. So that'll help narrow things down a little more. There can't be that many to choose from.'

'One other thing I did say,' Maria said after a momentary pause, 'I told Kon to make sure he used a branch far away from wherever he was staying. A different city. Just get in and get out. Collect the money and then head back.'

'Clever. Did I teach you that, too?'

'I don't know. Maybe you did. It just seemed logical.'

'Well, good instincts, then. Although it means narrowing down the options doesn't help us much after all. Is there anywhere in the country that Kon has been before? Anywhere he might head to out of familiarity?'

Maria did not answer immediately. Grace could tell that she was thinking, and she could see the change in her expression when she had the answer.

'There are two I can think of,' she finally said. 'Places we went together, when we visited Europe a few years back.'

'Where are they?'

'Amsterdam and Eindhoven.'

'OK. That's good. Any idea which one he liked better?'

'Definitely Amsterdam. But there's no way he'd have gone there.'

'Why not?'

'It's too obvious and Kon's not an idiot. Amsterdam's the big one. What did you always tell me, back when we were living in Credenhill? If I ever had to run, I shouldn't go to London or Manchester or Cardiff because major centres are the first place they'd expect.'

'True.'

'Plus remember what Kon used to do for a living, Joe. He was a systems expert, so he knows how the security set-up works in major cities. He knows how much easier it is to track someone in somewhere big and modern like Amsterdam. If he has to choose between the two, he'll choose Eindhoven.'

'You're sure?'

'Of course I'm not sure. How could I be sure? But if I had to bet, that'd be where my money went. Kon didn't even like the place when we were there, which makes me even more inclined to believe he'd pick it. That's how his weird mind works. He'd think no one could suspect he'd go to a dive like that when there are so many better options.'

'I suppose that's as good as it's going to get,' he said.

'Thanks,' Maria said, her tone sarcastic. 'You've made me feel like such a help.'

'I'm sorry. I was just thinking aloud.'

'Yeah. I got that.'

'Again, I'm sorry. You've genuinely been a big help. I think we can narrow down the options with what you've told me.'

'Is there anything else you need?'

'Just one thing: when do you think he'll go for the money?'

'To Western Union? Knowing Kon, as soon as possible. Could be today.'

'Already? You don't think he'd lie low a bit longer?'

'Maybe. But my guess is he'll have seen the cash depleting and panicked, and I told him I would deposit it today.'

'And have you?'

'Not yet.'

'Then don't. In case we don't cover the right outlet and we miss him on his first visit. It helps us if we do have to go back.'

'You're asking me to actively aid in his capture, Joe.'

'I'm asking you to do what's necessary for me to help your boys, Maria.'

The answer invited no response. And Maria clearly did not have one. Dempsey seemed to know as much and so he continued.

'I guess that means the clock's ticking. I'd best get to it.'

'Get to what?' This time it was Grace who replied. 'Every Western Union within, what, a hundred miles of Eindhoven? How are you planning to pull that off, Boss?'

'Leave the details to me.'

'As always.'

Grace moved her hand towards the phone, expecting Dempsey to clear the line as he always did when the next steps were settled. But before she could reach the handset she felt the touch of Maria's fingertips on her wrist. It made her look up and, as she did, she could see that Maria had more to say.

Grace stepped back, allowing the conversation to continue.

'Listen, Joe,' Maria began, her voice slow. Grace noticed that her tone had changed. The earlier hint of irritation was gone. Now she just sounded vulnerable. 'I know you have to find him. And I know he's done wrong. But please, don't hurt him. If something happens to him, I'll never be able to face my sons. He's their daddy, Joe.'

'You don't need to say that. I don't do that any more. Not for a long time.'

'And you won't let anyone else hurt him?'

'You don't need to ask me that, either.'

'Thank you.'

Another pause.

'And Joe?'

'Yeah.'

'Please stay safe, too. I couldn't live with myself if anything happened to you.'

This time it was Dempsey who hesitated. It seemed to Grace that he had something else on his mind. Something else to say. Whatever it was, he decided against it. Perhaps because he knew that Grace was right there, too, and would overhear.

When he finally spoke again, Dempsey settled for banality.

'I'll call you when I have him. Take care of yourself.'

The line went dead.

FIFTY-FIVE

Special Agent Alan Tyson checked the door of the empty, glass-walled office closest to his own desk and was surprised to find it unlocked. Very little had gone right for him the last twenty-four hours, and like any gambler he was always looking for a sign that his luck was about to change.

Maybe it finally was?

The encrypted phone secreted within his suit jacket had vibrated four times already. It left him with little time to find a secluded spot and so the open office was a godsend; this was not a call he could take in the open-plan workspace in which he usually sat.

A quick scan of the room confirmed no blind spots for a potential eavesdropper to be hidden. Satisfied he was alone, he pressed the connect icon and placed the phone to his ear.

'Give me a second.'

Tyson did not wait for a response. He placed the handset on the desk just across from the doorway and set about ensuring his privacy. It took barely seconds; first to close and lock the door, then to close the two sets of vertical blinds that would shield him from the main workspace.

He picked up the phone and stepped away from now obscured glass wall, towards the wide panoramic window that looked out on the streets of Woodland Park.

'Sorry about that. I had to make sure we couldn't be seen or heard.'

'Where are you?'

The tone of the Monk's voice made Tyson immediately

uncomfortable. But then when did it not? That weird Russian accent always put Tyson's back up.

'I'm at the Field Office in Woodland Park.'

'Are you secure?'

'In what way?'

'The investigation into the events of yesterday. Are you implicated?'

'No, not yet.'

Tyson felt a detectable increase in his blood pressure as he answered. He had been doing his best to keep his mind off the subject for exactly that reason. As inevitable as the outcome was, he could lie to himself if he did not have to think about it.

Right now, he had no choice but the truth.

'It's only a matter of time,' he continued. 'For the moment they figure Ben was on someone's payroll. The fact he was killed with Mancuso, it makes them think it was the mob. But that won't last.'

'Why not? With Mancuso's background, it's a solid theory.'

Tyson knew that the Monk was both right but at the same time very wrong. The mob connection *was* a solid theory. Mancuso had been a well-known New York gangland figure. A throwback to the mid-twentieth century when wise-guys like him acted with impunity. And so Ben McDonald being killed alongside a man like that, after breaking into a local family home?

It screamed bent cop.

Problem was, the Bureau would want to know just *how* bent.

'Corrupt agents get investigated like no one else,' Tyson explained. 'You know that. When this thing picks up pace, they'll find no further connection between Ben and Mancuso.

They will, though, see other things they were never supposed to. Things that implicate me.'

'And what do you propose to do?'

'I'm already doing it. I'm getting my affairs in order and then I'm gone. I need to be out of here before I find myself in a cell. Speaking of which, I want the money I'm owed.'

'The money was to be paid to your creditors. That was the deal.'

Tyson knew the deal. His gambling debts had been the price the Monk had paid for his services. But with his future on the line, well, now they hardly mattered at all.

'Do you really think I'm planning to pay those fuckers if I'm in the wind? Why? No, my little Rusky friend. You can pay me direct.'

The Monk said nothing for a few moments. And Tyson had no intention of breaking the silence. He had little left to lose and that gave him a freedom he did not usually enjoy.

'You know,' the Monk finally said, his voice free of emotion, 'the last person who spoke to me that way didn't live long to regret it. But unlike you, he had by that time outlasted his usefulness. You haven't. Yet. So let's dispense with the threats and the play-acting and instead let's focus on what I *can* do for you. And more importantly, on what you *will* do for me in return.'

It was not the response Tyson had expected. The Monk could tell that from the man's silence. Tyson had clearly been enjoying his own belligerence. No doubt he did not expect that he would ever be paid what was outstanding; that it was the last time the two would speak.

It took him almost ten seconds before he spoke again. When he did, he sounded less combative.

'OK,' he finally said. 'Shoot.'

'It won't be me doing the shooting,' the Monk replied. 'That will be *your* role.'

'Very funny. Where and when?'

'You don't want to know *who*?'

'What does that matter? The way things stand, I'm not saying no on principle. Only thing that matters is the practicality. You want a favour exchange from me, I need to know it's soon enough that I still have time to run.'

'Is today soon enough?'

'Today? Are you serious?'

'I am always serious. You should know that by now.'

'OK. Then yeah, that works. Where?'

'It's a ranch in Upstate New York,' the Monk said. 'Just outside of Cooperstown. I want it hit today. The civilian women and the children you find there, I want them taken alive. At least for now. Do what you want with the rest, although I'd suggest they'll be a lot less trouble dead.'

'And the captives? What do I do with them?'

'Keep them on the ranch. It's big. No one will come looking. Not in the timeframe I have in mind.'

'Which is what?'

'Twenty-four hours. Probably less. I'll be in touch. Then you're done.'

'And when that happens? When we're done?'

'Then I want every single person inside it dead – not a person left breathing – and I want every single building burned to the ground. Nothing left standing. Is that something I can trust you to do?'

'Not alone it's not.'

'We both know you won't be alone. This isn't amateur hour. You'll have a full team to work with. A big one, well equipped with everything you could need.'

'OK. How many people will this team and I find in there?'

'Six adult targets. Three children. Plus some hired farmhands.'

'And the children? You're sure about them? About what you want me to do?'

'Is that a problem?'

'Not at all. Their deaths are on your head, not mine. I just wanted to be clear. So how much are you offering for this?'

'Half a million dollars,' the Monk said. 'Paid into the account of your choice. And I will provide all the assistance you need to leave the country.'

'To where?'

'Where do you want to go?'

'Always did like the look of Cuba.'

'Consider it done.'

Tyson said nothing. A silence that worried the Monk. He was concerned for a moment that he had shown his hand too clearly. That the FBI agent had realised how dire his situation was.

'Five hundred grand's a lot of money for one job,' Tyson finally said. 'If you've got a big team and they've everything they need for this job, what makes me so valuable?'

'What I need is someone to lead them. Someone I know I can trust.'

The last few words were a lie. The Monk didn't trust Tyson one bit and both men knew it.

But he did *need* him.

The Monk's position in the US was not as stretched as it was in Europe. He had been forced to call on some of his North American operatives to deal with the fallout of the Ukraine situation but the majority of his US resources remained intact.

Money, however? Money was a problem everywhere. The economic hit of funding a 'patriotic Russian counter-offensive' against its own president had been huge. With so much tied into the cost of the paramilitary groups currently fighting inside Russia, the Monk could afford no one to lead the men he was sending to Cooperstown.

No one who would ask to see their payment up front, at least.

It left him needing someone as desperate as himself. Someone who would be too tantalised by the sum that he would not question either the Monk's ability or motivation to pay it. He hoped that man would be Alan Tyson and so he now moved to seal the deal.

'It's also very useful to me that you're familiar with the targets.'

'I am? Who are they?'

'The ISB agents you encountered yesterday. The ones who turned you and McDonald over. They'll be there. And they'll be ready to defend the place.'

'So this is about the Frankowskis again?'

'The Frankowski family is there, yes.'

Tyson was silent again for a few more moments.

'How many agents?' he finally asked.

'ISB? Four. On a working ranch with endless vulnerable points that's far too large for four agents to defend it. Especially against twenty-five men.'

'Twenty-five?'

'Twenty-six including you. Twenty-eight if we count the pilots.'

'Pilots?'

'I told you, the team is well equipped. And I don't want a single building left standing.'

'You're sending a plane?'

'A helicopter. To lay waste once you're done.'

'All this for four agents?'

'Four agents and the family. Maria Frankowski, her two children, her father and her sister. And perhaps a few enthusiastic cowboys, but they're paid help. They'll last until the first one falls.'

'Still, is it not overkill?'

'Those four agents are very good at what they do. And the father is former Marine Corps, even if he is an old man. So that makes five. They're still hopelessly outmatched but they will put up a fight. I've been careful to ensure the odds are in our favour.'

Tyson was silent once again. This time the Monk did not allow it to drag on.

'What's your answer?' he asked.

'Is there any chance you'll tell me what this is all about?'

'Absolutely none. Is that a problem?'

'For half a million dollars and a ticket out of here? None at all. Just curious is all.'

'Don't be.'

'OK,' Tyson replied. 'No more questions. You can consider them yours. And when you're done, you can consider them dead.'

FIFTY-SIX

Michael sat alone in the smaller of the two hospital canteens, his iPhone in his hand and its photo album app displaying memories from yesterday. All of them showed happy images of happy people; a family safe and content.

Twenty-four hours later and his world had been turned upside down.

He had called Sarah within seconds of leaving Scheveningen Prison, the words of Hannibal Strauss still fresh in his mind. Until then he had not considered the safety of his family or the dangers they might face.

But after what Strauss had described? The tactics the Monk was willing to employ?

It had left Michael without a choice.

Terrified at the thought of Sarah and the boys being targeted just to get to him, Michael did something he had hoped would never happen again: he asked Sarah to hide.

The request was simple enough. He needed Sarah to leave their family home – this time with the added burden of their sons – and to cut herself off from her everyday existence, including Michael himself. But simple was not the same as easy.

Michael realised just how huge a thing he was asking. But he also knew that there was no other way. As long as Sarah and the boys were some place they could be found, they were not safe. None of them.

And all because of a danger Michael had once again brought into their lives.

The arrangements were made quickly, the logistics dealt

with by Joelle Levy, with Michael told next to nothing about what they were. He was given no address or even a general location, and he had no phone or email contact. Until this was over, Sarah and the boys were out of his reach.

It was the only way he could ensure they were beyond the Monk's, too.

Michael considered that cost now, as he looked at the photos from the christening. It was a hell of a price to pay. Before coming to The Hague he had not been separated from any of them for even a night since their birth.

'Not one single night,' he said loudly to himself. 'And now this.'

'And now what?'

Michael looked up, his regretful thoughts interrupted by the arrival of Corbin Kincaid. The American was not unexpected; Dempsey had asked him to come. But Dempsey had stepped outside to make a call and so Kincaid had Michael alone.

It was not ideal nor was it the plan, but Michael did not let Dempsey's absence worry him. As much as this was Kincaid's world and not his, the lawyer was determined to start on the front foot.

'You took your time,' he said. 'We expected you an hour ago.'

'I didn't realise I was working to your clock,' Kincaid replied. His tone was exactly as belligerent as Michael expected. 'Where's your boss?'

Michael smiled at the question. He knew what Kincaid was trying to do.

'I don't have a boss. And that sort of divisive shit wouldn't work even if I did. You're the one who has the explaining to do, not us.'

'Explaining? About what?'

Michael ignored the question.

'Where's Sutton?'

'What's it to you?'

'We asked to meet you both.'

'You don't get to dictate how we operate. He's got his own responsibilities.'

'So it's just you?'

'Looks that way. Just the two of us.'

'For now, sure. So let's get started. Do you know where we were this morning?'

'You and your boss, you mean?'

Michael said nothing, refusing to take the bait. It forced Kincaid to play to his tune.

'OK, you've got me all curious. Where were you?'

'We were with Hannibal Strauss,' Michael replied. His eyes studied the American as he spoke, searching for a physical tell. 'He had a whole lot to say about what you and Sutton are really doing in The Hague. *And* why you're so interested in Will Duffy.'

Michael paused for effect. It was an old advocate's trick. Give the witness just enough time for the surprising new information to sink in, then hit them again as their heart begins to race.

Send them left after the first hit sends them right. Like guiding them into mental quicksand.

Michael sat forwards in his seat.

'You going to stop lying now and tell the truth? Or do I just accept Strauss at his word?'

'You're seriously calling a US government operative a liar? Based on what? The word of a goddamn war criminal?'

Kincaid's response was angry, exactly as Michael had expected. It was the natural response of a man with no real answer. Outrage as an alternative to honesty.

'We both *know* you're a liar,' Michael replied. 'Sutton as good as confirmed for us that your excuse about being here for US citizens was bullshit.'

'He did no such thing.'

'Actually, Corbin, I *did*.'

Both men turned towards the source of the voice. It was Sutton.

'I didn't see the point in the pretence,' he continued. 'Not when we could be helping each other. We're on the same team, surely?'

As happy as Michael was for the intervention, he could not help but notice that Sutton seemed shaken. The younger American's face, usually pale, was reddened. As if his blood pressure – or even his temper – had been raised.

'You OK?' Michael asked. 'You look kind of . . .'

'I'm fine,' Sutton replied. 'I just rushed to get here, that's all. I thought there was more chance of this meeting turning out useful if Corbin wasn't doing it alone.'

'What the hell is that supposed to mean?' Kincaid demanded.

'It's nothing personal,' Sutton replied. 'Just that, you know, you guys didn't exactly get along last time we were all together.'

Sutton looked around as he spoke, a quizzical look growing on his face.

'Speaking of which, where's Dempsey?'

'Right behind you.'

All three of them turned at the sound of Dempsey's voice.

The Englishman was already striding towards them, the only other person in the vacant dining room.

Kincaid gave him no time to be brought up to speed.

'You planning on joining your friend in this fantasy?' he demanded.

'If you're talking about what Strauss told us today, it's no fantasy.'

'And what the hell did he tell you, huh? What line have you gullible sonsofbitches bought off the man?'

'The line about the Mladorossi list.'

Michael had intended to say more, but he realised in that instant there was no need. The colour had drained from Kincaid's face. An indication of shock or – more likely – extreme anger.

Dempsey would have seen exactly the same reaction. Unlike Michael, he chose to say more.

'The same list you were supposed to collect from Mendel Prochnik,' Dempsey said. 'And probably the reason you came here last night; you came in case the exchange had been made and Will Duffy had it on him, didn't you? I take it you searched his room and his belongings in the night? And that you found nothing?'

Kincaid said nothing. His silence was all the answer they needed.

He looked from Michael to Dempsey and then to Sutton, his usual bold arrogance and belligerence somehow unmissable even in his silence. His displeasure at what Dempsey and Michael had revealed was clear; it was not information he wanted anyone else to have. Even agents from an allied agency. That much was clear from his stubborn refusal to respond. From his refusal to confirm that the Brits had called it right.

But still Michael tried.

'It's like I asked you earlier: Are you going to tell us the truth now? Or are we all just going to keep up this pretence?'

Kincaid lowered his backside onto the nearest table, his eyes fixed on Dempsey even as Michael spoke. He seemed either unwilling or unable to answer. Sutton, still standing, looked apologetically at both Dempsey and Michael.

An apology for which Dempsey had no time.

'Sod it,' he said. 'You can play spy games all you like, Kincaid. But I won't. There are lives at stake here so let's see if there's one last piece of news that might change your mind.'

'News about what?'

'News about the list.'

Kincaid sat upright.

'You know who has it?'

Dempsey nodded.

'We know who has it.'

FIFTY-SEVEN

Kincaid looked suspiciously around the empty canteen as all four men took their seats at the nearest table.

'Are you sure we can speak here?'

'No cameras in this room,' Dempsey replied. 'No reason to think it's wired and it isn't even staffed. No one uses it. Everyone goes to the main cafeteria downstairs.'

Kincaid looked round one last time, then fixed his eyes on Dempsey.

'OK. In that case, where's the list?'

'Not yet,' Dempsey said. 'First we need to know a few things.'

'Like what?'

'Like who knew that Prochnik and Duffy were meeting Frankowski to collect the Mladorossi list?'

'You think there was a leak our end?'

'There was a leak somewhere. Who knew?'

'No one.' The answer came from Sutton when Kincaid said nothing. 'Not even us. Prochnik and Duffy told us when it was happening, so we could arrange to meet them after; neither one wanted the list in their possession for any longer than they had to. But they didn't tell us where the meet was or who it was with.'

'Then how did you know the attack yesterday wasn't really a terrorist attack?' Michael asked. 'How did you know to follow up on it?'

'Because we know how the Monk operates,' Kincaid replied. 'And a gun massacre anywhere in The Hague, at the exact moment the handover was supposed to be taking place? There's no way that was a coincidence.'

Dempsey nodded his head. The reasoning made sense.

'What about the generality of the thing? Some idea of why you two were here in the first place. Someone must have known at least that.'

'In broadest terms, yeah,' Kincaid explained, his voice a little less arrogant than Dempsey was used to. 'But no more than that. This operation, it doesn't come with a whole lot of oversight.'

'Why?'

'Because the Monk and Mladorossi aren't exactly the top of the Agency's priorities right now.'

'Or at any time in the last thirty years,' Sutton added.

'I don't understand,' Michael said.

'I do,' Dempsey answered. 'Your side think he's a myth, too, right?'

'They do,' Sutton replied. 'Everyone but us. Although no one wants to make that call for sure, just in case. And so we've kind of been given free rein on this. No results expected. Anything we achieve is a bonus.'

Dempsey turned to face Kincaid.

'How long?'

'Twenty-five years, give or take.'

'How close did you ever get?'

'This. This is the closest.'

'And before this?'

'Nothing.'

'In all that time?'

'Yep.'

'That must have devastated your career.'

'It didn't do me much good, no.'

'So why?'

'Because I knew the sonofabitch was real. I knew the stories – the rumours – were real. I knew I'd get him one day, and look where we are today.'

'But how? Why were you so certain?'

'I was trained by a man who was certain. A man who had seen the bastard with his own eyes. I trusted him absolutely, through all those years and all those failings. Bill Sutton knew the Monk was real and he spent his career trying to prove it. I owed it to him to finish the job he started.'

'Sutton?' Dempsey turned towards Sean Sutton as he said the name.

'My dad,' Sutton replied. 'He was a spy-catcher. Runs in the family, I guess.'

'And he'd actually seen the Monk?'

'He did. Early in his career, in East Germany. He was obsessed with catching him ever since.'

'And the CIA just allowed that? Him, then Kincaid and now you both?'

'My dad was pretty good at what he did. He never found the Monk again, but he caught a hell of a lot of others. Including agents he was sure were Mladorossi. It bought him a lot of leeway.'

Dempsey turned back to Kincaid.

'And it was Bill Sutton who trained you?'

'It was. Like I said, I owe him this.'

Dempsey considered Kincaid's answers. There was something about the man that he still did not like, but he was unsure if that dislike equated to distrust. At the same time, the job that now lay ahead of them needed more than two men.

It needed four. At least four. And that left him with little choice.

He made his decision.

'Have either of you ever heard of a Konrad Frankowski?'

Kincaid and Sutton glanced towards each other, both faces blank. It gave Dempsey his answer before they even spoke.

'Who is he?'

'He's the man Prochnik and Duffy were meeting,' Dempsey replied. 'He's the man with the list.'

'The guy from the footage, the one Duffy pulls up? We couldn't identify him.'

'We know.'

'You're sure that's who he is?'

'As sure as we can be, based on what Strauss told us.'

'Plus Duffy said his name in a voice message he left me,' Michael added. 'When he thought things might go south. No other details. But taken together that's a pretty solid indication.'

'And you know where this guy is?'

This time it was Dempsey and Michael who shared a glance. Dempsey hoped it was enough to communicate his thoughts to his friend. It would have to be.

He turned back to the Americans.

'We have a way to find him.'

'Where?'

'He'll be in one of two locations later today. One's in Cuijk, the other Arnhem.'

'And how do you know that?' The question came from Sutton.

'No offence, Sean,' Dempsey said, 'but I'm not spilling all my secrets just yet. Here's what you need to know. At two p.m. today Frankowski will be visiting a Western Union outlet.

Based on where we believe him to be hiding out, the branches in Cuijk and Arnhem are the nearest two he could go to.'

'So all you really know is he'll be going to a Western Union somewhere in the Netherlands?'

'With some educated reasoning, we're confident about the two outlets we've named.'

'And how do you figure that? There's got to be more than two he could use?'

'He's not likely to head west from where he is,' Dempsey explained. 'That'd bring him too close to The Hague and he's hardly likely to go back to the place he's just escaped. So west is out. There are no outlets south of his location and there's no more Netherlands east of it. Plus he doesn't have his passport, so he can't leave the country. All of which means he'll go north.

'If he does that, the first Western Union he hits is in Cuijk. The next is Arnhem. They're relatively close to one another so it's impossible to make a call on which one it will be. But since there's no logical reason for him to travel any further than those, it's got to be one of the two.'

'How can you be so sure he'll be there at two p.m. when you don't even know which branch?' Sutton asked.

'Because that's when the Western Unions open in New York.'

'Jesus.' Kincaid's initial cynicism seemed to have gone completely, replaced by his earlier energy. His excitement was clear. 'You really think this information is right?'

'They're the only options that make any sense.'

'And the source of the intel?'

'Like I said, you don't need to know. But it's solid.'

'And what about the other Western Union outlets to the

west?' Sutton asked. 'Should we not cover them too, just in case?'

'In an ideal world we'd stake out every last one of them,' Dempsey replied. 'But we don't have the manpower. At least not from people we can trust. After what happened last night, I'm not willing to take the risk.'

'Agreed,' said Kincaid. 'It's just the four of us.'

'Yes,' Dempsey replied. 'Two of us in Cuijk, two in Arnhem. But not in the pairings you're thinking of.'

Dempsey felt all eyes turn to him as he made the statement.

'What does that mean?'

'It means that Corbin will be coming with me. Sean, you're with Michael.'

'Why?'

'Because I can't say I trust either of you just yet either,' Dempsey replied. 'And I'm not giving you two the opportunity to land Frankowski without us. So we split the teams. That way I've got a man I trust at both locations.'

'You don't get to tell us what to do,' Kincaid began. 'You can't—'

'I do if you want to be a part of this,' Dempsey replied. 'If you want your only chance to find the Monk in thirty years to go anywhere.'

'And if we go alone?'

'You go alone you can cover one outlet. Fifty-fifty chance you get what you're looking for. My way, the odds are one hundred per cent. Is that clear enough for you?'

Kincaid said nothing. And Dempsey knew why. The point was unarguable.

'You mind if I say something?'

Dempsey turned towards Sutton.

'Go ahead.'

Sutton glanced at Michael before he spoke, his expression apologetic.

'I don't want to offend anyone here, but you're sending me out with a civilian when there's a trained operative available?'

'Fine. You come with me. Corbin can go with Michael.'

'That's not what I meant,' Sutton explained. 'I mean that if I'm going into the lion's den, I'd sure as hell like to have a bear by my side.'

It took Dempsey a moment to realise what Sutton was saying. Michael was an instant quicker.

'You mean Sal,' he said. 'You want Sal with you instead of me.'

'No offence.'

'None taken. I'd want him ahead of you.'

Michael turned to face Dempsey.

'He's got a point, Joe. You guys don't know what you're going up against. It could be nothing, it could be everything the Monk can throw at you or it could be anything in between. You need the best you've got available and I'm not so vain that I think that's me. Not with Sal downstairs.'

Dempsey nodded his head in agreement.

'You're right. So Sean, you'll be with Sal. And Michael, you'll stay here and guard Duffy.'

Michael nodded back. Anything more was unnecessary.

'You've already met Sal?' Dempsey asked, his attention now back on Sutton.

'I had a talk with him earlier today. He's a man of few words.'

'Until he knows you. But you'll have plenty of time for that today.'

Dempsey stood up from the table.

'Since I have no introductions to make, let's get going. It's a ninety-minute drive to Cuijk and we need to be there by two p.m. We don't want to miss the man who can give us the Monk.'

FIFTY-EIGHT

Kon Frankowski leaned against the uncomfortable seating rail that stretched across the full length of Eindhoven Central Bus Station's glass and metal facade, his eyes cast downwards.

He had been at the station for a little under ten minutes. Long enough to feel uncomfortable in the intense heat of the day.

Kon was disguised once again in his newly acquired clothes. With the luxury of a bathroom mirror he had also attempted a wet shave of his head, which he now regretted. It had left his scalp raw with cuts.

Luckily they were hidden by the fedora. The contact irritation against his broken skin was uncomfortable as hell, but the hat was necessary. It covered his face from every elevated angle and so from most of the CCTV cameras that were positioned around the ageing station.

Kon glanced at his paper bus schedule and cursed his underestimate of the travel time between Hotel Olympic and the terminal. It had caused him to miss the 12.52 p.m. bus by two minutes. The wait for the next was just eleven minutes, but the 1.03 p.m. took almost half an hour longer to reach Uden Bus Station. From there he needed to catch a second bus to Cuijk, arriving at 3.13 p.m. It was an hour later than he had planned. Maybe even more, since he had not yet determined how far the station was from the Western Union branch.

Kon's eyes flicked to his watch and he considered again if he should wait a little longer for the next fast bus. It was tempting, but against it was the fact that the longer he waited the longer he was out in the open.

And the more chance I'm recognised.

People would be looking for him. He was sure of that. And he had to assume that search would eventually reach Eindhoven.

The reach and the ruthlessness of Hannibal Strauss's enemies were beyond any doubt. More so than he could have ever guessed; the attack at Grote Markt had made that very clear. Even a hint it could have been this bad and Kon would never have involved himself in what Strauss had persuaded him was a low-risk task.

And he still did not know who those enemies even were.

His thoughts drifted, not for the first time, to the computer file. To what Strauss had referred to only as 'the list'. He had no idea of the content – he had resisted all urges to read the thing; a precaution to protect himself from Strauss. Knowing nothing made it impossible to slip up and reveal information that could, in Strauss's eyes, turn him from an ally to a danger.

That same sense of self-preservation was why Kon had not followed Strauss's strict instructions and brought the file itself to the Grote Markt. Why he had instead purchased a new laptop and set it up to receive the list remotely, via the system he had put in place for that purpose. Kon had done that through his own initiative. A further 'Chinese wall' between himself and information that could be worth more than his life.

Now, as he stood defenceless in Eindhoven with no list, no laptop and no clue as to whose eyes he should be avoiding, he regretted the decision.

At least if I'd taken a look, he thought. *At least if I knew what the hell was on it . . .*

There was nothing to gain from dwelling on that decision,

he realised. Not when his focus was needed on the here and now. And right now he was safest indoors and alone, which meant getting under a roof as soon as possible. Even if that roof was on a slow, drawn-out bus ride.

But at least if I'm travelling, I'm not just a sitting target.

His mind was made up.

The Number 322 – the single deck, ultra-modern vehicle parked in the wide bay just ahead of him – opened its doors with three minutes to go before its scheduled departure time. The driver stepped off, ready to help passengers with their luggage as they boarded.

Kon needed no such assistance. With the exception of the book he had purchased inside the sparse terminal – bought as an excuse to not speak on the journey, rather than to read – he had nothing with him.

A minute later and he was in his seat inside the air-conditioned coach. A relief from both the outside heat and the fear of discovery. Only now did he realise how nervous he had been, out in the daylight with no idea of who might be observing him. But in here he had no such problem. As the first person to board, it was Kon who could assess other passengers as they embarked.

It was not a taxing task. Only six people. Two couples and two singles. None of them gave Kon a second glance and there was nothing about any of them that set off alarm bells. Hardly a guarantee of safety, he realised, but what else did he have beyond his instincts?

With his mind settled, Kon allowed his thoughts to drift to the one place they had returned each time he closed his eyes.

Home.

He had no doubt that Maria would be as good as her word.

That she would do what she had promised, depositing funds at the Western Union from which he could continue to survive. And that in doing so, she would take no risks that could bring trouble either to her own door or to that of her husband.

Maria would *always* do the right thing. Of that he was certain.

He felt a pang of guilt as these thoughts occurred to him, that it was not concern for his family he was focused on but instead what he needed his wife to do for him.

But Kon quickly dismissed the feeling. What else could he be expected to think about? He had no idea what was coming next or of how long this would go on. He needed to be prepared and for that he needed cash. It was all that mattered right now.

He pushed the thought of his family from his mind. It was a distraction he could not afford. Regardless of the safe signals coming from his instincts, he needed to keep his wits about him. To be aware of every passenger. Of every movement.

He took another look around the bus. At the six strangers travelling with him. No one was looking back.

Satisfied, Kon settled back into his seat, willing the journey to be over.

For this whole damn thing to be over.

FIFTY-NINE

Dempsey sat in the passenger seat of Corbin Kincaid's Audi A8, his eyes never leaving the door of the Western Union outlet that was across the street and fifty yards down from where they were parked.

It was 2.10 p.m. Ten minutes later than he had expected to see Konrad Frankowski, if this was the Western Union he had chosen. The delay was far from problematic – Dempsey would wait hours if he had to – but it did make him wonder if Maria knew her husband as well as she had assured him she did.

Conscious that the Cuijk outlet was one of two options, Dempsey's eyes kept drifting to the burner phone that sat between his legs. A cheap, contract-free mobile that could not be traced to him or used to track him. Like the other three operatives engaged with him in the hunt for Frankowski, he had left his own phone with Michael; Dempsey had discovered long ago that the best way to avoid the danger a contracted mobile tracking device posed to missions of this type was to simply not carry it.

It was from Gallo's burner, then, that he had been hoping to hear.

And the fact that he had not left just two possibilities. Either they had got this wrong or Frankowski was late.

He could only hope it was the latter.

'You getting nervous?'

'Nervous about what?' Dempsey did not even turn his head at the question, his eyes still facing the street as he replied. 'It's only ten minutes.'

'Still not what you expected, though,' Kincaid answered. 'You said two p.m. You sure about this source of yours?'

'Frankowski doesn't know this country. Maybe he got lost. Held up.'

'Maybe the Monk already has him.'

This time Dempsey did turn. Something in Kincaid's tone bugged him.

'You sound like you *want* that to have happened.'

'Don't be ridiculous. I'm just saying you never know. The guy's good.'

'Is that how he's stayed a step ahead of you all these years?'

'You think I'm embarrassed by that? He stayed out of Bill Sutton's reach too, buddy. And Bill was twice the agent you or I will ever be. Being even one step behind the Monk would be one hell of an achievement.'

'You sound like you admire him.'

'Wouldn't you? If you spent twenty-five years of your career chasing a man you know exists, but never getting close enough to prove even that? And all the while watching the shit he pulls – the damage he does – without anyone ever even knowing it's him? You telling me you wouldn't have even an iota of admiration for someone like that?'

'Not one little bit,' Dempsey replied. He turned a little more, for a fuller view of Kincaid. After what he'd just heard, he wanted to assess the man as he spoke. 'If anything I'd be ashamed of myself for not doing my job.'

'You think you'd have fared better?' Kincaid sounded annoyed. 'Do you even know what the Monk has achieved? What the Mladorossi have done?'

'Educate me.'

'They've brought down nations. They've torn up

decades-old alliances. Destabilised societies. And they're only getting better at it in the internet age. The misinformation tactics they've employed across the media and social media, all of that shit, they *are* impressive. Who do you think convinced the British people that they were better off going it alone instead of with the EU, like it was still the 1800s? Who do you think pushed the United States to start questioning NATO? That organisation kept peace in the West for seventy years, and still the Monk had our government thinking it wasn't pulling its weight. They're an insidious force. A shadow network that's been chipping away at us invisibly instead of fighting it out in the open. You really think *you* could go up against something like that?'

Dempsey watched Kincaid carefully, his interest piqued.

'And when that sort of thing isn't enough? Blackmail. Bribery. Sabotage. And, as you've seen, murder. There's no length the Mladorossi won't go to, if they think it will help them win. They are fucking ruthless, Dempsey. Way more than the likes of you and me. And they've had decades and more to get this shit right.'

'Then how is it Russia is in such a mess right now? If they're *that* good?'

'My theory? I think this is what the Monk wants.'

'A failed invasion and a civil war? Are you serious?'

'One hundred per cent. Remember, man, the Mladorossi has been there through every regime change for seventy years. Communist, non-communist, the oligarchy. The one constant is the Monk. Maybe that's no coincidence.'

'What does that mean?'

'Maybe he's behind those changes. The way he seems to glide from regime to regime, untouched and unaffected as others are toppled left and right? Maybe that's because the Mladorossi are driving the regime changes.'

'You mean they're working for Russia but against Russia at the same time?'

'Why not? Look at the history. The whole thing was set up by aristocrats. Tsarists. Why would anyone like that have loyalty to the regime that deposed their class? You're questioning how shaky things are for the bigwigs in Moscow, but what if that's the point? How the hell do we know the Monk isn't responsible for the internal resistance? How do we know he's not behind the coups?'

'So what, you think the Monk wants a throne?'

'I didn't say that. Just that maybe he wants a regime he can control. Which perhaps he could, back at the start of this one. But what's that old saying about power corrupting? Maybe he was able to control the Kremlin back in the day, when this administration started twenty years ago. And perhaps now he can't any more, and so he's decided it's time for someone new.'

Dempsey took a moment to think through what Kincaid was saying. He had to admit, it was not illogical. What had happened in the Ukraine, it had played out in a way that would suit someone seeking regime change in Russia. And with the intervention first of the Wagner Group and now of other, disparate paramilitary resistance – all of them essentially coups against the previously untouchable leadership – that change now looked likely. Never had Russia's president looked weaker and, if Kincaid was correct, that was what truly mattered: for the Monk, appearance was all. It was now near impossible that the current Moscow regime would survive both its massive failure in Ukraine *and* the anti-government coups from within its own borders.

If change at the top was the Monk's endgame, there were few better ways to guarantee it.

The theory went beyond what Dempsey had been thinking but now he considered it he arrived at a simple question: why not? If everything he had heard about the Monk was true, why would he and the Mladorossi *not* have ambitions on that level?

It made sense. But it also raised a problematic question:

How the hell does Kincaid know all this?

Dempsey looked at the American with suspicion.

'So how did we get to this point, then? If the Monk is bringing down governments and controlling what goes on in Moscow, how the hell are we just two steps from naming every last one of his organisation's assets?'

'Through sheer dumb luck and a traitor,' Kincaid snapped the answer. He sounded almost angry about it. 'Without Hannibal Strauss we'd be no further forward. And *that* evil sonofabitch ain't much better than the Monk himself. We can't claim credit for this. We're here because of Strauss. Not because of us.'

Dempsey felt his brow furrow. He immediately regretted expressing a visible reaction. He had not wanted to give away any hint of his concerns, but Kincaid could not have missed it, he was sure. And so he chose to be direct.

'Should I be worried about you, Corbin?'

Kincaid's expression changed at the question. As if he now realised what he had been saying. And, more importantly, how it was coming across. When he spoke, he gave no indication of that.

'About what?'

'You know about what. You sound like you're a fan.'

'Get fucked, Dempsey. You been on this for how long? This is my life, OK?'

'Still. I didn't hear much criticism just then.'

'Am I supposed to care what you think? I'm just steeped in this, that's all. And the truth is I'm a little ashamed of myself. A whole career, Dempsey. A whole working life and I only get close because this shit falls into my lap. I only get close because of you guys. Because of Strauss. It's not the stuff legends are made of, you know?'

'And your theories about the regime changes? The Wagner Group and the others?'

'Guesswork, for Christ's sake. What, you're the only one allowed to make logical deductions? What are we if we're not detectives?'

'Seems you know a hell of a lot more than you mentioned earlier, that's all.'

'And that's a surprise? After two and a half decades? Shit, I could fill a month telling you all the stuff you don't know.'

Dempsey said nothing in reply; it was plain that for every comment he made, Kincaid had an answer. Instead he just made a show of nodding his head, his mind far from made up.

With everything he had revealed, there was simply no way for Dempsey to know the motives of the man to his left. And so no way he could trust him.

With Frankowski potentially minutes away, it was *not* ideal.

SIXTY

Michael shifted uncomfortably in the lone chair at Will Duffy's bedside.

His injuries from the night before were bothering him more now than they had been through the day. Maybe it was how these things worked now he was a little older. Or perhaps this was just the first time he had been still enough to notice them.

Either way, he was once again cursing his run-in with the fake doctor.

The door to Will's room was closed, the space was silent. It allowed Michael time to think.

As ever, his first thoughts were for Sarah and the boys. He wondered again where they were. How they were. He would give almost anything just to speak to Sarah right now but he knew he could not take that risk. He could do nothing that could put his family in the crosshairs of the Monk.

Not until this is over.

Not for the first time, Michael found himself questioning when that would be. Even if Dempsey and the Americans did find Frankowski, what next?

He had no answers. No way to know how any of this would play out. All Michael did know — and he would only admit this to himself — was that he was grateful for Sean Sutton's sense of self-preservation.

Michael would have gone with them. He would have done whatever Dempsey asked of him. But he could not pretend the alternative was not preferable. Standing guard over Will Duffy beat wading into a fight every time. And twice over now he had a family to think of.

Now that he had something to lose.

Michael glanced towards Duffy as those thoughts ran through his mind. The sight of his friend fighting silently for life brought the inescapable question: 'what if?' The sheer amount of times that it could have been Michael himself in that bed, rather than sitting at its side. It did not bear thinking about.

Michael shook off the memories. He couldn't get distracted thinking about all the times in the past that he'd been in danger. Not when he still was. Sure, he wasn't running headlong into a gunfight the way Dempsey might be. But Michael wasn't safe yet, either.

Will was still in danger. Still a target. And that meant Michael was too.

He glanced towards the pistol on the bedside table; an unconscious reassurance as he considered what could still be coming his way. It was a parting gift from Dempsey, and Michael had placed it within easy reach, hidden behind an intentionally upturned box of tissues. He dreaded the thought of using it. But if the need arose, he would not hesitate.

They won't get to him again, he told himself, his eyes now back on Will. *They won't get another chance.*

That oath was still resonating as the silence was broken by an unfamiliar ringtone. For a moment Michael looked around in confusion. A second more and he realised why he did not recognise the tune. Dempsey, Gallo, Kincaid and Sutton had left their regular phones in Michael's care. A necessity to avoid being traced.

Michael stood and made his way around the bed, towards

the four handsets on the nightstand at the other side. As he came closer he saw it was Dempsey's that was ringing. A moment more and it was in his hand.

The screen displayed a number that began '+1'. American. But no name. Whoever this was, they were not saved within the phone's contact list.

He pressed connect and placed it to his ear.

'Joe?'

The voice belonged to a woman, the accent a soft, well-spoken East Coast American.

He took a guess at who it could be.

'Is this . . . is this Maria?'

'Who's this?' The sudden concern in the caller's voice was unmistakable. 'Is Joe there? Is he OK?'

'He's fine.' Michael's voice switched unconsciously to professional mode, honed through decades of reassuring clients whenever things took a turn for the worse. 'He's not here but he's fine. *Is* this Maria?'

'Who's asking?'

'My name's Michael Devlin. I'm a friend of Dempsey. A close friend.'

'Yeah? And how do I know that?'

'Well, I know that you're Maria Parker,' Michael replied. 'Now Maria Frankowski. And as well as being the wife of Kon Frankowski, you used to be engaged to Dempsey, back when you were living together in Credenhill. And I'm sure that *you* know there's not a man alive who could get that information from Joe unless he wanted to share it.'

After a brief pause Maria responded.

'You've got yourself a point, I guess. Close friends, then?'

'He's the godfather to my children, so I sure as hell hope so.'

'Joe? A godfather? Seriously?'

'My wife had the same reaction when I first suggested it.'

'Sensible woman. You should have listened to her.'

'He's doing fine so far.'

'Yeah? How long's it been?'

'A little over a day.'

Michael smile broadened as he spoke. He was now enjoying the unexpected distraction.

'Call me when it's been a week and he's been missing for six days of it.'

'Will do. This your number, is it?'

'It's my dad's. My phone's in pieces next to a New Jersey freeway.'

This time it was Maria who laughed. It sounded more nervous than Michael had expected; at odds with the confidence in her voice, but understandable in the circumstances.

'So why are you answering Joe's phone, Michael? Where is he?'

Michael paused for a moment, searching for the best way to answer. He opted for honesty.

'He's gone to get your husband.'

Maria said nothing. It was the reaction Michael had expected and so he allowed her the silence. No doubt she needed it. When she spoke again, her soft voice broke slightly.

'Are they . . . are they going to be safe?'

'It's Joe. If anyone's getting them both through this, it's him.'

'And his phone? Why do you have it?'

'He didn't want a tracker device in his pocket.'

'So he's alone and uncontactable?'

'Neither. He took back-up with him. Another agent. And he's got a burner. They all have them.'

Maria said nothing again. This time Michael broke the silence with a question of his own.

'Why did you call, Maria? Do you need something?'

'I . . . I . . . just needed to speak to Joe, that's all. Away from everyone else. I've heard his team talking. I know they've been in contact with you guys and so I know they're hiding things. I just wanted Joe to tell me straight.'

'What do you think they're hiding from you?'

'I don't know,' Maria said, sounding frustrated. 'I just know Eden's been speaking to Joe and she hasn't told me what about. And one of the others, Dylan, I heard him speaking to someone called Sil. I think he's part of the team too. But he hung up when he saw me.'

'You mean Sal?'

'Yeah, Sal. That's it. I just don't want to be kept in the dark. I need to know what's going on.'

Michael exhaled deeply. He saw no reason to lie. That would be unfair. But he knew too little of the truth to tell it all. And a partial truth could be as damaging as dishonesty.

All he could do, then, was to be honest.

'I just don't know, Maria. I haven't spoken to Joe or to Sal about their conversations with the rest of the team, but it makes sense, doesn't it? That they'd be in touch with each other for updates? This is one operation, even if it does cover two continents. They need to keep things coordinated.'

'So you think I'm just being paranoid?'

'I didn't say that. And even if you are, you've got good reason to be. My mind is racing a million miles a second just waiting for news, so I'm sure yours is too. But if you're really worried, go talk to Eden Grace. She's Joe's friend. He trusts her completely and she trusts him. If there's anyone who can answer your questions, it's her. Not me.'

'I know.' Maria's voice broke again. 'I know. And I will. But . . . I just . . . I just wanted to hear his voice again. To speak to him again, in case anything happens.'

Michael did not know how to respond; Maria's declaration had caught him completely off guard. He recovered his composure quickly, but he remained unsure of what to say.

'I . . . Look, I . . . I get that. But if anyone's coming through this, it's Joe Dempsey.'

Maria was silent, leaving Michael uncertain of what else he could say to reassure her. When she spoke again her voice was quiet.

'I know. Thank you.'

'Don't thank me. I haven't done a thing.'

'Will you tell him I called? When he comes back?'

'Of course. In the meantime, you take care of yourself.'

'Thank you. You too.'

Michael heard the line disconnect as he moved the phone from his ear, and in that same instant he felt his own handset begin to buzz.

He glanced at its screen.

This was the call he'd been waiting for.

SIXTY-ONE

Michael hit the icon, connecting to the number saved as 'SalGallo(Temp)'.

The first sound as the line came alive was a loud, crashing wind that made it difficult to hear. Probably no more than a heavy breeze in reality, hardy noticeable at the other end, but it was being amplified by the sensitive mic on Gallo's cheap burner phone.

Wherever the Italian was calling from, he was not inside a car.

'Everything OK, Sal?'

'No.'

The answer was blunt. Not that Michael would expect anything less. The Italian had so far proved himself to be nothing if not to the point.

'No, I do not think that it is.'

Michael felt his stomach tense at the answer.

'What's the problem?'

'It's Kincaid. I think we have made a mistake to trust him.'

'In what way?'

'I'm not sure. But I do not think he has the same objective that we have.'

'Sal, you're not where Sutton can hear you, are you?'

'I am not a novice. He is still in the car. I am outside and out of sight. I told him I needed to urinate.'

'Sorry. I shouldn't have even asked that.'

'Do not apologise for care. If we had taken more of it, we might not be where we are now.'

'And where are we? What's happened?'

'My time alone with Sutton, he has spoken much. Some of what he has said, it does not . . . it does not leave me convinced about Kincaid.'

'In what way?'

'I am still trying to decide that. But perhaps Kincaid does not want the Monk found. And if that's true, his intentions for Frankowski would be very different to our own.'

'But we *know* that's not true. Kincaid's been chasing the Monk for half a lifetime.'

'But has he?'

Michael did not fully understand the question. He wondered if the meaning was somehow lost in translation.

'What does that mean?'

'What if Kincaid looks for the Monk so that no one finds him?'

Michael hesitated. Now he understood.

'You mean what if his whole hunt for the Monk – all of those years – it was never intended to be successful?'

'Yes.'

'But why?'

'So that he remains free. So that no one else even looks. What if Kincaid is intentionally positioned where he can protect the Mladorossi from detection, all while seeming to lead the chase? A position from where, over enough time, he could begin to make the entire organisation seem like a fiction? He could make the rest of the world think—'

'That he's a myth,' Michael said. Dempsey's first reaction to the name – his disbelief at the man's very existence – was suddenly front and centre in Michael's mind. 'That *they're* a myth. Holy shit.'

'It would be a very effective means to protect him, yes?'

Michael nodded his head, oblivious to the fact that Gallo could not see his silent agreement. The theory was a neat one. He could not deny that. But neat was not the same as correct. He knew that better than anyone.

There were more questions that needed to be asked.

'Do you think Sutton's a part of it?'

'No. From what I have seen and heard from him. No.'

'Does he suspect the same thing?'

'No. In fact, he does not even realise what he has said. That man, he is a . . . a strange speaker. Wrixon would say he has no filter. And so I listened to him. I asked questions. And I was concerned with the answers.'

'Like what?'

'Like his description of Kincaid's search in the years before Sutton joined him. Before they worked together, Kincaid had made no progress. Operation after operation and he achieved nothing. Not a single . . . a single . . . *puntino* of evidence. In all that time.'

'But Kincaid was upfront about that. He told us they'd never really got anywhere.'

'Yes, but Sutton cannot explain why that was. He could not see what Kincaid had been doing in all that time. He told me he was surprised not just at the lack of progress. He was surprised at the lack of a plan. The lack of direction.'

'And what, he thought that was intentional?'

'No. He believes in Kincaid. Kincaid is the protégé of his father and so Sutton is blinded by loyalty. He did not find it suspicious, but he did find it . . . disappointing? Yes, disappointing. He knows how well his father taught Kincaid, but he thinks that Kincaid has followed none of those lessons.'

'OK. So he was worse at his job than Sutton anticipated. One explanation for that is that he's compromised, sure. But another is that he's just a shit intelligence agent. That's more likely, surely?'

'I thought that. But there is more.'

'What?'

'The arrangements with Strauss. Sutton had asked that they follow Duffy and Prochnik to their meeting. To witness the handover, identify the holder of the Mladorossi list and ensure that everything went to plan. If Kincaid had followed Sutton's suggestion, they would have been at the Grote Markt yesterday. They could have stopped the massacre.'

'And they didn't why?'

'Kincaid refused. He said the deal was that the lawyers meet their contact alone and he did not want to risk losing Strauss's trust. Sutton was unhappy with that. And more than unhappy after what took place.'

Michael did not reply. Even with only the details Gallo could provide, the conclusion seemed reasonable. And Kincaid's explanation to Sutton? That they could not risk losing the trust of Strauss? Trust had nothing to do with it. Strauss was desperate. However things went down, he was handing over that list; his future depended upon it.

It was far from being conclusive evidence, Michael realised. But it was damned concerning. And right now, with an armed Kincaid sharing a car with an unsuspecting Dempsey, he lacked the luxury of reasonable doubt.

Reasonable suspicion would have to be enough.

'I take it you haven't shared any of these thoughts with Sutton?' Michael asked.

'Of course not.'

'Good. So what do we do?'

'That is why I am calling you,' Gallo replied, 'rather than Dempsey.'

'Why?'

'Because Kincaid knows that you are friends. And he knows that I am a professional colleague. If you call and warn Dempsey, the call can appear personal. If I call – and if I do so without Sutton's knowledge, as I would have to – Kincaid could suspect something is wrong. It could put him on his guard.'

Michael nodded again. This time he realised he was doing it, and that Gallo could not see the silent consensus.

'Agreed,' he said. 'That makes sense.'

Michael thought for a moment, considering what he would say to Dempsey, what next steps he would suggest and what they should do to deal with the problem they now faced. It was a default reaction of his. To take charge and tackle the issue head on. An instant later and he caught himself. Of the two men on this call, it was not Michael who was best qualified to plot their next steps.

It made him almost sheepish when he spoke again.

'OK, Sal. Tell me the plan.'

SIXTY-TWO

Kincaid checked his watch for the twelfth time in five minutes. Dempsey was sure of the number, just as he knew what the CIA man's timepiece would tell him. Not to the minute, perhaps. But close enough.

3.40 p.m.

Dempsey found Kincaid's jitters concerning.

The two men had been parked by the Cuijk Western Union for just over two hours now, arriving thirty minutes earlier than Kon Frankowski could show. There was no possibility they could have missed him. No chance their target had already come and gone. And so fear of failure could not be the cause of Kincaid's restlessness.

This left just two possible explanations: it was either impatience or it was nerves. And to Dempsey, neither one was better than the other.

Kincaid would have faced death multiple times. That much was inevitable in a decades-long career in covert intelligence. He would have worked through situations far more dangerous than this one; there was no way he could be nervous about the seizure of a witness.

If it *was* nerves, then, they had to have been caused by something else. Something other than just the assignment. Something of which Dempsey was unaware.

The other possibility – impatience – was just as worrying. The career of every CIA officer was built around long, drawn-out operations. It was the very basis of intelligence work;

the nature of the beast. And yet here Kincaid sat, completely incapable of keeping his mind off the minutes.

Two possibilities. Both of which led Dempsey to the same concerning conclusion:

Kincaid's waiting for something else.

And only he knows what it is.

It was with that final thought in mind that Dempsey registered the unfamiliar ringtone of his burner phone. He noticed Kincaid glance towards the cheap burner handset, sat in the central console of the Audi. The American could not have missed the two words displayed on its illuminated screen:

Michael Devlin.

Kincaid looked away, towards the window, as Dempsey picked up the phone. It was a poor attempt to appear disinterested in the call.

Dempsey pressed down on the connect button.

'Everything OK?'

He used his right ring finger to subtly tap the lower volume key, reducing the sound of Michael's voice to a minimum. Whatever the reason for the call, he did not want Kincaid to overhear.

'You alone?'

Michael sounded worried.

'What do you mean they're moving him?' Dempsey forced a tone of irritation into his voice. He turned to Kincaid. 'The hospital wants to move Duffy. I need to stop them. We can't have him out in the open. They may as well put a bloody bullseye over his heart.'

Kincaid nodded his head.

'Agreed. Deal with it.'

Dempsey opened the car door, stepped out and closed it behind him.

'Give me a second.'

Only when he was fifteen feet clear, with his back to Kincaid, did he continue.

'What's wrong?'

'It's Kincaid. I think he's a problem.'

'You too?'

'What does that mean?'

'You're not alone in that opinion.'

'Who have you spoken to?'

'Just Kincaid. That was enough for me. Where are *you* getting it from?'

'Sutton,' Michael replied. 'Inadvertently through Sal. Sal's convinced Kincaid's bad news.'

'That's good enough for me. We can find out for sure later. Right now the only safe assumption is that Sal's right. What meeting point did he suggest?'

'You mean Sal?'

'Yes.'

'God, you guys think alike.'

'We've done this before, Mike.'

'Evidently. Sal left the choice to me, said he couldn't let Sutton see him checking for locations on his phone.'

'But he gave you search terms?'

'Yeah. He wanted it to be somewhere under cover and with limited access in and out, and as close as possible to being equidistant between your two locations, but still in the direction of The Hague.'

'Of course he did.' It was exactly the criteria Dempsey would have set. 'We need to be heading in the right general direction, otherwise we risk tipping Kincaid off that we're taking him to an ambush. Where did you find?'

'A private underground car park in Nijmegen. It ticks all the boxes. I've sent Sal the postcode by text. I'll do the same for you. Just don't let Kincaid see it.'

Dempsey smiled at Michael's advice.

'Yes, sir.'

'Sorry. I know you know. But if I didn't say it . . .'

'Don't apologise. It's the right instinct. Now what about Sutton? Does Sal trust him?'

'He does, but not enough to take the risk of even numbers when you guys meet. So he's sending him back to me, to keep him out the way.'

'On what basis?'

'He's told him there's been a security breach at the hospital and that I need support.'

'And Sutton's bought that? Enough to leave his assignment?'

'So Sal says. And why not? It's not like he could think Sal needs back-up to collar one computer geek, is it? Better to be where he thinks he's needed.'

'Still, it's disappointing. Sutton seemed more professional than that.'

'It's a potential problem solved, Joe. Don't overthink it.'

'I guess so. OK, so what's the next step? Whichever one of us takes Frankowski calls the other and then we all head to Nijmegen? So everything looks straight?'

'That's Sal's suggestion.'

'OK. Then I guess that's that. We just have to hope we don't get swamped by these Mladorossi bastards before we reach that car park.'

'Jesus, Joe. Don't say that.'

'Why not? It's the reality, Mike. There's no point lying to ourselves.'

Michael said nothing in reply. Instead he changed the subject. When he did, his voice was unusually uncertain.

'Do you really think Kincaid's bent? I mean, *really*?'

'We can't know that for sure. Not right now. But I've heard alarm bells. If Sal's done the same, we can't take the risk.'

'And if we're wrong?'

'Then I guess we'll be even less popular with the CIA for a while. Nothing new there.'

'What about—'

Dempsey did not hear the rest of Michael's question. The handset had drifted from his ear as his focus shifted completely.

A male figure, walking alone from the far end of the long, quiet street. Heading in the direction of the Western Union outlet.

He was just about the right size, but otherwise he looked nothing like the pictures Dempsey had seen.

And yet Dempsey had no doubt who he was looking at.

He put the phone back to his ear.

'Time for me to go, Mike. Frankowski's here.'

SIXTY-THREE

Kon wiped a stream of dripping sweat from the back of his neck and flicked it onto the road beside him.

As effectively as his outfit had turned him into someone else, it was hardly practical in the intense heat. The fedora was helpful; it gave him more respite from the beating sun than the baseball caps he was more used to. But everything else? The extra layers? The tight jeans?

Why would anyone choose to dress like this in the summer?

Like most thoughts that had crossed his mind since yesterday, the question made him think of Maria. It was exactly what she would have asked, her usual no-nonsense approach to things like fashion dismissing anything that took so much effort. She had been disparaging enough when Kon had first started to grow his beard, so he could only imagine what she would say about his current get-up.

The thought made him smile. It was a rare break from the mix of dread and excitement that had brought him this far, and it did not last. He had tried to avoid thinking of Maria since their last conversation. To avoid remembering the unmistakable tone of her voice. He had expected Maria to be afraid. He had expected her to be angry.

What he had not expected was a feeling that seemed so close to hate.

It wasn't *quite* hate. He knew that. If it had been then she would not have helped keep him alive. She would not have made the arrangements that brought him here today. No, she did not hate him.

But she sure as hell doesn't love me.

It was the only conclusion Kon could draw from what she had said. He was a fool to think he could have hidden his double life from her without her noticing anything. She was a clever woman, and he had been distracted. Distant. And now this.

How could she feel the same about me after all that?

It was a depressing thought and yet Kon had not completely lost hope. Because despite everything, Maria had still helped him. And if she cared enough to do that . . .

The symbol of that hope lay directly ahead. The Western Union outlet. Perhaps two hundred yards further along the pavement, its undersized logo now just about visible and its timely appearance a potential message from the universe.

Perhaps all was not lost.

Perhaps Kon could still regain his family.

For a man who regarded superstitious signs and omens as the very height of the ridiculous, he was surprised how much the timing lifted his spirits.

So focused was he on that sign that he was less than twenty feet from the small, shallow-fronted store before he registered the large man further along the road. The figure was not close but still. That was not the problem.

The problem was that he'd been visible for at least thirty seconds and yet Kon had only just noticed him.

That Kon had allowed himself to become so lost in his thoughts scared him. He squinted into the hot sun, to take a closer look at the figure. The man was probably entirely innocent – just a guy making a call – but Kon was concerned.

What if he's here for me?

What if there are others I missed?

A familiar panic set in as these questions and more ran

through Kon's mind. Before he could stop himself he had turned a full three-sixty circle on his heel, scanning his surroundings. He regretted it before he was even halfway done. He knew how strange the movement would seem. How much attention it would bring to him.

It was a relief, then, that he spotted no one else.

The road was quiet; the light smattering of traffic was moving freely and, besides the guy who was still on his phone, there was no one to be seen on either side of the street. That lessened Kon's anxiety, but still he chided himself. He could not let his guard drop like that again.

Not for Maria.

Not for anyone.

He took a final glance over his shoulder as he stepped through the open shopfront, then headed directly to the counter.

'Can I help you?'

The question was asked in Dutch, the first time since his arrival in the country. He guessed it was because he was no longer dressed like a typical American. The clerk's assumption that he was from the Netherlands was welcome confirmation that the disguise was working.

Kon was disappointed to break the illusion but he had no choice; his US driver's licence would reveal his nationality at a glance. As would his complete inability to speak the language.

'I'm collecting a money transfer from the US. It's from my wife. It would have been deposited today. In the last hour or so.'

'Can I have your identification?'

'Sure.'

Kon handed over the plastic card before stepping back, to wait while the clerk accessed the system. The process took longer than he had expected and the clerk's expression grew increasingly frustrated as she seemingly entered more data than was contained on the item Kon had provided.

At first he said nothing, keen that he would not stand out in her memory for anything more than his being American. But as the delay turned into minutes, a fearful feeling began to gnaw at his gut. Finally he could not help himself.

'Is there something wrong?'

The clerk looked up. She seemed grateful for the question. As if she had not wanted to be first to raise the issue.

'Are you . . . are you sure the money has been deposited?'

'Of course. I mean, it must have been.' The feeling was fast transforming into dread. 'She said . . . yeah. Yeah, it's definitely there.'

'Not according to the system. There is no record of a Frankowski on the system. Sending or receiving, today or ever.'

'That can't be right. She wouldn't have not done it.'

'Maybe you need to call this person, sir?'

'I . . . I can't.' Kon did not know what else to say. 'Could you check again?'

'I've checked four times. It isn't there.'

Kon could feel his emotions spike.

If Maria has broken her promise . . .

If she doesn't care enough to help me . . .

Taken together, the emotional and the practical implications of Maria's failure threatened to overwhelm him.

'Please,' he said. 'Please check again.'

The clerk looked at him for a moment, surely aware that a fifth attempt was a waste of both their time. But then sympathy seemed to overcome experience. With a nod of her head, she lowered her eyes back to the screen.

Kon watched as her fingers moved across the keyboard; by

now she knew the details she was inputting and so she worked quickly. Too fast for Kon to follow, but he had stopped watching anyway. His mind was somewhere else entirely, his focus on what Maria's failure could mean.

Did someone stop her from doing it?

Do they have her? Her and the boys?

Or did she just choose to cut her losses? To leave me to it, after everything I've done?

Each thought was as unbearable as the last. They left Kon in a daze as the clerk finally shook her head and handed him his driving licence.

'I am sorry,' she said. 'Perhaps she is delayed. Call her, sir. Or perhaps just come back a little later.'

The words meant nothing. Kon hardly registered they had even been said.

That Maria would let him down had not crossed his mind. Not once. And so he had not anticipated how much it would crush him.

He knew now.

Kon stepped into the street without a glance in either direction. In that moment he believed that his life could get no worse. That nothing could ever rid him of the darkness that now engulfed him.

That he would never make it past this despair.

A moment more and that belief was disproved by the pain of a pistol barrel pressed hard into the back of his neck.

SIXTY-FOUR

Dempsey moved the instant Kon Frankowski stepped out of the Western Union and onto the street.

He had been in position on the left-hand side of the outlet's open front since Frankowski had first stepped inside, with Kincaid mirroring him on its right. It was not the American's preferred plan; he had wanted to take Frankowski inside the building but Dempsey had overruled him, citing the presence of the clerk as a complication they did not need.

Easier, Dempsey had figured, than the truth: he wanted nothing obstructing his view of Kincaid himself as they took Frankowski. Not when he had such doubts over the American's loyalties.

Kincaid had moved quickly but Dempsey was closer and so he reached Frankowski first as he stepped out of the Western Union; within an instant Dempsey had grabbed a handful of his thick cotton waistcoat, pulled him close and pushed the muzzle of his Glock deep into the man's thin neck.

'Don't move a damn muscle.' Dempsey's mouth was inches from Frankowski's ear as he hissed the order. 'And don't say a word.'

More suspicious of Kincaid than ever, Dempsey's eyes did not leave the other agent even as he took custody of Frankowski. It was not where his focus needed to be and yet he could not risk a distraction, not when Kincaid could choose any second to show his true colours. He made his attention absolute, taking care to judge the American's expression and his body language, to be prepared for any sudden movements.

None came.

At least not yet.

'Get the door.'

Kincaid did exactly as ordered. No hesitation.

A second later and Dempsey had forced Frankowski headfirst into the back seat. The natural next move would have been for the Englishman to immediately follow, but he did not: Dempsey and Frankowski seated together with Kincaid standing outside would make them the very definition of sitting ducks. Instead Dempsey waited while Kincaid climbed into the driver's seat and secured his safety belt. Only then did he climb in the back, his pistol trained on the terrified newcomer.

His attention still fixed on Kincaid, he noticed that the American's eyes were rooted to the rear-view mirror as he put the car into drive and accelerated away from the kerb.

'Keep your eyes on the road,' Dempsey said. 'I've got this.'

Kincaid ignored the instruction and Dempsey chose to push it no further. An operative of his experience had to be competent enough not to kill them all in a car wreck. Dempsey could trust that much at least.

And besides, as long as he's using the mirror he's facing forwards. A shot backwards won't be worth a damn from that position.

Dempsey finally turned his attention to Frankowski, who by now had steeled himself enough to speak.

'Who . . . who are you?'

The man's voice was high-pitched with distress, but Dempsey ignored both that and the question he had asked. Instead he pinned Frankowski back into the seat with his left forearm, reached across him with his right, tugged the rear safety belt towards himself and secured it. Then he pulled his own belt across and clipped it shut.

A pre-emptive move. Protection, just in case Kincaid had any ideas about using a car crash as a way to incapacitate him.

Satisfied that option was now off the table, Dempsey glanced again at the rear-view mirror. With the Audi picking up speed, Kincaid was now paying more attention to the road ahead. But still his eyes kept returning to the reflection of the two men in the back.

As they did, Dempsey saw the gaze settle on Frankowski.

'You've been keeping secrets, Kon,' Kincaid said. 'That stops now.'

SIXTY-FIVE

Frankowski's attention shifted upwards from the pistol in Dempsey's hand, to the reflection in the rear-view mirror. A natural response to Kincaid's statement.

Just as natural was the shift back an instant later, to the gun still trained upon him. And that his response was directed towards the man holding it.

'I don't . . . I don't know what—'

'It's too late for that bullshit.'

Kincaid's voice was raised, but only by a little. And yet somehow the threat it carried had increased tenfold. It was an impressive trick, Dempsey thought. And it worked: this time Frankowski's eyes stayed on the mirror.

'Who . . . who are you people?'

'It doesn't matter who we are. We're here for the hard drive. Where is it?'

Dempsey said nothing because there was nothing he could add. Kincaid had made no mention of the CIA or the ISB; to cite either was to risk Frankowski resorting to his rights as an American citizen. It was an obstacle they could do without. And one which would not arise if Frankowski thought they might be the bad guys.

But Frankowski did not answer at all.

'I asked you a goddamned question.'

The vehicle's speed increased as the menace in Kincaid's voice shifted up another gear. Not that it seemed to be working. Frankowski still said nothing. And Dempsey was beginning to wonder why.

Is he standing his ground?

Or is he so terrified that he's unable to answer?

It took the barest of assessments for Dempsey to answer his own question. Frankowski was trembling, his gaze shifting wildly, his eyes settling on nothing. The actions of an individual near paralysed by fear.

'I won't ask you again,' Kincaid demanded from the driver's seat. 'If you don't—'

'ENOUGH!'

Dempsey had raised his voice to a level much louder than Kincaid. He needed to retake control of the exchange.

'Enough,' he said again, his voice now lower.

Dempsey made a show of turning his gun away from Frankowski and placing it to his right. Still within easy reach but no longer trained on his captive, the action was designed to do the opposite to Kincaid's approach.

He needs to be calmed, Dempsey thought. *He needs to feel safe. Or at least safer.*

Frankowski's eyes were finally settled, tracing the downward path of the Glock. Dempsey's technique was working.

'We're not who you think we are, Kon,' he began. 'We're not here to hurt you.'

'But . . . but . . . the gun . . .'

'We needed to get you off the street and into the car quick. In case we weren't the only ones there.'

'The only ones?'

'There are people looking for you. Dangerous people. But you already know that or you wouldn't be in hiding.'

'But . . . how . . . I . . .'

'We're not the bad guys. We're here to help.'

'Who are you?'

'My name is Joe Dempsey. I'm a senior field agent with the International Security Bureau, which is a department of the United Nations Security Council. And the guy up front, he's Corbin Kincaid. He's . . . he represents your government.'

Frankowski's eyes widened as he listened to what Dempsey was saying. His face was unusually easy to read. At first it showed his relief, but that was quickly replaced by doubt.

'But how . . . how do I know you're telling me the truth?'

Kincaid took a right-hand turn fast as Frankowski asked the question. Dempsey was sure that the violence of the manoeuvre was intentional. An unspoken rebuke of the softer approach Dempsey was taking.

'The truth? What the hell do you want from us?' The aggression in Kincaid's voice had not dropped at all. 'Will our badges do?'

Dempsey glanced at the rear-view mirror. The anger in Kincaid's eyes was impossible to miss. But it was easy enough to ignore.

He looked back at Frankowski.

'You're married to a woman who used to be called Maria Parker,' Dempsey said. 'A doctor. You have two sons. Anyone could know that. But we also know that Maria has taken your boys to her father David Burton's ranch, the Golden Calf in Cooperstown. She's there now, with a team of my agents on-site to protect her. It was Maria who told you how to get out of The Hague and it was Maria who told you to use the Western Union, and who told us you'd be there.'

Frankowski said nothing at first, but Dempsey could see his mind working. And he knew it could only lead the man to one conclusion.

'You've spoken to Maria?' he finally asked. 'Is she . . . is she safe?'

'She is.'

'And the boys?'

'They're all fine, Kon. They're all safe.'

Frankowski sat back into his seat with a deep sigh. From his body language he seemed as if a literal weight had just been lifted. Dempsey gave him a few moments to let it all sink in, knowing that Frankowski would be more calm and more trusting if given that time.

He looked towards the rear-view mirror and shook his head when he met Kincaid's still irritated, impatient gaze. A clear instruction that the American was to stay quiet, too. Kincaid did not need to speak to express his distaste for the silent order; it was written over what little was visible of his face.

Dempsey turned back to Frankowski. It was time to talk.

'Like I said, Kon. We're here to keep you alive. But we're also here to do our job. For that, we need the list. Where is it?'

Frankowski looked hesitant.

'The list,' Dempsey repeated. 'We need it.'

'How do you—'

'That doesn't matter. Where is it?'

'And what's on it?' The question came from the driver's seat. '*Who's* on it?'

'I don't know,' Frankowski replied. 'I never looked. I thought it was safest if I didn't know.'

'And yet you were willing to keep it safe for a man like Hannibal Strauss?'

'You don't say no to a man like him.'

This time it was Dempsey who took a moment.

Frankowski's answers were not assisting his attempt to play the 'good cop'. Instead they were making him angry. The fact that Frankowski would take money from an international war criminal on a no-questions-asked basis, without a thought to the danger in which he was putting his family?

It was not a mindset Dempsey could understand.

And sure as hell not one he was going to accept.

He glanced at Kincaid, who was looking back. Dempsey could not tell if the same answer had angered Kincaid, too, or if his irritation was just ongoing. But what he *could* tell was that, for once, they were in agreement; they both felt the same distaste for the man in their custody.

Dempsey took a calming breath, determined not to show his contempt for what had just been disclosed. It helped to keep his tone in check when he finally spoke.

'So where is it now, Kon?' Dempsey asked. 'The list?'

'It's not here. Not with me. It never was here.'

'What do you mean?'

'I played it safe. In case this whole thing was . . . in case it all went wrong. But I did set up an easy delivery system, over the dark web. Once I was sure it was all good here I could just get Maria to log in to my system back home and I could guide her through the transfer.'

'Are you telling me the file is still at home?' Dempsey did not like the way this was going. 'That it's with Maria?'

'Not the physical disk, no. I set up a copy of its content on my home system. Behind eight different firewalls and with the system physically disconnected from the web. Each of the firewalls was designed to wipe the file if someone attempted to bypass them without the correct passwords. So anyone going near that system without me to guide them—'

'Will wipe the copy,' Dempsey said, concluding Frankowski's sentence. 'And Maria knows all this?'

'No. No, Maria doesn't know a thing. Why would she? I didn't want her involved until she needed to be. Until I was sure it was all safe.'

Dempsey felt his pulse begin to spike, the scar on his left cheek beginning to itch as it always did when his blood was up. As hard as he tied to suppress it, the answers he was getting – the inadvertent involvement and the risks that Frankowski had forced upon his unknowing family – were pushing Dempsey close to the edge.

He had to force his anger aside and focus on what he needed to know.

'So if someone were to search your address, if someone were to take your computers and examine them . . .'

'You mean an ordinary someone. Someone who doesn't know what I know?'

'I mean the FBI, Kon.'

'My system is well above their grade. There's no one at the FBI who could bypass those firewalls. Not without destroying what was behind them.'

Dempsey was not sure how to feel about the answer. On the one hand it was a disappointment; there was no chance the FBI did not have Frankowski's hardware after what had occurred at his home the previous day. But on the other, with so many agencies already proving to be compromised, maybe it was better that none of them had access to the list.

Either way, it left an inevitable question.

'Enough about that, then,' Dempsey said, his tone betraying his growing impatience. 'I want to know about the hard copy. I want to know where it is.'

Frankowski hesitated. The change in Dempsey's demeanour, it seemed, had intimidated him. When he finally answered his friendliness was gone, replaced by something closer to his earlier fearfulness.

'The disk is in storage,' he said. 'Along with the rest of our stuff from our house move. It's all at David's place in Cooperstown.'

SIXTY-SIX

The noise in the kids' playroom was as disorienting as any training exercise Grace had ever taken. The Frankowskis' two hyper-energetic sons seemed like they'd be uncontrollable at the best of times, but the addition of their thirteen-year-old aunt made things exponentially worse.

Leisha Burton was as bursting with life as both boys combined, and she was enjoying the power and influence she had over the younger children. She had slowly cranked up the excitement and the decibel level, until it had reached a point where Grace could take no more.

She slipped out of the room without a word, closed the door behind her and exhaled heavily.

'Had enough?'

David Burton's voice made Grace spin on her heel. She had not heard him approach. The slight concern in his expression assured her that the question was no kind of criticism. If anything, it was solidarity.

'It's like a war zone in there,' Grace replied. 'Are all kids that loud?'

'Depends when you catch them. But those three together? That's heavy artillery. None of your own, then?'

'Is it that obvious?'

'Only because you're surprised by the mayhem. Plus it's not such an easy call, is it? Not for a lady in your line of work.'

'It's not what you'd call compatible, no.'

'Careers like yours, Eden, they don't last forever. Take it from me. You've still got time.'

Grace forced a smile at the reply, hiding the sadness the question of kids always caused her. As well-intentioned as Burton's words were, it was not a subject Grace wanted to discuss. And so she changed it.

'Speaking of careers like mine, it looks like you did pretty well after the Marine Corps.'

She indicated to the sprawling mansion around them as she spoke. Burton followed her gesture with an unmistakable look of pride.

'Yeah, it turned out pretty good for the most part. Goes to show you what you can do when you bring military values into the private sector.'

'In what way?'

'A ranch is no different to a company in the Corps. Same as almost any other business that's small enough for a boss to stay hands-on. This place was only ever gonna be as good as the men working it. And those men would only be as good as the training and the direction they're given. I realised that early on.'

'Smart move.'

'Eventually it was. When I bought the place, I brought in cowboys. And you know what? Every single one of them, to a man, they all knew better than I did. Every decision I made was questioned. Every order I gave was second-guessed. If I'd carried on like that, this place would never have been built. We wouldn't have made it past the nineties.'

'So you changed tack?'

'Yeah. Shipped out all but two of the original team and replaced them with veterans from the Corps. Men who understood command. Men I could rely on. That decision is what built all this. Wife and kids aside, best thing I ever did.'

Grace noticed Burton glance towards the playroom as he

finished speaking. It was an unconscious confirmation of his last statement: for everything he had, his family mattered most.

When he turned back to face her the previous sparkle in his eyes had gone. Whatever had crossed his mind in that glance had replaced his cheer with something more serious.

'How'd you feel about us having an honest conversation, Eden? Just the two of us?'

'Depends on the subject, sir.'

'I thought I told you to call me David?'

'Something tells me this one's gonna be a "sir" conversation.'

'Yeah. Yeah, I think it probably is. So let's get it over with: staying straight as straight, what do you make of all this? You really think someone's coming for my girl?'

Grace did not even hesitate. Burton had seen more action than Grace ever had. He had lived with at least as many threats to his life. He could handle the truth.

'Dempsey thinks they might be.'

'Thinks? Is that it?'

'Depends if they can trace her here. If they can, he's sure they'll come.'

'Shit.'

Grace could see the concern etched on Burton's aged but still handsome face.

'And if he is right? What's your take then?'

'Depends who comes. You're a military man, sir. I'm not telling you something you don't know when I say four of us isn't enough. I don't see how we defend a place this size against significant numbers.'

Burton nodded his head, his expression utterly serious.

'That's very true. But then it's not just four of you, is it?'

'Sorry, sir. Five, including yourself. I didn't mean to count you out.'

'I didn't mean just me.'

'Sir?'

'There's eighteen men working on this ranch, Eden. Sixteen of them ex-Corps. And believe me, I've been careful to only ever pick the best.'

Grace felt a glimmer of hope at Burton's words.

'You mean . . . ?'

'We've got a full-on fighting unit, Eden, at the ready. Like I told you last night, I've been expecting trouble for a very long time. Didn't expect it to be *this* trouble – didn't expect it to be about Maria – but prep for one and you prep for all. Anyone comes here in numbers expecting a cake-walk, they're gonna get the shock of their lives.'

A smile threatened the corner of Grace's mouth. Concerned it was inappropriate for the moment, she pushed the reaction down. But for the first time she could picture them coming through this thing in one piece. An image of how to defend the main house was half-forming, but still she had questions.

'Sir, can I ask—'

Grace was interrupted by the vibration from the phone in her jacket pocket. It could only be one person. She held it up, for Burton to see the name on the screen.

'Sorry, I need to get this.'

Burton nodded in response and moved away, to give Grace the privacy she needed. She gave him a moment before connecting the call.

'Do you have him?' Grace asked.

'We do.'

'And the list?'

'Is a lot closer to you than it is to us.'

'What do you mean?'

'It's on a portable hard drive, packed up with a bunch of other belongings. It's all stored away in one of the units on David's ranch.'

'You're kidding me!'

'I'm not. Is Maria there?'

'Not near me but yeah, she's here.'

'Get her to take you to where their stuff is stored. Find it for me, Eden.'

SIXTY-SEVEN

Dempsey eyed Kincaid as he disconnected the call to Grace, accessed the near-empty contacts list and scrolled to the number for Sal Gallo's burner. It was far from ideal that Kincaid should be hearing as much as he was.

It was also unavoidable.

The alternative was to stop the car and have the conversations privately, and Dempsey was not going to risk that. He would not risk leaving Frankowski in Kincaid's custody for even a moment. Not without him there too.

'I need to update the others,' he said, the comment directed at Kincaid.

'I can do that,' Kincaid replied. He already had his burner in his left hand. 'I can call Sean.'

'I've already hit Sal's number. Leave it to me.'

Dempsey put the phone to his ear. What was about to follow was a fiction – a ruse intended to redirect Kincaid to the safety of the private underground car park in Nijmegen – but it had to be convincing. Any warning to Kincaid, any indication that something was wrong, could scupper their plans.

'Boss.'

Gallo's deep voice was loud enough that Kincaid must have heard it. It added another dimension to the play that was to come. It required both Dempsey and the Italian to be convincing.

'We've got him, Sal.'

'And the list?'

'We know where it is.'

'He doesn't have it with him?'

'No. But it's safe.'

'Where?'

'Maria's father's ranch.'

'In America?'

'Believe it or not.'

Dempsey glanced at the mirror. Kincaid was keeping his eyes on the road but there was no way he was not listening.

It was time for the ruse.

'Time for you and Sutton to head back to The Hague. Meet us there, OK?'

'Sutton is gone already.'

Dempsey watched Kincaid's reaction. The American's eyes flitted to the mirror, confusion apparent. It seemed genuine.

'Sean's gone?' he asked. 'Why?'

'Why, Sal?' Dempsey asked, holding the handset out so that both he and Kincaid could hear the answer.

'An issue at the hospital. Michael called us, some problem with local security. Michael had no authority to deal with it so Sutton and I, we agreed one of us to go.'

'Why him?' Kincaid asked. 'Why not you?'

'His decision. And I agreed. If Frankowski was to be for one man to deal with, better it was me.'

'Makes sense to me,' Dempsey said. 'But this security issue, you think it's a problem, Sal?'

'No way to know. But better safe than sorry, no?'

'You mean Plan B?'

'Plan B?' Kincaid's reaction was intense, his eyes darting back and forth between the road and the mirror. 'What the hell is Plan B?'

'Consolidation of resources,' Dempsey replied. 'It means

we meet Sal at a rendezvous point up ahead. If we don't know what we're heading back into then we should at least do it together.'

'What rendezvous point?'

'Don't recall the address,' Dempsey lied. 'But I know the way. Let's just get close and I'll direct you.'

'Oh, this is bullshit.' Kincaid was angry. And he was not trying to hide it. 'I'm driving the damn car, Dempsey. My damn car. If we're going anywhere that isn't straight to The Hague then I want to know where that somewhere is.'

'You will. When we get there.'

Dempsey turned his attention back to the phone.

'Sal, we'll see you there. We'll wait for you.'

'Boss.'

The line disconnected. Kincaid must have heard it.

'Fuck this, Dempsey,' he said. 'I'm not being kept in the dark on my own operation.'

'This isn't your operation. This isn't *anyone's* operation. Like you said earlier, all of us just stumbled in to this. All we can do in those circumstances is our best. That means sticking to protocol and protocol right now is "need to know". Right now, you don't need to know the rendezvous point.'

'Do you seriously still not trust me?'

'Do *you* trust *me*?'

'That wasn't the question.'

'And yet it's the only answer you're getting for now.'

Dempsey intended that to be the end of the discussion. He did not want to take the exchange further, which would risk exposing his suspicions. Distrust was fine – distrust was expected – and so the issue of a withheld rendezvous point was not fatal.

An allegation that Kincaid was in league with the Monk, though? That was something else. And that was why he almost said nothing as his eyes settled again on the burner phone in Kincaid's hand.

Almost.

'You messaging someone, Corbin?' he asked.

'You're the only one who's allowed contact with his people?'

'Didn't say that. Just a dangerous thing to do while driving.'

'But necessary when the people you're working with keep you in the dark.'

'On one issue, Corbin. One little safety net. Like you wouldn't do the same.'

Dempsey waited a beat, his eyes not leaving what he could see of the handset.

'Has Sutton made it to The Hague yet?'

Kincaid said nothing. His eyes stayed fixed on the road.

'Has he?'

'I don't know,' he finally answered, no glance towards the mirror as he spoke. 'He hasn't replied.'

'Would you tell me if he had?'

Again, Kincaid said nothing.

In the circumstances, Dempsey could hardly blame him.

SIXTY-EIGHT

Alan Tyson whistled with appreciation as the Bell AH-1 Cobra came into view. A sleek, fifty-foot-long single-engine attack helicopter, it was exactly what he had envisaged. The perfect weapon for the end of what lay ahead.

The FBI agent stepped out of the passenger door before the Jeep had even come to a full halt. A few more seconds and he was up close, admiring the chopper from touching distance.

Tyson had been flown directly from Woodland Park in New Jersey to Knapp Airport, a small airfield just outside of Cooperstown, NY. From there he had been collected by one of the Monk's men and chauffeured the five-mile distance to the field in which they all now stood.

Dry, flat and around six acres in size, it was the perfect landing place for the Cobra. The field was far enough from the Golden Calf Ranch that they would not have seen the chopper descend, and it was sufficiently isolated that it could sit unobserved for the day or so that might pass before it was needed.

Most important, it was close enough to the ranch perimeter that it could be called in as soon as the mission changed and it was time to rain fire onto the Golden Calf.

Tyson looked around as he approached the massive vehicle, his attention now shifting to the men he would be leading. He had hardly noticed them as he had been driven in, so entirely was his focus on the Cobra. Now he saw them, though, and he was pleasantly surprised by the sight.

Twenty-six, he counted. One more than the Monk had

promised. All of them armed and ready for what was to come, he could tell, even while they lounged around on the yellowing grass and soaked up the sun as they waited for their day's work to begin.

Tyson took his time to size them up. Every one of them was young and fit, that much was undeniable. With not a man aged more than twenty-five, they were the usual mix of oversized steroid heads and undersized psychopaths their generation seemed so adept at producing.

What he could *not* tell was whether any of them were experienced. Had the Monk put together a team proficient with the weapons he had provided? Or was Tyson being paid his exorbitant fee to bring at least some combat expertise to the group?

In other words, is there even one genuine soldier here?

He could have no answer. Not before even the most basic of interactions. And yet as he looked at them now, Tyson had to ask himself:

Does it even matter?

Their success would come down to superior numbers and weaponry. And even if they were untrained thugs to a man, every army had room for berserkers. Just so long as they had a leader with real combat experience; someone who could operate at least some control over the animals.

That, Tyson now assumed, was where he came in.

He had served in the military before the FBI. The Monk knew that. Three tours and plenty of action. It did not make him the perfect candidate for the job, not least because the most recent of those tours was a decade and a half in the past. But he was sure as hell better than nothing.

He was experienced. Enough that he now noticed how

the men were beginning to fidget. They must have been told that their commanding officer was about to arrive and most would have deduced that Tyson was that man. And yet here he was, surveying but saying nothing. It was making them uncomfortable.

It was also increasing Tyson's certainty that these men were not military.

Soldiers are used to waiting.

And they sure as hell don't lounge in the grass when a commanding officer shows up.

It gave Tyson his answer. He would be leading game, violent amateurs against highly trained intelligence operatives. Twenty-six against four. It was a fight with only one winner, but it was a victory that would come with a cost.

A lot of these men are gonna die.

Shame for them.

With the odds calculated and thoughts of his own safety already running through his head, Tyson turned and headed directly for the Cobra. From here he could see the firepower the chopper was carrying. A sophisticated instrument of death, the afternoon's business could be settled from the sky far more easily than by men on the ground, if only the helicopter's long-range weapons could be deployed in the first stage of what was to come.

It was disappointing, then, that they could not.

The orders called for the capture of the woman and her kids, so the Cobra was too risky to use. It was here specifically for Stage Two: the destruction of the ranch itself.

Damn unfortunate, Tyson told himself. *It would have been a guarantee of getting through this alive.*

The Cobra's pilot was working on the aircraft's far side and so Tyson made his way round to speak to him. He studied the vehicle as he moved, noticing the configuration of the cockpit; a two-person design where one operator would sit behind the other, so more like a fighter jet than a typical helicopter design.

'You gentleman seem ready right now,' he observed. 'Shame about the wait.'

The pilot turned at the question. He was also older than Tyson had expected. Well outside the range for active service. And he looked confused.

'What wait?'

'The wait before you can deploy.'

'Our orders are to deploy with the rest of you.'

It was Tyson's turn to be confused.

'That can't be right. My order was—'

'Orders changed ten minutes ago.'

The pilot held up his own mobile phone for Tyson to read as he spoke. It was a short text message, sent from a number Tyson recognised as belonging to the Monk. And it changed everything:

> Ignore previous instructions. No capture necessary. Kill everyone. Burn everything.

SIXTY-NINE

D empsey watched unblinking as Kincaid turned in his seat. The movement was necessary for the reverse parking technique Kincaid was undertaking, but it also gave him an excuse to look directly into the back seat of the car. A position which would allow him a clean shot at the two men seated behind him.

It was an opportunity, if Kincaid was inclined to take it, and so Dempsey was ready.

Unlike Kincaid, Dempsey was facing fully forwards. He had no need to turn and he had no need to hide his weapon. All of which left him with a split-second advantage over Kincaid if he was forced to act. It was not a lot but it would be enough, and so he allowed no distraction as he watched the American's every movement.

Dempsey's hands gripped his pistol as he waited for even a hint of a betrayal.

None came. And nor did Kincaid seem to notice just how on edge the Englishman was as he pulled the car into the space.

A few seconds more and the Audi was parked; a comfortable fit in the generous bays that lined up against the back wall on the first subterranean level of the Kelfkensbos Parking Garage. Kincaid was facing ahead once more as he first turned off the quiet petrol engine and then unclipped his seat belt. Free of the restraint, the American made to turn in his seat again.

'Stay facing forwards.'

If Dempsey's tone suggested that his words were anything but an absolute order, the gun he pointed at the back of Kincaid's head would have cleared up the confusion. Only Kincaid's eyes and brow were visible in the reflection, but they were enough for Dempsey to see the shock registered on his face.

'What the fuck are you doing, Dempsey?'

'I'm playing it safe. I already told you, Corbin, I don't trust you. That hasn't changed.'

Kincaid gave the slightest of nods. When he replied, his voice carried none of the anger that Dempsey was expecting. Instead he just sounded confused.

'You really think I'm involved in all this?'

'Maybe. And right now, maybe's enough.'

Another nod. Dempsey was doing the right thing, exactly as Kincaid would have done if their positions had been reversed. From his muted reaction, the American seemed to acknowledge that.

'And this little detour you had us make. Is it really to meet with Gallo?'

'It is.'

'And the security breach in the hospital?'

'Didn't happen. Though Sutton doesn't know that yet.'

'So you trusted Sean just a little and me not at all?'

'Couldn't risk you. For all we know, you were driving us into an ambush.'

'I guess me just saying you're wrong wouldn't do much good, would it?'

'What do you think?'

'So what happens?'

'Nothing bad. You'll just be staying right here while we take Kon with us. Once he's safely in The Hague, we'll send someone to release you.'

Another nod. This time accompanied by a frustrated sigh.

'What do you think any of this gains you, Dempsey?'

'It keeps me and Kon alive, in the event you *are* in on this.'

'And if I'm not?'

'Then no one loses out, do they? We all want the same thing. And this way we all come out of this in one piece.'

Kincaid nodded one more time.

'You know the Agency won't take this lying down, right? We're the CIA. You just don't pull this kind of shit with us.'

'I'm expecting some fallout if I'm wrong. But I'll take the cold shoulder in the office over an ambush every day of the week. Wouldn't you?'

'I guess so. But I've got to ask you, man: do you *really* think I'm involved in all this? After chasing the Monk my whole damned working life?'

'Probably not. But I'm not betting my life on a probably.' Dempsey glanced at Frankowski. 'My life *or* his. And this way only your ego gets hurt. Seems to me to be the logical step.'

'Hard to argue with that.'

There was still no anger in Kincaid's voice even now. Just resignation. It left Dempsey unsure of what to think, but not for a moment did he question his decision. There was no going back. Any consequences he would deal with later.

He placed a hand on Kincaid's right shoulder, so he could feel any increase or decrease in tension that would suggest a sudden movement. The other hand gripped the pistol that was still aimed at his crown.

'OK, time to do this. Keep your left hand on the steering wheel, then lean across with your right, open the glove box and take out the cuffs you keep inside.'

Kincaid chuckled to himself as he followed Dempsey's instructions. Dempsey knew why: it had been Kincaid who had first mentioned the restraints. In case they had been needed for Frankowski.

Moving slowly, he used his one free hand to reach in and pull them out.

'Shouldn't have told you about these, should I?'

He held them up for Dempsey to see.

'This would've been more difficult if you hadn't. Now keep moving slow and put that first cuff on your left wrist.'

Kincaid did as instructed.

'Now lean back to the glove box and take out the key.'

Kincaid obeyed again, passing it back to Dempsey when told to do so.

'OK. Feed the cuffs through the wheel and secure your right wrist.'

A few moments more and the task was complete. Kincaid was fully restrained with an arm on either side of the Audi's steering wheel, his movement fully curtailed. Any threat he might have offered was gone.

Satisfied they were safe, Dempsey lowered his pistol, climbed out of the car and made his way to the front driver's side. Once there, he leaned inside and took the burner phone from Kincaid's pocket.

'You know you've got this wrong,' Kincaid said.

'I hope so,' Dempsey replied. He moved his head back out of the car and stood upright. 'For both our sakes.'

Dempsey did not speak again as he next moved to the rear passenger door nearest to Frankowski, opened it and pulled him out of the car by the collars of both his shirt and his waistcoat.

Frankowski offered no resistance. He had stayed silent throughout Dempsey's exchange with Kincaid but he could not have missed a word. It could only have convinced him even more that Dempsey was truly there to protect him.

'Stand right there and don't move.'

Dempsey did not wait to see his order followed. Instead he focused on scanning their surroundings, looking for any sign of danger ahead of their next move.

The sweep was a habit. A precaution taken almost subconsciously, even in this safest of surroundings. A place where no one could possibly find them.

Not for the first time, that habit saved Dempsey's life.

With no other human and no other occupied vehicle visible within the parking garage, there should have been no cause for the glint of light that hit the far wall to Dempsey's right. And yet there it was.

No more than an instant. A bare glimpse of reflected glass, gone as quickly as it had appeared.

But not so quickly that Dempsey missed it.

He had turned before his conscious mind even registered the sight, an act of pure instinct. Grabbing Kon Frankowski, Dempsey threw them both to the concrete floor beneath their feet, just as the distinctive whistle of a supersonic projectile sailed past his ear.

Someone was out there. And that someone was *not* a friend.

SEVENTY

The secure storage unit looked like any typical stable from the outside. Not the safest place to store cherished family items, Grace had thought as Maria had led her to it. But now she saw how misleading that first impression had been.

Built into the original frame of a wooden stable block, the room was essentially a reinforced concrete box with a single way in and out. And even that entrance was not what it appeared from an exterior view. The traditional wooden split-level doors unbolted and opened to reveal a thick metal shutter that could only be raised via a digital coded entry system.

It was an impressive set-up. As insecure as it looked from outside, no one was accessing this space without the right six numbers being entered in the correct order. Exactly as Maria had done to get them inside just moments earlier.

The interior lights came on automatically as the shutter slowly raised, revealing an area that was smaller than Grace had expected. The reduced size was the inevitable result of the reinforced interior; what the thick concrete walls and roof added in strength, they subtracted in square-footage. But even that was an advantage right now.

The smaller the space, the less it can hold. Which means fewer boxes needing to be searched.

'Any tips on where we start?' Grace asked.

'Not really,' Maria replied. 'But every box is marked. We must be looking for any that say "Kon" or "Kon's Stuff" or maybe "Office Stuff". There's no need to go through anything marked with anything else. Not unless we don't find what we're looking for in one of the more obvious containers.'

Grace just nodded her head, disappointed that Maria had not just remembered the location of her husband's stashed hard drives. There were, she guessed, between forty and fifty boxes piled ahead of them. It was enough to keep them occupied for a while, depending on how many were marked in the way Maria had said.

She took a deep, reassuring breath as she contemplated the task ahead.

'Then I suppose we'd better get started.'

SEVENTY-ONE

Time seemed to slow as Dempsey fell and yet his momentum guaranteed a painful landing in his immediate future. He knew what was coming but he could do nothing to stop it.

An agonising bolt of what felt like electricity shot through his left arm as his shoulder hit the floor hard. He had damaged something. He realised that instantly, even if he didn't know how badly. And he had no time to waste on working it out; the near-deafening gunfire that was echoing around the car park saw to that.

'JESUS FUCK!!'

The shout came from Frankowski, causing Dempsey to turn awkwardly on his injured arm.

Frankowski had hit the ground hard as well, but face first. It had caused a shallow four-inch cut to run from one eyebrow to another, joined across the bridge of his nose. Blood was seeping from the wound, temporarily blinding him as it ran down into his eyes.

No doubt panicked by both the gunfire and his inability to see, Frankowski began to crawl to his knees, the first stage of an inevitable effort to climb to his feet. It was a natural reaction but it was also one that Dempsey could not allow. He reached out, grabbed the back of the man's neck and slammed him back down into the concrete.

'Stay there,' Dempsey hissed. 'You want to live, you don't move. I don't need you in my way.'

Frankowski indicated his compliance as best he could; it was difficult to speak with his blood-soaked face pressed into the cold, hard floor. Satisfied, Dempsey turned his attention back to the shooter.

Or, more accurately, where the shooter had been.

Dempsey had to move fast – not staying in one pinned-down spot was the surest way to stay alive – but he had no idea of the direction he should be moving. The echo effect of the solid garage walls had made it impossible to zone in on the source of the shots fired.

I'm not even sure of how many he got off.

Two at least.

But it could have been three.

All he knew for sure, from the feel of the bullets as they had passed him, was that the shots had come from somewhere up ahead.

It was not nearly enough. But for now it was all he had.

Gripping his pistol in his right hand, he steadied himself with his left by pushing against the car in the next bay. The natural cover of his position was helpful for staying alive, but it also restricted his sight-lines to a minimum. The odds of spotting the shooter from here were near to zero.

Kincaid, though, was in a different position. Restrained in the driver's seat and facing outwards, his view would have none of the obstructions that hampered Dempsey. That fact would have made him a useful resource.

Except he must have brought this bastard here to begin with.

Dempsey glanced upwards and towards the wing mirror. The angle gave him only a glimpse of the American in the driver's seat. It was not enough to make a proper assessment of Kincaid's reaction to the shots and so Dempsey began to adjust his position, intending to gain a fuller view.

The process was trial and error, made all the more difficult by the need to keep behind the cover of the surrounding cars. But finally Dempsey was able to achieve the most effective line of sight, and when he did he saw something he was not expecting.

Kincaid was panicking.

Dempsey was unsure of what to think. Could it be an act? Was Kincaid really *that* good a conman? And even if he was, would he be putting on a show even now, with Dempsey out of the car and at the mercy of whoever the hell was out there?

It was unlikely. But it was not impossible.

And besides, how can it not *be him?*

Who else even knows we're here? Who the hell . . .

His thoughts were interrupted by more shots, the intensity of their sound amplified many times over by the concrete walks on every side. As before the effect was deafening, but this time Dempsey was prepared and so he could shut out the disorientating impact of the volume and focus on what he could learn.

Three shots this time.

And the sonofabitch is right there.

The echo had still made it difficult to work out details by sound alone, but this time the sight of the muzzle flash allowed Dempsey to count by sight. It also told him exactly where the shooter was positioned.

He reacted in an instant. Raising himself high enough to fire over the bonnet of the closest vehicle, Dempsey let off five rounds in quick succession, every one perfectly centred on the point of fire from moments earlier.

An instant later and he was down again. Back behind the cover of the car.

There was no way to tell if any of the rounds had hit their

target. He doubted it, but even so — even if they had not — at least the shooter knew he was in a fight.

Now let's see how good he is with someone firing back.

The thought was still in Dempsey's mind as he glanced again to his right, to Kincaid.

What he saw removed every doubt that had driven him since Cuijk.

The Audi windscreen had stood up well to the three-shot onslaught. Its shatterproof glass had justified its name; instead of falling into a thousand pieces it had been pierced in three places only, each one of them within inches of the others.

And all of them centred directly in front of Kincaid's seat.

Dempsey could not risk his own safety by raising himself level with the window. Nor did he need to. From this angle his view of Kincaid was back to being partial, but partial was enough.

Kincaid was a bloody, motionless mess, with the thick, viscous red that dripped from his open mouth confirmation that he had breathed his last.

SEVENTY-TWO

Michael stood up and raised his arms as high as he could reach. It was the fullest stretch he could manage, as if his upper body was trying to break free from its lower half.

The movement was much needed. Michael had been seated in Will Duffy's room for almost four hours now, in a chair plainly designed to discourage a lengthy residence. The inactivity had combined with the damage he had picked up last night to leave his back and his shoulders aching.

The stretch, though enthusiastic, did him little good. He needed to walk it off.

Heading towards the door, he stepped out of the room and into the quiet corridor outside. The hallway was maybe ninety feet long. Too short for anything that would really get the blood pumping, but it would have to do. Michael was here for a reason – to protect Will – and so he needed to keep his friend's room in sight at all times.

At least this way he could walk off some cobwebs without leaving Will unwatched.

The end of the corridor, where the elevator bank sat, was barely twenty feet to his right and so Michael turned left. It still took him no time at all to reach the far end – ten seconds at best – and so he was already heading back when he heard the sound of an arriving lift.

Sean Sutton stepped out, a look of concern across his face and his hand already inside his jacket, where Michael assumed his holster to be.

'Is everything OK?' He headed straight for Michael.

'Gallo said there'd been a security breach. He said you needed back-up.'

Michael held up his hands, palms out, to stop Sutton from drawing his weapon. He had expected the American's arrival since his phone call to Gallo and so he had prepared what he would say to hide the Italian's lie. Sutton was here a lot sooner than he had anticipated, but Michael was ready to play his part.

'No, I'm sorry, it was a mistake, Sean.'

'What do you mean a mistake?'

Sutton seemed irritated. It was hardly a surprise. He must have driven with his foot to the floor the whole way from Arnhem to have reached The Hague so soon. And he would not have done that if he had not been genuinely worried.

It left Michael feeling a little guilty at the deception.

'It was the hospital security team. A few of them came up earlier, to check on the ward, and I thought I recognised one of them.'

'From where?'

'I don't know. But I thought there was something about him and the way he was looking at me. Let's be straight, Sean; this isn't my world. I'm not like you and Kincaid and Joe. I don't know how any of this works and I panicked. I shouldn't have, I know that now. And I shouldn't have said anything to Sal.'

Sutton listened, his annoyance undisguised.

'You realise you've dragged me away from the assignment?'

'I know. I'm sorry.'

'Sorry doesn't cover it. I left Gallo alone so I could get back here for you.'

'I know. And again, all I can say is sorry. And thank you. I'm sorry I panicked, I really am.'

Sutton said nothing for a few moments. He just looked around them, at the quietness of the ward.

'A lot less people around now,' he finally said.

'Fewer emergencies, I guess. Yesterday was kind of once in a lifetime.'

'Not where I come from. Still, the place seems deserted.'

'Near enough. Everyone here seems pretty stable. It's probably the first chance staff and families have had a chance to rest since it happened.'

'I guess so.' Sutton looked over Michael's shoulder, back along the corridor towards Will's room. 'What about Duffy? Any sign of improvement?'

'The swelling on his brain has gone down a lot. If it keeps improving at this rate, they'll be able to bring him out of the coma tonight.'

Sutton seemed to visibly perk up.

'And he'll be able to speak to us?'

'I don't know. I expect he'll need to rest first, before he can start answering questions.'

Sutton nodded.

'Yeah. Yeah, I guess that's right. But after that, you know? That's a big step.'

Michael paused, confused by what Sutton expected to learn.

'Surely we know everything Will does? He can only tell us what Hannibal Strauss told him, and Strauss has told us that himself.'

'It pays to be thorough. Who knows what Strauss was holding back.'

'It didn't seem that way.'

'You never know, Michael. There's always questions worth asking. You should know that yourself, being a lawyer.'

'I guess so.'

Sutton's bad mood seemed to be lightening. It made Michael feel better about the underhanded move he and Sal Gallo had pulled.

'So this security guard,' Sutton began, 'you're sure he's *not* a problem?'

'I'm sure.'

'How?'

'He came back,' Michael lied. 'Alone. I took the chance to speak to him and it was pretty obvious I'd got things wrong.'

'When was this?'

'Maybe twenty minutes ago.'

'Did you call Gallo to tell him?'

'I did. He didn't answer.'

'So you've not been in contact with him since that first call?'

'No.'

'What about Dempsey?'

'No,' Michael lied. 'He didn't answer either.'

Sutton stayed silent for a few moments. He seemed to be thinking.

'Well, then I guess I should bring you up to speed, huh?'

'Is there news?'

'Yeah, there's news. They've got him. They've got Frankowski.'

'Really? That's fantastic. Where was he?'

'Cuijk. Where Dempsey expected him to be.'

'So what happens now? Did he have the list? Is it all over?'

'I only know what little Gallo told me. I'm not sure if they've even questioned him yet. They were going to rendezvous halfway and then bring Frankowski back to The Hague.'

'So what do *we* do?'

Sutton did not answer immediately. Instead he took his time to look around again. Finally, after a long, tired sigh, he had a suggestion.

'Look, why don't you go back and get some rest. I can tag you out here.'

Michael thought about it. It was an enticing offer after the last forty-eight hours. But he also wanted to see this thing through to the end, particularly when it now seemed to be in sight.

'No,' he finally said. 'Thanks, but no. I want to be here when they get back.'

'They won't be coming here, Michael. They'll be taking Frankowski into custody.'

'But *then* they'll come here. I want to be here for that. I want to be here until they tell us Will's really safe.'

Sutton looked at him quizzically.

'You're sure about that? Seriously, I can cover this while you get some sleep, man.'

'And what if anything happens while I'm gone?'

'You think I'm not up to the job?'

'Not at all. Jesus, you'll be way more use than me when it comes to it. But I can't rest until Dempsey's back, Frankowski's in custody and we have the hard drive in our hands.'

Sutton eyed Michael for a few seconds. There was a look of amusement in his eyes that Michael could not miss.

'What?'

'Nothing. Just that you're as paranoid as Dempsey.'

'We think alike sometimes, yeah.'

'It ain't healthy, you know?'

'Kept us both alive so far.'

'OK. So double duty it is, then.'

'Double duty it is.'

Sutton smiled.

'I guess I'd best go get us both some coffee.'

SEVENTY-THREE

'**I**'ve got it.'

Grace turned at the sound of Maria's voice and saw her knelt beside a large open box close to the far wall of the unit, her arm deep inside the cardboard container. Maria seemed to be struggling to pull it back out. Whatever she was gripping was not coming out easy.

'You sure it's what we're looking for?'

'Hundred per cent.' Maria freed herself as she spoke. In her hand was what looked like an innocuous black plastic box. 'Kon labelled it.'

'He what?'

Grace could hardly process what she had just heard; could Kon Frankowski really have labelled the most vitally confidential item he would ever possess?

'Kon labels everything,' Maria said. 'Mr Organisation.'

'But . . . this?'

'Especially something like this.' Maria stood up and walked towards Grace as she spoke, handing her the hard drive as she reached her. 'It's his way. There was no chance something this important wouldn't be identifiable.'

'Jesus. Did he really not think this through?'

'It's not his world, Eden. Even if he was dumb enough to try and live in it for a while.'

'I'm not gonna lie, I'm surprised he lasted this long before trouble started.'

'You and me both,' Maria replied.

Grace looked at the sleek metal and plastic slab, then turned it over in her hands. It revealed a crudely applied white strip, marked with one poorly written word: 'Strauss'.

She looked at Maria, then back again at the label.

'I know what you're thinking. You're wondering how the hell I married a man like that.'

'I already know why you did that.'

'My dad did warn me, you know.'

'I'm sure he did.'

'Maybe I should have listened.'

'You'd be a younger son down if you had. Everything has an upside.'

Maria smiled, seemingly grateful for the positive spin. She looked like it had cheered her up.

It was an emotion that would not last.

The sound and sensation of the nearby explosion was unmistakable, even through the protection of the thick concrete walls. The whole room rattled as the shockwave hit its outside, as if there was something trying to rip it clear of the very ground beneath.

Grace drew her pistol and threw the hard drive back to a shocked Maria before sprinting to the unit's open door.

The main residence was straight ahead and a little to the right. Six hundred yards, give or take. Grace could see the entire building from this angle, as well as the biggest of the ranch's six working barns, two hundred yards closer and to her left.

Both were intact with no sign of damage, which told Grace that the explosion had to have come from *behind* the storage unit. Whatever the cause, she and Maria were between it and the main house.

'WHAT THE HELL JUST HAPPENED?'

Maria was shouting. It was a normal reaction to the

deafening sound that had just hit them, and it was made all the more necessary by a further cacophony that now seemed to surround them. Whatever it was, the pulsating sensation of the noise was overwhelming.

Grace turned as she registered the screamed words, and as she did she saw the terror in Maria's eyes. Fear had driven every drop of blood from her skin, but it was not fear for herself.

'IS IT THE HOUSE?' Maria was frantic. 'IS IT THE BOYS?'

'NO!' Grace shouted back. 'THE HOUSE IS OK. THE BOYS ARE SAFE.'

Grace looked out again as she answered, trying to spot the source of the explosion.

What she glimpsed answered every question.

Grace did not need to see the full vehicle to identify it as an attack helicopter. The sound alone should have been enough, particularly with the devastation that had been caused outside of her sight-line. And yet it was the unique configuration of the chopper's tail, visible for just an instant as it passed overhead, that clinched it.

It was hardly a welcome development, but at least it told her what they were up against.

She turned back to Maria, her tactical training now taking over.

'It's them, Maria. They've found us.'

A split second later and the statement was confirmed by an explosion even more deafening than the first. The walls shook again as the shockwave hit, but this time the temperature inside the room spiked with the sound. It seemed to suck the air from the atmosphere around them, causing what was left to burn like an oven.

That one was closer, Grace thought. She surveyed the exterior one more time. *Still behind us, but closer.*

She turned to Maria. With the explosion still ringing in her ears, she had no choice but to shout.

'STAY IN THIS ROOM. THIS PLACE WILL TAKE A HIT BETTER THAN ANYWHERE ELSE ON THE RANCH.'

'WHERE ARE YOU GOING?'

'I NEED TO GET TO THE HOUSE. TO GET YOUR BOYS OUT.'

'LIKE HELL YOU'RE DOING *THAT* WITHOUT *ME*. THOSE ARE *MY* KIDS.'

'MARIA, LISTEN—'

'IT'S NOT A DEBATE, EDEN. I'M NOT HIDING IN HERE WHILE ANOTHER WOMAN RISKS HER LIFE FOR MY SONS. I'M COMING WITH YOU.'

Grace said nothing.

This was not an argument she could win. Even if she did have time to try.

Choosing the path of least resistance, she grabbed Maria by the wrist, pulled her to the door and then held her in place as she plotted the fastest course from stable block to residence.

It took less than an instant; there was just one obvious route.

With her gun in hand, her body primed to sprint and the sound of the passing chopper starting to lessen once again, she turned back to Maria.

'WHATEVER YOU DO, STAY CLOSE.'

SEVENTY-FOUR

Grace gripped Maria's wrist with one hand and dragged her the length of the L-shaped stable-yard. The secure room they had left was directly behind them, the furthest point from the house. It was one of five that made up the longer line of the 'L'.

Much to Grace's frustration, they had forty yards to go at least, after which they would hit the open space between the stables and the main residence.

'Stay close to buildings,' Grace said as they moved forwards. 'It's the only cover we've got.'

She looked forwards as she spoke, her Glock held out ahead of her in a hand less steady than was ideal; it was never best to hold a pistol in a single-hand grip and that was especially true when moving. But she had little choice. There was no way she was letting go of Maria. Not with the danger that would soon be above them.

And God knows what else on the ground.

Grace listened intently as they ran, as the sound of the approaching chopper grew ever louder. She did not look back. For this to work, she needed her timing to be right. And even more than that, she needed the helicopter to stick to the pattern it had already established.

That meant staying hidden, to give them no reason to deviate.

A few seconds more and they had reached the end of the stables. Once there she released her grip on Maria's wrist and placed her forearm across her chest, pushing Maria against the final unit.

'STAY OUT OF SIGHT,' she shouted, the noise of the chopper now loud enough to deafen, 'AND OPEN YOUR MOUTH WIDE.'

'WHAT?'

'TRUST ME.' Grace opened her own mouth and pointed inside. Then she closed it again to speak. 'LIKE THAT, OK. ONLY KEEP IT OPEN.'

Maria did as she was asked, and Grace said just one more thing before she did the same.

'NOW BRACE YOURSELF.'

The instruction was not a moment too soon. The noise of the explosion hit at the same instant as its shockwave; at just a few hundred yards, the distance was too small for the slower sound waves to be outran. With the shorter row of stables taking the brunt and the others soaking up much of the residue, the impact of air on Grace and Maria was much reduced but still powerful enough to knock both women off their feet.

The air seemed to burn around them as they both struggled back up, still hidden from the helicopter as it flew overhead to begin its third turning circle.

'HOW DID YOU KNOW THAT WAS COMING?'

Maria had pulled herself closer to Grace in order to be heard.

'ROUTINE. THEY DID THE SAME FOR THE FIRST TWO BUILDINGS. APPROACH, FIRE, TURN.'

'AND THE OPEN MOUTH?'

'EQUALISES THE PRESSURE. STOPS THE SHOCKWAVE FROM MESSING UP YOUR INSIDES.'

Maria looked around, horror etched all over her face. Grace followed her eyeline and saw the same sight: armed men – David Burton's men, Grace was sure – were now streaming out of the residence and moving in every conceivable direction.

'WHAT'S HAPPENING?'

'GROUND ASSAULT,' Grace replied. 'THEY MUST BE COMING FROM EVERY DIRECTION, SPLITTING YOUR DAD'S MEN.'

'WE NEED TO GET TO THE HOUSE.'

'WE WILL.'

'NOW, GRACE.'

Grace grasped Maria's wrist again, more tightly than before, and used every ounce of strength she had to hold the woman back.

'WE MOVE NOW, WE DIE NOW. WE NEED THAT CHOPPER TO PASS OVERHEAD, THEN WE GO.'

Grace looked up as she spoke, careful to remain hidden under the overhang of the stable roof. Her position gave her a first full view of the vehicle that was doing so much damage all around them. She recognised it instantly: a Bell AH-1 Cobra assault helicopter; she had seen plenty of them growing up on the many bases her father's deployments had taken them. And so she knew exactly what the machine was capable of.

A few seconds more and it had passed them, heading away to complete its turning circle and set itself up for its next death run.

Grace looked at the distance ahead of them. The path to the main residence. Then she looked again at the retreating Cobra.

It's too far. We won't make it.

And yet she knew they couldn't stay where they were. With

the rearmost barns and the slaughterhouse gone, the stables were surely next.

It wasn't even a choice.

She glanced towards Maria and nodded her head.

'TIME TO GO.'

Maria did not need to be told twice. Within seconds they were out in the open, sprinting as fast as they could towards the sprawling mansion that now seemed to fill the horizon ahead, such was Grace's focus upon it. At least five hundred yards away, it was unlikely they could maintain their initial pace for the full distance. But Grace was determined to try.

She looked to Maria as they covered about fifty yards. Older and thicker-set than Grace, she had expected Maria to be slower, too. But so far the doctor was matching her stride for stride.

Another fifty yards and they were still shoulder to shoulder, the detail of the house and the surrounding grounds becoming ever clearer. Grace was breathing hard as she covered the distance, her eyes scanning the full panorama ahead as she searched for any sign of a threat.

What she saw shocked her.

There were scores of men ahead, some near, some far, dotted across her field of vision in groups of twos and threes, and engaging one another in what could only be described as a pitched battle. From here Grace could not tell the attackers from the defenders. She figured the tighter, more professional-looking groups to be David Burton's men, but that was an uneducated assumption; she had no way of knowing how good the others might be.

What she *did* know was Alpha Team, and so it was no surprise as she saw gunfire coming from the upper windows and the roof of the residence. Her ISB colleagues had done what they did best: they had positioned themselves high with clear sight-lines into the distance, and from there they were sniping attackers left and right.

Another fifty yards covered and Grace had not lessened her pace one bit.

She glanced back at Maria, who in turn had slowed only slightly, and noticed for the first time that she was limping. The ankle injury from earlier, Grace realised. As minor as it was, there was no way it could take this kind of punishment. Not on the sun-dried, stone-hard mud beneath them.

Grace slowed by a fraction, determined to stay together. As she did she looked into the sky behind them and her racing heart missed a beat.

Oh shit.

The Cobra had completed its turn and was bearing down on the stable block. It would be just seconds before it opened fire again, after which it would move into its turning circle for a fifth approach. And when it did, the pilot would spot them.

And then this is all over.

She looked back at Maria, her eyes flitting to the hard drive still in the doctor's hand. Grace wanted both of them safe – Maria and the list – and she would make sure that happened, even if it meant doing the impossible.

'FASTER,' she shouted, desperation overcoming her lack of breath. 'IT'S COMING.'

It was a desperate instruction. One Grace was sure could not be achieved. And yet somehow, as their feet hit the dirt beneath them, they managed it. Together they hit a speed greater than either had moved before, an injection of pace that came from a sheer will to survive.

It was fast. Faster than Grace had ever moved before. But it was not fast enough.

Not even close.

This time the shockwave hit before the sound and, as before, the sheer force of the air that punched into their backs forced both women off their feet.

Grace fell hard, the impact made worse by the speed she had been moving. She had no idea if Maria had hit the ground as painfully, but she was aware that the doctor was up first.

Grace staggered to her feet a moment later, every inch of her body hurting and no time to check if any part was more injured than the rest. Instead she grabbed Maria and pulled her forwards.

'WE'VE GOT TO GO. COME ON.'

They ran again. Slower this time. Still a sprint by any standard, but the exertion and the impact had taken a toll. The ground was not passing beneath their feet at the same rate and there was nothing Grace could do to change it.

We're not going to make it.

She looked back. Just a glimpse, but enough to notice that the Cobra had changed its trajectory. And not in the way it had done before.

This time, it was coming for them.

'COME ON!'

Grace had no idea now if she was shouting at herself, at Maria or at them both. Or maybe it was none of those. Maybe it was at the chopper itself. A challenge; a demand to get this thing done. She was beyond rational thought. She was beyond help.

They both were.

She stumbled as she looked around again, barely managing

to regain her footing before she fell forwards. She felt Maria at her elbow as she fought to find her balance, then felt herself being pulled upright.

'KEEP GOING,' Maria shouted, 'WE'RE ALMOST THERE.'

Grace did not do as instructed.

They had two hundred yards to go and the Cobra had positioned itself perfectly. She and Maria were now directly in its sights, precisely aligned with its front-mounted machine gun; the perfect weapon for clearing the road.

There was no way they were both getting to that house.

But maybe one of them could.

'WHATEVER HAPPENS,' Grace shouted, 'DON'T STOP RUNNING!'

Maria hesitated for only a moment. She seemed to understand exactly what Grace was about to do. And to accept that it was the only choice. There was no argument. No debate. No emotion. There was nothing but cold, logical acceptance.

And two simple words.

'Thank you.'

Grace turned around as Maria sprinted away. With her pistol now held firm in a two-hand grip, she raised it skywards, towards the Cobra, and opened fire.

One.

Two.

Six.

Ten.

As many rounds as she could unload in quick succession, again and again until she saw the telltale dip in the Cobra's nose. The subtle alteration in its trajectory that told her what she needed to know.

Maria and the hard drive would reach the house.

Because the Cobra was coming for *her*.

Confident in what she had achieved, Grace stood her ground. There was nowhere for her to run now. She was a sitting target, at the mercy of a machine built to kill.

There was no way out of this. And that certainty was somehow comforting.

Grace smiled as she raised her pistol one last time. If she was going to die, she would do so shooting back.

Eleven.

Twelve.

Thirteen.

Fourteen.

Fifteen rounds in quick succession, fired without reply in just seconds. Not a single one doing any significant damage to the chopper.

Not until the sixteenth.

Grace turned at the sound of the extra bullet. A lone shot that she knew had not come from her: she had exhausted her own fifteen, and the unique whistle ruled out a pistol.

It was, Grace realised, a sniper's bullet.

And it had done what she could not.

Grace did not see the impact but what happened next made that unnecessary. The Cobra lurched with a sudden loss of control, juddering in mid-air like a drunk unsure of which way to fall. And then, its decision made for it by the laws of physics, it began to spin downwards.

The direction of the chopper's descent took it away from Grace, away from Maria and away from the house. That much was luck, but it was a break Grace was grateful to accept. She watched as the Cobra's spin became ever more violent, before it finally hit the ground with a force that dwarfed the explosions from its rockets.

Though grateful to be alive, Grace had no time to linger on thoughts of her survival. The most obvious threat was gone but plenty more remained. The gunfire she could hear coming from every direction was evidence enough of that.

She chanced a single glance to the roof of the residence and saw exactly what she expected. A figure that could only be Dylan Wrixon, the finest marksman Alpha Team had, was looking directly at the decimated Cobra. There was no doubt in Grace's mind that Wrixon had fired the bullet, just as there was no doubt that he would be unbearable about the fact he had saved her life.

Conceding that this time she would have to allow Wrixon his moment, Grace refocused on the residence to see that Maria was barely one hundred yards from the back door.

And she was not alone.

SEVENTY-FIVE

Dempsey's legs were burning with strain as he moved behind the line of parked cars. The need to remain crouched made his progress much more physically demanding than if he had been upright, with the problem made worse by his need to move at speed.

The combination made each step a little harder than the last.

It was a pain Dempsey could easily ignore. Little more than an irritation when compared to the physical traumas he had tolerated over the years. And certainly not as debilitating as the agony in his left shoulder. His heavy landing had damaged his rotator cuff, that much he knew for sure. But he suspected from the sharp, electric-like pain that the injury went further.

Whatever it was, it would have to wait. Dempsey could not allow anything to slow him. Not until he had flanked whoever had killed Kincaid.

Not until the sonofabitch is dead.

Dempsey had already concluded that he was up against a single shooter. The rounds had been fired from a single spot, and when Dempsey had fired back he had given any second shooter a clean kill. That it was a gift untaken came with one simple explanation.

There was no one else there to take it.

A maze of shot trajectories and covered angles were running through Dempsey's head as he moved, visualising every conceivable permutation of the exchange to come. It was his usual reaction to a combat situation; the thing that set him apart from the rest. While most resorted to a mix of instinct and drilled-in training when bullets began to fly, Dempsey planned.

The same mental images occupied him until he neared the rear corner of the parking garage. Puzzles to be solved, until they were replaced by a problem.

A big problem.

The two empty parking bays at the end of the line of cars were unexpected. The space Kincaid had taken had been the first available after driving two thirds of the floor. It had led Dempsey to assume that the building was near capacity. One empty bay, then, was unwelcome, but two?

That was twice the distance. Twice the exposure. Twice the danger.

Dempsey looked back over his shoulder. He was at least forty feet from where he had left Frankowski, safe behind Kincaid's Audi where the shooter could not yet have a clear line of sight. Right now it seemed like an attractive place to be; a safer option than the twelve-and-a-half-foot gap ahead of him.

He dismissed the thought. Neither he nor Frankowski were visible from where the rounds had been fired, but there could be no guarantee the shooter would stay in that same spot.

For all Dempsey knew, he or she could have moved already. And so every moment of inaction increased the risk to both their lives.

It left him no choice. Dempsey had to keep going. He had to risk crossing the two open parking bays and the prolonged moment of visibility that came with it. It was the only way to get ahead of this. The only way he could stop being the shooter's prey and instead become their hunter.

The decision was made.

Dempsey gripped his pistol tight and burst into movement

without a moment of hesitation. Hitting full speed in barely a step, he covered the two open spaces in less than a second.

It was the fastest he had ever moved and still it was barely enough.

Two rounds hit the concrete wall beside him, the dust thrown up sending a cloud of grit into Dempsey's face. It was as close a call as he could remember having, but it was not the near fatality that concerned him. It was what the shots revealed.

Whoever it is, he's good.

He's really good.

The bullets had come from directly ahead. Closer and at least twenty feet to the right of the ones that had killed Kincaid. It led Dempsey to an unavoidable conclusion: the shooter had anticipated exactly what he would do and had changed position to counter it.

Dempsey stopped moving the moment he was back behind cover. His mind was working fast as he tried to regain some control of the situation. As he considered what he should do next. His actions so far had proved too predictable to the shooter and so he needed to rethink the plan.

Whatever he did next, it would need to be something unexpected. Something that would catch even Dempsey himself off guard, if the roles were reversed.

He looked again at the path ahead. The changed angle from the shooter's new position provided a clear line of sight between the cars that were providing his cover. Moving between them would have left him vulnerable before. Now it was suicide.

But what was the alternative? Dempsey could not wait here, pinned down to one position. All the shooter had to do was move a few cars further to the right, from where a kill shot was possible. And it was not like Dempsey could just rush the guy. Not from here. Not when the shooter knew . . .

The last thought brought his racing mind to a halt. He was in a no-win no man's land, where no rational decision would get him through this. There was nothing sane he could do that would not be anticipated.

And that, he now realised, was perhaps his best chance.

He took a deep, invigorating breath as he pushed all logic aside. He had to do what the shooter could not possibly expect. Something that would cause the brief hesitation that could save his life.

If he could do that, he could make that moment count.

Dempsey did not wait even an instant more. The shots that had missed his head had told him the location of the shooter, and little enough time had passed that they couldn't have moved far.

The distance could not be more than twenty-five feet. Hardly the blink of an eye for a clear, unobstructed sprint. But what lay ahead of him was *not* that. With parked cars blocking both his path and his view, there was no straight line from A to B.

And Dempsey was not even sure of where B precisely was.

It made a direct frontal rush an act of madness; a full-on dash into certain death. It was not a decision any rational man would even consider.

And so it was the last thing the shooter would expect.

With the decision made Dempsey moved fast, hitting a full sprint before he had reached even the front wheel of the vehicle that covered him. His speed would have surprised *any* enemy, but surprise was not enough. It would gain him a heartbeat at most.

Dempsey needed more.

He needed the shooter to be diving for cover, and there was only one way to achieve that.

Dempsey fired the first round as he burst into a run. The second a step later. The third as he cleared the cover of the car.

Three shots down. Seven more to go; all the ammunition he had left to cover his movement.

It was going to be tight.

He covered the hard concrete ground at a blistering pace, fuelled by desperation, each round of suppressing fire followed within half a second by another. At this rate he knew he could keep the shooter pinned down, preventing him from firing back.

But only for as long as his clip lasted.

Dempsey did the arithmetic as he moved.

Four seconds.

He made them count.

He closed the distance within five shots. By the fifth, he could almost feel the presence of his would-be killer; that unnamed sense of another person's proximity, even with parked cars blocking his view.

It was an instinct Dempsey had learned to trust and so he did not slow at all as he hit his final obstacle. Instead he leapt onto the bonnet of the nearest car and vaulted forwards, and firing one more covering round as he hurtled through the air.

The elevation did only half of what he intended. It gave him a clear view of the space at the rear of the cars where he expected the shooter to be. But it did not provide him with a final, killer shot.

Because, to his horror, the space was empty.

But the spot next to it was not.

Still moving through the air and having caught a glimpse of movement in his peripheral vision, Dempsey just had time to turn his head and finally see the man who was here to kill him.

It was Sal Gallo.

SEVENTY-SIX

Michael looked up at the sound of the opening door and immediately recognised the logo on the two takeout cups Sean Sutton was carrying. It was identical to the one sold by the coffee vendor outside the entrance to the hospital. The same man Michael had paid just this morning for the worst cup of the stuff he had ever tasted.

'You go outside for these?' he asked, careful to not sound negative.

'I needed to make a call,' Sutton replied. 'Two birds, one stone.'

He held out one of the cups.

'Yeah. Why not.'

Michael placed the cup on the table to his right instead of taking a sip; he had no intention of letting the sludge inside touch his tongue ever again, but Sutton did not need to know that.

'You hear from Dempsey or Kincaid while you were out?'

'No,' Sutton replied. He took a pull of his own coffee. It resulted in a slight grimace, suggesting that the American might silently share Michael's opinion. 'You?'

'No. Nothing. What about Sal? Has he called?'

'No, nothing from him either.' Sutton indicated to Michael's cup. 'You not drinking?'

'Letting it cool,' Michael lied. 'So do you think we should call them?'

'Not the way it's done. We have to wait until they're ready to contact us.'

Sutton looked around the room as he spoke.

'Is there only one seat in here?'

Michael nodded.

'That's accommodating. I'll go get another.'

Sutton put his cup on the opposite table to Michael's and left the room. He was soon back with an identical uncomfortable wooden chair in his hands. He set it next to Will Duffy's bedside, across from Michael, and took a seat.

The two men sat in silence for a few minutes. It was an uncomfortable quiet. They hardly knew each other and neither seemed able to think of what to say. It wasn't helped by Michael noticing the occasional suspicious glance.

Probably wondering why I'm not drinking that muck he brought up, he thought. *Either that or he's wondering if I can be trusted.*

When Sutton finally spoke, Michael realised that the American, too, was finding the silence a little awkward.

'Look, Michael, are you sure you don't want to take the chance to get your head down?'

'You want me out the way?' Michael was only pretending to joke. He was quite sure that Sutton wanted to do his stint of guard duty alone.

'No, it's not that.' The denial was not convincing. 'I'm just conscious of the day you've had. Like you said earlier, even the medics in this place have gone home to rest. You've got a chance to do the same. Why not take it?'

'I'm staying,' Michael replied. 'Until Dempsey gets back, at least. I got him into this. The least I can do is see it through with him.'

'What do you mean you got him into this?'

'I mean it was me who was coming to look for Will after the shooting. If it wasn't for that, Dempsey wouldn't even be here.'

'You're serious?'

'Of course I'm serious. Why?'

Sutton shook his head, a smile spreading across his face.

'I thought he was here on an ISB operation.'

'He is now. But only because he declared it one. If we hadn't been together when Will was hurt, this wouldn't even have been on his radar.'

This time Sutton laughed out loud.

'I don't get it,' Michael said. 'What's so funny?'

'Just . . . just how the world spins, I guess. Without Dempsey we wouldn't be any closer to the Mladorossi list or to the Monk. We'd be running in circles like we always do. When Prochnik and Duffy were taken out of the equation we hit another wall. That only changed with you guys. Without you, we'd be nowhere near Frankowski. We'd be nowhere.'

'And?'

'And it's just how the chips fall, that's all. If you didn't know Duffy or Duffy hadn't survived the attack, the Monk would have had nothing to worry about.'

'Of course he would,' Michael replied. 'With or without us, he still wouldn't have the list.'

'Yes, but come on. How long was Frankowski going to be a problem for them? A computer geek against the Mladorossi, Michael? With none of us looking out for him because none of us would have known who he was?'

'Except for Will and Strauss.'

'A man in a coma and a war criminal. OK, OK. Maybe I'm oversimplifying it. But come on, you must see my point. If you didn't know Duffy then this whole thing would have turned out very, very different.'

'Maybe. But I *do* know Will, don't I? And he *did* survive. So here we are.'

'I guess so,' Sutton replied, his grin fading. 'It's just . . . it amused me, is all. The way the world works sometimes. I'm sorry. It's just my weird sense of humour. Plus, truth be told, I'm pretty beat myself. I'm not thinking too much about what I'm saying.'

'So why don't *you* go get some rest?' Michael asked. 'What's good for the goose . . .'

'What?'

'Just an expression.'

Both men stopped speaking for a few moments. Michael had found their conversation more than a little jarring, although the renewed silence was equally off-putting. He was considering which was worse when Sutton spoke again.

'Can I ask you something?'

'Sure,' Michael replied. 'Fire away.'

'It's about Gallo.'

'What about him?'

'Do you know him well?'

'I met him this morning. He's Joe's friend, not mine.'

'Right. In that case forget it . . .'

'No, tell me. What is it?'

'It's maybe nothing,' Sutton replied. 'I just . . . I found him a little weird is all.'

'Weird how?'

Michael was conscious that both he and Sal had lied to

Sutton to get him out of the way, so that Gallo could meet with Dempsey alone and deal with the possible threat of Kincaid. He wondered now if Sutton had somehow detected that dishonesty.

'It's hard to describe. It's just . . . I don't know. Just an instinct I had. I kind of thought he wanted rid of me.'

'Why would he want that?'

'Who knows. There are any number of possibilities. One of which is not so welcome.'

'I don't follow.' Michael was doing his best to seem ignorant. 'What possibility?'

'Well, what if he wanted me out of the picture because he had bad intentions?'

'Bad intentions?'

'You know how the Mladorossi work, Michael. The Monk has people everywhere.'

'You're saying Gallo . . .'

'Who knows? Which is kind of the Monk's deal, right?'

Michael thought for a moment.

'And what? You think he wanted you gone so he had a clean shot at Dempsey and Kincaid?'

'One less gun to worry about.'

'No. No way. Joe trusts him. He's one of Joe's hand-picked men.'

'Then who better to have on the payroll? If you're the Monk, I mean?'

Michael said nothing, his mind now a whirl.

Could Sutton be right?

Could Sal have manipulated this whole thing?

Could he have used me to get Sutton out of the way, so he could have a clear run at Joe?

He shook his head, trying to dislodge his own thoughts.

'No,' he finally said, as much to himself as to Sutton. 'No. Sal's one of the good guys.'

'I hope you're right.'

'I *am* right.'

'In that case we've got nothing to worry about.'

Neither man said another word, the same uncomfortable silence falling once again. Only this time Michael did not notice it. This time, his focus was elsewhere.

It was on Sal Gallo. And it was on his own fears and doubts.

What if I've sent Joe a problem even he can't handle?

SEVENTY-SEVEN

'MARIA! WAIT!!'

Grace pushed herself ever harder as she called out Maria's name. She knew her voice was unlikely to be heard; she was running headlong into a gun battle with automatic weapons firing all around her. A battle to which Maria was even closer, if only now by twenty yards.

But still she had to try. She shouted again as she gained on the slower woman ahead of her.

'MARIA!'

Maria had taken the direct route towards the residence after splitting with Grace, but that line had become impossible to hold the closer she came. As desperate as she no doubt was to get to her children inside, Maria could not have missed that she was running into a war zone and so she had reacted as any normal person would. She had changed course and she had taken cover whenever the fighting got too close.

It had made the last one hundred and fifty yards a crawl instead of a sprint.

The change in pace had been welcomed by Grace; it gave her time to catch up. But that was about as far as the positives went.

She had admired Maria's natural combat instincts as she watched her avoid cluster after cluster of fighting men. Even without training, the doctor had a talent for self-preservation. But talent without training would only get her so far. To get through this – to even have a chance at survival – Maria needed Grace beside her.

A fact that was proved just moments later.

With Maria slowed almost to a stop, Grace had covered the final fifteen yards between them in seconds. And as fast as that was, it was still almost too late. Less than two hundred feet from the residence now, Maria's path was blocked by a three-man detachment of David Burton's men as they engaged a group twice that number close to the building's outside pool.

To avoid the hail of bullets passing between them, Maria had taken cover next to a ten-foot-wide wooden pool house that hid her from the view of either group. From there she must have felt safe, like a child who equates not being able to see with being unseen.

Grace knew different. Still approaching from behind, she had a wider view. A view which including the young gunman who knew exactly where Maria was standing and who was moving around the pool house to make the most of his advantage.

Grace would never know that gunman's intention. Whether he meant to fire on Maria or to use her as leverage, to call off David Burton's men.

Grace would never know because she gave him no chance to do either.

With the gunman less than two feet from his unsuspecting target, Grace aimed her body directly at him and launched herself forwards. The momentum of her full sprinting pace propelled her onwards and they collided just as the gunman cleared the last inch of the pool house, with Grace using her right forearm to drive his head hard into its wooden wall.

She felt his body buckle with the impact but she could not make the mistake of claiming a victory already. The gunman was more than a third again her size and, as hard as his head had struck the wall, he had not dropped his weapon.

But then neither had Grace.

Holding her empty Glock in her hand like a club, she struck the hard metal butt across his face not once but six times, each time aiming for his temple as she sought to do as much damage as possible. Multiple blows, all of them in quick succession, all of them with as much power as she could bring to bear.

She stepped back after the sixth, breathing hard, and watched the gunman fall. From the state of his bloodied and broken skull and the dead stare of his open eyes, Grace knew he would not be getting back up.

'Jesus Christ.'

Grace turned at the sound of the words, her blood and adrenaline pumping too hard to assess their tone. All she knew was they had come from Maria, who – she guessed – must have seen what she'd just done.

'I had to, Maria,' Grace began. 'I had no—'

Maria held up her hand, a sign to stop speaking. Then she bent down without a word and picked up the dead man's abandoned M16 assault rifle.

'Don't apologise,' she said, once she was upright. 'That sonofabitch deserved exactly what he got.'

Grace gestured to the weapon as Maria carried out a fast check which seemed far more professional than she would have expected.

'You . . . you know how to use one of these?'

'You've met my daddy, right?'

'Silly question, then.'

'Yep.'

Maria looked back towards the pool. The fight that had

blocked her path was over. From what little was left of the other side, Burton's outnumbered men had come off best. Not that Maria seemed interested.

All that mattered was that the path was clear.

She turned back to Grace.

'Let's go get my boys.'

SEVENTY-EIGHT

Sal Gallo was six feet to the right of where Dempsey had guessed. It was hardly a distance at all, but it was enough. Dempsey had committed completely to his estimate on the shooter's location and so there was no way he could accurately re-aim his weapon before Gallo could react.

But he could redirect himself.

Gallo was already moving. The shock of Dempsey's suicide rush had made him hesitate for an instant, long enough for Dempsey to lay down suppressing fire. But any advantage that had given Dempsey was now gone. Gallo was armed and ready to act.

It was Dempsey, though, who had the momentum. Still moving fast through the air, he used the edge of the nearest car roof as a springboard and kicked out with his left leg, sending himself lunging to his right.

It was a desperate movement, quite literally do or die. But even if it worked, the odds of a win were still not in Dempsey's favour.

Against Sal Gallo it was more likely do *and* die.

The thought did not occur to Dempsey in the bare instant between seeing and engaging the Italian. He had no time to consider the physical mismatch between them; no chance, even, to wonder why one of his own team had betrayed him. Instead his every instinct was focused on staying alive beyond the next few seconds.

And to stand any chance of *that*, he needed Gallo disarmed.

If Gallo had been holding a pistol, Dempsey would have

been dead. Instead it was a rifle that Dempsey now saw in the Italian's oversized hands. A much superior weapon in so many ways, it was longer and more cumbersome. And so it took just that little more time to be turned.

Gallo almost made it. He was quick enough to open fire, but not quick enough to take aim first. The two discharged rounds sailed just inches to Dempsey's left as the Englishman came crashing down hard into a man he had trusted with his life.

Dempsey had no time to think as he made the first violent contact and so he did not consider the freakish physical strength of Gallo. If he had, he would still have been surprised by the Italian's reaction to his attack.

The collision should have done *something*. It should have staggered him, at least. Dempsey was two hundred and twenty-five pounds of taut, practical muscle, and every ounce of that had hit Gallo from above, as fast and as hard as Dempsey could manage.

Any normal man would have been knocked down by the impact. Most would be rendered helpless for at least a few moments. Maybe more than that.

But Gallo? The Italian stepped back just an inch or two, his own footing never anything but solid. It was like hitting an immovable rock face, only this was a mountain that came equipped with tree-trunk arms it could use to fight back. He halted Dempsey's forwards momentum as if he were nothing more than a rag doll, before throwing him off with what seemed to be zero effort.

Literal explosions aside, it was a physical force beyond anything Dempsey had ever felt. There was nothing he could do as his trajectory was changed for him. Helpless to resist, he felt himself propelled backwards through the air, his lungs emptied by the impact of Gallo's palms against his chest and his momentum beyond his own control.

It took the hard metal of the car behind to halt his backward movement and his legs buckled as his feet finally hit the floor, a bolt of intense pain firing up his spine as he fought to stay upright, his pistol smashed free from his hand.

The source of his agony was instantly apparent. The car's wing mirror had snapped as it drove into his back, but what was left had pushed deep into his kidney. Somehow it did not pierce the skin, but Dempsey knew that internal damage had been done.

He felt a sudden need to vomit – an involuntary response to his injury – but somehow he fought it off. There was no time for that. Not if he was going to live through this. Not if he was . . .

Dempsey's survival instinct interrupted his own thoughts. It was screaming at him. There was something his conscious mind had missed. A moment more and he had it.

Sal caught me and he pushed me with open hands.

If he did that, he must have dropped the rifle when we collided.

Sal's unarmed.

The realisation gave Dempsey hope and with it a surge of adrenaline pumping through his bloodstream. It nullified both the searing pain in his lower left side and the immobility of his rotator cuff. He would pay a price for the masked pain. Dempsey knew that. In fact, he welcomed it.

Because future pain means I've survived this.

He stopped thinking as he saw Sal begin to lean downwards towards the floor, reaching for his rifle. The weapon had dropped between the back of the nearest car and the trunk of the vehicle behind it. It would take him least two seconds to reach it, Dempsey figured. He could not be given that time. The fight was going badly enough already. Add a firearm into the mix and Dempsey was a dead man.

It was all the motivation he needed.

Gallo looked up at the sound of movement. Soon enough to see Dempsey's rushed approach but too late to do anything to stop it. He reeled backwards from the impact of Dempsey's right knee to his face; it was the first time he was made to stumble by the physical force of the smaller man. He was not impervious to pain after all.

The sight of Gallo's stumble spurred Dempsey on. He could give the Italian no time to recover. Instead he would keep fighting – punching, kicking, striking, attacking – for as long as his already damaged body would allow.

The knee strike that had sent Gallo backwards had also sent him upright and exposed his head, allowing Dempsey to follow it up with the most powerful left cross he had ever thrown. It landed clean and was joined an instant later by a right that was every bit as hard, then a perfectly executed left hook to finish the combination.

All three blows hit with every drop of the desperate force Dempsey could find; the last punch was so hard that he felt two of the knuckles on his left hand shatter with the impact. Each one should have been enough to stop even the strongest fighter, but Dempsey did not forget who he was up against.

He was not going to stop now.

Lunging forwards one more time with his right knee, his open hands reached upwards to grab Gallo by the back of the head. The intent was another knee strike to the face but somehow the Italian was still able to fight back, retaining the presence of mind to rush forwards as Dempsey lifted his leg.

Keeping low, Gallo drove his shoulder deep into Dempsey's

gut, the impact like a train. It forced the oxygen from Dempsey's lungs and sent yet another crippling shockwave through his insides.

And neither the movement nor the pain stopped there.

The sheer force of the blow sent Dempsey careering backwards and, before he could recover his footing, Gallo grabbed him and lifted him clean from the floor. Dempsey could do nothing to resist as his body moved higher into the air, his equilibrium turned inside out as he was slammed spine-first onto the roof of the vehicle to his right.

The force of that collision was staggering, enough to sap every ounce of strength his body could hold. But still Dempsey had his wits. A moment of helplessness against a man like Gallo was a moment too many; it could only end in death. And so, against the roaring objection of his body, he forced himself to move.

Intending to lift his damaged left side away from contact with the dented roof, he twisted his body onto its right. It did little to help – the effort of movement matched the agony of physical touch – and he realised now that he was moving far too slowly for what lay ahead. But still he was ready to react. Ready to defend himself from Gallo's next onslaught.

He could not understand, then, when the Italian did nothing.

For the briefest instant Dempsey questioned if Sal was gone; a thought brought on by nothing but desperate, irrational hope. He dismissed it as quickly as it had arrived and replaced it with the obvious truth:

Sal's not hitting me because he's reaching for the floor.
He's reaching for his rifle.

Dempsey's last few drips of adrenaline fired through his

veins as he realised Gallo's intentions. Enough for one last shot at survival. He knew he had no more than a moment.

Using his grip on the edge of the roof and every muscle in his torso that still worked, he flung his lower half outwards and his right foot around in a long and powerful sweep that was timed to coincide with Gallo's rise.

Sal came up with his rifle in hand exactly as Dempsey had predicted, which allowed the Englishman's boot to collide cleanly with the weapon. The impact ripped it from Gallo's grip and sent it hurtling across the garage and out of sight.

Dempsey wasted no time watching it go. He had next to nothing left and so what he *did* have, he had to make count.

With Gallo momentarily distracted by the loss of his weapon, Dempsey took advantage of the bigger man's hesitation. He brought that same leg sweeping up and back, ramming the thick, hard heel of his boot into Gallo's nose.

The feeling of shattered bones kept him moving, fuelling Dempsey as he launched himself from the edge of the car roof. He knew this time that Gallo was strong enough to catch him.

In fact, he was counting on it.

Sal halted the leap in mid-air, just as Dempsey had anticipated, and so his head was defenceless as Dempsey began to rain down blows with his fists and with his elbows. He targeted Gallo's skull and neck, landing hit after hit from above until, finally, the Italian's legs began to give way.

Gallo staggered backwards, slinging Dempsey aside as he did.

The throw was almost an afterthought from a badly injured man but still had enough force to send Dempsey careering into the same car he had leapt from less than a minute earlier. He landed in the spot where the two men had first collided and this time there was no way he could stay upright. With nothing left to keep him on his feet, Dempsey slumped to his knees, his insides on fire; only the frame of the car next to him prevented a total collapse.

It was to Dempsey's relief, then, when he saw Gallo do much the same. With his rifle out of sight and with injuries of his own, the giant staggered backwards and slumped onto the boot of a car parked in the row behind. It seemed that he, too, had little left to give.

Dempsey did not allow Gallo's condition to give him false hope. He suspected that his own injuries were much worse than Sal's. It left him needing to find some new advantage. But for now, as they both tried to regain their strength, there were things he needed to know.

'How long's it been, Sal?' he finally asked. His injuries made it difficult to speak, but he was determined not to show it. 'How long you been working for the Monk?'

'You think . . . you think I am a traitor?'

Gallo's voice sounded pained. Perhaps he was more injured than Dempsey had realised. The blows to his neck, most likely.

'It's kind of hard to think anything else right now, you know?'

'I am no traitor. I am loyal.'

'So all this?'

Gallo missed a beat before he replied. When he did, he cast his eyes to the floor.

'I am loyal to my family first of all.'

Dempsey frowned at the answer. In that moment, he understood.

'He threatened them?'

'He *has* them.'

473

'The Monk?'

'Yes.'

'How do you know?'

'Because he showed me proof.'

'You spoke to him yourself?' Dempsey was stunned. 'In person? Do you know who he is, Sal?'

'Yes.'

'Who?'

'What good will it do you? You can't survive this. You are too hurt to fight.'

'Humour me. For old times' sake.'

Sal sighed sadly as he looked at his friend.

'You will not like it.'

Dempsey felt his blood run cold at the answer. Because it suggested that Dempsey had met him too.

That it was someone who had been under his nose the entire time.

'Tell me,' he said.

'The CIA agent,' Sal said quietly. 'The Monk is Sean Sutton.'

SEVENTY-NINE

Dempsey stared at Gallo, too shocked – too lost in his own disbelief – to respond.

Sutton.

Sean Sutton.

That sonofabitch. He's played us for fools. He's played . . . Jesus Christ, Kincaid. That man . . . all his life, searching for a ghost . . . for a legend, who was right beside him the whole time. Probably throwing him off track at every bloody step.

He looked back towards Gallo.

'But . . . How?'

'I do not know. Once he had my family, I was only concerned for them.'

Gallo's words brought him back to the reality of his situation.

Of *Gallo's* situation.

'Where is he keeping them?'

'If I knew that I would be there. Not here. It's because I do not know . . . That is why this has to happen.'

'What's the deal, then?'

'You are.'

Gallo indicated towards the Audi. Towards the still hidden Frankowski.

'You and him. If I kill you both then my family go free. If I do not . . . you know what happens if I do not.'

'And you? What happens to you?'

'I don't matter. As long as they're safe.'

'Jesus, Sal.'

Gallo said nothing, but Dempsey could see his strength returning. The Italian was putting less weight on the car and becoming steadier on his feet. It was the opposite for Dempsey. As much as he was hiding it – as much as he tried to ignore it – his injuries were making him weaker by the moment. Whatever had happened to his kidney, it required medical attention.

That knowledge made his heart race. He needed to think fast. He needed . . .

Dempsey shifted his right hand on the floor – an attempt to move his weight and take some pressure away from his injured side – and as he did the feel of cold metal on his fingertips derailed his thought process. It gave him a surge of hope.

He kept his expression blank. He had to keep Gallo talking.

'When?' he asked. 'When did he take them?'

'Today.'

'But how did he even find them? How did he . . .'

'I know as little as you, which is why I have no choice. If this man can act with such speed, what chance do we have? What can I do but obey?'

'Sal, I could have helped you. You didn't . . . you didn't have to . . .'

'You know that's not true. Could you save them? Maybe. You have done many things that make me think maybe. But would you risk your family for that? Everyone you love for a maybe?'

'I . . . I don't know, Sal. I just . . . I just wish you hadn't done this.'

'So do I. But I have no choice. It is you or it is them.'

Gallo's voice grew stronger as he spoke. More determined. Dempsey knew what that meant.

'And so it had to be you.'

He began to push himself upright. His unnatural power was back. This was going to happen.

'I promise you, Sal. Whatever happens now, I will stop him.'

'You can't stop anything. You can't even stop me.'

He stood to his full height and looked down on the still-kneeling Dempsey. From his face alone, Gallo's inner conflict was unmistakable. He did not want to do this.

And neither did Dempsey.

'Can't you trust me? We know who he is, we have Frankowski. We have the upper hand. Come on, Sal. How often have we gotten through impossible situations together?'

Gallo shook his head. He believed he had won. He believed the smaller man was too injured to fight on. And in those circumstances, that made Dempsey a dead man.

When he spoke, his deep voice broke a little.

'I cannot take that risk. That life is gone now.'

Dempsey could see that Gallo's mind was made up. There was only one way this could end and it had to happen now.

The Italian managed just two determined steps and then he stopped, his eyes now fixed on the Glock 19 that was held rock-steady in Dempsey's right hand.

The gun Dempsey had used to cover his sprint just minutes earlier.

The gun that had fallen beneath a car after their first collision.

The car that was now holding Dempsey upright.

Dempsey did not blink as he aimed the weapon at the centre of Gallo's forehead.

'You don't need to do this, Sal. Whatever happens next, I'm

going to stop him. He won't hurt your family. I promise you that.'

Gallo shook his head.

'The gun. It is empty. You fired too many.'

'It's not.'

'I don't believe you.'

'Then you'll die, Sal. I've got one shot and I can't aim to wound, not when it's you. So please, don't make me do it.'

'I have no choice. The only guarantee for my family is your death.'

Gallo moved again. Fast and determined, he managed two more steps.

He would never take another.

EIGHTY

Dempsey struggled to his feet, his legs unsteady under his own weight. As he pushed his ravaged body upright, he looked down at the corpse of Sal Gallo.

He had always thought of the Italian as being so much more than a man, physically speaking. It was an opinion that had now only strengthened. Gallo had completely outmatched Dempsey, in a way no one had ever done before. Not even close.

If Dempsey had ever considered it, he would have expected to be the underdog in that particular fight, yet he was still shocked by just how wide the gulf between them had been.

It took him a full three minutes just to build the energy to stand upright. The damage Gallo had caused in their short exchange had left him literally broken. The injury to his kidney, if that *was* what Dempsey was feeling, made every movement an ordeal. He found himself having to steady his body against the nearest parked car, swaying as waves of nausea threatened to bring him back down.

He fought off the weakness, determined to put even the thought of it out of his mind. The sight of Sal's corpse helped with that. It was one of the most terrible images Dempsey had seen in a life coloured by death and by loss.

More sobering right now, however, was Gallo's betrayal. Both its speed and its cause.

Dempsey had been double-crossed before. More than once and sometimes by men who had meant even more to him than the Italian. But never before had a friendship gone from absolute trust to a fight for survival in just a matter of moments.

When Kincaid had driven into the parking garage less than ten minutes earlier, Gallo had been Dempsey's lifeline. The one-man army on whom he could rely through whatever lay ahead. Not even a quarter of an hour later and that lifeline was dead, his very existence snuffed out by a single round to the centre of his forehead.

That turnaround alone was difficult to take, but it was made immeasurably worse by Gallo's motive. Because unlike others in Dempsey's past, his reasons were understandable. Gallo had done what he had done for his family. He had tried to guarantee their lives, even at the cost of his own.

It was a motive Dempsey could truly understand. And it was why he had made his own promise before taking the Italian's life.

He would do what Gallo could not.

He would save the dead man's family.

He would find Sean Sutton and he would kill the sonofabitch.

With that oath ringing in his ears, Dempsey looked back across the parking garage and towards Kincaid's Audi. It was forty feet away, close enough that the three holes in its windscreen were unmistakable.

The holes partially obscured Kincaid's body beyond them, but there was no doubt that it was there. And no doubt the American had been killed on Sutton's orders. If any fact disgusted Dempsey the most, it was that one. Sutton had known Kincaid his whole life. He had seen him grow from his own father's protégé into the . . .

Dempsey stopped at his own thought of Sutton's father. Because if Sutton was the Monk . . .

His mind scrolled back to the conversation with Hannibal

Strauss. What was it he had said? That the Monk was an *inherited* title? What if that was literal? What if it was passed from father to son. That would mean . . .

That would mean these bastards have been hiding in plain sight for generations.

They're a myth because they *made themselves a myth.*

They protected themselves from spy-hunters by being *the spy-hunters.*

He shook his head at the realisation. Strauss had called the Mladorossi's funding by the Soviet and then Russian regimes its greatest achievement, but that paled in comparison to positioning its leader at the heart of the United States intelligence community.

Dempsey stumbled as this last thought crossed his mind; his stream of reasoning had distracted him from the usually effortless task of staying upright. Realising that he was breathing hard from just those few steps, he forced himself to focus on the Audi.

From here there was no sign of Frankowski, but that was to be expected. Chances were he was still curled up in a sobbing ball where Dempsey had left him, taking cover between the rear of the car and the back wall of the parking garage.

It took Dempsey longer than it should have to cover the forty feet between them. Much longer. Every step was an exertion, every stride a victory. By the time he reached the Audi's bonnet he was exhausted, ready to fall again. That he stayed on his feet was a triumph of sheer mental will over the reality of his physical condition.

He could go no further.

'Kon.'

Dempsey was surprised to hear his own voice as he called

out the name. It sounded weak. Pained. He knew he could not allow that. Frankowski could not know how badly hurt he was. It was a weakness that could encourage the man to run. And if he did, there was no way Dempsey would be able to catch him.

When he spoke again, he made sure that his voice was his own.

'Kon, it's over. Come out.'

No answer.

'Kon.'

Again there was no answer. It was irritating, even though he knew the likely reason. Frankowski was no doubt too traumatised to register that his name had even been called. As understandable as it was, Dempsey had no time to be delicate.

'Frankowski, get your arse out here now or I'll come back there and drag you out.'

The tone was tried and tested, designed to be deployed in even the most high-pressure situation. Dempsey was unsurprised to see it work. He watched as Kon slowly appeared from his hiding place, raising first his head and then his upper body from behind the car until he was finally standing.

'Is it . . . is it over?'

Dempsey nodded his head.

'For now. But others could be coming. We need to move.'

Frankowski remained motionless, his eyes fixed on Dempsey.

'You're hurt.'

'You should see the other guy.'

Dempsey said the words without thinking, a rote repetition of Michael's reply the previous night. He immediately regretted them. It was far too flippant for what he had just lost.

His tone was serious when he spoke again.

'We need to go.'

He opened Kincaid's door without another word and pushed the dead American upright with his right hand, before patting his bloody torso with his left. He quickly found what he was looking for: Kincaid's pistol and four clips of ammunition.

Dempsey took one look at the weapon. It was a Glock 17. He discarded it and kept the bullets. The clips were compatible with his own Glock 19 and he had no need for a second firearm.

Moving with care, he stored the magazines on his belt and turned back to Frankowski.

'We're going to need a car. Can you drive stick?'

Frankowski looked confused. He gestured to the Audi.

'What's wrong with this one?'

'Apart from the bullet holes in the windscreen, the dead guy in the front seat and the blood that's decorating the back window? The Monk knows what car Kincaid was driving. So, can you?'

'Can I what?'

'Drive stick?'

As Frankowski nodded his head, Dempsey turned and began to scan the vehicles around him. In seconds he had found what he was looking for. A twenty-year-old red Honda Civic hatchback. It had two traits that were essential for the task at hand: the reliability of turn-of-the-century Japanese engineering and a security system two decades older than the newer, more formidable cars that surrounded it.

It took Dempsey almost a full minute to reach the car at his slowed walking pace. Thirty seconds more and he was through its locked driver's door. Another fifty and the engine was hot-wired into life. The whole exercise took at least a minute and a half longer than it would on any normal day.

Frankowski had followed and stood alongside throughout, so he was barely a foot away as Dempsey dragged himself out of the door.

'You *are* hurt.'

Dempsey ignored him.

'You're driving.'

'Where?'

'Back to The Hague.'

'Are you sure? You look like you need a hospital.'

'We're going to a damn hospital,' Dempsey snapped back.

Dempsey felt his right knee give way as he spoke. He managed to catch himself before he fell, but Frankowski could not have missed it. He could no longer pretend.

'Look, you can see I'm hurt. That's why you're driving. But before you do, I need you to climb in the back and pick up my phone. There's people I need to speak to.'

'No way, man. You need a doctor.'

'I know what I need. Now get in the goddamned car and get me my phone.'

'Why? What the hell is more important than keeping yourself alive?'

Dempsey felt his blood pressure rise at the question.

'Keeping the people I love alive, that's what.' He stopped himself before saying more. He needed a moment to construct his next sentence carefully. 'And your wife, too. I need to keep *her* alive.'

Frankowski's eyes widened at the mention of Maria.

'You mean she's still in danger?'

Dempsey nodded his head slowly.

'More than she ever has been.'

EIGHTY-ONE

Michael could hear the incessant tapping of his own foot, his nervous energy overflowing in his system. He had no control over the movement. No way to stop it, just as he could do nothing about the gnawing feeling in his gut.

He could not take his mind off of Sal Gallo and Dempsey.

He could not shake the thought that he had helped the Italian to catch his friend at his weakest.

He glanced across at Sutton. Not for the first time. Probably not for the twenty-first. As ever, the American's eyes were down. Fixed to his phone. He was, Michael knew, waiting for the call they were both expecting. Confirmation that the rendezvous had been successful and that they were now bringing Frankowski in.

The rendezvous . . .

Michael wondered if Sutton was as nervous as he was. If he was as worried about the threat that Sal Gallo might pose. Sutton was close to Kincaid, Michael knew that. Not as close as Michael and Dempsey, but there was at least a residual loyalty there.

Enough that he won't want to see him dead, anyway.

He looked across again. If Sutton *was* nervous, he was much better than Michael at hiding it. As he should be. That kind of deception was the man's career.

'I want to call them.'

Michael said the words out of nowhere and without so much as a conscious thought. They surprised even him.

'I want to call Joe,' he repeated.

'No,' Sutton replied. 'I've told you, that's not how operations work. They'll call us when they're ready.'

'I know what you said. I don't care. I want to call.'

'I can't let you.'

'You can't bloody stop me. You've no authority here, Sean.'

'Michael, let's not do this. You're tired and you're emotional.'

'You really don't care what Sal Gallo could do?'

Sutton's eyes narrowed. For just a moment he seemed confused, then he seemed to understand.

'You're still thinking about that? Jesus, Michael. What I said about Gallo was just a thought. I didn't say it was likely.'

'That's because you don't know the full story. Truth is, Gallo *did* con you. We both did. He didn't want you with him when he met with Dempsey and Kincaid, so he told you a bunch of bullshit about a security breach here. And he had me go along with it.'

'What? But why?'

'Because he didn't trust Kincaid. And so he didn't know if he could trust you.'

'Holy shit. So what, it was Gallo's idea to get rid of me?'

'It was.'

Sutton got to his feet. Michael could see the anger in his eyes.

'You realise what you might have done here?'

'Of course I bloody realise. Why do you think I want to call Joe?'

'You're calling no one. You're doing nothing. I knew we shouldn't have involved a fucking civilian in any of this.'

'You didn't involve me. It's got nothing to—'

'Sit the fuck down and shut the fuck up.'

Sutton's voice was as firm as Michael had ever heard it but still it would not have stopped the Irishman from doing exactly as he had planned. Sutton reaching for his phone, however, did make him pause.

'You're gonna make the call?'

'Of course I'm gonna make the goddamn call,' Sutton snapped back. 'Someone has to warn them.'

Sutton tapped the screen and put the phone to his ear. Michael could not hear the other end of the line, but the expression on Sutton's face suggested he was missing nothing.

Michael waited, hoping for some indication that Dempsey had answered.

None came. And the longer it took, the more his stomach turned over. His butterflies were now a barrel of snakes, fighting themselves within his gut.

A familiar sound interrupted his thoughts. A sound which made his heart race.

A sound which gave him hope.

It was the sound of *his* phone, sitting on the nearside table. He reached out and picked it up with his back to Sutton, flipping the handset over so that he could see the caller's name displayed on its screen.

JoeD(Temp)

His relief was palpable and he turned back to Sutton to share the good news.

'Sean, it's Dempsey.'

The phone was already to Michael's ear as he turned and so he could hear Dempsey's voice at the same moment his eyes fell on the barrel of Sean Sutton's raised gun.

A voice that now sounded a million miles away.

'Michael, it's Sutton. Sutton's the Monk.'

EIGHTY-TWO

Michael's attention was drawn naturally to the pistol that was aimed directly at his heart, but he forced himself to look upwards. Not because it gained him any advantage; he had no doubt that Sutton would happily look him in the eye as he pulled the trigger. No. There was nothing to gain from meeting his gaze.

But Michael did it anyway.

Sutton would have to see Michael's defiance as he took his life.

'So Dempsey is alive,' Sutton said.

Michael noticed that an accent had entered his voice. His usual American drawl now clearly mixed with Russian.

'That's a shame for you. I was going to let you live.'

'Bullshit.'

'Not bullshit at all, Michael. Why do you think I wanted you to go and get some rest? Why do you think I bought you the coffee when you wouldn't?'

'The coffee?'

'You were supposed to drink it. When you did, you'd have fallen asleep.'

'You drugged it?'

'I needed you out of the way, but at the same time it would have been useful to keep you alive.'

'Why?'

'Because you were my cover. You saw me kill Luuk Jansen, Michael. You saw—'

'Who?'

488

'Luuk Jansen. The man I sent to finish Duffy last night. You saw me kill him.'

'I didn't know his name.'

'Why would you?'

Michael found his eyes drifting back down to the gun. Again, he forced himself to look up. To engage Sutton.

'What does it matter that I saw that? So did plenty of others.'

'I know. But no one else could have given the complete picture, could they? No one else spoke to Sal Gallo. No one else could report being manipulated by him, to keep me away while he murdered the rest of the team. No one else could have exonerated me so completely of everything the Monk had done to cover his tracks. You were the patsy I needed, Michael. With everything you would have told them, no one would have been looking at me. It would've been all eyes on Gallo.'

Michael hesitated, searching his racing mind for the next question. He knew what he wanted to say: he wanted to point out how none of this mattered anyway with Dempsey alive. He wanted to point out that his friend had won. That for every advantage the Monk had, Dempsey had beaten him.

But none of that would have served his purpose right now. Michael was playing for time, and pissing Sutton off was not the way to gain it.

Instead he kept it trivial.

'And what makes you think Sal wouldn't have confessed? That he wouldn't have told everyone the truth?'

'You think I had no end game for Gallo?'

'What, then?' Michael asked.

'Gallo could never have confessed. That was the price for

his family.' Sutton continued with a smirk, his voice disdainful. 'And as for your desire to draw this little exchange out, what do you think that will achieve?'

Michael said nothing.

'You think if you can get me to monologue like some second-rate Bond villain, that I'll still be here in time for Dempsey to come to your rescue, all guns blazing?'

'The thought had crossed my mind.' Michael did his best to sound calm. 'The image of it, truth be told.'

'Then you need to read up on your Dutch geography. I could talk at you for thirty minutes and still be long gone before his car even reaches the outskirts of The Hague.'

Michael forced his face to stay free of any expression. It wasn't easy; the news was disappointing. But he was determined that he would not let it show.

'Shall we test that?' he asked, his tone intentionally flippant. 'I reckon I've got at least that much chat in me.'

'No, Michael. No. I don't think we will.'

Sutton visibly tightened his grip on his pistol, his forearm stiffening. Michael recognised the signal. He was steadying himself for the recoil, which suggested he was preparing to fire. And yet Michael had an instinct that Sutton wanted to talk. The very nature of what the Monk did would make it impossible for him to share his conceit in normal circumstances.

This, then, was a rare opportunity to boast. A unique chance to revel in his own brilliance.

And Michael's survival depended upon helping him to take it.

'So what now?' he asked.

Sutton looked puzzled.

'What do you mean?'

'I mean Joe's alive and he knows who you are. Which must mean that Sal Gallo's dead. So, what now?'

Sutton did not miss a beat. He seemed unfazed by the situation Michael had described.

'Sean Sutton disappears. That's all. It's time for a new fiction.'

'You expect me to believe that's it? After all these years? All this time building the Monk and the Mladorossi? You can abandon it that easy?'

'Abandon the Mladorossi? Why would I do that?'

Michael was confused by the man's confidence.

'Because Joe's coming for you. He's coming for all of you.'

'Is that right? And how exactly is he expecting to find me, Michael? How is he expecting to find all of us?'

'The list. The one Frankowski has. Strauss was clear on that. Every one of you bastards is on there. It leaves you nowhere to hide.'

'You're right. That list *would* be an end to us; it includes everything you just said and more. What a shame, then, that Dempsey doesn't have it.'

Michael felt a cold chill at the answer. It was not the response he had expected. It was also the last thing he wanted to hear. The Mladorossi list was everything. Their ultimate weapon against the Monk.

If they did not have it . . .

He had to hide his shock at what he had just been told. To do that, he forced a tone of amused disbelief into his voice.

'And just who *does* have it, then? If not Frankowski.'

'It never left the United States,' Sutton announced. 'And until about fifteen minutes ago it was sitting in a storage unit in upstate New York that belongs to Frankowski's father-in-law.'

Michael's heart rate increased even more. The reference to the ranch removed any doubt he had that Sutton was lying.

The place Maria ran to for safety . . .

The place Joe sent what was left of his team . . .

He knew he had to ask his next question, no matter how much he feared the answer.

'What do you mean "until fifteen minutes ago"?'

'Give or take.'

'What?'

'The ranch, Michael. David Burton's ranch. Did you really think I would take that risk?'

'What have you done?'

'It's gone. Wiped off the face of the Earth. Along with everyone and everything in it.'

Michael said nothing, but there was no way he could hide his emotions this time. His horror. His fury. He did not even try.

'So there *is* no list any more,' Sutton continued. 'There is no way to identify my network. There is no way to find me, not once Sean Sutton's gone. All of this effort, Michael. All of this loss. It was for nothing.'

Sutton stood up to his full height. The pistol barrel swept upwards with him, until it faced Michael's forehead instead of his chest.

'And it's cost you your life.'

EIGHTY-THREE

G race was a few steps off the pace as Maria closed in on the open rear door of the residence. She had stopped for a moment to arm herself with an M16 from one of the Monk's dead mercenaries; one of the large group who had been taken out by David Burton's trio of far better trained ex-Marines.

It was a necessary delay but one which left her playing catch-up once again.

It was obvious by now that the attack was not going well for the Mladorossi contingent: their bodies littered the area around the house and pool. There were maybe fifteen corpses all within sight and at least three quarters of them were strangers to the ranch.

There would no doubt be many more dotted around the wider grounds that surrounded the house. Grace was certain of that. Just as she was sure, by the lessening sound of gunfire, that even those few who were still alive were in the process of being decimated.

The Monk's men were losing this and they were losing it badly. But it was not over. Not as long as a single one of them remained alive.

Until every threat's gone, none of us are safe.

The thought had barely crossed her mind before it proved to be true.

Maria was a little over twenty yards ahead of Grace, running flat-out with no obstruction between her and the residence, her focus on reaching her sons seemingly absolute. Which was why she did not notice the two men who raised their weapons as one.

Grace had not seen them either. Not at first. But as Maria closed in on the building's back entrance, they both moved into view.

Their positioning could not have been better if they had planned it. With one gunman appearing ten yards to Maria's right and the other half again as close to her left, they instantly had her in an inescapable crossfire.

Maria had run headlong into an inadvertent death-trap. And she still didn't know it.

Grace raised her own rifle and flicked the fire mechanism to a three-round discharge as she slid to a halt. For her to be able to fire first would be a near-superhuman feat.

It would also not be enough.

Even as Grace took aim at the closer man, she knew beating *him* to the shot would not save Maria. Because even if she was faster than he was, Grace only had time to take out one of the two men now taking aim.

And they were both so close that neither man could possibly miss.

That knowledge, though, did not slow Grace for a moment. She still had to try.

She pulled the trigger without hesitation, for just long enough to fire all three rounds; a fraction of a second at most. She did not wait to see them hit their target, but nor could she turn quickly enough to open fire on the second shooter.

Grace was fast. But no one was *that* fast. And so, at the sound of a second burst of three shots, she braced herself for the sight of Maria's fall.

It was a sight that never came.

Instead it was the second gunman who went down, the victim of three rounds directly to the heart. An instant later and

David Burton had hurdled the fallen body of the man he had just killed, a display of athleticism unnatural for a man of his age and no doubt fuelled by concern for his daughter.

Maria, for her part, had frozen at the sound of the shots, each so close that they must have seemed to surround her. The disorientation must have been extreme and for a moment Grace was concerned how she would react; whether she would start shooting back, in misjudged self-defence. Thankfully Burton reached her before she could do any such thing, throwing his arm around his daughter and pulling her into his chest, and saying words that Grace could not hear, not even as she finally came close enough to touch them both.

'IS EVERYONE OK?'

Grace was immediately aware that she no longer needed to shout. Not with the sound of surrounding gunfight now so diminished. Even so, after so many explosions in so few minutes, she had no real control over her own volume.

Both Burton and Maria turned at the hollered question, and upon seeing her Burton reached out and pulled Grace in close. She could almost taste his sweat as he hugged her with an arm that felt like steel.

'Thank you,' he said, his grip impossible to escape. 'Thank you.'

The grateful embrace lasted for longer than it should have done in the heat of a battle. Grace realised that early and was trying to pull away even before Burton finally let go. All three stepped back from one another as they came apart, with each of them taking a moment to look around.

'What do you think?' she asked Burton.

'Nearly over,' he replied.

'How are your men?'

'We've lost more than I'd like. Nowhere near as many as them.'

'What about the house?' The question came from Maria. 'Is anyone in there with the boys?'

'Leisha has them in the safe room. They're locked in and I've got a man stationed right outside.'

Maria nodded fast, a look of exhausted relief on her face. It was the first time Grace had seen her look anything but frantic since the sound of the first explosion. It was as welcome a sight as she had seen all day.

But it was not one she had long to enjoy.

With Grace now facing the residence, she could not miss the flicker of movement over Maria's shoulder. She shifted her gaze towards the back entrance to the house, raising her rifle as she did. But it was too little too late.

Grace had seen what she had seen in the blink of an eye. The last glimpse of men moving fast.

Three men.

None of them Marines.

All of them heading inside.

She turned to Maria and to Burton.

'We've got to move.'

EIGHTY-FOUR

Grace could hardly keep up as Maria burst through the open rear door of the east wing and sprinted headlong into the hallway beyond.

The woman was moving with the determination of a mother fighting for her children. It seemed to add strength and speed and energy. Grace had read articles that described some near-mystical maternal boost but she had always dismissed them as fanciful.

Now that she was seeing it in action, she was inclined to think again.

Maria and Burton knew the layout of the house and so Grace was content to follow, turning left and right and left again as they ran towards the safe room. None of them knew if the three gunmen were even headed in that direction, but no one was taking any risks.

Twenty seconds and three turns more and they were there.

The entrance to the safe room was an innocuous wooden panel, indistinguishable from the rest of the walls that surrounded it and notable only for the armed guard who stood beside it. He greeted Burton with a gesture that was somewhere between a wave and a salute.

'Everything OK, Boss?'

'Not yet,' Burton replied. 'There's three shooters inside the house. Any sign?'

'Not a one. What's the plan?'

'We need to flush the sonsofbitches out.'

Burton turned to Maria.

'Sweetheart, I want you to get inside the safe room with Leisha and the boys. Anyone comes through that door that's not one of us, you empty that rifle dead centre, you hear?'

'Got it, Daddy.'

He turned to Grace.

'We're gonna find these bastards.' He indicated the guard. 'I want you and Rob to stick together and take the East Wing. I'm going to call up some of the others and patrol the rest.'

'Sir.' Grace turned to the man she now knew to be Rob. 'OK, come with—'

She did not get to finish the sentence, her words interrupted by the burst of three bullets that shattered the young man's head barely feet from her face. It showered her in a mixture of blood, brain and skull.

Grace's training did not allow her to react as any normal human would. She had no time to retch. No time to scream. Instead she did the one thing that had been drilled into her during her time with the Presidential Protection Division of the United States Secret Service. She dived for the body that was under her protection – she dived for Maria – and took her to the floor before another round could be fired. And once down she pinned Maria beneath her own bodyweight, preventing her from moving as Grace herself turned to get a sight of their attackers.

It was during that last stage that she saw the result of David Burton's equally intense training.

Drilled to attack rather than defend, Burton had done what any member of the US Marine Corps would do. He had raised his own assault rifle, taken a knee and fired back. And even exposed in the open hallway with no obstruction he could use for cover, he had done well.

One of the three gunman had gone down to perfectly placed shots to the chest. Another had taken one to the shoulder and one to the neck.

Unluckily for Burton, his successes did not come in threes.

Grace had turned just as Burton was hit twice, the second shot leaving him motionless on the floor. She grabbed for her fallen rifle to return fire but, as her eyes moved from Maria's father to the man who had shot him, she felt herself freeze.

'You?'

Even hundreds of miles from where she had last seen him, Grace instantly recognised Special Agent Alan Tyson. It was the shock of his appearance – here and now, so completely out of his previous context – that distracted Grace's attention for one crucial moment.

'DADDY!!!'

The scream broke through Grace's confusion, but it was too late for her to keep Maria on the ground. Maria was on her feet before Grace could do anything to stop her. Fearing that Tyson would react to her movement with a bullet, Grace lunged again for her rifle in the hope she could beat him to the shot.

It would not be necessary.

Maria's emotions must have overridden her conscious mind at the sight of her fallen father, because she ran directly at Tyson. It was a hopeless attack. And it blocked any chance of a clean shot for Grace.

It was lucky, then, that Tyson seemed bemused at the audacity of his would-be attacker. Enough that he chose non-lethal force.

Stepping forwards so that the butt of his rifle faced Maria, he raised it to shoulder height and struck her hard across the face as she came close. The combination of Maria's speed and

Tyson's power sent her reeling backwards and to the ground. She landed unconscious on top of her father.

Grace was hit with a surge of angry adrenaline at the sight. It drove her upwards, from the ground to a knee, her eyes fixed on Tyson. She raised the barrel of her rifle and dug its stock into her shoulder for the cleanest possible shot. She was determined that Tyson would pay for what he had just done.

That he would pay for all of this.

She was determined, but she was not fast enough.

The sound of a single shot coincided precisely with the sharp, burning agony that cut deep into Grace's left shoulder. Her shooting position had left her at an angle and so the bullet had more flesh to rip through before it could exit, increasing the damage. Not that Grace knew that yet. For now, it was the impact that proved the biggest problem: it had sent her careering backwards, slamming her down hard onto the floor behind.

With her weapon dropped from her hands, Grace lay helpless as Tyson approached. He stepped over Maria and Burton – both of them unmoving – and came close enough that his shoe was on the tip of Grace's hair where it touched the wooden floorboards beneath. Then he placed the still-warm barrel of his rifle on her forehead.

'Nice to see you again, Agent Grace.'

Grace did not respond. She was still struggling to focus.

'You not going to say hello to an old friend?'

'Get . . . get fucked.'

'Well, that's not very polite, is it?'

Tyson pressed down hard with his rifle, the bite of the barrel causing Grace to scream out in pain as the back of her head was pushed into the floor. The compression of her skull was agony, made many times worse by the undersized area on which the pressure was being applied.

For a moment she did not know what would give way first: the small circle on her forehead or the whole back of her head. And then, as quickly as it had started, the pressure was gone. But it was a momentary respite only. Tyson had spotted her bullet wound. With a cruel smile he slowly pressed his foot down onto it.

Grace screamed again. Louder this time. As much as she wished she had stayed silent, there was nothing she could do to stop herself. The pain was unbearable, even after Tyson had removed the pressure and returned the barrel to her forehead.

'Now,' he said, his weight on the rifle minimal for the moment, 'how about we try that again? If we're going to work together, we'd better be on good terms.'

Grace did not blink. She had no idea what Tyson meant by 'work together', but neither did she care. There was nothing he could do that would make her cooperate with him.

'I told you to get fucked.'

This time Tyson did not speak. Nor did he move the rifle barrel. Instead he stared deep into Grace's eyes, as if he was assessing her very soul. He was, she guessed, deciding if repetition would earn him a different reaction.

And he seemed to conclude that it would not.

'Screw it,' he said, pulling the rifle away fast and without warning. 'Suit yourself.'

Grace braced herself for what was coming. She did not know why; there was no tensed muscle in the world that could repel a three-round burst from an M16. She could only flinch, then, as she heard the shots fired. Exactly as many and exactly as fast as she had expected.

It did not occur to Grace in that moment that three shots fired into her head would *not* be something she would hear. Nor did it occur to her that conscious thought on the subject should be impossible. It was only when she heard and felt the impact of a large, lifeless body hitting the ground next to her that she knew for sure she was not dead.

Grace slowly opened her eyes, her focus only partially returning. She did not need it; she could not fail to recognise Tyson's corpse, now crumpled on the floor to her side, three bloody bullet wounds grouped at the top of his spine.

But she *did* need it to see beyond him. And so it took a few seconds more for the blur just feet away to coalesce into an image Grace could understand: Maria, back on her feet and now lowering David Burton's rifle. And in that moment, Grace remembered what Dempsey had called Lesson Number One.

Never turn your back. Not unless you know they're dead.

It was a lesson Tyson would now never learn.

EIGHTY-FIVE

Michael's mind was racing as he searched for something – for anything – that would delay Sean Sutton from ending their conversation with a bullet.

It was an almost impossible task. What was left to discuss when they both already knew the outcome? The Sutton persona would go. The Russian had already accepted that. But the Monk would live on. The Mladorossi would survive.

Sutton, Michael saw, had won.

For the first time in a long time Michael could think of nothing to say. And it was that failure, ironically, that would keep him alive a little longer. Because Sutton had recognised Michael's silence for what it was: defeat. And now he wanted to enjoy it.

His lips broke out in a cruel, crooked smile. It was an expression Michael had not seen before: the Monk's true face under the Sutton mask.

'You're wondering what you can say to keep me talking.' His accented voice was filled with mockery, and it was all the more effective for being accurate. 'What you can use to buy a little more time.'

'Wouldn't you be?'

'I wouldn't be in this position in the first place.'

'Course you wouldn't. Not a genius like you, eh?'

Sutton frowned, a reaction which gave Michael an equal mix of hope and fear. The barrister's undisguised sarcasm had clearly hit a nerve. And to that there were only two possible reactions.

Michael was grateful when Sutton chose the less fatal one.

'And what is that supposed to mean, funny man?'

'It means you got this far out of luck,' Michael replied. 'Luck and a support network that someone else built. You think you're special? You're nothing more than a kid playing in your daddy's work clothes.'

The smile was now gone. Sutton was no longer finding this situation funny. Not now Michael had found his pressure point.

'Luck? Do you . . . do you have any idea how much planning goes in to what I do? How much . . . what it takes to be *me*?'

'Way more than you're capable of, that's my bet. I mean, look how close you came to losing the lot. If Frankowski had only had that list with him—'

'Well, he *didn't*.' Sutton's voice was now raised. As close to a shout as he could risk in the quiet but not deserted ward. 'He didn't have it, Michael, did he? And now no one does.'

'Like I said: Luck.'

Sutton stared at Michael with hatred in his eyes, his grip on his weapon visibly less steady. The physical reaction spurred Michael on. He knew he was taking a risk, but he sensed he had found the one thing that would keep Sutton arguing instead of shooting.

'And you'd have done this better, would you?' Sutton asked.

'I didn't say I would, no. Your father, though? That's a different story.'

'What about my father?'

'Well, did *he* ever come this close to disaster?'

Sutton did not reply. He just stared. For a moment Michael thought he might have pushed too hard. That Sutton would choose to end the conversation now. His heart rate spiked as his eyes drifted towards the spot where his own weapon lay hidden. It was less than ten feet away.

Close but not close enough. Michael would be dead before he could make it halfway.

Dead as soon as Sutton wanted it.

He was relieved, then, when Sutton finally responded.

'You know nothing about my father.'

'I know you're only who you are because of him. This whole thing: Sean Sutton, the CIA, the Monk. You're nothing but a cheap knock-off of a better man.'

'You know nothing.' Sutton's accent was now thicker than ever, his answers spat out like venom. 'You and all of you . . . *inorodtsy*. You think so small. You think so . . . so . . . *prosto*. You think my father created this? My father *inherited* this, just as I did. And just as *his* father once took it from his own. One man did not create the Mladorossi, Michael. One man did not create the Monk. It's the work of a century. It is . . . it is . . .'

Sutton took a step back. He seemed to too angry to continue. It was exactly what Michael wanted.

'And you think that's better? That you've let down whole generations instead of just your father?'

Sutton's face was a mask of silent rage. It fuelled Michael. This was working.

'A hundred years of planning – success after success after success – and you bring it all crashing down around you in how long? It can't be more than a decade, surely? Not at your age?'

'Nothing is crashing down on anyone. You have achieved nothing.' A small smile began to grow again as Sutton found his voice. '*Ty nichego ne dobilsya.*'

Michael did not allow the change in demeanour to stop him.

All it proved was that he had exhausted one line. That was no defeat. He would simply find another.

'Russian again,' he said. 'Who's that even for, Sean? There's only you and me here. You don't need to fake the accent and show off a few words. We both know it's an act.'

'It is no act!' Sutton's voice was raised. Michael – as intended – had touched yet another raw nerve. 'It is who I am. It is who my family are. We are Russian.'

'Born and raised in America. Like your father and his father before him. You're more American than the damned US president himself. Whether you like it or not. So cut the show, eh?'

'Show?' Sutton's blood was rising. 'Show? This . . . this is my . . . my everything. My heritage is real. My family, we held our nose and we lived among your Western filth because we had to. But once the door to our home was closed and the outside world was excluded? Then we were in Russia. Then *we* were Russian.'

'Bullshit. You think my boys back in London will grow up speaking like they're from Belfast? Just because they're mine?'

'If your patriotism was strong enough.'

'Like I said. Bullshit.'

'What would you know anyway?'

'I smell lies for a living, Sean. If you don't think—'

'ENOUGH!'

Michael could not prevent a visible flinch at the sudden shout. He knew he had been getting to Sutton. He had not realised quite how much until the self-proclaimed Russian had raised his gun once again in fury.

Michael forced himself to hold Sutton's gaze. It took every ounce of his self-control to hide his fear. To keep his eyes from drifting back to the pistol. He was determined that he would not show weakness. Even as he realised that this was it.

Sutton, he could tell, was through being distracted.

'Joe will find you,' he said. 'You know that, right?'

'Really? And how do you think he'll do that?'

'It took him twenty-four hours this time. You think he can't do it again?'

'This time? The circumstances were . . . unique. They won't be again.'

'Unique how?'

Sutton shook his head. He had no intention of answering more questions.

'And besides, next time won't be a one-way hunt.'

'What does that mean?' Michael asked.

'It means it won't just be him looking for me. It means *I'll* be looking for *him*. And for everyone he loves. And, just so you don't think you're getting off light, I'll be looking for everyone *you* love, too.'

Michael said nothing. He could feel his blood beginning to rise. That old primal anger rearing its head once again. He did what he could to suppress it; right now he needed his brain, not his fists.

'You heard what I said, didn't you?' Sutton continued. 'Yes, you heard me. That woman of yours, Michael. Her and those two little boys. You think this ends with you? Think again.'

'You won't find them.'

'Oh no? You think I don't have people in England?'

'If you had all you claim to have, we wouldn't even be here.'

'Is that so?'

'We both know it's so. All your resources and yet you still had to come here and get your own hands dirty? You're here to kill Will because you've no one else to do it. You've overstretched yourself, Sean.'

'You think so?'

'I *know* it. You've taken what you were given – you've taken what your predecessors made for you, what they built for you – and you've screwed it all up. So am I afraid of what happens after I'm gone? Am I afraid that Joe won't find you? That he won't be able to protect my family? Like bollocks I am. You'll be dead within the week.'

Sutton seemed unsure of how to react. For a moment it seemed he would give in to his previous anger. That he would once again take the bait. But then he seemed to think better of it. He redoubled his grip on his pistol and took the slightest of movements forwards, his gun now aimed at Michael's head.

'Not again, barrister.' His smile returned. 'It worked once. It won't work—'

The unexpected click of the door's locking mechanism interrupted Sutton before he could finish. More importantly, it also caused him to turn.

The reaction was little more than a flicker. Just a moment's break in his concentration as his instincts kicked in and told him to check on the new arrival. He seemed to resist the urge almost as soon as it took hold, turning back to face Michael once again.

All in, it was no more than an instant. But that instant was enough.

Michael moved as soon as he heard the door. He did not glance to see if someone was about to come through. Nor, if they were, who that someone was. His every instinct screamed that he had no time for that, just as he had no time to turn and collect his own gun from the bedside table.

He had one chance. One way to live.

He had to move forwards.

Towards Sutton.

And he did exactly that.

Michael covered the distance between them in a fraction of a second, somehow hitting full speed as Sutton forced his focus back upon him. It left Sutton with time to react but no time to aim, and so the single round he got off before the impact of Michael's fast-moving body sailed harmlessly over the Irishman's shoulder.

Michael did not even flinch at the sound. He knew what he had to do to survive. For the second time in a day, he had to fight at Will Duffy's bedside.

Only this time he had to win.

The collision of their two bodies knocked the pistol clear of Sutton's hands and towards the doorway, but Michael paid no attention to its trajectory. Sutton had been knocked backwards and into the wall by the weight of Michael's rush, leaving him off balance and open to the crunching headbutt that Michael aimed downwards, into his unprotected face.

The sound of shattered bone seemed to fill the air. Most likely it was a trick of the contact – that Michael was feeling rather than hearing the sensation of bones giving way – but either way it did not slow him. The bigger man by three inches and twenty pounds, Michael put both his hands around Sutton's throat, pinned him against the wall and with a strength Sutton could only wish to match, he began to squeeze.

As hurt as Sutton was, he did his best to fight back. He struck out at Michael. Hard at first, into the Irishman's injured body and then up to his head, reopening the wound above Michael's eye from the previous night. The blows were powerful and they were well placed; Sutton knew how to fight.

But nothing he could do was going to be enough.

Michael's anger had been growing through the confrontation, kept barely in check by the knowledge that he could not reach Sutton before Sutton could fire, and that his only option was to keep the man talking. It had been a close-run thing: his underlying berserker fury had sat just beneath the surface, present but suppressed.

Until the moment came.

Michael's rush had been fuelled by the sudden unleashing of every one of his base primal instincts, with every bad action he had forced down for the last twenty-four hours pouring out in one long, sustained moment of violence. Sutton had as much chance of resisting as he would a wild animal. But still he fought, each blow weaker than the last.

Each blow wasted on a man who wanted him dead.

There was no thought behind Michael's actions now, as he ignored the hits and gripped ever harder, his hands a vice that crushed into Sutton's neck muscles and beyond them his windpipe. He did not even recognise the mantra that was coming out of his own mouth as he constricted Sutton's airways ever tighter.

'I won't lose any more of my family . . .,' he said. 'I won't lose any more of my family . . . I won't lose . . .'

'MICHAEL, STOP.'

The shout came from the doorway, but it may as well have been from another floor of the building for all Michael heard it. It did not register with him for a moment. All that mattered was Sutton. All that mattered was removing the threat he posed.

'MICHAEL!'

This time the shout came with a physical intervention: someone grabbed him from the side and tried to pull his hands from Sutton's throat. For a few seconds he ignored it, his focus fully fixed on one thing alone, but finally his grip was broken. Unable to ignore it any more, Michael swung up his left elbow and hit the interloper in the eye, a blow he immediately followed with a crushing right cross that sent Alastair Compton to the ground.

Michael turned his attention back to the now fallen and unconscious Sutton. Nothing would stop him from finishing the job.

It was a return to action that would last just seconds. Michael had not noticed as Compton climbed back to his feet. Nor did he pay attention to the noise that came from the Englishman's direction. But what he could not ignore was the feel of cold steel on his temple.

Compton had picked up Sutton's dropped gun and was now pressing it against Michael's head.

It was enough to break through Michael's loss of control. Taking a few seconds to compose himself, Michael allowed Sutton to slump back to the floor. But he himself did not move.

'So what is this?' he asked, his hands down and his eyes facing defiantly forwards. 'You one of his too, are you?'

'One of whose?' Compton sounded confused. 'What the fuck is going on here, Michael? I've just walked in and found you choking a man to death. What the hell—'

'Take the gun from my head and I'll tell you.'

'Would *you* do that? Honestly? If the tables were turned?'

'He's behind all this, Clubber. That piece of shit down there. Everything that happened yesterday. He's behind the attempt to kill Will. The attempt to kill us. Everything. This sonofabitch, he deserves to die.'

'He's CIA, Michael. He's here to help.'

'The CIA is a cover. This bastard, everything bad that's happened, it happened on *his* orders. He's too dangerous to be left alive. He has to die.'

'You're serious?'

'I'm serious.'

Compton began to lower the weapon.

'And you're sure?'

Michael turned to face him.

'I'm sure.'

'Then if you're right, Michael, what he deserves is a trial.'

'Not for this. Not for what he's done.'

'Listen to yourself. Listen to what you're saying.'

Michael took a moment, his heart rate slowing, his civilised self returning.

'Clubber, he—'

'This isn't how this conversation is supposed to go. I'm the shitty one here. It's supposed to be *you* telling *me* about the importance of justice. *You* telling *me* that every man deserves a trial. That's *your* thing. That's who *you* are. You're Michael fucking Devlin. The most irritatingly moral bastard I've ever known. You can't just kill him. That's not you.'

Michael looked down at the unconscious Sutton. His higher brain was taking hold once again. His rational mind taking back control. But still, Sutton's threats kept returning. As did what he knew of the Mladorossi.

They have people everywhere, his lower brain was telling him. *Everywhere.*

The thoughts made him paranoid.

'What are you even doing here, Clubber?'

'I came to check on Will. I wanted to see how he was.'

'Why?'

'We worked together. I like the guy.'

Michael nodded. The answer was a fair one.

And if he wanted me dead, why did he lower the gun?

He turned his attention back to Sutton.

'He can't be trusted, Clubber. He needs—'

'He needs a fair trial. And he's going to get one.'

Michael said nothing.

Compton was right.

Sutton would live.

He would live. And he would face justice.

EIGHTY-SIX

Dempsey opened his eyes as he felt the car come to a stop. He glanced through the windscreen and then through the passenger window, looking for some sign of where they might be. At first his sight was too blurred for him to spot anything telling, until he settled on the words printed just overhead.

He adjusted his body position so he could face the driver's seat, doing his best to ignore both the agony of movement and the complete lack of strength he needed to power it. Sitting next to him, his hands on the wheel, and with look of despair on his face, was Kon Frankowski.

'We're here?' Dempsey asked, no longer able to mask the weakness in his voice.

'It's where you wanted to come. And like I kept telling you, you need a doctor.'

'Was I out?'

'For about twenty minutes.'

Dempsey said nothing at first. The fact they were here at all was a surprise.

'But you brought me anyway. You didn't run.'

'You need a doctor.'

'You could have just dumped me out anywhere.'

'Jesus fucking Christ. How many times, man? You need a goddamn doctor.'

Dempsey had assumed that Frankowski would abandon him at the first opportunity. That he would take off to save his own skin, rather than come to The Hague and face the consequences of his actions for Hannibal Strauss.

But Frankowski had proved him wrong. He had willingly brought Dempsey into the heart of The Hague. Towards the last place he could really want to be. And towards justice for his own criminal actions.

It was not what Dempsey would have expected.

The confusion hung over his mind for a few moments more as he fought off the residual effects of sleep and of his own debilitating injury. He tried to focus. To overcome the pain and the immobility and to do what he was here to do.

But what was that? Why did we . . .

The answer came to him out of nowhere, and with it a surge of energy through his battered body. It could not have been adrenaline – there was no way he had any left, not after the battle with Sal Gallo – but still, something pushed him up. Something pushed him on. All of it triggered by a single thought.

Michael.

Dempsey was out of the car and staggering for the hospital entrance with no thought to the damage he was doing to himself; his gun in his hand, his only focus was on getting to the ICU. He could feel how slow he was moving. How his limbs were refusing the instruction of his mind. But still he pushed on. Into the hospital, past the reception and onwards to the bank of elevators.

The lifts seemed to get further away with every step, his vision narrowing to a tunnel as he moved. Dempsey could hear voices of surprise around him, and the sound of Frankowski trying to persuade him to stop and wait for medical attention.

Dempsey knew he could not do that. He did not have time.

He had to save Michael.

It was that thought alone that kept him upright as he finally reached the lift, his big, battered body staggering into the hard brickwork beside it as he came to rest. He hit at the machine's button, oblivious to the lights above it that indicated its imminent arrival, before finally allowing himself to lean against the wall.

It was intended as a momentary release. Just an instant of support as he waited for the lift. And it was a mistake. With his body relaxed, Dempsey felt himself sliding downwards with no way to stop his own momentum. His legs were giving way, refusing to obey the order to stand. And they were taking the rest of his body with them.

Dempsey would later remember little about the next few minutes.

He would not remember the feeling of his own weakness as he tried and failed to pick himself up off the floor. As he tried to push himself onwards, to finish the task for which he had come.

He would not remember the agony as he was lifted from his resting place by the elevators and placed on a gurney, ready to be rushed to the Emergency Department.

He would not remember the sight of Kon Frankowski beside him all the way, for some reason choosing to stay rather than save his own skin.

No. Dempsey would remember one thing and one thing only. He would remember the sheer, unrestrained relief as his friend – his brother – found *him*. The sight of Michael's face as he stood above him in the Emergency Department and tightly gripped his hand would be the only memory Dempsey would have of that moment.

And the only one he wanted.

Michael was safe. And Dempsey could finally rest.

EIGHTY-SEVEN

Two weeks later

Michael stepped out of his kitchen and into the sunshine that bathed the garden beyond. The intense heat of the past few months had cooled since his time in The Hague, to a temperature more typical for a London July.

But still there was not a cloud in the sky.

He walked down the stone staircase that led from the property's rear ground-floor door to the mini courtyard that sat at the basement level, his laptop open in his hands. Just feet from the final step was the same wrought-iron table where he had sat with Sarah and their closest friends on the night of the Grote Markt attack.

Sarah was there again today, but this time she was joined only by Dempsey. They were deep in conversation, enough that Michael was hesitant to interrupt them. He looked at his watch, checking if there was time for him to leave them to it.

There was not.

Dempsey had arrived from The Hague the previous evening, having travelled in far less luxury than he and Michael had done fourteen days earlier. Warned not to fly for several months, he and Will Duffy had made the journey together by train. It had not been comfortable for either man.

While Duffy remained the more injured of the two, Dempsey was far from healthy. He had suffered a laceration of his left kidney during his confrontation with Sal Gallo. An injury so severe that he had come close to acute renal failure.

His ten-day hospitalisation in the HMC Westeinde ICU had just about prevented that, but his recovery was going to be slow.

It was also going to be here, in London, at Michael's insistence. After everything his friend had done for him and for Duffy, the Irishman had insisted that Dempsey recover with his family. And for once, Dempsey had chosen to do as he was told.

Michael took the seat next to his injured friend and placed his laptop on the tabletop, the screen open and facing them both. Sarah was sitting on the other side and so she had no view of the machine's display.

'You want to move round so you can see?' Michael asked.

'Your two big heads are more than enough,' Sarah replied. She drank down what remained of her water and got to her feet. 'Besides, you shouldn't have the press here for this.'

Michael smiled. It was the answer he had expected. He opened his mouth to agree but before he could he was interrupted by an electronic chirp. The warning that their Zoom meeting was starting.

Dempsey reached out and clicked the laptop's mousepad as Sarah walked away from the table. A moment more and Eden Grace's face appeared on screen.

'Jesus, Boss. You've lost some serious weight.'

'That'll happen when you can't eat solid food, Eden,' Dempsey replied, his usually strong voice strained. 'Don't worry. A few steaks and some mashed potatoes and it'll pile back on.'

Michael said nothing. Grace was right, he knew. Dempsey had dropped a good twenty pounds. And most of that had been muscle, mainly because there had been little else to go. He was now closer in build to Michael himself, which looked wrong on his naturally thicker frame. Michael could only hope it would go back on as quickly and as easily as Dempsey seemed to think.

But that was a question for the future. They were here to deal with the present.

'Nice to meet you face to face, Eden,' Michael said. He had spoken to Grace many times in the past two weeks, but the video call was his first glimpse of the American. 'You don't mind me sitting in?'

'You're the man who brought Sean Sutton in, Michael. You deserve to know the outcome. Plus I know Dempsey's gonna tell you anyway.'

'Only once you were gone,' Dempsey replied. 'I'd have at least *pretended* to do this by the book.'

'Easier if we're honest, though, right?'

'Always.'

'So where is he?' Michael asked. 'There's been nothing on the news.'

'There won't be,' Grace replied. 'The decision's already been made. This won't go public.'

'But . . . then what happens? Where will he be tried?'

'There won't be a trial.'

'Why?'

'Because he confessed. He confessed to everything he had done. And he told us how to find Sal Gallo's family.'

'How are they?' Dempsey asked.

'They're safe and they're unhurt. So to that extent, at least, you kept your promise.'

'But how *are* they, Eden?'

'They're devastated, Boss. Like you'd expect.'

'What do they know?'

'Everything. Just like you insisted.'

Dempsey nodded his head, his expression grim.

'It's right that they know. That he died for them.'

Grace said nothing in reply. When Dempsey stayed silent too, Michael took the chance to speak. To ask a question that was burning to come out.

'I don't understand. Why would a man like Sutton just confess?'

'Because once we had the Mladorossi list and the names of all of the embedded agents, plus all of the other information on that file? He had no choice.'

'But he's a fanatic,' Michael said. 'Surely he wouldn't—'

'He's also a man who wants to live,' Grace interrupted. 'And to do that, he had to avoid being handed back to the Russians. They've conned successive Russian governments into paying them billions over the years. Essentially funding a hundred-year coup against themselves.'

'Kincaid's theory was that the Monk was funding the Russian paramilitary groups who were lining up against their own government,' Dempsey said thoughtfully.

'He was right,' Grace confirmed. 'The Wagner Group and the rest. All of them are just resources of the Mladorossi. The list confirmed that. There are some people in Moscow who would be very interested in having a little chat with Sutton if we handed that information over. And he knows that. He had no choice but to cooperate.'

Michael sat back into his chair, amazed by what he was hearing. It was difficult to grasp the scale of what they had stumbled into. To appreciate just how powerful Sean Sutton and his family had been.

Equally, it was difficult to accept that it could now be over. Michael needed to know more.

'So what happens to Sutton now?' he asked. 'How do we guarantee that this is the end?'

Dempsey fixed his eyes on the screen rather than on Michael.

'The Facility, right?'

'That's right,' Grace replied.

'What's the Facility?' Michael asked.

'It's a maximum security prison in Texas. For men like the Monk. Men who've done things the world can't know about.'

Michael's brow furrowed. The idea of a prison for the untried and un-triable did not sit easy with his defence lawyer sensibilities. He had left Sutton alive in the belief that the Monk would face justice for what he had done. And justice, Michael believed, required a public face. It was a philosophy that had been drummed into him at law school:

Justice must not only be done, it must be seen to be done.

This was *not* that.

'And what about the embedded Mladorossi agents?' Dempsey asked, seeming not to have noticed his friend's unease. 'How many have been identified?'

'All of them, as best as we can tell.'

'Where?'

'Everywhere, Boss. The US mostly, but they were all over the world. It's going to take a much longer debrief to go through them all, but there were hundreds.'

'And the UN?'

'Yeah, we had our share. The driver who set you up at the apartment for one. Yuri Shevchuk for another.'

'Shevchuk was Mladorossi?' This was one Michael had not seen coming.

'Yes and no. He wasn't an agent but he was an asset.

Sutton had leverage over him, so as to manipulate Strauss's prosecution.'

'Leverage?'

'His family.'

'Where are they now?' Dempsey asked.

'Safe. Sutton gave them up.'

'And Shevchuk?'

'Custody. The duress will help with his sentence but it's not a defence. Not for what he was doing.'

'And beyond those two?'

'Plenty more, Boss. Too many.'

'What about the ISB?'

'None of ours, outside the situation with Sal. But close enough. People we've worked with.'

'Have they all been pulled in?'

'A lot of them have. Enough that it's going to be tough to keep this whole thing quiet. It's kind of hard for senators and congressmen and members of your parliament to just fall off the radar, you know?'

'How will it be done?' Michael asked.

'That's well above my pay grade,' Grace replied. 'Above all of ours. We'll leave that headache to the higher-ups.'

'How many got away?' Dempsey asked. 'How many do we still have to worry about?'

'A lot. They took as many in one coordinated swoop as they could, but the Mladorossi network was big. And a whole lot of Sutton's assets were already in Ukraine and Russia. We reckon we missed about thirty per cent of them.'

Dempsey nodded his head. He did not seem surprised.

'Long road ahead to track them down,' he said.

'Yeah, but at least from now on we'll have back-up. It's

not the Mladorossi versus Alpha Team any more. Not now we know who we can trust.'

Dempsey smiled at the reply. And Michael knew why. Dempsey had trusted a handful of people his whole life and far too many of those had betrayed him. Mladorossi or no Mladorossi, he was not about to expand what little remained of his circle of trust.

But he was also not going to discuss it. Not over a computer screen. He changed the subject.

'What's the situation with Strauss?'

'He'll be released within a month,' Grace replied. 'We just need to create the right fiction for the charges to be dropped.'

'I'll look forward to that. And Kon Frankowski?'

'He's being given some leeway on the money laundering, like you asked.'

'Like you asked?' Michael did not hide his surprise as he turned to Dempsey. 'Why the hell would you ask for that?'

'The man saved my life, Mike. And he played a key part in us nailing Sutton.'

'But what about Maria?'

'What about her?'

'You're just going to throw that away? Let her arsehole of a husband just go back there, to pick up where he left off?'

'I got to agree with Michael on this one, Boss.' Grace this time. 'You and Maria, you owe yourselves an honest conversation at least.'

'What I owe her is respect. She's a married woman with kids. If I can bring her husband back to her – if I can bring their father back to them – then that's what I'm going to do.'

'Oh, come on, Joe. It's—'

'It's the right thing to do, Mike. Whatever the two of you

think. I sent her away once because I was a danger to her. That hasn't changed. If anything it's now even worse. Strauss is coming for me. You know that and I know that.'

'What?' This time the question came from Grace. 'Boss, what does that mean? He's coming for wh—'

'I'll explain later, Grace. For now just trust me that it's true. That it's true *and* that it was necessary.'

Dempsey turned back to Michael.

'I did what I had to do to protect her, Mike. I can't put her back in the crosshairs after that.'

'Jesus, Joe.'

'It's the right thing. In fact, it's the only thing. She's safe where she is, without me in her life. And if I can give her back her family into the bargain, what man would do less?'

'Most men,' Michael replied. 'Most men.'

Neither Michael nor Grace said anything more for a few moments. Instead the Irishman considered what his friend had given up. The possible future he had lost with the woman he loved, all in order to save her life. A sacrifice she would never know.

He glanced back to the screen without a word. Grace was equally silent. Michael guessed that she was thinking the exact same thing.

A few seconds later and she confirmed it. Her attempt to veer the subject in a light-hearted direction was a giveaway of what was really on her mind.

'David Burton won't like it,' she said. 'He thought he was finally rid of the snivelling little sonofabitch. His words, not mine.'

'He'll just have to lump it until he's back on his feet,' Dempsey said. He was laughing as he spoke, the mention of

Maria's father and his distaste for her choice of husband clearly welcome. 'There's nothing he can do about it until he's back in fighting shape.'

'I wouldn't be so sure. If it came down to throwing hands, I'd pick Burton at sixty-five with two bullet holes in him ahead of the best version of Kon Frankowski.'

'You're probably right,' Dempsey admitted, clearly still amused by the very idea.

'So what about you, Boss? When can we expect you back in Manhattan?'

Dempsey looked at Michael, then up towards the back door of the house. What he saw there made him smile and so Michael followed his gaze. Sarah was at the foot of the staircase, a nine-month-old child in each arm.

A few more steps and she was with them.

Dempsey reached out and took Liam Devlin from Sarah, while Michael did the same with Daniel. The Englishman examined his godson in silence before finally turning back to the screen.

'You know what? You hold the fort for a while. I need a proper holiday this time.'

'In London?'

'In London. With my family.'

Grace smiled back at the screen. A wide, happy grin.

'Exactly what I was hoping you'd say. Take your time and get better. And believe it or not, the world will still be here when you get back.'

'Just you make sure it is, Eden. I'll see you soon.'

ACKNOWLEDGEMENTS

And so we reach Book Five.

As many ideas as I still have for this series – and I hope at least some of you will be happy to know that there are lots of them – I don't think I ever believed I would reach this point. That people would still be wanting to read about the adventures of Joe Dempsey and Michael Devlin. Or that my publishers would still want to print them. It's the natural pessimism that comes with a solitary pursuit like writing, I guess.

Whatever the reason, I am immensely grateful that I still get to do this, *and* that I'll still be doing it for many more books to come. For that, I owe a debt to more than a handful of people. And so without further ado . . .

To the whole Elliott and Thompson team. To Lorne Forsyth, to Marianne Thorndahl, to Donna Hillyer and to Emma Finnigan. And to Pippa Crane in particular. It goes without saying that these books simply would not exist without your involvement at every level. From the freedom you give me to write what I want to write – a very unusual freedom, I have come to realise – to the quite extraordinary understanding you have shown for the delays caused by and time commitments inherent in my day job at the Criminal Bar. And, perhaps most importantly, to the never-to-be-underestimated contribution the editing team brings to making these books readable (Five books, Pippa! Five!! You poor woman . . .). I honestly doubt I could do this with anyone else and I am very aware just how lucky I am.

Next, Ewing Law. To Scott, to Nicola, to Rebecca, to

Dawn and to Dillon. Again, this would be absolutely impossible without you guys. The slack you cut me is the only reason I can find time for this writing malarkey. When Scott and I set out to create Ewing Law all those years ago, one of our ambitions was that it would give me time to write. But we never, ever thought we would grow the way we did – that we would become as busy as we are – and so the fact that this promise is still honoured is nothing short of incredible. This second career of mine would not be possible without your help and I am grateful every day.

To my 'name providers': one of my biggest struggles when writing is coming up with names for my characters. I have various tricks to get around it, but the best – where possible – is simply stealing. So thank you to the real Kon Frankowski, to the genuine Dylan Wrixon, to the actual Leisha Burton and to the almost Alastair Compton (Allan Compton KC) for allowing me to steal your identities, if only for a book or two. And thank you in particular to the real-life Kulvinder Vic Sethi, who kindly bid a great deal of money to the amazing charity Caudwell Children to appear in *The Shadow Network*. Vic, I hope we did you justice. And that you don't hold a grudge.

Now to the other kinds of help I've been given. First, Carl Buckley for your guidance on the workings of the International Criminal Court in The Hague. Most of which didn't find its way into the book as the plot became more political and less legal, but still, the grounding was invaluable. Next, Grant Benjamin. What can I say? Fourth book running where you've been the final beta reader. I don't think I could submit a final draft without your opinion, so you best not have any plans to be anywhere else in about twelve months' time. And then there's Neil Speight, the man who keeps my feet very much on the ground on those rare occasions that I start thinking of myself as a real writer.

One of the big lessons I have learned since my first book is the importance of support from other writers. Be it for professional advice, for plotting guidance, for research into the myriad of areas of expertise into which a story can drift, or even just to share a joke to break up the day. And so thank you to Colin Scott and particularly to Neil Lancaster and to Ed James for doing exactly that and more. Probably much more.

Which brings me to family and the support they provide. The most important factor of all.

To my sister Kate. Book number three as a beta-reader, I think. And she has become no less enthusiastic and no less demanding of 'more books'. Thank you, Kate. The encouragement and the support mean far more than you realise. As to the inevitable 'it's the best one yet' reviews. Right or wrong, they are very necessary!

To my Mum. Five books now for you. All the way back to those first three chapters of what became *Killer Intent*, which you read back when I was twenty-one. You have never been anything other than completely frank and honest and utterly supportive in the twenty-four years since then. I wouldn't be doing this if it were not for you. And not just because of that whole 'birth' thing; you didn't rest on those laurels!! So thank you, Mum. I know I don't say it enough.

And to Victoria and to Joseph. The latter of whom is no help whatsoever but who I'll include with his mum because then he at least gets a mention. Victoria, I have said three times already in these acknowledgements that I could not do this without the help I get from certain people. About no one is that more true than you. I realise how much of my time is spent working, whether it's writing and promoting books or preparing and defending Crown Court trials. And I am very well aware that our family's life – which just seems to sail along effortlessly in spite of my distractions and absences – is not just something that happens. You make it happen. You give me the time to do all the too-many things that I do. You give me the unwavering support without which everything else would be impossible. And you do it all while raising Joseph and running a career of your own. I do not know how you do it but I am incredibly grateful that you do.

And finally, as ever, to you. To the reader who has bought and read and I hope enjoyed *The Shadow Network* (and, either before or later, the rest of the series). You are the most important part of this jigsaw. Without you, no amount of loyalty and love and help from everyone I've mentioned so far would keep these books on the shelves. I cannot thank you enough for sticking with me and with Dempsey and with Devlin, and I really do hope that you'll continue to do that for many years to come.

ALSO BY TONY KENT

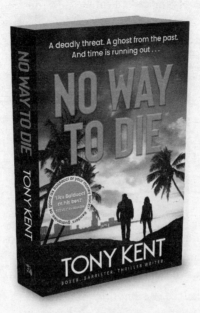

'A pulsating action thriller'
Sunday Times

When traces of a radioactive material are found alongside a body in Key West, multiple federal agencies suddenly descend on the crime scene. This is not just an isolated murder: a domestic terrorist group is ready to bring the US government to its knees.

The threat hits close to home for Agent Joe Dempsey when he discovers a personal connection to the group. With his new team member, former Secret Service agent Eden Grace, Dempsey joins the race to track down the terrorists' bomb before it's too late. But when their mission falls apart, he is forced to turn to the most unlikely of allies: an old enemy he thought he had buried in his past.

Now, with time running out, they must find a way to work together to stop a madman from unleashing horrifying destruction across the country.

RRP: £8.99 • ISBN: 978-1-78396-553-3

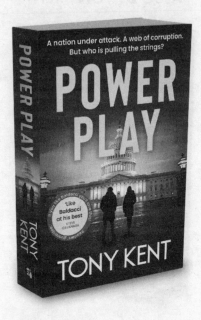

'An intricate, twisty minefield of geopolitics and absolute power gone rogue. Kent has outdone himself with this one.'
David Baldacci

When controversial US presidential candidate Dale Victor is killed in a plane explosion, along with hundreds of other passengers, it appears to be a clear-cut case of terrorism. But as criminal barrister Michael Devlin and intelligence agent Joe Dempsey are about to discover, everything is not as it seems.

As the evidence begins to mount, everything appears to point to the very top of the US government. And now someone is determined to stop Dempsey and Devlin from discovering the truth. At any cost.

Together, they must find a way to prove who's really pulling the strings, and free the White House from the deadly grip that has taken hold of power.

RRP: £8.99 • ISBN: 978-1-78396-491-8

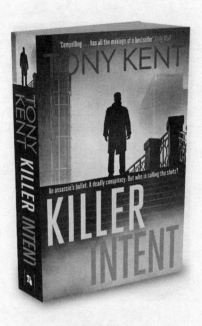

'A compelling combination of
political drama and lethal action.'
Daily Mail

When an attempted assassination sparks a chain reaction of explosive
events across London, Britain's elite security forces seem powerless to
stop the chaos threatening to overwhelm the government.

As the dark and deadly conspiracy unfolds, three strangers find their
fates entwined: Joe Dempsey, a deadly military intelligence officer;
Sarah Truman, a CNN reporter determined to get her headline; and
Michael Devlin, a Belfast-born criminal barrister with a secret past.

As the circle of those they can trust grows ever smaller, Dempsey,
Devlin and Truman are forced to work in the shadows, caught in
a life-or-death race against the clock, before the terrible plot
can consume them all.

RRP: £7.99 • ISBN: 978-1-78396-382-9

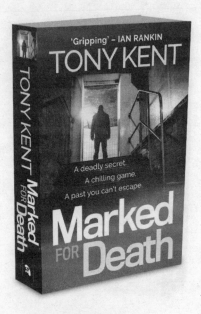

'Gripping.'
Ian Rankin

When London's legal establishment is shaken to its foundation by the grisly crucifixion of a retired Lord Chief Justice, Detective Chief Inspector Joelle Levy is tasked with finding his killer. The identical murder of former solicitor Adam Blunt offers a ray of hope – but what connects these victims who met such a gruesome end?

Assigned to the story from the start, news reporter Sarah Truman sets out to investigate, not suspecting that the trail will lead straight back to her own front door and her fiancé Michael Devlin. A criminal barrister determined to prove the innocence of his own client, Michael is at first oblivious to the return of the murderous figure from his past – until tragedy strikes closer to home.

Struggling with his grief and guilt, and now caught up in a madman's terrible quest for revenge, Michael must race to bring the killer to justice – before it's too late.

RRP: £7.99 • ISBN: 978-1-78396-449-9